Shadow
on the
Crown

Shadow on the Crown

Patricia Bracewell

Viking

VIKING
Published by the Penguin Group
Penguin Group (USA) Inc., 375 Hudson Street, New York, New York 10014, U.S.A.
Penguin Group (Canada), 90 Eglinton Avenue East, Suite 700, Toronto, Ontario, Canada M4P 2Y3
(a division of Pearson Penguin Canada Inc.)
Penguin Books Ltd, 80 Strand, London WC2R 0RL, England
Penguin Ireland, 25 St. Stephen's Green, Dublin 2, Ireland (a division of Penguin Books Ltd)
Penguin Group (Australia), 707 Collins Street, Melbourne, Victoria 3008, Australia
(a division of Pearson Australia Group Pty Ltd)
Penguin Books India Pvt Ltd, 11 Community Centre, Panchsheel Park, New Delhi – 110 017, India
Penguin Group (NZ), 67 Apollo Drive, Rosedale, Auckland 0632, New Zealand
(a division of Pearson New Zealand Ltd)
Penguin Books (South Africa), Rosebank Office Park, 181 Jan Smuts Avenue, Parktown North 2193,
South Africa
Penguin China, B7 Jiaming Center, 27 East Third Ring Road North, Chaoyang District, Beijing
100020, China

Penguin Books Ltd, Registered Offices: 80 Strand, London WC2R 0RL, England

First published in 2013 by Viking Penguin, a member of Penguin Group (USA) Inc.

10 9 8 7 6 5 4 3 2 1

Map illustration by Matt Brown

Publisher's Note
This is a work of fiction. Names, characters, places, and incidents either are the product of the author's
imagination or are used fictitiously, and any resemblance to actual persons, living or dead, business
establishments, events, or locales is entirely coincidental.

LIBRARY OF CONGRESS CATALOGING IN PUBLICATION DATA
Bracewell, Patricia, 1950–
Shadow on the crown / Patricia Bracewell.
p. cm.
ISBN 978-0-670-02639-5
1. Emma, Queen, consort of Canute I, King of England, d. 1052—Fiction.   2. Ethelred II, King of
England, 968?–1016—Fiction.   3. Great Britain—History—Ethelred II, 979–1016—Fiction.
4. Queens—Great Britain—Fiction.   5. Normans—Great Britain—Fiction.   I. Title.
PS3602.R323S53 2013
813'.6—dc23   2012028932

Printed in the United States of America
Designed by Nancy Resnick

ALWAYS LEARNING   PEARSON

For Lloyd, Andrew, and Alan

The English Court, 1001–1005

Æthelred II, Anglo-Saxon king of England

Children of the English king, in birth order:

Athelstan

Ecbert

Edmund

Edrid

Edwig

Edward

Edgar

Edyth

Ælfgifu (Ælfa)

Wulfhilde (Wulfa)

Mathilda

Leading Nobles and Ecclesiastics

Ælfhelm, ealdorman of Northumbria

Ufegeat, his son

Wulfheah, his son (Wulf)

Elgiva, his daughter

Ælfric, ealdorman of Hampshire

Ælfgar, his son

Hilde, his granddaughter

Ælfheah, bishop of Winchester

Godwine, ealdorman of Lindsey

Leofwine, ealdorman of Western Mercia

Wulfstan, archbishop of Jorvik and bishop of Worcester

The Norman Court, 1001–1005

Richard II, duke of Normandy
Robert, archbishop of Rouen, brother of the duke
Judith, duchess of Normandy
Gunnora, dowager duchess of Normandy
Mathilde, sister of the duke
Emma, sister of the duke

The Danish Royals

Swein Forkbeard, king of Denmark
Harald, his son
Cnut, his son

Glossary

Ætheling: literally, *throne worthy*. All of the legitimate sons of the Anglo-Saxon kings were referred to as æthelings.

Ague: any sickness with a high fever

Augur: to predict from signs or omens

Braies: French term for trousers, made of linen

Breecs: Anglo-Saxon term for trousers

Burh: an Anglo-Saxon fort

Byrnie: a mail tunic

Ceap: the market, or high street

Chasuble: an ecclesiastical vestment, a sleeveless mantle covering body and shoulders, often elaborately embroidered, worn over a long, white tunic during the celebration of the Mass

Chausses: French term for hose, or long stockings

Cope: an ecclesiastical vestment, often of silk and elaborately embroidered; it resembled a long cloak

Culver: Anglo-Saxon term for pigeon

Cyrtel: a woman's gown

Danelaw: an area of England that roughly comprises Yorkshire, East Anglia, and central and eastern Mercia where successive waves of Scandinavians settled throughout the ninth and tenth centuries

Ealdorman: a high-ranking noble appointed by the king to govern a province in the king's name. He led troops, levied taxes, and administered justice. It was a political position usually conferred upon members of powerful families.

Fyrd: an armed force that was raised at the command of the king or an ealdorman, usually in response to a Viking threat

Gafol: the tribute paid to an enemy army to purchase peace

Geld: a tax levied by the king, who used the money to pay the tribute extorted by Viking raiders

Godwebbe: precious cloth, frequently purple, normally of silk; probably shot-silk taffeta

Handfasting: a marriage or betrothal; a sign of a committed relationship with no religious ceremony or exchange of property

Headrail: a veil, often worn with a circlet or band, kept in place with pins

Hearth troops: warriors who made up the household guard of the king or a great lord

Herepath: a military road

Hird: the army of the Northmen; the enemies of the English

Host: army

Kalends: the first day of the month in the ancient Roman calendar, which always fell on a new moon

Leech/leechcraft: a physician; the practice of the healing art

Leman: lover; from Old French

Pennons: banners

Pulses: dried peas and beans

Reeve: a man with administrative responsibilities utilized by royals, bishops, and nobles to oversee towns, villages, and large estates

Rood: the cross on which Christ was crucified

Scarp: a steep slope formed by the fracturing of the earth's crust

Scop: storyteller; harper

Screens passage: a vestibule just inside the entrance to a great hall or similar chamber, created by movable screens that blocked the wind from gusting into the hall when the doors were opened

Seax: knife

Sending: an unpleasant or evil creature sent by someone with magical powers to warn, punish, or take revenge on a person; from Old Norse

Skald: poet or storyteller

Tafl: a popular board game in early medieval England and Scandinavia with some similarities to modern-day chess

Thegn: literally "one who serves another"; a title that marks a personal relationship; the leading ones served the king himself; a member of the highest rank in Anglo-Saxon society; a landholder with specified obligations to his lord

Wain: a wagon or cart

Wergild: literally "man payment"; the value set on a person's life

Witan: "wise men"; the king's council

Wyrd: fate or destiny

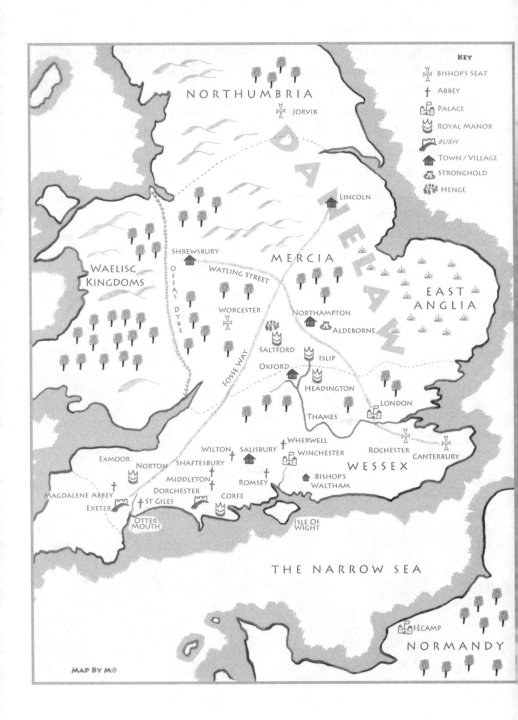

A.D. 979   In this year was King Edward slain at even-tide, at Corfe-gate, on the fifteenth before the kalends of April, and he was buried at Werham without any royal honors. Nor was a worse deed than this done since men came to Britain. . . . Æthelred was consecrated king. In this same year a bloody sky was often seen, most clearly at midnight, like fire in the form of misty beams. As dawn approached, it glided away.

—The Anglo-Saxon Chronicle

Shadow
on the
Crown

Prologue

Eve of St. Hilda's Feast, November 1001

Near Saltford, Oxfordshire

She made a circuit of the clearing among the oaks, three times round and three times back, whispering spells of protection. There had been a portent in the night: a curtain of red light had shimmered and danced across the midnight sky like scarlet silk flung against the stars. Once, in the year before her birth, such a light had marked a royal death. Now it surely marked another, and although her magic could not banish death, she wove the spells to ward disaster from the realm.

When her task was done she fed the fire that burned in the center of the ancient stone ring, and sitting down beside it, she waited for the one who came in search of prophecy. Before the sun had moved a finger's width across the sky, the figure of a woman, cloaked and veiled, stood atop the rise, her hand upon the sentinel stone. Slowly she followed the path down through the trees and into the giants' dance until she, too, took her place beside the fire, with silver in her palm.

"I would know my lady's fate," she said.

The silver went from hand to hand, and against her will, the seer glimpsed a heart, broken and barren, that loved with a dark and twisted love. But the silver had been given, and at her nod, a lock of hair was laid upon the flames. She searched for visions in the fire, and they tumbled and roiled until they hurt her eyes and scored her heart.

"Your lady will be bound to a mighty lord," she said at last, "and her children will be kings."

But because of the darkness in that heart across the fire, she said nothing of the other, of the lady who would journey from afar, and of the two life threads so knotted and tangled that they could not be pulled asunder for a lifetime or forever. She did not speak of the green land that would burn to ash in the days to come, or of the innocents who would die, all for the price of a throne.

There would be portents in the sky again tonight, she knew, and high above her the stars would weep blood.

A.D. 1001   This year there was great commotion in England in consequence of an invasion by the Danes, who spread terror and devastation wheresoever they went, plundering and burning and desolating the country. . . . They brought much booty with them to their ships, and thence they went into the Isle of Wight and nothing withstood them; nor any fleet by sea durst meet them; nor land force either. Then was it in every wise a heavy time, because they never ceased from their evil doings.

—*The Anglo-Saxon Chronicle*

Chapter One

December 24, 1001

Fécamp, Normandy

The winter of 1001 in northwestern Europe would have been recorded as the coldest and fiercest in seventy-five years, had anyone been keeping such records. In late December of that year, a storm tore out of the arctic north with terrible speed, blasting all of Europe but striking hardest at the two realms that faced each other across the Narrow Sea.

In Normandy, it began with a sudden drop in temperature and a freezing rain that coated the limbs of the precious fruit trees in the Seine's fertile valley. A driving wind swept behind the rain, snapping brittle, frozen branches and scattering the promise of next summer's harvest over wide, sleet-covered fields. For a full day and night the storm raged, and when the worst of it was spent, a light snow fell upon the wasted landscape as quietly as a benediction.

Watching from within their abbey walls, the monks of Jumièges and of Saint-Wandrille contemplated the loss of their apple crop, bowed their heads, and prayed for acceptance of God's will. Peasant farmers, huddling together for warmth in frail, wooden cottages and fearing that the end of the world was come, prayed for deliverance. In the newly built ducal palace at Fécamp, where Duke Richard and his family had gathered to celebrate the season of Christ's Mass, the duke's fifteen-year-old sister, Emma, quietly pulled heavy boots over her thick woolen leggings and prayed that she would not waken her sleeping sister—to no avail.

"What are you doing?" Mathilde's voice, raw and resonating with elder sister disapproval, emerged from a thick nest of bedclothes.

Emma continued to tug at a boot.

"I am going down to the stables," she said.

She threw her sister a sidelong glance, trying to gauge her mood. Mathilde's thin brown hair was pulled into a tight braid that gave her face a drawn, pinched look and added to the severity of the frown that she cast upon her younger sister.

"You cannot go out in this storm," Mathilde protested. "You will catch your death." She started to say more but was racked by a sudden, cruel fit of coughing.

Emma went to her, snatched up the cup of watered wine from a table beside the bed, and held it for her sister to drink.

"The snow has stopped," she said, as Mathilde sipped from the cup. "I will be fine."

And unlike Mathilde, Emma thought to herself, she rarely took sick. Poor Mathilde. It was her misfortune to be the only small, dark-haired, sickly child in her mother's brood of blond, vigorous giants—eight brothers and sisters, all told.

When her sister had drunk her fill, Emma snatched up a shawl from the foot of the bed and threw it over her thick, bright hair.

"You are going to check on your wretched horse, I suppose." Mathilde's voice was little more than a throaty growl. "I do not see why. God knows all of those creatures are tended with as much care as if they were children. It is mean of you to leave me here all alone."

Emma, who loved the outdoors, who loved horses, dogs, and hunting, and who was happiest when she was riding along the Norman shore beneath high chalk cliffs, knew better than to try to explain her errand to Mathilde, who detested all of those things. Emma was sorry that Mathilde was ill and bored, but she would go mad if she could not breathe some fresh air and be alone for just a little while. The two of them had been pent up together within doors for three full days.

She lifted a heavy, fur-lined black cloak from its peg on the wall and threw it over her shoulders.

"I will not be gone long," she said.

Mathilde, though, had thought of another objection.

"What if the shipmen return while you are down there?" she demanded. "You cannot trust those Danish brutes not to molest you if they come upon you alone and unprotected."

Emma fastened her cloak beneath her chin, pondering this warning.

The Danish king, Swein Forkbeard, had petitioned her brother for winter harbor along Normandy's northern coast, and Duke Richard, unwilling to offend the fierce warrior king, had granted it. To Richard's fury, though, Forkbeard's own ship and a dozen more had sailed into Fécamp's harbor two days ago, forcing her brother out of courtesy to invite the king to join his family at the palace.

The king had accepted swiftly and had settled into her brother's great hall with a score of his companions—rough, hard-faced warriors with only the thinnest gloss of civilization about them in spite of the wealth of gold that they flaunted on their wrists and arms. Mathilde, sick with the ague, had kept to her bed. Richard's wife, Judith, only a few weeks out of childbed, had done the same. So it was Emma's mother, Dowager Duchess Gunnora, with only her youngest daughter at her side, who had offered the king the welcome cup upon his arrival in the hall. The duchess, proud of her Danish heritage and her blood ties to the Danish throne, nevertheless had no illusions about Swein Forkbeard. She presented Emma to him with formal courtesy, then banished her daughter to the private quarters with all of the other young women.

Emma had not been sorry to go. Forkbeard had greeted her with cold, fiercely calculating eyes and a silent nod. His brooding gaze seemed to weigh her, as if she were not a woman but a commodity that could be bought and sold—a trinket that he might purchase in the market at Rouen. She had colored beneath his fixed, brutal stare, and had wanted to take to her heels to escape it. But she had forced herself to walk slowly from the hall, chin held high, acutely aware of the shipmen all around her who raked her with merciless eyes.

These were men who made their living by murder and rape, men who had been baptized to Christ but whose souls still belonged to heathen gods, or so she had heard. Their grim, weather-scarred faces had haunted her dreams that night, and like her brothers, she wished that Forkbeard and his shipmen had never come to Fécamp. Today, though, the palace was emptied of Danes.

"The shipmen have gone to the harbor to inspect their vessels for storm damage. They will likely not return until dark. I will be back long before that, and I promise I will keep you company then until we put out the candles." With that she slipped from the room before Mathilde could think of any other objections.

The courtyard was deserted as she made her way toward the stables, and the air was so frigid that it hurt to breathe. She followed the wall, grasping at its stones with one hand as she navigated the slippery mud and slush that had been churned up by men and horses. Emma's snow-white mare, Ange, whickered a greeting, and Emma nuzzled the horse's neck, warming her face against its thick winter coat. A moment later, though, she heard a commotion in the stable yard that worried her.

Could the men have returned so soon? Surely not all of them. They would have made a great deal more clamor.

Using Ange as a screen, Emma peered toward the wide doorway and saw Richard and Swein Forkbeard leading their mounts toward the stable. She had always thought her brother quite tall, but the Danish king bested him by half a head. They were the same age—both of them very old by her reckoning, for Richard had been born more than twenty years before Emma. But the king of the Danes, with his white hair and long white beard, worn forked and braided, looked far older. There was a sternness about Swein Forkbeard's countenance, a hard-eyed ruthlessness that frightened her. He even frightened Richard, she was certain, although he masked it with courtesy.

She had no wish to greet the Danish king again, or to face her brother's wrath at finding her here, so she shied behind her horse to wait for them to go away. They seemed in no hurry, in spite of the cold. Richard, in halting Danish, was relating the pedigree of the king's mount and doing his best to explain what he looked for in breeding his horse stock.

She smiled at her brother's clumsy efforts with Swein's tongue. Like all of the Duchess Gunnora's children, he had learned Danish at his mother's knee. And like most of his siblings, he had abandoned it at an early age. Emma had been the only one to embrace it, and she could speak as fluently in Danish as she could in Frankish or Breton or Latin. She had even learned some of the English used by prelates who sometimes visited her brother from across the Narrow Sea.

Neither Richard nor her brother Robert, the archbishop, knew of Emma's gift of tongues, as her mother called it. Gunnora had advised Emma to keep this remarkable skill a secret. *Use it to listen,* she had said, *rather than to speak. You will be surprised at what you will learn.*

Emma listened now and realized, with a start, that the conversation between her brother and the Danish king had moved from the breeding of horses to the breeding of children.

"A marriage alliance would be in both our interests," Swein Forkbeard said. "I have two sons who need wives. One of your sisters might do, and you would gain much from such a marriage, I promise you. Of course, were you to reject it, you could lose a great deal." There was silence for a moment, and then the king said, his voice speculative, taunting, "How much, I wonder, are you prepared to lose?"

Emma covered her mouth with her hand, shocked by the clear threat in Forkbeard's words. What would he do? Send shipmen to ravage Normandy unless Richard sent one of his sisters to Denmark to wed one of Forkbeard's sons?

She held her breath, waiting for Richard's reply.

"My sisters are overly young to wed." Her brother's fumbled words were so casual that Emma wondered if he had understood all that the Danish king had said.

"Age matters little," Forkbeard replied, his tone amiable now. "My youngest son has seen only ten winters, but like his elder brother, he is already a skilled shipman and warrior. As for your sisters," he paused, and Emma twisted her fingers nervously in Ange's mane as she waited for him to go on, "you must not be too tender in your care of them. The Lady Emma seems ripe for bedding. You would do well to breed her now, for a good price, or you might find that you have left it too late."

Emma felt the blood rise to her face, humiliation and anger warring with shock and fear. Surely Richard would not agree to sell her to Denmark! It was a harsh, brutal place, barely Christian. Her family could trace their bloodline back to the northern lands, but that was in the past. Surely it was not part of their future. Denmark was a land of fierce men ruled by a ruthless king. Swein Forkbeard had not inherited his crown but had won it in a battle to the death waged against his own father. Richard could not allow her to marry into a family such as that!

Her blood pounded in her ears, and she had to strain to hear her brother's response to Forkbeard's words.

"Your proposal does my family great honor," Richard said. "You will understand, of course," he went on, his voice smoothly persuasive in spite of his broken Danish, "that a betrothal is too delicate a matter to be settled quickly. There are many things to consider and to weigh, and as you know, I have two sisters. You have yet to meet the elder, who, by tradition, should naturally be the first to wed."

She did not hear the Danish king's reply, for the men's voices faded, replaced by the clink of bridles as grooms led the horses to their stalls. Emma remained rooted to the spot where she stood, her face buried in Ange's neck, her thoughts in turmoil over what she had heard.

Swein Forkbeard's proposal must carry great weight with her brother. Richard was a realist. He would consider the sacrifice of a younger sister a small price to pay for Norman peace with Denmark. It would be terrible for the bride, though—banished to a hostile, distant land. Mathilde would hate it, even as Emma would. She felt her throat constrict at the very thought of it.

No, her brother could not do such a thing to either of his sisters. He would not send them so far away. He had wed their elder sisters to great lords in Brittany and Frankia, securing his borders and adding considerably to his treasure. Surely he would use Mathilde and herself in a similar manner, for Normandy's border was long and Richard had need of allies.

But Richard was ambitious. A royal marriage, even to a son of the barbarous Swein Forkbeard, would enhance her brother's prestige throughout Europe. Forkbeard may be a Viking warlord rather than a godly Christian king, but all of Europe feared him, and that made him a valuable ally. She could easily imagine Richard succumbing to that argument, and she feared what he might be plotting with the Danish king in his private chamber.

She whispered a few endearments into Ange's ear, then, afraid that Forkbeard's men might arrive hard upon his heels, she hurried back toward the palace. She would say nothing of what she had heard to Mathilde. Their mother, surely, would have some say in the matter, yet Emma was frightened for her elder sister.

A slender needle of anxiety began to prick her insides. She did not trust Richard.

Chapter Two

December 25, 1001

Rochester, Kent

In England that December the fierce snowstorm blinded and buried countless travelers caught on the high chalk downs of Wessex, even within a few short steps of shelter. Near Durham in Northumbria the snow piled so high on the thatched roof of Lord Thorkeld's great hall that it collapsed of its own weight, burying the lord and his family and retainers, twenty folk in all. On the Isle of Wight a storm surge swept an entire village into the sea. In Devon the once prosperous towns of Pin-hoo and Clyst, their houses, workshops, and storerooms razed to the ground during the previous summer's Danish raids, were buried beneath fifteen feet of snow, as if they had never existed.

In the king's hall at Rochester, Æthelred II of England and his councilors sat at table for the winter feast swathed in furs against the bitter cold. Their mood would have been dour even had the weather been more moderate. They drank their Christmas ale with grim determination rather than pleasure, their company unleavened by the presence of any women. The king's mother, a force at court for nearly twenty-five years, had gone to God some five weeks before, in November, on the Feast of St. Hilda. The king's lady wife, brought to childbed on Christmas Eve for the eleventh and final time, had breathed her last on Christmas morning. Her cold body lay beneath the vaulted wooden ceiling of the king's chapel, mourned by her attendants. The child, born too soon and perhaps sensing his loss, found no comfort in the arms of his wet nurse. Whenever the roaring of the wind and the desultory muttering of men momentarily abated, his feeble cry wafted through the hall like the wail of a soul wandering between heaven and earth. The women tending the babe shook their heads, lips pursed. The child was not long for this world, they deemed, for he would not suck.

The men who kept company with the king at the high table gave little thought to the infant and his prospects, for Æthelred had sons a-plenty, several of them fully grown. What he lacked now was a wife, and they were determined to find him one, whether he would or no. They disagreed, however, on where to look for her.

King Æthelred, a man haunted by his past and troubled about his future, sat among them, his tall frame hunched over his silver plate and his right hand clenching a gilded drinking horn. Twenty-three years on the throne had seared creases into his face that were unusual for a man who had not yet seen forty winters. Telltale streaks of gray in his tawny hair testified to the hardship of rule, and the bent angle of his head beneath the thick, gold crown suggested that it was more burden than ornament.

The king, regarding his advisers with watery blue eyes, was well aware of the line of division among them with regard to his marital prospects. The men with lands in the north, led by Ælfhelm, ealdorman of Northumbria, would urge him to wed Ælfhelm's daughter Elgiva—a beautiful witch of a girl as ambitious, he suspected, as her father. A marriage there would strengthen the bond between the king and the northern lords, whose allegiances to Ælfhelm and to each other were somewhat stronger, Æthelred knew, than their fealty to him.

The men with lands in the south would urge him to look beyond the Narrow Sea to Normandy for a bride. Wed the duke's sister, they would tell him, and persuade her brother to side with Æthelred against the Danes who pillaged English towns and abbeys. Æthelred suspected that it might take a great deal of persuading. The Vikings paid Duke

Richard well to harbor their ships on his coast and to trade their spoils in his great market in Rouen. If Æthelred should marry one of the duke's sisters—and if he sealed the alliance with enough gold—Richard *might* be willing to bar the Danes from his ports, and so stop the Viking rape of English coasts.

Then again, Æthelred knew, he might not.

The hubbub in the hall, which had been muffled while the men filled their bellies, rose again as the meal came to a close and the drinking began in earnest. Æthelred motioned to his cupbearer to refill his drinking horn, then eased himself back in his chair and glowered at the men around him from hooded eyes, focusing at last on Ælfhelm of Northumbria. The ealdorman had risen from his bench and stood now in earnest consultation with a knot of nobles and clergy. His face was as craggy as a weathered scarp and just as difficult to read. Æthelred had never been able to decipher the subtle workings of the mind behind that stonelike visage, but he would wager half of Wessex that tonight Ælfhelm was garnering support for his daughter's marriage to the crown.

And he would find it, certainly. It was customary for England's king to choose his bride from one of the noble families of the realm. Æthelred's wife and his mother both had been daughters of northern lords. Their fathers, though, would have been more pliable than Lord Ælfhelm. It seemed to the king that Ælfhelm was not mortal, but carved from granite and stone. Æthelred neither liked nor trusted the man, although he was careful to hide this. And while the king understood that it was wise to bind his enemies close, it seemed to him that the marriage bed might be too close for comfort. Ælfhelm had sons as well as a daughter, sons who, like their father, hungered for the power that came with a royal marriage. That power, combined with the family's wealth and northern allegiances, could be more trouble than any girl was worth.

As for the girl herself, the last time the king had seen Elgiva she had been all of thirteen summers old. She had looked far older though, her body full and womanly, her mouth as red and voluptuous as ripe fruit.

She was a woman born for bedding, and had she been older he might have forgotten himself and obliged her. But her youth had stopped him. That and her obvious awareness of the power she had over men, which had chilled his ardor somewhat. Now, at sixteen, wealthy and beautiful, with powerful kin and with family lands that rivaled his own, if he did not marry her himself he should have to watch her carefully. Whatever man she did marry must have no pretensions to the throne, or Æthelred might find his very crown at risk.

The king took another long pull at his cup. As for the unmarried sisters of Richard of Normandy, there were two of them, and that was all he knew about them. He knew something of Richard, though—a pretentious upstart sprung from Danish raiders who had decimated the northern territories of the Frankish kingdom, and then settled there to breed horses and brats. Richard's pedigree was nothing like Æthelred's noble ancestry, and although Richard himself was a Christian and styled himself "duke," he was little more than a Danish pirate. In his youth he had even gone a-viking, raiding the Irish coast for gold and slaves, and he had ever welcomed the dragon ships to his harbors. Even now, rumor had it, there were Danish longships, their holds filled with English plunder, sheltering along Normandy's coast. So to wed one of Richard's sisters and plant a babe in her belly might be wise. It might give the Norman duke a more personal interest in the security of England's shores.

Æthelred frowned. To take a Norman bride would offend his northern lords and bind them more strongly to each other—and against him. To wed Ælfhelm's daughter instead of the Norman girl would be to throw away perhaps his only opportunity to quell the Viking threat to his kingdom. There was peril whichever way he turned, north or south. Taking any wife at all would be a devil's bargain, and if it were up to him, he would not do it. He was the king. He wanted no woman in his hall.

He drank again, deeply, from the gold-rimmed horn, but the sweet mead that should have sent fire racing through his blood did not warm him. Instead, a chill, cold as the mouth of a grave, snaked along his arms and grazed an icy finger up his spine. A heaviness oppressed him, an inescapable black dread, and he whispered a curse against the sending that he knew was come upon him and that he could not escape. His vision blurred to haze, the sounds of feasting stilled, and from every dark corner, shadows streamed toward him until they reached the dais and formed a pulsing darkness before him. From its murky heart, his dead brother's face, eyes glowing and malignant, stared into his.

He tried to pray, to curse, but he could make no sound except the formless, silent howl that was the voice of nightmare. The drinking horn slipped from his hand, yet he did not hear it fall. He heard only a low keening, like the sound of the wind hurtling against white cliffs above a pounding sea. It grew until it filled his brain, and again he tried to cry out, clutching his head in his hands as other hands grasped him, and the black phantom before him rippled and then faded at last.

Alarmed voices rang in his ears, and someone held a cup to his mouth, urging him to drink, but he dashed the cup away and shook off the hands that would tend him. Desperate to distract them, he called for music and was rewarded by the strum of the harp and the chanting of his *scop*.

His men scattered back to their places, but as Æthelred cast a furtive glance around the room, the eyes that met his were guarded and troubled. What did they think they had seen? A king besotted and drowned in his cups? A man overcome with grief at the death of his wife?

Better that than a king haunted by his brother's ghost.

Three times now the thing that had been his brother had appeared thus before him, staring with glistening eyes. He had seen it first a month ago, hovering like some monstrous bird above his mother as she lay dying. Three days later, when he followed the dowager queen's body to its resting place at Wherwell Abbey, he had glimpsed Edward's face glaring at him, a darker shade among the chapel shadows. And tonight it had come again to torment him. Was it to be his *wyrd*, his fate, to be visited forever by his dead brother now that he alone remained alive of those who had seen Edward die?

What was it that drew the dead forth to walk among the living? And what would it take to send the thing back into its grave?

His thoughts flew to his dead wife, Ælfgifu, lying cold and still upon her bier. Tomorrow he would take her body by ship to its resting place at Minster Abbey. Would the specter of his brother be waiting there for him, as it had waited at Wherwell? He shuddered at the thought of it. Tonight he would pray for redemption, beseech forgiveness and mercy from God for the death of his brother. He would even plead for the repose of his mother's soul, although he had no doubt that she was tasting the torments of hell.

Chapter Three

December 25, 1001

Aldeborne Manor, Northamptonshire

Elgiva of Northampton—great-granddaughter of Wulfsige the Black, granddaughter of the Lady Wulfrun of Tamworth, and only daughter of Ælfhelm, ealdorman of Northumbria—stood at her chamber window and saw with satisfaction that a heavy snow was once more piling up against her father's manor walls. The massive drifts would keep the men indoors for several days, and that suited her purpose exactly.

She sat down upon a stool and gestured to a servant to latch the wooden shutter against the cold. Pulling her thick woolen shawl closer about her, she tried to control her impatience as her old nurse stood behind her and used deft fingers to tame her mass of dark curls. She must look her best at tonight's Yule feast. There were royal visitors awaiting her in the hall, and if events played out as she intended, she would soon be sharing her bed with the eldest son of the king. After that it would be a simple enough matter for her father to negotiate whatever details were necessary to arrange a royal marriage.

She picked up a silver mirror and contemplated the perfect arch of her dark brows, then angled the disk to reflect Groa's aged face beneath her gray linen headrail. That face was as familiar to Elgiva as her own, yet there were secrets behind the shadowy gray eyes that she had never been able to fathom.

"Tell me again," she said, "about the prophecy."

Groa's normally brooding expression lit up with a rare, knowing smile.

"You are destined for queenship, my lady," she said. "Your children will be kings. You have but to reach out your hand and grasp what you desire."

Elgiva pursed her lips, studying their fullness in the mirror.

"I intend to," she said. "I intend to make Athelstan desire me tonight." She wanted him to hunger for her body in exactly the way the priests railed against in their sermons.

"How can he not?" Groa asked. "You are as beautiful as you are wealthy. Even the king desired you, and you were but a child then."

Elgiva smiled, relishing the memory of her meeting with the king at Yuletide three years before. She had bribed a servant to help her escape from an evening of prayer in Lady Ælfgifu's chamber, and in the dark passage outside she had unwittingly stumbled into the king. Æthelred had saved her from a fall by pulling her hard up against him, holding her there for far longer than necessary while he inquired if she was hurt. She had answered him with her most beguiling smile, had eagerly pressed her body against his as he held her close. Then, with a skill she could not help but admire, he had slipped a hand through the neckline of her cyrtel to fondle her breast. She had let him do it, of course, because he was the king, and because she had been too astonished to protest. Besides, she had liked it. Who would have guessed that a man so old could have such eloquent, liquid hands?

She had dared to hope that he would lead her to his chamber, but it was at that interesting moment that one of his attendants had come to drag him to some meeting or other, and so her brief little tryst with Æthelred had ended.

Angling the mirror a little lower she studied her full breasts and the necklace of thick gold that had been a gift from her brother Wulf. It had been Wulf who had told her father about her little interlude with the king. Her father, who had ever been one to strike first and ask questions later, had cuffed her so hard that her mouth and nose had bled. He would have hit her again had Groa not come between them, fingering the pagan amulet she wore at her throat and threatening him with a curse. That had stayed her father's hand, for he was wary of Groa and her curses and potions. Still, her father had hurled filthy words at Elgiva, calling her a cunt and a whore, and he had sent her from court that very day. She still hated him for that, but she had learned a lesson. She was very careful now about what secrets she confided to her favorite brother.

"I am glad," she said, "that I did not give my maidenhead to the king. It would have been a waste."

"As he already has a wife," Groa replied, her face in the mirror gone all grim again, "it would have done you little good, to be sure."

Well, it might have gotten her more lands and more money if she had become the king's leman, but she was already one of the wealthiest women in the realm, and one of the few who owned her estates outright. Still, it would not have made her queen, and that was what she truly wanted. Groa had said she would be the mother of kings, after all, so it must mean that she was meant to wed Athelstan, who would surely take the throne when his father died.

And for the next two weeks, Athelstan and two of his brothers would be under this roof for the Yule feast. It was perfect.

Even better, her father was not here, although he had nearly ruined everything by insisting that she go south with him to attend the king's Yule. He would have had her spend Christmas Day on her knees mouthing prayers with the king's wife and her ladies. She had gulled him out of that, though, and she smiled to herself as she remembered how her father's brow had darkened when she casually said that she hoped to become much better acquainted with the king during her time at court. He had raised a threatening hand, and she had feared that he might strike her, but Groa had whisked her out of the chamber, scolding like mad, and that had saved her. After that nothing more had been said about taking her south, and with her father and elder brother now gone, she could do as she pleased. Wulf certainly would not stop her.

"I think that Lord Athelstan has a look of the king about him," she observed. They had the same golden hair and square, pleasing face.

Groa snorted. "When I saw him in the yard this morning he had the look of a man who spends more time grooming his horse than he does himself."

"I did not ask for your opinion," Elgiva snapped. "And you are not being fair. Any man looks unkempt when he has been riding." Besides, there was an air about Athelstan, an unconscious swagger that she found infinitely appealing. At sixteen years old he was the heir to the throne of all England, and no one knew it better than he did.

She had watched from the hall steps as he rode through the gate, and he had lifted his eyes to hers and snared her in an unsettling blue gaze. She had seen it then, that awareness of just exactly who and what he was. He had worn it like a mantle, and from that instant she had wanted to wrap herself in it.

One day Athelstan would be the most powerful man in the realm, and her destiny, she was certain, must be bound to his. For two weeks he would be her guest—time enough, surely, to make him desire her, and to convince him that he must have her for his wife.

Chapter Four

December 31, 1001

Aldeborne Manor, Northamptonshire

It was the seventh night of Christmas feasting, and Athelstan stood with his brothers amid a throng of revelers near the central fire of the great hall at Aldeborne. The bad weather had finally broken, and it appeared that every estate holder in the hundred of Northampton had ventured out of doors to join Lord Wulfheah and his sister Elgiva at table. The timbered hall, its carved rafters garlanded with greens, was redolent with succulent aromas, and the haunches of roasting meat above the coals made his mouth water. The high table at the top of the hall had been laid, as it had been every night since he'd arrived, with a snowy cloth, silver plates, and fat candles. Tonight numerous extra tables had been set up in the hall as well, and the noise from the crush of guests was almost deafening.

As Athelstan turned to say something to his brothers, the hall quieted, and he saw that Elgiva and Wulf had appeared on the dais to begin the business of formally greeting their guests. They made a striking couple. They were both black-haired and handsome, although Elgiva's petite figure and small features gave her an elfin grace that was missing from her brother's taller, warrior's frame. They were both clad in deep scarlet, and Elgiva's shimmering gown clung to her in a way that was guaranteed to make every man in the room uncomfortable inside his breecs. Her hair was dressed in loose, wanton curls that framed her face and cascaded down her back, and when her voluptuous lips curved into a beguiling smile, a man would have to be made of stone not to smile back.

He ought to know. She had been favoring him with that smile—and somewhat more—from the moment he'd ridden through Aldeborne's gate a week ago. On Christmas night she had welcomed him with the ale bowl that was traditional and a molten kiss that was anything but. It had surprised the hell out of him, but he had not been fool enough to take it seriously. Not at first. She had placed him by her side at the table, though, and the casual grazing of knee and shoulder and hand all through the long meal had nearly driven him mad with a desire that food would not satisfy. By then he had caught on to her little game, and although he'd been playing it for seven nights now, it had lost none of its allure. She aroused him still, and he would find relief again tonight with the pretty blonde he had plucked from the kitchens—a girl who expected no reward beyond a few silver coins.

And that was the difficulty with Elgiva, he thought, watching her as she made her way through the hall with the brimming ale cup. Bedding her would cost him far more than a little silver. If he got her with child—even without a Christian marriage or a handfasting—it would have political repercussions that would further shift the weight of power in England to the northern lords.

Elgiva's brother Wulf had to know that. He was five years older than she was, and he had a place on the king's council. Since he was making no effort to curb his sister's little game, he must approve. Did her father know of it? Had he even put her up to it? The ealdorman was not here and so could claim innocence if any spark flared between Elgiva and one of the æthelings. The blame—and the king's wrath—would all fall on *him*.

He had not taken his eyes from Elgiva, and his brother Ecbert leaned toward him and whispered, "The hell with it. Why don't you just bed her and put yourself out of your misery?"

Athelstan threw him a dark look. "The lady comes with far too much baggage, and you know it," he muttered. "Do not let me drink more than a single cup of mead tonight, or I might lose my senses and take what she's offering. Why don't you bed her, Ecbert, if she is to your taste?"

Ecbert snorted. "She would not have me on a platter," he said, "more's the pity."

"It is the eldest ætheling that she wants," Edmund said, "and do not flatter yourself that your good looks have anything to do with it."

Edmund had the right of it. Athelstan was only too aware of the mantle of responsibility that he bore as the eldest son of the king. When he wed, and that would likely not happen while his father lived, it would be for political expediency, not personal inclination. To form any kind of attachment with a girl of noble birth would be to hand the girl and her family a weapon to use against the king. He could bed any girl in the kingdom, as long as she was not crown worthy.

Elgiva, who at that moment stepped in front of him to offer him the ale cup, was forbidden fruit. Her dark eyes held his as he drank, but for once her face was grave, and she was careful not to touch his fingers with her own.

Was this another move in the game, or had she learned about his trysts with the kitchen wench? He hoped the girl would not be punished. He would have to make sure that she was well compensated, just in case.

Whatever was behind this sudden coolness, he must play his part. He returned Elgiva's gaze with a grave bow and said, "Your beauty, lady, is a gift to us all."

Elgiva, gazing into Athelstan's guarded blue eyes, accepted his compliment with a curt nod. She knew he desired her. She could see it in his glance, could feel it in her fingertips whenever she chanced to touch him.

But he would rather bed a kitchen wench than the Lady of Northampton. Wulf had told her that, sneering that Athelstan obviously preferred a woman with experience in bed play. *I can give you some of that, sweetheart,* he had whispered, kissing her forehead and laughing when she stalked away from him.

Wulf stood beside her now, his hand at her waist, distracting her with a light caress. She slipped away from him, ignored Athelstan, and smiled at Ecbert, who she had determined would sit beside her at the feast tonight. Let the king's eldest son gnaw on the knowledge that he was not the only ætheling in her hall.

At the table, the younger brother seemed gratified by her sudden favor, and he responded by regaling her with a series of ribald tales that he, at least, seemed to find enormously entertaining. He reminded her of nothing so much as a boisterous puppy, gaunt and clumsy, with none of the grace of his brothers. Even Edmund, the youngest of the three and built like a tree stump, had more to recommend him than the lanky Ecbert, who was all arms and legs and, she thought, very little brain. His horselike face and braying laugh added nothing to his charm. It was a pity that he was too young to grow a beard, for she judged that it would improve his looks considerably. There would be less of him to see.

Still, he seemed open enough and completely guileless. Perhaps she could get him to reveal something about Athelstan that would be the key to bewitching him.

She signaled to a serving girl to fill Ecbert's cup, which he had already emptied three times, and she noticed that a servant had slipped behind the table to deliver a wax tablet each to Wulf and to Athelstan. She recognized her father's seal on the tablet that Wulf opened, and the question she had been about to pose to Ecbert died unspoken on her lips. She turned to her brother instead.

"What does my father say?" she asked him. To have arrived tonight the messages must have been sent from Rochester at the very first moment that the weather allowed. Surely they contained news of some import.

Wulf did not answer her but glanced at Athelstan, who was reading his own missive.

"It is heavy news," her brother said, his face grave. "I am sorry, my lord."

Elgiva held her breath. It must be a death. Nothing else would make her brother look with such concern toward the ætheling. Was it the king? Dear God, if he were dead, then the *witan* would surely offer Athelstan the throne. The implications of that for her own future could be enormous. The new king would need a wife, and her father would make sure that Athelstan looked to Northampton for his bride. She might be a queen before Eastertide.

But Athelstan had set the tablet down in front of him, and now he rose and faced the throng in the hall. His expression was solemn, and his movement drew all eyes toward him. A hush fell over the revelers as they waited to hear what he would say.

"I am bid by my father the king," he said, his voice echoing through the silent hall, "to announce that on Christmas morning my mother, the Lady Ælfgifu, died after giving birth to a son. The babe, alas, followed his mother in death. I ask that all present here tonight pray for both their souls." He turned to Elgiva and Wulf. "I would speak with my brothers alone. Please excuse us."

Elgiva watched the three brothers make their way from the table. Their mother's death was a sorrow to them, she supposed, but her passing was of little significance to anyone else. The king's wife had borne him numerous children, but as his consort and not his queen, she had done little else. Her death would have no effect on the kingdom or on Elgiva's world.

She turned to her brother, who was looking thoughtfully at the tablet in his hand.

"What does my father say?" she asked again. "I suppose that the king's sons will leave for Rochester tomorrow." This news must put an end to the feasting, in any case.

"They do not go south," Wulf replied. "There is no reason to do so, for their mother is already in her grave. My father writes that the æthelings are to take charge of our house troops and go to the king's manor at Saltford. He will meet them there, but he does not say when. Not immediately, I think." He tapped a finger against the tablet, then he looked speculatively at Elgiva. "The king, it seems, will take another wife, and very soon. I am ordered to stay here with you, in case you are

summoned to court. It appears, my dear sister, that my father enter-
tains the hope that you will be Æthelred's bride."

Elgiva gaped at her brother, while her mind played with new possibilities. To be wed to the father and not the son was not the destiny
that she had been anticipating. Would it suit her? Well, it would certainly put her in a position of power much sooner than she had looked
for it. Yet it was not an honor that she was certain she would like, and
it was not exactly the power that she had hoped for.

"To what end would the king marry?" she asked Wulf. "Æthelred is
an old man with seven sons. What need has he of a bride who would
give him yet more sons?"

"He is not so old," her brother said. "And, as you have good reason
to know, he enjoys his earthly pleasures. Better to marry than to burn,
the Scriptures say."

She frowned. She wanted to wed a king, and yet . . .

"His first wife was never crowned queen," she protested. "What
good to wed a king and not get a crown?"

Wulf's hand snaked behind her as if he would caress her, but instead she felt his fingers grasp her neck in a painful, viselike grip that
she could neither escape nor shake off without making a scene.

"Do you never think beyond your own petty concerns, my dear sister?" he hissed into her ear. "Do not delude yourself into thinking that
this alliance would be for your benefit. Its sole purpose would be to
strengthen my father's influence with the king, not cater to your mon-
umental vanity. You will do whatever you are bid to do, wed whomever
you are bid to wed, and let your father and brothers handle whatever
details are to be negotiated."

He let her go, and she rubbed her neck surreptitiously, smiling up
at him for the benefit of anyone in the hall who may have noticed their
little interaction.

"May I ask, then, if my father is negotiating my betrothal? Am I to
be allowed to make preparations for my nuptials?" She would need new
gowns, jewels, more attendants, and her own furnishings for the lady's
chambers at the Winchester palace. How much time did she have?

"It is somewhat more complicated than that," Wulf replied.

She did not like the sound of that.

"What do you mean?"

"You are not the only maid that the king is considering."

Now he leered at her, and she realized that he was toying with her, forcing her to tease the news out of him bit by bit, reveling in the power he held over her.

"You are lying," she said, refusing to be baited anymore. "There can be no one else, for I am the obvious choice." And now that she had grown somewhat used to the idea, the prospect of wedding Æthelred, the king with the liquid hands, was suddenly extremely appealing.

"Are you so confident, my dear?" Wulf asked, his dark eyes dancing with amusement. "I would not be so, if I were you. My father does not provide any names, but he states quite clearly that other possible brides exist. Their advantages are even now under consideration by the king." He leaned toward her to whisper in her ear. "If you had gone to Rochester you might have been able to use your many charms to sway Æthelred in your favor. But, alas, you stayed here. Poor Elgiva. It looks as though you should have accompanied our father to the Christmas court after all." He nipped her ear and then got to his feet. Moments later he had joined a group of guests below the dais.

Elgiva, following him with her eyes, still wondered if he had told her the truth. If he had, and if the king chose to look elsewhere for a bride, then her decision to remain here for the Yule feast was, quite possibly, the worst mistake she had ever made in her life.

Chapter Five

January 1002

Fécamp, Normandy

The cold, hard frosts of early January clung tightly to the lands that bordered the Narrow Sea, and for many days after the turn of the year, the tall masts of the Danish longships bristled in Fécamp's harbor. When the ships set sail at last, following the whale road back to their homeland, folk in the town breathed a collective sigh of relief, and in the ducal palace life settled into its winter routine.

The women of the duke's household spent their daylight hours together in the chamber of Richard's young wife, Judith, attending to their needlework. The lighter-weight summer tunics, mantles, fine linen shifts, even *chausses* and *braies* that belonged to members of the ducal family, had been drawn from their coffers, inspected carefully for rents and tears, and sorted into piles for repair.

Emma, who had some skill with the harp, played softly for the women who were seated in a companionable circle around the brazier. As she plucked the strings her glance drifted to where Mathilde had taken advantage of a shaft of daylight filtering through the high, horn-covered window. She had recovered from the ague that had troubled her over the last weeks, and now her face, although still thin, had regained some color and vibrancy. She was bent over an embroidery frame, where she worked a grail in pure gold thread upon a cope of white silk. It was to be a gift for their brother, Archbishop Robert, and

Mathilde's lips curved with satisfaction as the beautiful thing came to life beneath her fingers.

Judith, pacing the chamber with her six-week-old son on her shoulder, paused to inspect Mathilde's handiwork.

"It is a magnificent and generous gift, Mathilde," she pronounced in a tone of grudging approval. "I hope that when it is completed you will turn your skill toward something more practical. You will require some fine new gowns, I think, when we return to Rouen."

Emma, watching her sister, saw her mouth purse. They both found it irksome to be ordered about by their brother's wife, however well-intentioned her directives might be. Twenty years old, with nut-brown hair and a pleasingly rounded figure, Judith of Brittany's benign appearance belied her strident personality. She had shouldered the role of duchess of Normandy with a vigor that irritated even the Dowager Duchess Gunnora. Months of internecine skirmishes between the duke's wife and his mother had threatened to turn into all-out war, until finally the two women had managed to forge a workable truce. Gunnora continued to advise her son on matters of state, and Judith ruled his household. Emma and her sister had found the terms of the unspoken treaty not especially to their liking, but they had not been consulted.

"Are the gowns that I already own not fine enough for my attendance at your court in Rouen, my lady?" Mathilde's voice rang high and sharp, with an unmistakably brittle edge that made Emma wince.

"It was not meant to be a criticism, Mathilde," Judith snapped, shifting her child from one shoulder to the other, "but it is time to think about preparing for your betrothal and marriage. Now that Richard has a son I am certain that he will wish to provide for you and for Emma in the same way that he did for your elder sisters. You, Mathilde, will surely be the next to wed, and it may be sooner than you think."

Startled by Judith's remark, Emma struck a false note, then set the harp aside. Her mind fastened on Judith's words, and now she recalled the conversation she'd overheard between her brother and Swein Forkbeard. Had Richard, after all, promised his sister to the son of the

Danish king? Or had that conversation with Forkbeard merely spurred Richard to bend his thoughts toward his youngest sisters' marriage prospects?

"Is my brother contemplating an alliance for my sister?" she asked, keeping her tone light. "Pray, Judith, if you know something, do not keep us in suspense."

"Your brother," Judith said, "has Mathilde's welfare, and yours, Emma, always at heart. Whatever provisions he makes for you will be explained to you at the appropriate time. I only bring this up now because, as you are both of an age to marry, you must comport yourselves differently than you have in the past. In particular, you, Emma, will not, under any circumstances, accompany Richard on his progress this summer. Best you put it out of your mind completely."

Emma stared at Judith in shock. "But I have always made that journey!" she protested. From the time she was a little girl and, even she had to admit it, her father's spoiled pet, she had been allowed to accompany the duke and her brothers on the summer progress to the ducal forts, abbeys, and manors that lay scattered across Normandy. Emma had been the only one of the sisters to make the annual trek, and she had reveled in the relative freedom of those excursions. It was true that she was accompanied by a small phalanx of personal attendants, who never left her side, but the rhythm of that itinerant existence provided a welcome contrast to the sequestered life inside the castle walls.

"You are a child no longer," Judith said. "I have advised Richard that your place must be here, with the women of the court, and he has agreed. We will speak of it no more."

Emma bit her lip. Beside her, Margot, the healer and midwife who had assisted Emma into the world and had accompanied her on those summerlong journeys, patted her hand in commiseration. Heavyhearted with disappointment, Emma began to sort through a pile of her gowns, searching for signs of wear. She would appeal to her mother about this, although she suspected it would do her little good.

Judith, meanwhile, had handed her babe to a wet nurse and seated herself among the women again. They worked in less than amiable silence for some time, until it was broken by the sound of commotion from the castle yard below. Clearly some visitor of importance had approached the gate and was requesting audience with the duke. The calls of the gatekeeper and the door warden were too muffled, though, for anyone in the chamber to make out what was said.

Judith gave a quick nod to Dari, an Irish slave who had accompanied her from Brittany. Tiny, soft-footed, and clever, Dari made an excellent little spy. She brought the ladies word of activities occurring in the duke's hall long before any messages were conveyed along more formal lines. Judith rewarded Dari with ribbons, trinkets, and even silver pennies, depending on the import of the information that she carried, saying that it was well worth it in order to receive news almost as soon as it was heard in the kitchens.

Emma, still brooding over the loss of her summer's adventure, took up a cyrtel of her own and, inspecting it, found a rip at the hem. It was one of the gowns she wore when riding, very full and loose. She placed it on the pile to be mended, then looked up to see that Dari had returned, wild with excitement.

"The messenger is English, my lady," Dari said breathlessly. "A company of men from across the Narrow Sea has landed at the harbor and will be with us soon. There is an archbishop among them, and an ealdorman. What is an ealdorman?" She spoke the unfamiliar word with a wrinkled nose.

"It is an English title of some kind," Judith said. "Something like a duke, I believe, only not so powerful as Richard. An archbishop, though . . ."

There was no need for her to complete the sentence. All the women understood the importance of an archbishop, who represented both temporal and spiritual power. Appointed to their sees by the reigning monarch of the land, they controlled enormous wealth, administered large estates, and maintained a retinue of fighting men. Emma's brother Robert, archbishop of Rouen, was second only to his brother, the duke, in terms of prestige and power. The arrival of an English archbishop in Normandy meant that some matter of great import was at hand.

"Go down to the kitchens, girl," Judith said to Dari, "and learn whatever you can. Hurry now!"

Dari slipped away, and the women returned to their work, although Emma guessed that each of them was as distracted by the arrival of the English as she was.

"Will he be offering a treaty, do you think?" she asked. The presence of an archbishop seemed to imply that. In her father's time the pope himself had brokered a treaty between England and Normandy regarding the trading of stolen English goods in Norman ports. She had been too young to pay close attention to the talk that swirled around the hall, about the wisdom of bowing to the pressure exerted by the pope, and by England's king. She could remember, though, heated discussions between her mother and her two brothers when the issue of the treaty had been raised again a few years ago.

Archbishop Robert had insisted that Richard, as the new duke, need no longer abide by their father's treaty with England. It infuriated Robert that King Æthelred, reportedly the wealthiest monarch in all of Christendom, would demand that the duke of Normandy forego his quite lucrative trade with the Danes or the Norse or anyone else. He had convinced Richard of the wisdom of this point of view, and since then Richard's coffers had grown heavy with silver from a brisk trade in slaves and booty looted from England.

"I expect," said Judith dismissively, "that it will be some matter of trade or policy that your brother and the dowager duchess will settle. We will learn about it in good time, but I will wager that it has nothing to do with us."

Judith's lips stretched into a thin line, suggesting to Emma that Richard's wife was not yet at peace with the fact that she sat here sewing while Richard's mother sat at his right hand in the great hall. The politics of marriage, Emma thought, appeared to be every bit as complicated as the politics of kings.

Chapter Six

Athelstan, Ecbert, and Edmund rode at the head of a small company of men along a track that wound through a snow-smothered landscape. Above them thin white clouds driven by a light breeze streaked the sky. For two weeks the æthelings had been awaiting the arrival of Ælfhelm, ealdorman of Northumbria, at the royal estate near Saltford, the men restive and chafing under the enforced inactivity brought on by repeated bouts of foul weather. In that time the æthelings had received no further word from either the ealdorman or the king, and Athelstan felt as if they had been abandoned, awaiting word of their father's pleasure. He wondered what was in the king's mind to keep his eldest sons distant at such a time.

It had not concerned him that news of their mother's death had reached them only after she had been laid to rest, for he understood that the deadly Christmastime storm had made it impossible for a messenger to make it through any sooner. He and his brothers had mourned her in their own way, yet her loss had touched them almost not at all. Although she had borne eleven children she had tended none of them in their infancy or their youth. Her impact upon her sons and daughters had been of no greater weight than that made by a single snowflake when it touches the earth. She had been but a shadow in their lives, almost invisible in the far larger shadow cast by their father, the king.

Now, though, Athelstan found it worrisome that Ealdorman Ælfhelm and the other great lords of the land remained with the king in Winchester while the eldest æthelings had not been summoned. What matters of moment were being discussed among the king's counselors?

What secrets was their father keeping from his sons?

"He will marry again," Edmund had said flatly, when they had discussed it among themselves.

Ecbert had guffawed in disbelief, but Athelstan was inclined to agree with Edmund. Their father was not a young man, but he was vigorous and hale, and his carnal appetites were an open secret among the nobles of his court. The bishops, certainly, would urge him to marry.

Such a step could have momentous consequences for the æthelings, and the fact that Athelstan and his brothers were not privy to their father's deliberations gnawed like a canker. Even as he turned his face up to the pale light of the winter sun, Athelstan's thoughts were as cold as the wind that blew at their backs.

He urged his horse up a gentle rise, toward an ancient stone that stood black against the sky. It marked the final leg of this morning's quest, a journey that had been suggested by Ecbert, half in seriousness and half in jest. He had heard tell of a crone living alone in a fold of the hills, a wisewoman who could read events far in the future.

"We should seek her out," he had urged last night, as he faced Edmund across the *tafl* board, deliberating his next move. "She might tell us something to our advantage."

Athelstan and Edmund had both scoffed at their brother's suggestion, but Ecbert had persisted.

"The local folk swear that she has the Sight," he insisted. "Even the prior from the abbey hereabouts has been known to visit her cottage."

"Probably to persuade her to leave her pagan ways," Athelstan said drily, from where he sat watching their play.

"They say that she knows things," Ecbert persisted, "that she can decipher men's hearts."

"You might want to ask her for advice on how to win at *tafl*," Edmund said, making a move that captured Ecbert's king and ended the game. "That is your third loss, man. You are utterly hopeless tonight."

The normally genial Ecbert threw up his hands in frustration.

"I am bored, Edmund! I am fed up with waiting here like a kenneled dog. If the weather is fine tomorrow, I shall ride out to consult the old woman. Athelstan, will you come with me? Who knows? She may be able to tell us what is in the mind of the king."

Athelstan thought that unlikely. Nevertheless, the journey, at least, might not be such a bad idea. He glanced around the hall, where men clustered in small groups over games of dice or nodded over cups of ale. They were all of them bored and not a few of them surly. They would be at each other's throats soon if he did not find something to occupy them.

He nodded briskly to Ecbert.

"It can do no harm," he said, "and the men and horses will benefit from the exercise, fair weather or no."

And so they had set out midmorning, following landmarks that a local man pointed out as he led the way—a tree blasted by lightning, an abandoned mill, an ancient mound that the folk thereabouts called the Devil's Barrow. They had arrived at last at a long, low ridge where the snow lay less thick than it did on the surrounding countryside, and where the standing stone, its edges scored in primitive runes, pointed skyward.

Athelstan checked his horse beside the ancient, lichen-covered stone. Gazing into the shallow vale beyond, he caught his breath at what he saw: a circle of what he guessed must be a hundred standing stones, each one the height of a man or a little more, mushroomed from the valley floor. Like monstrous, deformed fingers, black against the blanket of snow, the stones cast long shadows that speared, ominously, straight at him.

They might not be as massive as the giants on Sarum's plain, he thought, but there were far more of them, and they had the same menacing power. He did not like it, and he felt his gut begin to churn.

Ecbert and Edmund came up beside him, and he watched their faces as they surveyed the scene before them. From their stricken expressions it was clear that they were having second thoughts about this venture—as was he. There were enough dark things in this world. One needn't seek them out.

"Are you sure about this?" he asked Ecbert.

"No," Ecbert muttered, "but it would be stupid to turn back now." He flicked a glance at Athelstan. "You go first, though."

Athelstan scowled at him, then peered into the valley again, looking for signs of life. The stone circle was fringed by moss-bearded oaks, and on its far side he could see a small croft sheltering among the trees, its thatching frosted with snow. He realized with a shock that what he had taken for another stone, standing in the gloom near the hut, was a living figure staring back at him.

She had been waiting for them, then. He was certain of it, although he could not say how he knew. There was something else he was certain of as well, and it added to his anxiety. He was meant to go down there. Ecbert was right. There was no turning back now.

He led the way down into the grove, threading his horse through the trees toward the croft, purposely avoiding the clearing and its hulking, glowering stones. As they neared the cottage he saw that the figure waiting there was swathed in layers of coarse, black wool, her head covered by the folds of a shawl so thick that the old woman's face, if it was a woman, was all but invisible.

"God be with you, my lord," she called.

The voice was surprisingly deep and harsh—roughened, Athelstan guessed, by wood smoke and disuse. He dismounted and went toward her, Ecbert and Edmund trailing behind him.

"God be with you, mother," he said. "It must be hard faring for you this winter, living so far from your neighbors as you do. Will you accept a small gift, some supplies to replenish your larder against lean times?" He gestured to one of his men, who placed a large sack filled with cheese, bread, and pulses beside the hut and then hastened back to his mount.

The eyes watching Athelstan showed neither surprise nor gratitude.

"What would you have of me?" she asked. "You have come far from your appointed road, for you are bound north, I think. The *herepath* lies that way."

She gestured to the west, where the old road built by the Roman legions, the Fosse Way, ran from Exeter in the southwest to Jorvik in the north. Presumably, whenever Ealdorman Ælfhelm arrived to lead them to Northumbria, they would, indeed, follow that same northward road.

Still, Athelstan reassured himself, it did not take second sight to hazard that a group of armed men wearing the badge of the ealdorman of Northumbria would likely be headed that way.

"Perhaps you have already given me what I seek," he said, "if you can predict nothing more for me than a road that leads north. But it is my brother here," he motioned to Ecbert, "who wishes to consult you."

She peered up at him then, and he saw the gleam of shrewd eyes from within the folds of her shawl.

"Nay, lord," she said, shaking her head slowly. "You are the one who has need of guidance. Will you give me your hand?"

He hesitated, brushed by a whisper of foreboding. The knowing eyes fixed on his, though, flashed a challenge that he could not ignore, and he placed his hand within her outstretched palms. Her fingers felt thin and clawlike, as roughened and calloused as his own.

She peered at his palm, and for some time she was silent while Athelstan's disquiet grew. The standing stone on the ridge, the menacing stone circle, the skeletal touch of the old woman's hands—all of it was forbidden, pagan magic. He felt a wild urge to flee, but in the next moment she spoke, and in a voice far different from the one with which she had greeted him. Now it was vibrant, full and feminine. The timbre of it pulsed through him in the same way that a tolling bell vibrates through the blood.

"There is great strength in this hand," she proclaimed, loud enough for all his men to hear, "strength enough to wield even the great Sword of Offa."

Next to him he felt Edmund give a sudden start of surprise, and he could guess what his brother was thinking, for the words struck him, too, with a force as sharp as a blow. Offa's Sword, once wielded by that legendary Saxon king, even now hung on the wall behind their father's chair in the great hall at Winchester. By tradition it was bestowed by the ruling king upon his designated heir. It had not yet been promised to Athelstan, but he expected that one day it would be his.

Yet how had this woman guessed that she spoke to the eldest son of the king? Had word reached her somehow that the æthelings were at Saltford? Possibly. Possibly this was all an act, but if so, to what end?

Now the woman curled his fingers into his palm and leaned close to him.

"Sword you may wield," she said, so softly that only he could hear her, "yet the scepter will remain beyond your reach."

It took him a moment to grasp the import of her words, and by then she was already turning away to enter her croft. Quickly he covered the space between them, caught her arm, and held her.

"Who will take the scepter, then, when the time comes?" he hissed softly. "Who will wear the crown?"

She turned, and for a long moment she looked past him, at each of his brothers in turn, until at last she faced Athelstan again and slowly shook her head.

"There is a shadow on the crown, my lord," she murmured, "and my Sight cannot pierce the darkness. You must be content with the knowledge you have been given, for I can say no more."

No, of course she would say no more, he thought. She was wily, this one, toying with her supplicants as skillfully as a practiced harlot so that they sought her out again and again. Yet she could have no real power, not unless one granted it to her. And he would not journey down that dark road.

He released her with a curt nod.

"Go with God then, mother."

She turned away from him, and he followed her with his eyes until the dark maw of her croft swallowed her.

Ecbert had already mounted his horse, but Edmund was waiting for him, studying him with dark, speculative eyes.

"What did she say to you, there at the end?" he asked. "What did she say about us?"

"Nothing of import," Athelstan replied gruffly. "You did not really expect anything, did you? She is nothing but a fraud, Edmund."

He mounted his horse and made for the ridge top, but in spite of what he had said to his brother, his thoughts ran on the old woman's words. Her prediction about Offa's Sword was no more than he already knew. He had been born the eldest son of one of the richest kings in Christendom, and Offa's Sword was his due.

As for the rest of it, if there was any truth in the future that she bespoke him—that he would never be England's king—then he must find a way to change his destiny.

Chapter Seven

February 1002
Fécamp, Normandy

The purpose of the English delegation to Normandy became clear as soon as the news spread of the recent death of the consort of the English king. Although Duke Richard maintained a stony silence about what had occurred during that first meeting in the great hall, everyone assumed that the archbishop and the ealdorman had brought a proposal of marriage for Mathilde, and that it would be accepted. A liaison with the English throne would raise Richard's prestige in all of Christendom. He would be a fool to turn it down, and Richard was no fool.

Nevertheless, the negotiations dragged on for weeks, wreathed in secrecy behind the cloistered walls of nearby Trinity Abbey. Gunnora, who attended each session, returned every night to the palace so grim-faced that neither her daughters nor even the intrepid Judith dared to question her.

When eventually Ealdorman Ælfric was seen to board his ship and set sail with a document that bore the ducal seal, the palace hummed with excitement and anticipation. Emma waited with her sister for word that Mathilde must attend her mother and brothers to be counseled regarding King Æthelred and the role that Mathilde would play, but no summons came. Instead, the web of secrecy that had been cast about the proceedings between the Norman duke and the ministers of the English king remained impenetrable. The dowager duchess went into seclusion at Fécamp's Priory of St. Ann, while Richard and Robert left Fécamp altogether, riding with the English archbishop to the abbey of Saint-Wandrille to pray for the success of their endeavor.

Judith, who had no more inkling than anyone else about what had taken place in the abbey cloisters, nevertheless followed through on her plan to order new wardrobes for both of Richard's sisters in preparation for their future nuptials. Fabrics of the finest silk, linen, and wool arrived daily from Rouen. Gowns, chemises, stockings, and headrails spilled from busy fingers until every chamber at Fécamp became a storehouse of wedding finery.

Mathilde, who should have been at the center of all of the preparations, had taken ill again, laid low by headaches that would not let her sleep. Emma spent long hours at her sister's bedside relaying every scrap of rumor and gossip that she gleaned about the English king and his court, although her own heart was heavy at the coming separation. Mathilde, she guessed, must feel it even more, for she would leave everything familiar behind her. Worse yet, beyond that parting lay the reality of the king, so many years older than his new bride, and in addition to that, the challenges of an English court filled with strangers speaking a foreign tongue.

Much would be expected of the king's new wife, Emma thought, burdens that she could only begin to imagine. How would Mathilde, who had never been physically strong, cope with the pressures of that new life? Often Emma lay awake in the cold watches of the night thinking about those burdens, her heart filled with dread for her sister, knowing that beside her Mathilde, too, lay awake in the dark. Yet each sister kept her own counsel.

And so the weeks passed until, late one February afternoon, the dowager duchess returned from St. Ann's, and Emma was summoned to wait upon her. She found her mother alone in her chamber, circlet and headrail cast aside and the long gray braid of her hair coiled atop her head. She was warming her hands at the brazier, and the light from below accentuated fine creases around her mouth and eyes. She nodded to Emma, then turned her gaze back to the glowing coals, and for a time was silent. Emma saw an unfamiliar weariness in her face, and a resemblance to Mathilde that she had never before noticed in the sharpness of her nose and the thin line of her mouth.

Finally her mother spoke, almost as if to herself. "Events have overtaken us, and I cannot wait for your brothers' return to set things in motion." She glanced at Emma and nodded toward a nearby stool. "You had best sit down, Emma, for I have a great deal to say to you."

Emma's heart clouded with dread. She sat upon the stool and waited for whatever hammer stroke was to come.

"As you have no doubt guessed," Gunnora said, "the king of England has sued for your sister's hand in marriage." She glanced at Emma, then began to pace the room. "King Æthelred wants something in return, of course—something more than a nubile young bride to grace his bed. And so, in recompense for the great honor that he bestows upon us in taking a Norman wife, he will expect your brother to close his harbors to the Danes. His emissaries have not said as much directly. They have danced around the issue like virgins round a maypole, but it is clear what they want, and your brother has given them every reason to believe that he will grant it."

Emma leaned forward in her chair, her eyes on her mother, her mind racing. She had been so preoccupied with the challenges that this marriage presented for her sister that she had forgotten the peril that her brother risked by agreeing to it. Æthelred of England was the mortal enemy of King Swein of Denmark. With Mathilde's marriage to Æthelred, Richard, too, became an enemy of the infamous Swein Forkbeard, making Normandy a target for Danish raiders.

"In fact," Gunnora went on, "your brother cannot deny the Danes access to our harbors and our markets. If he should do so, Swein Forkbeard would turn his shipmen upon us like starving dogs on a wounded stag. He would harry our coasts for plunder, and then barter it quite happily in Hamburg or Bremen. The English king could not come to our aid, for he has no fleet. The French king would merely rejoice in our misfortune. It would be a catastrophe for every Norman settlement that lies within reach of Danish longships. And so," she stopped her pacing and stood before Emma, "it will not happen. Your brother will never close his harbors to the Danes. Nevertheless, he will agree to do so, and his sister will be given in marriage as his bond."

Emma stared at her mother as the wretchedness of her sister's fate struck her. Mathilde would be little more than a royal hostage, sent to guarantee her brother's submission to the will of the English king. And if Richard broke his pledge and defied the king, Mathilde would be defenseless in a foreign land, with no means of protecting herself from whatever retribution her royal husband might choose to inflict.

"He cannot do it," Emma whispered, her mouth gone dry with horror. Her brother could not sacrifice Mathilde this way, could not place her at the mercy of the English king.

"So I told your brother," Gunnora said, and now Emma could hear the weariness in her voice. "But Richard is a ruler and a man, and the life of a young girl, even that of his own sister, weighs little when balanced against the fate of an entire people. I could not sway him from his course."

Emma felt sick at the thought of Mathilde alone in a foreign land, perhaps a prisoner of the king.

"What will happen to her?"

Gunnora began to pace the room again, her hands twisting one inside the other, and Emma grew more and more frightened by her mother's obvious distress. When Gunnora spoke at last, she did not answer Emma's question.

"Richard is not oblivious to the peril that his sister would face in England. It took little effort on my part to persuade him that we must provide her with a weapon that she could use to protect herself should her husband turn against her. The solution was obvious, but we agonized for hours over how it was to be accomplished. In the end, we offered Æthelred my dower lands on the Contentin. It is a princely gift that he could not easily refuse, for it gives him a toehold on this side of the Narrow Sea." She stopped her pacing and drew in a long breath. "In return, Richard demanded that his sister go to England not as Æthelred's consort but as his queen."

She looked at Emma with a kind of triumph in her eyes. "Emma, Ealdorman Ælfric has returned with word that the English king has accepted the contract. Æthelred's Norman bride will not be a mere consort but will be crowned as his queen. She will have wealth and stature far beyond that of his first wife. She will stand at the king's side accorded privileges that he cannot easily rescind however much he may be provoked."

Emma saw at once the wisdom of such a provision, but she also recognized the additional burden that a crown would place upon her sister.

"Does Mathilde know?" she asked.

A shadow crept across Gunnora's face, and Emma watched, bewildered, as her mother stepped forward and knelt in front of her. Slender fingers clutched Emma's own, fingers so cold that they seemed to burn against Emma's skin.

"It is not Mathilde who will go to England, Emma," her mother said. "It must be you."

The words flowed over her like water at first, and then they seemed to form into waves that buffeted her until she could no longer pull in even the smallest breath. She did not dare look away from her mother's solid gaze, because it was the only thing that kept her from drowning in that treacherous sea.

She felt as if the world she knew had suddenly changed from a place of safety and sanctuary to something unknown and terrifying. She did not want to go to England, did not want to wed a king, did not want to bear the weight of a crown. Yet, gazing down into her mother's stern and unrelenting face, she knew that she would be given no choice.

She slipped from her stool as panic engulfed her. Dropping to her hands and knees she began to retch, burning bile scalding her throat. A basin appeared before her, and her mother's steadying hand grasped the back of her neck. She closed her eyes, but she could not stop the spinning panic that had her in its grip.

"It is the shock of it," her mother said, her voice gentle but firm. "You were not prepared for it. But you will receive much worse than this in the years to come, my daughter," and now the voice seemed to Emma implacable and uncompromising. "You must ever be prepared within yourself to face what trials may await you. Let this be your first lesson: No one else must see you like this, Emma. Do you hear me? However great the provocation, you must never allow anyone to see your fear."

Emma, crouched upon the floor, her body braced upon her forearms, her stomach churning, squeezed her eyes tight against the tears that threatened.

"Why must I be the one to go?" she demanded. "Mathilde is the eldest. She wants it. It is her right."

"Your sister has neither the strength nor the will to pit herself against the . . ." Gunnora stopped, as if she regretted her words and would take them back, ". . . against the trials that face a queen," she finished slowly. "Only you, Emma, of all my daughters, have the gifts for that."

Many hours later, as Emma lay sleepless at her mother's side, Gunnora's words echoed endlessly in her mind. She had no illusions about the fate that awaited her. That much her mother had made perfectly clear. As Norman bride and English queen she would walk a fine line between the interests of two rulers—her brother and her lord. Both men would demand her fealty. One, at least, would exact a heavy price if she were to prove disloyal. That was what her mother feared, and what she had been willing to reveal.

But there was something else that her mother would not say, and Emma felt certain that it had to do with the English king. She sensed that Gunnora knew something about Æthelred of England that she did not want Emma to know, at least not yet. It was that unshared knowledge about the man she would wed that frightened her most of all.

In the streets of Fécamp and Rouen, in Caen and Évreux, the populace hailed Emma as the flower of Normandy, the bride who would become England's queen. Within the ducal palace, though, where the duke's sisters once shared a bedchamber, the news of Emma's betrothal was no cause for rejoicing. Mathilde, bitter and angry that a royal marriage had been contracted for Emma instead of for her, took to her bed, refusing to speak to her sister in spite of Emma's tearful entreaties and Gunnora's measured reproofs. Finally, Gunnora sent her to Rouen, where Mathilde would not be daily bombarded by the frenzied preparations for her sister's marriage.

Emma wept at Mathilde's departure, but Gunnora did not let her grieve for long. There was much that Emma had to learn before the ships would carry her across the Narrow Sea.

She spent long hours with the ealdorman, Ælfric, who schooled her in the finer points of the English language and the traditions of the court. He was an able tutor who treated her with grave courtesy, and she came to like him well. Not a young man by any means, his genial face was framed by thick gray locks that hung to near his shoulders. His beard, too, was gray, and his dark eyes gleamed beneath bushy gray brows. The fist-sized golden broach that clasped his cloak at one shoulder and the jeweled rings adorning his fingers bespoke wealth and influence, and she wondered how close he was to the king.

Ælfric told her of the ancient kingdoms of Northumbria, Mercia, East Anglia, and Wessex, and of the great King Alfred, who began the task of binding the separate kingdoms into one—a task completed at last by King Edgar, Æthelred's father. That king, he told her, had died at an early age, leaving his throne to a young son. Ælfric's face had darkened then, as if some memory from that distant past had suddenly cast a shadow over the present. He would not say what troubled him, though, and Emma's suspicion grew that there was something about her betrothed husband that was being kept from her.

During this time she received guidance from her family as well. Richard advised her regarding the estates for which she would be responsible, reminding her to pay close attention to income and expenditures, to rents and to yields.

Archbishop Robert counseled her regarding God's expectations of her as queen, particularly her duties to the Church and the men and women who served it.

Judith helped her choose the attendants who would accompany her to England and assisted with the packing of all her belongings: clothes, furniture, bedding, supplies for the journey, gifts for the family and for the nobles who awaited her. It was no insignificant task. It would take three longships to transport Emma, her retainers, and her goods to Canterbury. Two more ships would carry a dozen horses bred in the Norman stables—Emma's own gifts to the members of her new family.

It was Gunnora who, summoning her daughter to her chamber, raised the matter of the marriage bed and of Emma's role as bedmate of a king.

"It is your duty to be submissive to your lord, Emma," she said in clipped tones, as she sat facing her daughter. "It would be perilous for you to refuse the king your favors or to rebuke him, for your crown will be little more than an ornament at first."

Gunnora's expression softened then, and she cupped Emma's cheek with her hand.

"You are very young, my girl. That is your weakness as well as your strength. The king will cherish you for your youth and your beauty, and you must use both to gain his favor." She drew a deep breath and placed her hands on Emma's shoulders. "Never forget that your first and most important task is to bear a son. It is your son who will be your treasure and your protector, even while he is yet a babe. It is your son who will give you power, who will bind the king to you in a way that he can be bound to no other living woman."

In the brief moments that she was alone, Emma pondered her mother's words. Would her child, she wondered, really be of much importance to a king who already had numerous sons and daughters? Could Æthelred of England ever be bound to her as he had been to that first wife?

It was a question she did not ask aloud, for even her mother could not know the answer.

On the night before she was to leave for England, there was no great feast held in Emma's honor, for it was Lent and feasting was forbidden. The ducal household, though, gathered in the great hall at Fécamp, where the betrothal gifts sent by the English king had been spread out over six long tables. Among the treasures there were caskets filled with gold and silver; bolts of silk, linen, and the finest wool; silver bridles and saddles of tooled leather; fur pelts of martin, ermine, and sable; cunningly carved wooden boxes that held delicate musical pipes; necklaces studded with amethysts and emeralds; and an assortment of books magnificently bound in gold. When the gifts had been admired, Richard's bard recited a poem about a flower that was borne on the tide from Normandy to England, where it bloomed and prospered and was loved by all.

Emma listened to the poem with dry eyes and a mild expression, for that was what was demanded of her. In her heart, though, she carried a weight of grief, uncertainty, and fear that filled her with dread and seemed to press upon her very soul.

A.D. 1002   Then, in the same Lent, came the
Lady Emma, Richard's daughter, to this land.

—*The Anglo-Saxon Chronicle*

Chapter Eight

April 1002

Canterbury, Kent

The voyage from Fécamp to Canterbury took five days, and every one of them was cold, wet, and miserable. The heaving of the ship and the unremitting stench of fish oil that the shipmen used to waterproof their clothes and rigging sickened Emma and her companions. It was a relief when they left the open sea and finally entered the placid waters of the River Stour. As they sailed past the wattle huts and wooden enclosures marking the outskirts of Canterbury, Emma stood at the entrance of the shelter that had been rigged midship. She gazed through a steady rain at a flat, sodden, dreary landscape. In the distance, cathedral towers seemed to pierce the forbidding clouds that hung low and gray over the city.

Beside her Lady Wymarc was muffled in the folds of a woolen cloak, and as a blast of rain hit them, she pulled Emma's fur-lined hood up to keep the rain off her hair.

"Do you suppose," Emma murmured, her heart as gray and heavy as the swollen clouds, "that the sun ever shines in this dismal place?"

"To be sure, my lady," Wymarc replied briskly. "It cannot always be this wet or the English would have feathers and webbed feet." She placed a hand on Emma's arm. "Do not lose heart, I beg you. Not now, when the worst of the voyage is behind us."

Emma could not help but smile as she looked into the wide brown eyes that regarded her with a mixture of sympathy, pride, and excitement. Wymarc was ever one to look for the sun behind the clouds. She had an irrepressible exuberance—a quality that had not found much favor with Duchess Judith but had endeared her to Emma. The two of them were much the same age, and during the mad weeks of preparation it had been Wymarc's unbridled enthusiasm for the adventure that lay before them that had buoyed Emma's spirits and kept her from despair.

"I will be grateful to leave this ship," Emma said, "but I fear that the worst is likely yet to come." She dreaded this first meeting with the king, and she wanted it behind her. Yet even that, she reminded herself, would not be the worst that she would have to face in the coming days. There was the bedding to get through, but she put that out of her mind for now. "When we go ashore, do not leave my side," she commanded, "even for a moment."

A bridge spanned the river ahead of them and led to a wide, tower-crowned stone gateway from which banners hung, limp and dripping. Emma could see a throng of folk crowded at the tower's foot and massed upon its parapets, waving kerchiefs and hats enthusiastically in spite of the rain. A rumble of voices floated across the water toward her in a general roar of excitement and cheers. Armed men in mail tunics and scarlet cloaks lined the path that led from the riverside to the city wall, their black shields overlapping to keep the crowd at bay.

At the water's edge, four black-clad acolytes, oblivious to the steady downpour, held a scarlet canopy over a scarlet-robed archbishop. A knot of brightly clad noblemen, their fur-lined mantles and hoods testifying to their high rank, clustered behind the prelate, their faces turned expectantly toward the approaching ship.

"Which of them is the king?" Wymarc asked.

Emma scanned the men again but none of them fit the description that Ealdorman Ælfric had given her of Æthelred—a tall, well-built man with long golden hair and a trim beard.

A little shiver of foreboding crept along her spine to mingle with the anxiety already there. Was it possible that he had not come to greet

her? She recalled how her brother Richard had made the five-day journey to Bayeux to wed Judith and escort her back to Rouen, and how
the count of Turenne had traveled for near a month to sue for the hand
of her sister Beatrice. Æthelred, though, had sent a delegation to Normandy to bid for his bride rather than come in person. Could he not
even trouble himself to meet her at the city gate?

"I do not think that he is here," she murmured to Wymarc.

"Perhaps he is waiting to greet you in great state inside the palace,"
Wymarc said, "or at the church. Perhaps he thinks you will not wish to
see him until you have had a chance to rest from the journey."

Or perhaps, Emma thought, he is somewhat less than eager to meet
his bride. Whatever the reason, it was an affront to her, and her anxiety grew.

The boat drew up to the dock, and Emma recognized Ealdorman
Ælfric standing foremost among the nobles waiting to greet her. He
had left Normandy some days before she had, and now the sight of his
gaunt, old face, already smiling a welcome, cheered her somewhat. He
helped her over the gunwale and into the shelter of the canopy, then
took both her hands and bent to kiss them.

"The king sends you greetings, my lady. Your bridegroom wished
to come himself, but pressing matters of state have kept him from your
side. I am bid to welcome you and escort you to your lodgings in the
abbey precincts."

He had barely finished speaking when the archbishop raised his
hands and intoned a blessing, and the noise of the crowd hushed as the
Latin words floated on the air. After that Emma was introduced to
each nobleman in turn, and she greeted every man with a gracious
word and a smile in spite of the misgiving that clutched at her heart.
She had been anxious at the prospect of meeting the king. That he had
not come to greet her, whatever the reason, only increased her unease.

"I thank you, my lords," she said, in a voice as strong as she could
muster, carefully enunciating the tongue-twisting English words, "and
I thank the people of England for their welcome. May the Lord shower

his blessings upon us all." The crowd gave a roar and, satisfied that she had pleased them, Emma turned to Ælfric. "I beg you, my lord, to tell me when I may look forward to meeting with the king."

The archbishop, an ancient man with a sour expression, raised an eyebrow and pursed his lips in disapproval. "You would do well to curb your impatience, my lady," he said gruffly. "Be content that the king will attend to you in his own good time."

Stung by his rebuke, Emma had to bite her lip to keep from saying something she might regret. Here was one who disapproved of her. Was it because she was young and a woman, she wondered, or because she was Norman?

It was Ælfric who jumped in to mend the awkward moment.

"On Sunday," he said, "the king will greet you at the church door to recite the marriage vows. Immediately afterward he will escort you into the cathedral for the coronation ceremony."

Not until Sunday! That was five days hence. What kind of man was this Æthelred that he would not meet with his bride in private for even a few moments of conversation before he wed her? Was this how things were done in England? The sense of panic that she had kept at bay for the last six weeks began to clutch at her again.

"I wish to meet with the king tomorrow," she insisted, smiling, although it was an effort. "Surely he can grant me a few moments of his good time."

"I am sorry, my lady," Ælfric said gently. "That will not be possible, for the king has not yet arrived in Canterbury. He has sent word that he will not be here before Sunday."

She could feel the eyes of each nobleman fix upon her, taking her measure, curious to see how she would receive this unwelcome news. She said no more, but nodded to Ælfric in acknowledgment of his apology, doing her best to disguise both her displeasure at the king's slight and her fear of what it might mean. She doubted that she was very successful. Her hands, she realized, were clenched as tightly as the muscles of her stomach. Drawing a deep breath, she made an effort to relax as she followed in the wake of the archbishop, who had started toward the city gates. She would have turned to search for Wymarc behind her, but she knew instinctively that she must keep her back straight and her head forward.

Ælfric escorted her to a litter draped lavishly with furs beneath a silk-lined canopy. Making a low bow, he handed her into it, and then she was borne on the shoulders of eight noblemen through the streets of Canterbury. She forced herself to smile, lifting her hand to the crowds of folk who lined the way or waved at her from thatched rooftops. She heard cries of "Welcome! Welcome to Richard's daughter!" over and over again as she was carried through the streets and past the great cathedral toward the abbey.

Her head ached from the noise, and from the effort to hold back tears that clouded her eyes—tears of both gratitude and dismay. The people of this realm had welcomed her with joy, yet the king who was to be her husband had not welcomed her at all. In the midst of this jubilant crowd, she had never felt so achingly alone.

That evening Emma dined with her Norman household in the guest quarters of St. Augustine's abbey. With so many familiar faces about her Emma could almost imagine that she was still in Normandy. She could not dispel, though, the anxiety that she felt at the king's absence today. He should have been there to greet her, and he had slighted her by staying away.

She called to mind Richard's parting words five days before, as he accompanied her to the waiting ships.

"You are not the first bride, Emma, to go to the bed of a foreign king, and you must be very clear about what is expected of you. Bear in mind that you go to your lord not as a woman, but as a queen. In the same way, he comes to you not as a man, but as a king. He will not be father to you, nor lover, nor even friend. Do not expect it. All you can expect from his hands is what any of his subjects can expect, and that is justice and mercy. You, as queen, though, must demand one thing more. You must demand his respect. Never forget that for a moment, and never do anything that might cause you to forfeit it."

Today Æthelred of England had not shown her the respect that she deserved, although she did not know why. She wished that one of her brothers had accompanied her to England. Surely Duke Richard or Archbishop Robert would have been able to give her some insight into what might be going on in the mind of the king. Instead she was without counsel, and she felt as if she had been thrown rudderless into high seas. She could not reach safe haven, even if she knew what it looked like.

In the meantime, the people in this room depended upon her for direction, and she had very little to give. What she needed was information—not the history lessons that Ealdorman Ælfric had given her but news of the court and of the people in it. If she were at home she would send someone to the kitchens to listen in on what was being said, but she could hardly do that here.

She considered the men and women around her. Only a few members of her household could understand English, much less work their mouths around it well enough to speak it. Wymarc was one, for her stepmother was the daughter of a Kentish lord. Young Hugh of Brittany, who had been one of Richard's stewards, was another. Her bard, Alain, could recite their poetry, but she was not sure how much of it he actually understood.

And there was her priest, Father Martin. She did not know him and had had little time to speak with him in the weeks before they left Normandy, but he had served her mother well. She knew that he was a scholar, good with languages, and that he had studied for a time in an abbey somewhere here in England. Her mother had said that he was an excellent clerk, for he wrote a fair hand.

At the moment Emma did not need a clerk. What she needed was a spy. Father Martin, clad in fine, dark-colored wool and with a crucifix hanging at his breast, was the likeliest candidate to gather news within the cathedral precincts. The community there would likely welcome a priest and scholar who was part of the Norman retinue.

She called the priest to her side, and then, after some thought, she summoned Hugh as well. As they knelt before her, she studied their upturned faces, both of them clean shaven in the Norman style. Aside from that they were a study in contrasts. Father Martin's lined face and gray hair bespoke his age, and his solemn brown eyes studied her with the gravity of experience. Hugh was youthful and dark, strikingly handsome, with an engaging charm that, she had reason to believe, had captivated Wymarc on the voyage here. Her friend had spoken of him with such admiration that Emma had warned her to have a care for her heart. Still, Hugh's genial manner was well suited to the task she had in mind for him.

"I am in need," she said, "of information about the English. I must know what their concerns are, what they think, what they believe, and, particularly, what they fear." She looked at the priest. "Father Martin, I want you to mingle with the cathedral community in any place where you can engage them in conversation. Hugh, I want you to go into the market square tomorrow, down to the port and into the alehouses. Find out what the folk of England think of their king. Discover what is being said about his marriage. You must not be afraid to tell me what you learn, even if you fear it will displease me. Do you understand?"

When she had dismissed them she felt more composed. She had set something in motion, and soon she would have results. She reminded herself that she was not alone here, and that she had resources, if only she took the care to use them.

The next evening Emma met with Hugh and Father Martin in a once barren abbey chamber that her attendants had transformed into a quiet retreat suited to a queen. A brazier burned in the center of the room, and embroidered hangings covered the cold stone walls. Emma sat in a high-backed chair with cushions behind her shoulders, furs on her lap, and a stool under her feet. As she considered the two men before her, she saw that the priest looked particularly grave, so she turned first to him.

"Tell me," she said.

"There are . . . evil rumors, my lady," he said slowly, ". . . about the king, and how he obtained his throne."

Emma frowned. "But surely Æthelred inherited the throne from his father," she said. "Ealdorman Ælfric said that King Edgar died young, and that his son was crowned after that."

"That is true," the priest said, frowning, "but the boy who was crowned after King Edgar was not Æthelred. It was his elder half brother, Edward. In the cathedral scriptorium there are chronicles that report," he paused, "unsettling events that occurred in those days."

So Ælfric, whom she had liked so well, had told her only part of the truth. Could she not trust anyone in England then?

"Go on," she said.

"King Edgar had three sons by two different wives. The middle son died very young, while his father still sat the throne. Some years later, when King Edgar died of a sudden illness, no heir had been named, and the two sons who survived him were born of different mothers. Edward, the eldest, was crowned, but many of the great men in the land questioned his right to the throne, for his mother was not a consecrated queen, and Æthelred's mother was." He paused and heaved a weary sigh before continuing. "After he had ruled but three years, King Edward was murdered—brutally, the chronicles say. He was young when he died—only sixteen. It was then that his half brother, Æthelred, was named to the throne by the *witan*, the group of nobles who advise the king."

"And what happened to the murderers?" she asked. As a brother and a king it would have been Æthelred's particular duty to punish such a terrible crime.

"The murderers were never discovered," Father Martin said. "No one was punished and no restitution paid." He hesitated, his expression grim. "I persuaded one of the brothers here, an old man now, to tell me what he recalled from that time."

Again he hesitated, clearly unwilling to burden her with his knowledge. Emma waited, her heart filled with misgiving, and at last Father Martin continued his tale.

"It was believed by many that Æthelred's mother, the dowager queen, plotted the murder of her stepson. That was a terrible time, with bloody portents in the night sky that even the priests could not ignore. I am told that last autumn, just before the dowager queen died, the night skies ran with blood again, although the old man I spoke with did not see it."

Emma sat very still, pondering his words. She knew well the power of rumor and superstition. When her father was alive, Rouen had buzzed for a time with tales that he wandered the streets at midnight, going into darkened churches to battle phantoms and demons. Indeed, it was true that her father had visited the churches by night, for his final illness had bereft him of sleep, and he sought the intercession of one saint after another in his search for healing. But the duke had wrestled with no demons, only with the knowledge of his own coming death. The rumors about him had contained a kernel of truth that had been misshapen by wild conjecture. Perhaps this was the same thing.

"How long ago did this happen?" she asked the priest.

"King Æthelred has ruled England for twenty-three years."

She did the sums. Æethelred, who was now in his thirty-fifth year, could have been no more than a child when his brother had been murdered. What possible role could a child play in such a heinous act?

"Tell me, Father Martin," she said, "do you believe that the king had a hand in his brother's death?"

The priest fingered the cross at his breast as he pondered her question. At last he said, "This is a Christian land, my lady, yet through all the years of Æthelred's reign, godless men from across the North Sea have raided and burned and tortured this realm. Why would God allow such a thing, unless there was great sin in the land?"

And what greater sin, she thought, than the murder of an anointed king? Was this the truth about Æthelred that no one had been willing to reveal to her?

Her anxiety about the man she was to wed grew, yet troubled as she was, she would rather be armed with knowledge than go to him cloaked in ignorance. She murmured her thanks to the priest. Then, as an afterthought, she reached down and touched his hand. "Please pray for me, Father," she said, "and for the soul of the king."

As she turned her attention to Hugh she wondered what horror story he might have to tell.

"The word in the marketplace," Hugh volunteered, "is that the king has just sent nearly thirty thousand pounds of silver to a Danish host camped on an island off the southern coast. I'm told that the Vikings spent all of last summer burning and robbing in the southern shires, and that the silver," he paused and smiled wryly, "is meant to discourage them from picking up where they left off when the weather turns fair again."

"So the king bribes the Vikings to leave his lands," she said. "Jesu, it is a vast amount of money."

"Aye, my lady," Hugh agreed. "And the common folk, and even the nobles, it seems, begrudge having to pay the high taxes that the king has imposed to raise it. They complain that first the Danes raid the land, and then the king's men come and take whatever is left to bribe the Danes to go away."

"But where are the warriors?" she asked. "This is a rich land with a wealthy king. Can Æthelred not defend his people?"

Hugh shrugged. "The king has his personal guard, as do many of the nobles, but in times of great need he must summon warriors and arms. By the time word of an attack is spread and the levies called up, the Vikings have taken their plunder and made their escape." He frowned and shook his head. "It is whispered, too, that the king is unlucky. Whenever his soldiers meet the enemy some hapless thing occurs to sway the battle in favor of the outlanders."

Was it bad luck, she wondered, or, as Father Martin believed, was it God's curse? And, merciful heaven, what was the difference?

"My lady," Hugh said, "my news is not all dismal. There is general rejoicing over your nuptials. The common belief is that the arrival of a new queen can only bring good fortune to England."

"I expect the new queen's dowry will not come amiss, either," she said, "if the king defends his land with silver instead of steel."

She dismissed the men and sat a while, pondering all that she had heard. Where was the truth in the rumors, and what secrets lay hidden in the soul of the man she must wed? Even if the king was innocent of his brother's murder, his throne was bathed in his brother's blood. She must share that throne. Whatever the fate that lay before Æthelred the king, as his queen she would share that as well.

Chapter Nine

April 1002

Canterbury, Kent

On Easter Sunday, Æthelred of England took his Norman bride to wife, and he watched with hundreds of others as a circlet of gold was placed upon her head and she was named England's queen. Afterward, he presided over his wedding feast in the royal hall near the cathedral. Seated upon the dais, his new queen at his side, Æthelred looked about him and was not entirely pleased with the situation in which he found himself.

He had spent a great deal of coin over the last weeks in an effort to purchase peace for England. Some of it had been settled upon this chit seated next to him, and if her brother kept his promise, England's coasts would be far more secure than in years past. Whether Richard could be trusted, though, was a question that niggled at him like a sore tooth.

As for the girl, he liked the look of her well enough. She had a smooth, clear complexion, enormous green eyes, and a long, straight nose. Her mouth was too wide, but she seemed to have good teeth, and her voice did not vex him—not yet. Her hair was pale beneath the silken headrail that was held in place by his gift of a golden crown.

He frowned. He should never have agreed to her coronation. His council was to blame for that. Their infernal wrangling had driven him to make a hasty decision. Within hours of signing the marriage documents he had regretted the act, but by then the official scrolls were on their way to Normandy, and it was too late.

His first wife had demanded no crown and had suffered no harm from the lack of it. This one, though, wanted assurances for any children that she might bear, wanted them first in line for the spoils after he died. It would lead to disputes as to which of his offspring were more throne worthy, and if Emma bore a son there would be bad blood between his first family and his second, all because he had given this Norman bitch a circlet of gold.

It had happened before, and his sons knew their family history well enough—knew of the factions that had formed around himself and his brother when their father died. Edward had been the elder, but men had questioned his claim to the crown because Edward's mother had been a consort and no queen, unlike his own mother, who had bewitched the king into her bed and then convinced him to grant her a crown. It had led to years of unrest between rival nobles, who had backed either Edward or himself—and it had ended in Edward's murder.

He closed his eyes and, with an effort of will, turned his mind from his dead brother, lest his very thoughts draw him from his grave again. He considered the slim girl beside him, mentally discarding her glimmering gown and the delicate garment beneath it until she was naked but for the pearls that hung in ropes about her neck. He imagined those pearls resting against her high, proud breasts and cascading past the delicate curve of her hips to the pale thatch between her thighs.

Soon he would be lying between those thighs, and the thought made his mouth go dry with anticipation. He emptied his mead cup and called for more.

Be fruitful and multiply, the archbishop had admonished them when they took their vows. Well, Emma looked as though she could do that well enough, and if she should bear only daughters, so much the better.

He drank again from his cup and again he called for more. At one of the tables below him he could see old Ælfric mouthing something at him. Christ! Another duty to perform, as if taking a Norman slut to wife hadn't been enough.

Reluctantly he pushed himself to his feet and lifted his golden goblet high, quelling the murmur of the wedding guests.

"To the Lady Emma of Normandy," he bellowed, "queen of all England!"

The company responded with cheers, and next to him, his new young queen blushed.

As the revelers stood and raised their cups to her, Emma searched among them for her own people, but she found no familiar faces in the throng. She trusted that they would have found their way to tables somehow. Certainly there was enough food here that no one would go to bed hungry tonight. The king, she had learned, had ordered food tables set up all over the city in celebration of his nuptials, so even the poorest folk would sleep with full bellies for this one night at least. She was glad of it.

She let her gaze wander, over the heads of the guests seated at endless rows of tables, and then along the intricately carved oak columns that marched in two rows down the length of the hall and soared upward so high that they disappeared into darkness. This was a huge edifice, far larger than her brother's hall at Fécamp, or even in Rouen. It had obviously been built to inspire awe, and to intimidate. It succeeded on both counts, and in its massive, dim interior she felt small and insignificant . . . and cold. A breeze fingered its way through the roof thatch to tease the brightly colored banners hanging from the crossbeams. In its wake, the wall torches and the banks of thick candles danced and flared, throwing shadows that loomed menacingly and then shrank to nothing. A constant draft from somewhere behind her chilled her backside, and she regretted not wearing a second chemise beneath her gown.

She took a sip of mead from the silver cup, which was intricately etched with a tracery of vines—one of several wedding gifts from the king, along with the two finger rings and the crown she wore. The sweet liquor burned her throat but warmed her from within, giving her the courage to consider the man seated beside her, whose brooding expression seemed a fit accompaniment to the cold, dark hall.

She knew that he was several years younger than her brother, but he looked much older than Richard. The long golden hair that Ælfric had described to her was streaked with gray at the temples, and the king's face was creased and seamed across the forehead and around the mouth and eyes. It struck her, as she studied him with quick, furtive glances, that he was not a happy man. Careworn, she might have said, although Father Martin's tale of the unpunished murder of a king made her wonder if it was guilt, and not care, that had etched the lines in his face.

On his head he wore a massive golden crown studded with gems that glinted in the firelight, and she pitied him for that. The thing looked heavy, and it must be a punishment to wear it for any length of time. His white tunic, belted at the waist, was woven of fine linen, its sleeves elaborately embroidered in bright colors. The deep blue mantle of shimmering godwebbe that he wore was lined with gold silk and clasped at one shoulder with an enormous gold brooch that was studded with rubies.

The king, taken all in all, looked a powerful and imposing figure. Yet he would have been comely even had he been clad in coarse wool. He carried himself with a fine, noble grace in spite of the weight of that daunting crown. She could not tell from looking at him, though, if he was kind or patient, if he had a sense of humor, or if he could have killed a brother in cold blood.

That last thought, streaking into her head just as she raised her drinking cup to her lips, made her hand tremble so that she nearly slopped the liquor onto her gown. She set the cup down until she could compose herself. For some time now she had been trying to think of something to say to her husband, but he looked so forbidding that she did not know how to begin. The story of the death of King Edward continued to trouble her, boring through her brain like an insidious worm. She could not forget it, and she could not very well ask the king if it was true that he was a kin slayer and king slayer.

For his part, he had said not a single word to her, and she began to wonder if he even realized that she could speak his language. But surely, she thought, Ælfric must have told him that. Nevertheless, all that had passed between them so far had been ceremony, scripted in Latin, and neither one of them had strayed from their assigned words. She had been advised that she must wait for him to initiate the first conversation, and so she had done. But the king had remained dourly silent.

Determined that she would wait no longer, she had been casting about for some topic of conversation, and now she decided to ask about his children. Some of them, at least, had attended the wedding and coronation, for she had seen a flock of gorgeously gowned youngsters, accompanied by what she presumed were nurses and tutors, in one of the side alcoves of the cathedral. She did not see any of them here, though. This was something of a surprise, for she would have expected that at the very least his older children would attend the feast.

"My lord," she said, "I do not see your children here. I had hoped to meet them all today. Are they not allowed to attend the feast?"

The king, using a large chunk of bread to fastidiously mop up the juice from a thick slice of roasted lamb, attended to his culinary duties as if she had not spoken. She had begun to despair that he would answer her at all when, still attentive to his plate, he asked, "Why did your brother send you instead of your elder sister? Had she no taste for the favors of an English king?"

Emma froze, sensing in his words a danger that belied the casual tone of his voice. So it begins, she thought. Already she must dissemble, tell him enough truth to appease him but not so much that he could guess her brother's intention to break the pledge he had made.

"My sister and I," she said lightly, "do as we are commanded, whether it is our inclination or no. We do not ask for explanation, and I asked for none from my brother regarding his decision to send me here." In effect, this was the truth. She had asked her mother, not Richard. "Were I to guess, however, I would say that he feared that my sister, who suffers frequently from ill health, would not be strong enough to undertake the duties of a queen." She thought about what those duties would demand of her before the evening was over, and took another sip of mead.

"Perhaps, then," said the king, "I should have insisted on your sister as my consort, so that I would not be saddled, as I am now, with a wife who demanded the title of queen."

Stung by his discourtesy and his apparent dissatisfaction with the marriage bargain he had struck, Emma could only stare at him for a moment while she caught her breath. Then she felt the weight of the circlet upon her head as well as the weight of her brother's final words to her. *You must demand the king's respect.* She roused herself to respond.

"I expect my brother would have made the same demand, whichever sister he sent you. And as you did not insist upon my sister," she said, hiding her displeasure with a smile, "instead of a wife who might have been a burden to you, you have a queen who can share any burdens that fate may send you. Such is my *wyrd*, I think." She purposely used the term that Ealdorman Ælfric had taken such great pains to explain to her, hoping that it would goad her husband to courtesy, if not respect.

Finished with his bread and gravy, the king took up his goblet, and she wondered how many times he would empty it before the night was over. Still he did not look at her but trained his eyes out over the throng of folk in the hall below them.

"You are but a child," he murmured. "What can you possibly know of the burdens of . . ." He stopped in midsentence, and his face blanched.

Emma followed his gaze and saw that a newly arrived group of several men and a lone woman were striding now up the central aisle.

Æthelred stared at the apparition coming toward him, at his brother's wraith striding through the smoky haze of the hall. His heart seemed to shatter in his chest, and then, to his even greater terror, he realized that this was no phantom sending. This was a man of flesh and blood. Sweet Christ, this was Edward come alive again from the grave to condemn him. His brother's familiar visage pinned him with merciless accusation, and although he mouthed a protest, the menacing figure did not stop.

His grip tightened on the goblet in his hand, and his heart pounded so hard that the girl at his side must have heard it, for suddenly he felt her fingers clutch his wrist.

He thrust her away from him, passed a hand across his eyes, then looked again. Edward still advanced upon him through streaks of light and shadow, and Æthelred rose to his feet, poised to summon his guards. But even as he raised his hand he grew uncertain, and he checked the cry upon his lips.

The figure neared the dais, and he saw, bewildered, that it was not Edward who approached but one very like him. And then his confusion cleared and he recognized his son, Athelstan, who, by some trick of chance or the devil, had assumed an uncanny resemblance to the dead king.

He mouthed a curse at the bitter irony of it. Surely this was another punishment sent upon him, to see the wraith that haunted him in the dark looking back at him now from the countenance of his eldest son. His mind flicked to his queen's assurance that she would share his burdens. What would she think if he were to share with her the burden of his dead brother's vengeance?

Athelstan reached the dais, and Æthelred hauled in a breath. Good Christ! How long had it been since he had last seen the boy? It must be near a year, yet in that brief space of time his son had matured, in looks at least, from boy to man. Why in Christ's name did he have to look like *that* man?

At last he dragged his gaze from his son's face, and only then did he mark the others who attended him.

"Ælfhelm," he murmured, for it was the ealdorman who stepped forward now to bend the knee with the others and speak.

"My lord king," Ælfhelm said, "I beseech your pardon for our late arrival on this auspicious day. We were delayed upon the road." He looked up then with not the least sign of regret evident upon his craggy face. "I return your sons to you," Ælfhelm said, but he was casting an appraising glance now on the young bride, and his mouth twisted into a sneer. "They would greet their new . . . mother."

Æthelred did not reply. His eyes were drawn again to Athelstan, for he still marveled at his son's resemblance to the dead Edward. Finally he considered the others. Ælfhelm's cubs he knew—the two sons and the daughter. He let his gaze linger on the girl briefly before he fixed his attention on his own whelps.

They should all have been at the ceremonies today. This tardy arrival in the midst of the feast and the scowling faces of his three offspring were meant to underscore their opposition to the marriage. He had been right to think that granting his bride a crown would lead to friction. It had already begun, and Ealdorman Ælfhelm had no doubt fanned the flames of dissension. The old devil would like nothing better than to pit his sons against him, setting them upon him like a pack of hounds.

Well, let them howl their outrage to the moon for all the good it would do them. The deed was done. They would have to live with the consequences, just as he would.

He fixed his eyes upon the thunderous face of his eldest son and said, "You are welcome to our feast. It would have done my queen greater homage had you arrived in better time, but go, refresh yourselves. We will speak of this another time."

He resumed his seat as the whispering began among the guests. There would be rumors in the city tomorrow about the king's strange behavior at his wedding feast. He raised his cup, and when he drank he felt the warmth course through him, soothing his tortured nerves. Let them whisper. His brother, the king, was safely dead and in his grave.

He watched his sons melt into the crowd, and he did not miss the look of smoldering resentment that the girl, Elgiva, cast upon the new queen. That amused him. Elgiva's high rank and wealth assured her a place in the queen's household. All by herself she would likely be a significant burden for his new bride to shoulder. Emma was welcome to it.

He glanced at his queen and saw that she was watching him, her eyes huge with amazement and speculation. He scowled. She wearied him, and he wanted rid of her.

He stood again and, drawing her up beside him, he announced, "The queen will now retire, and she bids you all good night."

The assembly rose amid the usual bawdy shouts and applause, while Emma raised an eyebrow in surprise. But she said nothing, merely offered him a gracious courtesy before turning abruptly to follow the servants who would lead her to his private chamber.

Satisfied at having the dais to himself, Æthelred sat down and applied himself once more to his food and drink. He would tend to his queen soon enough.

Emma surveyed the great royal bed, which was sumptuously draped with curtains and bedecked with furs and intricately embroidered pillows. It had been arranged here just this morning, she knew, for all of the accoutrements of the king's bedchamber accompanied him wherever he went—hangings for the walls, pelts for the floor, the finest linens and furs for the bedding, even the candle sconces and braziers for light and warmth. She felt a shiver of foreboding, though, as she looked solemnly about her. There could never be enough candles, she thought, to light this chamber. All the furnishings were dark and oppressive, in spite of their richness.

Her own household goods were already on their way to Winchester, for she would have no need of them here. Tonight, and while the king stayed in Canterbury, she would share his chamber and his bed. It made her feel like she was just another piece of chattel, like a gilded coffer or a handsomely embroidered cushion.

She tried to put that thought aside as the dozen women who had escorted her from the hall began the business of preparing her to greet her husband. Emma had assisted with this same task herself when her sister Beatrice had wed, and she recalled how Beatrice had chattered and laughed all through the undressing. Emma felt too numb to speak, and she submitted dumbly to her attendants' ministrations.

Most of the women were strangers to her, for it was an honor granted by the king to assist his bride at the bedding. She had been allowed to choose only two attendants from her Norman retinue, and so Wymarc was here with her, and her old nurse, Margot, looking like a little brown wren amid all the fine ladies.

When Emma had been stripped of her wedding finery and garbed in the delicate shift that Gunnora had embroidered with her own hands, Emma was escorted to the bed. She exchanged the appropriate courtesies with the women of Æthelred's court, and then she dismissed them. It was not politic, she knew, but she could no longer bear their curious stares. When only Wymarc and Margot remained in the room, Emma collapsed backward upon the bed cushions, exhausted.

A moment later Margot was at her side, offering her a cup of wine. "It is good Norman wine, that," she said, "from your own stock. Drink it all, my lady. It will do you good."

"God bless you, Margot," Emma said, sitting up and grasping the cup. She took a greedy gulp of the wine, then considered the flagon still in Margot's hand. "Put that here, near the bed, and you'd best pour some for yourselves. I expect we might have a long wait. Something tells me that the king will not be in any hurry to lie with his new queen tonight."

Wymarc's unflagging smile dimmed a bit. "Why do you say that? He should be eager to attend you. You are the most beautiful woman in this hall."

"Beauty, I fear, is no great advantage," Emma said slowly, staring into her wine cup. "The king seems to regret his . . . purchase."

She looked up at Wymarc, whose face clouded with misgiving.

"That cannot be true," Wymarc said. "Why would he regret it?"

Emma sighed, exasperated. "I do not know why! I only know that he is in an ill temper, and it is directed at me. He all but threw me out of the hall."

"Dear God," Wymarc breathed. She exchanged a worried glance with Margot, then suggested hopefully, "Could it be that he is just a nervous bridegroom? He is so much older than you; perhaps he is afraid that he will disappoint you."

It was kind of Wymarc to look for an excuse for the king's odd behavior, but she had not heard Æthelred's curt words. Emma took another swallow of the wine, thinking with dread of the bedding to come. If he had been so cold at the table, what would he be like in the bedchamber?

Then she remembered the stricken look on the king's face when he saw his sons. He had been more upset with them even than with her.

"There was something else," she said, "something to do with his sons. They came late to the feast. When the king saw them he was so distracted that I thought he had been taken by some kind of seizure. He recovered himself in a moment, but it gave me a fright."

She described the undercurrent of tension between the king and his offspring. Even now it flayed her nerves to recall it. The king's sons had been hostile, but Æthelred had not looked angry as much as frightened. His eyes had grown wide and his face had gone pale with terror, as if he were facing Death itself.

"Mayhap it was one of their companions that frightened the king," Margot suggested.

"That may be so," Emma said slowly, remembering the older man who had addressed the king. His face had been seamed and rugged, with a flat nose and small, mean eyes—a hard, nightmarish face behind a thick, black beard. But could even a man such as that strike terror in the king?

"Oh, God," she said, pulling her knees up and dropping her face against them, "there is so much that I do not know." She raised her head and thrust her empty cup at Wymarc for more wine. "The man's name is Ælfhelm," she said. "In the morning I want Hugh to discover everything that he can about this Ælfhelm and report to me. You must find Hugh tonight and tell him."

"Of course," Wymarc said.

Emma sat back against the pillows, clutching the goblet with both hands, reviewing all the events of the day and trying to keep her thoughts away from what must occur next.

"My lady queen," Margot said softly from her stool beside the bed, "do you know what to expect from the king tonight?"

Emma laughed. Suddenly it all seemed funny to her. She looked at the cup in her hand and decided that it must be the wine, for there was really nothing funny about it at all.

"My mother spoke to me," she said, "and Judith told me of her wedding night. I think, though, that my own experience is likely to be somewhat less," she groped for a word, "friendly."

Margot nodded. "Likely Judith knew her husband's touch already before they were wed, as they were betrothed many months. It will be different for you," she said gently, "for you know nothing of your husband. May I give you a word of advice, my lady?"

Emma nodded, eager for any counsel—anything to erase the appalling image of one of her brother's fine stallion's mounting a mare that came all too easily to her mind.

"You must not be afraid," Margot said, "no matter what he says or what he does. He may be gentle with you," she took a little breath and looked hard at Emma, "or he may not. I have no knowledge of the English, or of kings, or of this Æthelred as a man. But whatever he does, it will go better for you if you are easy and calm." She smiled. "The wine will help with that, to be sure. But in this room, my lady, and especially on this night, you must make yourself go soft in every part of you, the better to accept his hardness, if you take my meaning."

"Yes," Emma said, "I think I understand you." It seemed an impossible task, though, given how brittle she felt, as if she might break into a thousand pieces at the slightest touch.

"You must use your mind," Margot went on. "You may not have to, of course. He may be the kind of man who gentles a woman the way a good rider gentles a horse. If he does that, if he uses his hands to soothe you, it will be easy for you to respond in kind. Just follow his lead. But you are a horsewoman, my lady. You have seen some men, surely, who use their horses with a fury that has no gentleness in it. The more the horse resists, the harder it goes for him."

"She is no horse!" Wymarc objected, her face stricken at the old woman's words.

"No, she is not," Margot agreed, "for she has a sharp mind, and she can use it. If need be, my lady, let it take you to whatever time and place you choose that will ease you. I hope you will not have to, but you must remember that your mind can provide you with refuge, should you need it."

The large, scored candle in the bedchamber had marked the passage of two weary hours before Emma heard the heavy door open. Margot and Wymarc scrambled to their feet as the king entered, escorted by six of his councilors. Emma watched Æthelred warily from her place on the bed, bearing Margot's words in mind and trying not to stiffen. Still, she felt the pulse beat hard in her throat as the king made his royal entrance, crownless now, although still draped in the magnificent blue and gold cloak.

"Leave us," he said peremptorily to the attendants, with a wave of dismissal. And in a moment the room was empty but for the two of them.

Æthelred stood a few feet from the bed, looking down at her. Emma searched for telltale signs that he was somewhat the worse for drink. She knew well enough that wedding feasts often ended in debauchery, and she had allowed herself to hope that the king might be too overcome with ale or wine or mead, or all three, to want anything to do with her. But he did not weave or sway as he surveyed her, and it occurred to her that he might very well be more sober than she was.

"Get up," he ordered, "and take off your shift. I want to see what I've purchased."

The command sent a wave of shock through her. Nothing that anyone had told her had prepared her for this. It confirmed her opinion that Æthelred regarded her as little more than chattel. She masked her resentment, though, and she tried to loosen her muscles, doing her best to follow Margot's advice. Without a word she slipped off of the bed, untied the ribbons at her throat, and let her shift pool on the floor at her feet.

She blessed Margot under her breath, because the wine she had consumed made the task seem ridiculous rather than onerous. She had to stifle the urge to giggle. She had stood naked like this often enough in front of serving women who washed her from head to foot, and she willed herself to think of this as no different. The chamber was cool, though, in spite of the charcoal brazier, and she felt her nipples harden. She lifted her chin a bit and, giddy with wine, was sorely tempted to ask the king to disrobe so she could inspect him as well, but she thought better of it. It would be a new sight for her, and she had no idea how she would respond to her first glimpse of a naked man. In any event, he would have to undress sooner or later. She had but to wait.

Æthelred gazed sullenly at his bride, desire warring with suspicion. It disturbed him that she had complied with his crude command so readily. He had spoken out of anger—at his councilors for inflicting this marriage upon him, at her brother for demanding a coronation, and at Ælfhelm, damn his soul, for turning his own sons against him. None of it was the girl's fault, yet now that she had disrobed so brazenly in front of him, he was forced to wonder why.

Cursing, he made for the small table that held a flagon and poured a cup of wine.

"Are you a maid?" he asked. That would explain why Richard had foisted this younger sister upon him. She was used goods. For all he knew she might be carrying a Norman brat in her belly.

He stared at her over the rim of his cup and saw that her entire body had flushed in response to his question.

"I am a maid," she said. "I am also your queen, and I will not be treated like some slut from the gutter."

He downed the wine, tossed the cup to the floor, and began to remove his garments. "You are queen by my pleasure," he said. "You would do well to remember it. And in the morning, when the council inspects the bed linens, we will know for a surety whether or not you are a slut from the gutter, as you so colorfully put it. Now get into the bed and let us get on with the matter at hand."

Later, when she lay asleep at his side, Æthelred stared wide-eyed into the flames of the candles that flanked the bed. He had done his duty as king and husband in as efficient a manner as possible. The girl, to her credit, had done the same. She was no whore, if he was any judge. She had lain beneath him as unresponsive and boneless as a sleeping cat. He had expected something better, after seeing her naked before him like some Viking goddess; but she had disappointed him.

It was just as well. He wanted as little to do with her as possible—only enough to satisfy the demands of church and kingship.

He closed his eyes, and in that darkness his thoughts strayed to his dead wife. He had been but seventeen when he wed her, and she was twenty. In all the long years of their marriage he had never seen her naked. When he lay with her she had responded like a nun, tensing with repugnance at the act that she was forced to endure. Although she had never refused him, she had borne his attentions every time in virtuous silence, had likely prayed her way through each ordeal. Whenever she quickened with child she informed him immediately, with undisguised satisfaction, for while she was breeding she did not have to accommodate the carnal activity that she found so odious. She was always happiest when she was pregnant. He was content then, too, for he found his pleasure elsewhere, with women who spread their legs for him with relish.

He sat up in the bed to study the girl curled beneath the furs, her hair spilling over the pillows like silver in the candlelight. She did not seem to be repulsed by the act. He had even caught her studying his face with detached bemusement as he entered her, and it had made him wonder what was going through her mind.

It might be possible to forge a bond with her, if he took the time to do it. She was young enough and inexperienced enough to be trained as a lover. It could be quite pleasant to share his bed with her.

But that would give her some measure of power over him, and as his queen she had too much power already. He did not want a queen—did not even want a wife, curse it—yet here she was.

He lay down again, on his side, his back to the other body in the bed.

He owed this girl nothing. He would use her for his pleasure because her nakedness aroused him. He would fill her belly with a child and would order his Mass priest to beseech heaven for a daughter. Beyond that he would give her no more than what the terms of the marriage contract required of him. Her title of queen would have to satisfy her, for that and a child were all that she would get from him.

Chapter Ten

April 1002

Canterbury, Kent

On Easter Monday over one hundred women crowded into the great hall of the archbishop's palace to greet Æthelred's bride. Elgiva arrived late, with Groa in her wake. As she tried to make her way toward the dais, a fat matron stinking of cloves pressed hard against her, and the sharply sweet smell of the spice was almost Elgiva's undoing. In an instant she was a child again, hiding in her mother's clothes coffer—unable to move, scarce able to breathe, too weak to free herself, and enveloped by darkness, the scent of cloves, and a mindless panic.

That same panic clawed at her now, and she began to whimper as she tried to twist away from the stench of the spice and from the crowd that engulfed her. Sickened and faint, she pulled her own cloak against her face, but it did little to block the pungent smell of cloves. She felt her gorge rise and she thought she would be sick, but Groa took her hand and squeezed it to steady her.

"Let us make for the wall," Groa said urgently. "You will be able to breathe there."

Frantic and dizzy, she blindly followed Groa as the old woman doggedly elbowed her way past a score of protesting noblewomen. She felt herself growing more and more faint, but she clung to Groa's hand, and at last they reached the wall. The next thing she knew Groa had cleared a bench of gawkers and helped her up. A blast of frigid air from a narrow window scored her face, and she drew in a long breath that was deliciously free of the stink of cloves and wet wool.

Slowly her light-headedness began to dissipate, and she rested her now throbbing head against the wall as Groa joined her on the bench to watch the proceedings taking place at the top of the room. When Elgiva saw the new queen, though, her gorge rose again. Emma, flanked by guards and attendants, sat enthroned beneath a golden canopy. Regally swathed in a deep blue mantle, her blond hair braided into two long plaits, she wore upon her head the same golden circlet that the archbishop had placed there yesterday.

"It should have been you," Groa said softly.

And that was the truth of it. That bland, pasty-faced Norman witch had cheated her out of her destiny. Who would have imagined that Æthelred would take a foreign bride, and then make her a queen? It should never have happened. The king had made the wrong choice, and her father was not the only one who said so. By now even the king must realize his error. She had not missed the way his eyes had lingered on her face yesterday when she stood with his sons below the royal table. If he did not already regret his choice of bride, he surely would in time.

An endless parade of women made obeisance before the queen, presented their gifts and received tokens from the queen in return—a pin or a brooch, and always of silver. The queen, it seemed, knew how to purchase affection. Well, Emma would not purchase Elgiva's affection, no matter how precious the gift.

Dear God! How long would she be forced to live in the queen's household? Months, certainly. Maybe even years.

She felt ill again at the thought of having to scrape and bow before Emma, but even that, she supposed, was better than moldering away in Northamptonshire. This queen, at least, was young—not like Æthelred's last wife, who had been older, even, than the king.

And like it or not, she would be one of the queen's household. Her father had made that clear when they broke their fast together this morning.

"You must be my eyes and my ears at court," he had said, "for I journey north at week's end until the *witan* gathers again in summer. I want you to make every effort to gain the trust of the queen. She is little more than a hostage for her brother's good behavior now, but if she gives the king a son, there is no telling what power she might wield."

"God forbid," Elgiva had murmured, "that she should give Æthelred a son."

Her father had merely shrugged and left her. She had dawdled over her food, pondering her father's words and wondering if she might eventually maneuver herself into Athelstan's bed, and if not his, mayhap the king's. She was toying with that possibility again as Groa touched her arm.

"You had best go forward, my lady," Groa urged, "if you wish to make your obeisance before the queen. I will lead you through the crowd." She held out the gift that Elgiva would present to the bride.

Elgiva took another long gulp of air and allowed Groa to help her from her perch. She cared not what her father wanted. She would not smile and fawn before this queen like the other fools here. She had heard their talk yesterday—the whispers about the beautiful young queen and her noble lineage. Emma, they said, had been named after her mother, the Frankish king's sister, who had wed Emma's father when the two were little more than children.

That was nothing but a *skald*'s tale, invented out of sunbeams and moondust and probably spread abroad by the king himself to enhance his bride's prestige. Groa had nosed out the truth of it, and Elgiva intended to make sure that the women of the court learned the queen's secret.

When she finally reached the canopied throne, and the steward had announced her name and titles, she made her obligatory courtesy before Emma, but she did not smile. She would not simper for this queen, although she had chosen the bridal gift with great care. She rose from her obeisance and held up the small, intricately carved ivory casket. On its lid a fierce dragon ship sailed upon an ivory sea, and along the casket's back and sides a monster of the deep twisted and writhed.

"I bring you a treasure from Jorvik, the capital of my father's vast district of Northumbria," she said, pitching her voice so that the women all around her would be able to hear. "It is of Danish workmanship, and therefore a fitting tribute for our Danish queen. Your mother, I am told, is a Dane. Is this not so?"

The words echoed in the room, and Emma felt a tremor in their wake, like the tingling in the air just before a lightning bolt strikes. There was little love for the Danes in Æthelred's England, and Emma suspected that her Danish mother had probably been kept a royal secret—until now. Few outside of Normandy would concern themselves with the marriage practices of the Norman duke who had had two wives at the same time—one a Danish heiress who brought him lands and children and the other a barren Frankish princess whom he had not wanted.

Emma looked into the dark, triumphant eyes of the girl who stood before her and saw there the same contempt that she had read in Ealdorman Ælfhelm's face the night before. Like father, like daughter, then. She had yet to discover the source of their enmity, but she would have to begin to deal with it this very moment.

"It is true, Lady Elgiva, that my mother was born a Dane. I, however, was born a *Norman*," she emphasized the last word, and now she stood up so that she could be seen easily, directing her next words to all the women in the hall. "Yesterday, when I wed your king, I was born anew before God and all the world as an English woman and an English queen." The room erupted in riotous applause, and Emma acknowledged it with a smile before she turned solemn eyes upon the Lady Elgiva. "I thank you, lady, for your gift. It symbolizes, I trust, your allegiance to me and to my husband. In token of my acknowledgment of your honored position among my attendants, I bid you accept this ring."

Emma slipped a gold ring from her finger and placed it in Elgiva's palm. She doubted that the gesture would win the young woman's friendship, never mind her allegiance. Nevertheless, she had to make the effort, for Elgiva was to be part of her retinue, and live in the queen's quarters. It would be, she feared, akin to living with a beautiful bird that had an unfortunate tendency to bite.

Æthelred let his three eldest sons stew for several days before summoning them to his private chamber. As they had been in no hurry to attend his nuptials, he would let them wait upon his pleasure to question them about it.

He knew that they resented his queen, fearing that any son Emma might bear would have a stronger claim to the throne than their own.

Nevertheless, he was still the one wearing the crown, still the one his sons needed to placate, not the other way round. Apparently they needed to be reminded of that.

Eyeing them as they came into the room, he said not a word. Let them sweat a little while longer. Athelstan met his gaze unblinkingly, but there was an uneasy question in his eyes. Edmund, the dark one, did not dare to even lift his head. Ecbert smiled sheepishly until Æthelred's glare wiped the idiotic grin from his face.

"What is it that you would say to me?" Æthelred growled, addressing Athelstan, whose uncanny resemblance to the dead Edward continued to gall him, like a constant reproach.

"Why did you give her a crown?" Athelstan demanded.

Edmund flinched, and well he might. The question was far too raw. Æthelred kept his temper, but only just.

"Is it thus that you question the policy of your king, as if you were my equal? Who in Christ's name do you think you are to do so?"

"I am your heir," Athelstan replied, bristling like a hedgehog. "I have every right to ask such a question. You have taken a Norman bride to your bed and made her your queen. What do you expect me to do, wish you happiness? Shall I pretend that my own interests are not at stake?"

"You have no interests beyond those that I give you," Æthelred thundered back at him. "You have no monies nor estates nor powers other than those that have been granted by me. Christ! You are too young to even have a thought in your head that does not agree with my wishes."

"You are wrong there, my lord. Indeed, I have many thoughts, and almost none of them, I expect, agree with your wishes."

"Then it should have come as no surprise to you," Æthelred spat, "that I did not seek your counsel before I made my decision to wed."

His son flushed, his expression wounded. "And yet," he said, "it did surprise me. It surprised all of us. For weeks we waited for a summons from you, my lord, requesting us to attend your council. Yet it did not come. Tell me then: Whose counsel did you seek? Which of your brilliant advisers encouraged you to grant a crown to a foreign bride? I warrant it was not Ealdorman Ælfhelm. He makes no secret of his belief that you are either mad or a fool."

So, here it was. Here was what he had suspected all along. Ælfhelm had turned even his own sons against him.

"Has Ælfhelm persuaded you, then, to his point of view?" he demanded. "All of you?" He raked them all with his glance, but no one would answer that query. Even Athelstan looked somewhat taken aback now, by his own audacious words. "I knew when I placed you under Ælfhelm's leadership that he would try to twist your minds against me, but I had hoped that my sons would show more fealty to their father and king. It seems that my trust was misplaced."

"My lord," Athelstan's tone was placating now. "I did not mean to—"

"I know exactly what you meant. By word and deed you have declared yourself. Since you hold my marriage and my queen in such low esteem, you are banished from my presence and from my court. Get you to St. Albans, all three of you, until I send for you again. Lord Ælfhelm has taught you to question your king. Let us see if the good brothers at the abbey can teach you patience and humility. Now get out."

Outside the king's chamber Athelstan halted, stunned by his own temerity and what it had wrought. He felt his brothers' accusing eyes on him, and he dreaded the censure that he knew was coming.

"That went well," Ecbert said. "Banished to St. Albans until God knows when. Thank you for that, brother."

"Only a fool," Edmund volunteered, "calls the king a fool."

"I did not call him a fool," Athelstan protested.

"No," Edmund replied, "you called him a fool and a madman. Even better! Whatever possessed you to speak to him in such a way?"

"He bid me speak my mind, and I did. Yes, all right, I made an error. I believed that he truly wanted to know what I thought."

"Jesu, Athelstan! He had no need to ask for that. It has been writ on your face for days."

"What would you have had me do? Kiss his hand and bid him be happy between the legs of his new queen? He would see it for a lie."

"Could you not have found some middle ground?" Edmund persisted. "You undermine your own cause by being so blunt! Your wish is to have some influence upon the king's decisions, yet how are we to do that if we are banished from the court?"

"It could be worse," Ecbert said brightly. "He could have sent us to Glastonbury, where we'd have to spend the summer in the bog lands fighting the midges. At least St. Albans is on solid ground and easily within a day's ride of London, with plenty of inns and alehouses along the way."

"Shut up, Ecbert," Athelstan snapped. "The king still thinks of us as children, and as long as he does, we will never be able to influence him."

"His bride is the same age as you are," Edmund replied. "Clearly he does not think *her* a child. We had better hope, though, that she has no more influence upon him than we do."

That, in particular, made Athelstan wince. They would be spending the next weeks or months at St. Albans while the new queen would be spending them in his father's bed. If she gave him a son, then what? The prophecy of the seeress still rang like a warning bell in his head, and he could see no way to explain it, unless his father's Norman bride should persuade the king to disinherit his elder sons.

Chapter Eleven

July 1002

Near Winchester, Hampshire

Emma, tucked into the royal wain with Wymarc and Margot, surveyed the sun-dappled Hampshire countryside—a vista framed by draperies that had been tied back to let in light and air. The view was the only thing pleasant about this leg of the journey, for the thick cushions lining the seat beneath her did little to absorb the shock of the wagon's jolting passage along the deeply rutted road. She could not decide which was more uncomfortable— travel aboard a heaving longship or inside a teeth-jarring wheeled box. The box, at any rate, was always dry, but the heavy, cumbersome vehicle moved so slowly behind its plodding oxen that Emma was convinced it would have been faster to walk.

She was relieved that this long trek to the royal seat of Winchester was nearly over. They would spend tonight in an abbey, and tomorrow, escorted by a delegation of clergy and prominent citizens, she would enter the city that was to be her new home. Father Martin knew Winchester well, and he had described it as a beautiful walled town set amid folds of forest, field, and pasture in the king's heartland of Wessex. Yet, as she looked out at all the different shades of green below a wide blue-and-white sky, she felt a pang of longing for the sea. Here there would be no shore where she could ride with the salt spray upon her face, no white cliffs, not even the call of seabirds that had sometimes filled the skies above Canterbury.

Just then the road curved, and for a few moments she could see Æthelred mounted on the horse that had been her wedding gift to him—a dappled gray stallion that Richard had helped her choose. She had begged to be allowed to ride with the king today but had been refused for a host of reasons that his steward had tediously itemized for her. And so it was the king's favorite, Elgiva, who rode beside him, her skirts pulled up across her knees to reveal shapely legs that her thin hose did little to hide.

It did not surprise Emma to learn that it was Æthelred's custom to have favorites among the ladies of the court. It was something her brother had warned might happen, and he had told her that she would be foolish to show any displeasure because of it. It was a king's prerogative, he had said.

Emma would have found her husband's prerogative far easier to live with if he had chosen someone other than Elgiva for his attentions. She had learned very quickly the root cause of Elgiva's thinly disguised contempt: The Lady of Northampton had herself hoped to wed the king and as she could not punish Æthelred for spurning her, she chose to turn her malice upon Emma, the usurper.

There were a thousand ways to sow discord among a household of women, and Elgiva seemed determined to utilize every one. Haughty glances, unkind remarks, baseless rumors, and spiteful tales had led to a clear divide between Emma's English and Norman attendants, and she despaired of ever finding a way to repair it. Elgiva's blatant efforts to attract the king's eye did not help.

Even beyond that, though, there was something about Elgiva's nature that troubled Emma. She could not make out if it was the careless cruelty of a spoiled child or if something darker lay concealed beneath the fair skin and fine eyes. She wondered that the king did not see it. Or perhaps he did, and that was what intrigued him the most—darkness drawn to darkness.

For although she still knew very little about Æthelred as a man, she knew that across his soul lay a shadow that she could not fathom. He was very much afraid, this king. She had seen it at their wedding feast, and in the three months that she had shared his bed, he had been troubled by dark dreams. She had sometimes wakened in the night to find the bedchamber bright with candles and the king slowly pacing, murmuring to himself—whether prayers or curses she could not say.

She wondered what he saw there, in the long watches of the night, but she did not have the courage to attempt to probe the dark visions in his mind—whether shadows of memory or of things yet to be. Æthelred had barred her from his private thoughts, and even from his presence, as surely as if he had built a wall between them—or built a wall around her, for she was more prisoner than wife or queen.

She saw him only in the formal feasting in the hall or in the strained, cold silence of their bed. In Canterbury she had not been allowed to ride or hunt with him—for fear of her safety, she had been told. She was no more than a foreign hostage—mistrusted by her lord. She was watched constantly by the women who served her, and every missive she sent or received from Normandy passed first through the hands of the king.

She woke each day dreading that some ill tidings would reach the king about her brother or about some monstrous Viking raid that could be laid to Richard's account. And what, she wondered, would Æthelred do to his hostage then? Up to now those fears had been groundless, but the sea lanes would be open for many weeks yet, and until winter storms kept the dragon ships from venturing onto England's shores, she, like the king, would not rest easily at night.

She gazed out at the green land that was so beautiful and told herself that she must not despair. Yet she doubted that she would ever feel that she belonged in this place, or that she could ever care for the dark king who ruled it.

The road curved again, and again she saw Æthelred with Elgiva beside him, her black hair tangling in the breeze.

"I wonder," she said aloud, "if the king confides in Elgiva, and if she is truly fond of him."

Wymarc's mouth twisted in an uncharacteristic scowl.

"Elgiva is fond of no one but herself," she said. "Come to that, the only person who loves her more than she loves herself is that old witch Groa. I expect she thinks that Elgiva pisses holy water."

Margot shot her a reproachful glance. "That will do," she said.

"But it is true," Wymarc insisted. "Groa worships the girl. Can you not see it? I think Elgiva must have cast a spell on the woman, and on the king as well, come to that."

"Do not judge Groa too severely," Margot reproved her. "If she loves the girl overmuch it is hardly to be wondered at. Elgiva has been the only bright thing in that poor woman's life."

Wymarc looked, astonished, at Margot.

"Why do you say that? What do you know about Groa that we do not?"

Margot pursed her lips, glanced from Wymarc to Emma, and then heaved a little sigh.

"When Groa was a young woman she was taken in a raid from her home somewhere in the far north. Her captor was one of Ælfhelm's thegns, and he kept Groa as his concubine. She bore him six children, all of whom died before they were a year old. Her man died, too, while Groa was pregnant with her last child, and when that babe died at her breast she was given Elgiva to suckle." She sighed again. "Since then the girl has been her all in all."

Poor Groa, Emma thought. She was a grim-faced creature, as hard, cold, and sharp as a sword to all but Elgiva. Did bitterness and loss truly do that to a woman? Must she become hard when misfortune struck, so that she did not break?

Wymarc, too, seemed subdued by this glimpse into the life of Elgiva's old nurse, for she was silent for some time, gazing out at the passing fields of new grain.

"I grant you that she has suffered," Wymarc muttered, "but Groa does her mistress no service by defending her even when she knows Elgiva is in the wrong. I'll warrant that Elgiva does what she pleases because she has always been allowed to do so. Look at her now, riding next to the king with her skirt hitched up almost to her waist. It is not seemly."

"If the king bids Elgiva ride with him," Emma murmured, "she cannot easily refuse him."

And if the king were to command even more from Elgiva—what then? Emma did not believe that Ealdorman Ælfhelm would sanction an illicit relationship between his daughter and the king. Elgiva was much too valuable in the marriage market to waste. But Ælfhelm had gone to his lands in the north, and if the king wished to bed Elgiva, there was no one to stop him.

Almost unconsciously, her hand pressed against the belt cinched tightly at her waist. Her womb had not yet quickened with the king's child, and it had been three months. She could not help but think of her own family history. Her mother had borne six children while she was the unwed consort of a duke whose Frankish wife had died young, childless, and brokenhearted. If Elgiva were to seduce Æthelred from Emma's bed, it might be Emma's lot to remain childless. And without a son to protect her, she would be at the mercy of the king and *his* sons.

She had tried to befriend them—the three eldest—after their return from their eight-week exile at St. Albans. The eldest, Athelstan, had treated her efforts with a frosty disdain that occasionally warmed into chilly courtesy. Sometimes in the hall he would not bother to disguise his dislike. He would stare coldly at her, as if she were some outlandish creature from another world—which, in some ways, she supposed she was.

His brother Ecbert, a year younger than she was, did not seem to know what to do whenever he found himself confronted with her. He was a genial fellow by nature, his normal expression a lopsided grin. Whenever he was in her presence, though, he took care to rearrange his face into a frown. He could not maintain it for long, though, and she sometimes caught him observing her with shy interest.

It was Edmund who seemed to resent her the most. He was fourteen summers old, but a dour lad who seemed far older. He never greeted her with anything but a scowl, and he never spoke to her if he could help it—and then only in monosyllables.

She had far better luck with Æthelred's youngest children. To her surprise and relief they seemed to accept her with dispassion, if not enthusiasm, looking to her as if she were just another one of the many functionaries who oversaw their schooling and daily care. She thought that they could not have been very close to their mother, for they never spoke of her, and even the girls did not seem to miss her.

There was one other child—Mathilda, the youngest and barely two years old—whom she had not met, for the girl had been installed in a convent shortly after her mother died. It was not unusual for the daughters of kings and wealthy magnates to be consecrated to God, but Emma thought it hard that this child would have to live such a circumscribed life from so early an age. She could not imagine giving up a daughter of her own to such a life.

None of Æthelred's children would be at Winchester just yet. The eldest had left on business of their own, and the youngest had been sent to some estate in the country. The purpose, ostensibly, was to give the king and his bride time alone together, unencumbered by the children of his first wife. Emma had laughed when she heard that, for she liked the king's younger children far better than she liked the king.

In August, though, the children would return to Winchester. When they did, she must welcome them as a mother and a friend. If she could not give the king a child, then she must befriend her stepchildren, because her own safety—her very life—might one day lie in their hands. She was confident that she could win the affections of the girls and the youngest boys. It was the king's three eldest sons—Athelstan, Ecbert, and Edmund—who presented the real challenge. Somehow she had to convince them that she was not a threat. How was she to do that, though, when everyone knew that her whole purpose was to give birth to a son who would be their rival for the king's affection and largesse—and perhaps, one day, for the throne itself?

Chapter Twelve

August 1002

Winchester, Hampshire

Æthelred stood beside a light-filled window embrasure in his private chamber and greeted the arrival of his eldest son with a grunt. He half anticipated another outburst of resentment like the one he had had to endure before he'd banished the pup to St. Albans, and he did not relish the prospect.

Christ, he was weary of it all—the restless, sleep-troubled nights, the days of wrangling with councilors and churchmen, and underneath it all the incessant rumor of trouble that he knew was far more than rumor. He had dispatched this recalcitrant son of his to gather information, and now, eyeing Athelstan as he bent the knee with sober regard, Æthelred took heart. Perhaps the whelp was beginning to learn humility. Perhaps he would be of some use after all.

"You followed my instructions?" Æthelred asked, coiling himself into his chair and gesturing for his son to stand.

"Yes, my lord."

"And do you understand the problem that I face?"

Athelstan inclined his head. "Some years ago you forged an alliance with Viking raiders who were ravaging our lands, you bade them serve you as mercenaries, and rewarded them with gold and properties. Now you have bands of well-trained, well-armed Vikings, most of them Danes, settled throughout your kingdom."

Æthelred scowled. His son had grasped the situation well enough, if not the policy behind it.

"I had little choice at the time," he said, "nor am I the first ruler to settle mercenaries in his realm. The Frankish king did it. Even the great Alfred was forced to allow Danes to settle north of the River Humber."

"But in Alfred's time," his son said, his expression carefully bland, "the Danes settled in lands where few of Alfred's people dwelt. Your mercenaries are in Devonshire, Hampshire, and Oxfordshire—in the very heart of your kingdom."

His son did not say it, but Æthelred heard the unspoken accusation. He had placed a pack of wolves in the sheepfold.

"I gave them estates," he growled, "and they gave their oaths that they would not turn against me."

Yet they had done so, and with a vengeance. After several years of abiding by the pledges they had made to him, the dogs of war had been loosed upon England.

Æthelred, remembering, grimaced, and rubbed at a suddenly painful temple with his fingertips.

One of those dogs, Pallig, was wed to the half sister of Swein Forkbeard, and when Forkbeard had attacked the southern coast last year, Pallig and his men had joined in the assault. They had pillaged and burned all across Wessex, and the English host that rallied against them had failed to stop them.

He'd had no choice but to bribe the lot of them yet again to leave his realm in peace. Forkbeard had taken his gold to his ships and sailed east, but Pallig had merely made new pledges of peace and retreated to his estates. He and others like him were like boils upon the land that would someday erupt to plague him once more. He could not trust them.

"You spoke to Pallig?" he asked.

"I spoke with Pallig and with his wife, Gunhild."

"Think you he will keep his oaths to me?" He watched his son closely and spotted the hesitation before the answer was given. So the lad, too, saw the threat.

"My lord," Athelstan said, "Pallig is no farmer. He is a mercenary down to his soul—an adventurer who thrives on danger and excitement. If you do not put him to some use, he will make more mischief in spite of his pledges to you."

Æthelred waved the suggestion away.

"Once before I set the fox to guarding the chickens and I paid the price. I will not make that mistake again. Pallig may be living on estates that I granted him, but he is Swein's man at heart. He is like a knife at my throat."

"No, my lord," his son objected. Æthelred glared at his presumption but let him have his say. "Pallig is more like a kingdom unto himself," Athelstan went on, "not bound to any man. He takes whatever he feels is his by right and by force of arms. It is not the having that he loves, it is the getting. If you could but find a way to bend him to your will—"

"Men like Pallig do not bend!" he snarled. "Best you learn that now, boy. If money will not sway him, nothing will." Good Christ, he had dealt with vermin like Pallig for two decades; he knew them far better than this cub of his, who had not yet seen eighteen summers.

Athelstan frowned at his father, sympathy for the king's dilemma warring with exasperation. That England was beset by enemies from within as well as from without was the king's own doing. Granted, the marriage to Emma might stem the tide of Viking raids, but Æthelred had made a devil's bargain when he had given land to men like Pallig. They were like feral dogs that must be tamed and muzzled. He could think of only one way to do it.

"Pallig has a son, my lord," he said urgently, "newly born. Take the boy as hostage for his father's good behavior." If the boy were raised at court, he would become English and no Dane. Build trust with one child, and others, no doubt, would follow.

"Hostage?" Æthelred almost spat the word. "It is far too late for that now. We might have made it a condition in March, before we made the *gafol* payment, but now we have nothing with which to bargain. Pallig will not willingly hand his son over to me." He fingered his beard, his face brooding and dark. "He is safe on his own lands, surrounded by his warriors, a law unto himself. Nor is he the only one. There are a dozen more like him, spread across the southern shires. Who is to say what schemes they may be plotting?"

Listening to his father's groundless suspicions, Athelstan's exasperation finally overcame his sympathy.

"Who is to say that they are plotting any schemes at all?" he demanded. "What if they are not? What if Pallig merely craves action? He is a shipman! Can you not put together a fleet and charge him with guarding our coast? My lord, what other choice have you?"

His father made no answer, and Athelstan, looking into a face that he suddenly realized was haggard and far too pale, felt a sudden chill along his spine, as if a blade had been drawn through ice and laid against his skin. The king was staring, red-rimmed eyes fixed and frightened, at something behind Athelstan. He whipped around, fearing to see some horror there, yet he saw nothing save a bank of candles whose meager flames trembled in a shadowy corner, where the daylight did not reach.

He turned back to the king, and still his father stared, his face working as he mouthed a soundless cry, knuckles whitening as he clutched the carved dragon heads beneath his hands.

"My lord!" Athelstan cried. Was this some fever of the mind sprung from the cares that beset a king? Some disease that struck suddenly and left nothing but the shell of a man in its wake?

He reached out and clasped his father's hand, and he was stunned by how cold the taut flesh felt beneath his palm. His own blood seemed to freeze in response, and he felt suddenly afraid that he was watching his father die.

He grasped the king's shoulders and shook him, not knowing what else to do. In response the watery blue eyes came to rest upon his own, but the king's distress seemed to become even more acute. His father bent forward, his body rigid as he beat his breast and moaned a wordless cry, tortured by some invisible enemy.

"My lord!" Athelstan cried again, raging at his helplessness. Why did no one hear him, no one come to offer aid?

Yet even as he formed that thought, his father's body relaxed, and the bent head dropped into the king's slender hands. Athelstan's panic eased, and he felt as if he had just wakened from a nightmare.

Slowly his father raised his head, and now his face was creased and gray as the wide eyes fixed purposefully on Athelstan.

"What did you see?" the king demanded in a hoarse, urgent whisper.

Athelstan hesitated, unnerved by the intensity of his father's gaze, his mind groping desperately for a response that would appease the king.

"I saw shadows, my lord," he replied at last. "Only shadows." And I saw a king half mad with fear, he thought. But of that he dared not speak.

His father drew a long breath and released it as he repeated Athelstan's response.

"Only shadows," he whispered, and he pressed his hands against his eyes, as if he would banish whatever baleful vision lingered there.

Athelstan roused himself to fetch wine from the nearby table that held cups and a flagon. He watched while his father drank, and a hundred questions formed in his mind.

"Were you in pain?" he asked. "Has this"—he searched for some way to describe it—"affliction struck before?"

His father, much revived, it appeared, by the wine, threw him a dark, almost furtive glance.

"It was but weariness, nothing more," he murmured. "It has passed now. There are far weightier matters to occupy both my mind and yours. You will forget it." He left his chair and began to pace, restless and distracted. "There have been signs," he said heavily, "of trouble to come. I have seen portents—" He flung up an arm as if to sweep away his own words. "Nay, I need no portents to know that Pallig is dangerous. As you say, he is no farmer. Neither are the men who answer to him. They will become restless, and then they will strike."

The next moment the chamber door opened, and his father's steward, Hubert, entered carrying a packet of documents. The king raised a hand to forestall whatever Hubert might say and looked gravely at Athelstan.

"Did you see any indications that Pallig was preparing for battle?"

"No, my lord," he said, mystified both by what he had just witnessed as well as by his father's apparent determination to ignore it.

The king grimaced, as if that was not the answer he had anticipated. "Then there is nothing more to do, for now." He brushed past Athelstan as he made for his chair and beckoned to the steward. "Leave me. I have business with Hubert."

Athelstan stood there for a moment, troubled, unwilling to leave before he had gained a better understanding of what he had just seen. But both men ignored him, and he knew better than to disobey his father's command. He strode slowly from the chamber and, glancing back, he saw his father's eyes now fixed hard upon him, and in those eyes was a warning that it would be perilous for him to ignore.

As he made his way through the great hall, something that Bishop Ælfheah had said to him in the spring came back to him: *The king is troubled in his mind.* Had the bishop been witness to a similar occurrence, then? Ælfheah had not explained himself, and Athelstan dared not question him about it now. That threatening glance from his father had commanded his silence. He stepped from the royal apartments into the sunshine of late summer, his mind still wrestling with the king's strange behavior and his talk of signs and portents.

Yet he, too, had been given a sign by the seeress near Saltford—albeit one he was unwilling to believe. And last winter there had been rumors from the north that men had seen columns of light shimmering in the night sky—fierce angels with swords, it was said, come to punish men for their sins.

Truth to tell, his father was not the only one disturbed by such portents, yet what steps could anyone take to vanquish foreboding or to prevent some cataclysm that was lurking in the future? And then, recalling his interview with the king, he knew with certainty that his father must be planning steps of some kind. Why else had he been sent to speak with Pallig? Yet if his father did have some presentiment of disaster might not his very efforts to avert it bring about the misfortune that he so dreaded?

Try as he might, Athelstan could not penetrate the mysterious workings of the king's mind any more than he could unravel the dark threads of the future spun for him by the cunning woman beside the standing stones. It was a futile endeavor, and when he heard the shouts of children's laughter, he willingly relegated his father's troubling words and actions to the back of his mind. He had forgotten that the children would have returned to Winchester, and he followed the sound of laughter into the queen's garden. There, the sight of his brothers and sisters playing at dodge the ball seemed innocent and blessedly carefree. He was astonished, though, to see that the queen had joined them in their game. It was not something that their own mother had ever done.

He glanced around the garden, noting the absence of any of the English noblewomen who should have attended the queen. So the rumors that had reached him at Headington were true. There were two courts at Winchester, one made up of the king's retinue, the other of Emma's mostly Norman entourage. That, he guessed, was the result of his father's dissatisfaction with his bride. The king had expected to wed a child who would speak only Norman French, and so could be kept ignorant of the currents of information swirling around the hall and the palace—information that she might impart to her brother and, through him, to the king's Danish enemies. Emma's skill at English had astonished them all and must have infuriated his father.

But if the queen could be a conduit for information going from England to Normandy, and thus to Denmark, then she could be a conduit in the other direction as well. His father, so focused on Pallig and the enemies he perceived within his borders, had probably made no effort to learn anything from Emma about Duke Richard—about his ambitions or his allies. But someone ought to do it, and soon—before the king's misguided animosity toward his bride made her despise all of them.

Emma scooped up the leather ball, took aim at Edgar, and threw, but the lithe nine-year-old easily dodged her poorly aimed missile.

His brother Edward taunted her cheerfully from his position next to her in the circle. "You throw like a girl."

Emma laughed. "I did not have any brothers to teach me how to throw."

"But you have a brother, do you not?" Edward asked, deftly using his foot to stop the ball that skipped toward him. "Is he not the king of Normandy?" He hurled the ball at Edgar, but he, too, missed.

"He is the duke," Emma corrected him. "Normandy is a part of France, and so my brother's overlord is France's king." Not that her brother ever took much notice of the opinions of the French king. "But my brother, like your father, rules a great land filled with many people, very much like a king. He is much older than I am, though. When I was a girl he was already a grown man and had no time to teach me to throw a ball. I am very good on a horse," she said, hoping to impress Edward, who was regarding her skeptically. "I learned to ride when I was quite, quite small," she said, catching the ball that Wymarc, in the center of the circle, had nimbly sidestepped.

"Then we must go riding this afternoon," Edward urged, his face lighting with enthusiasm. "It is much better than playing with a ball."

Emma frowned, wondering if she should attempt it. She longed to ride, but every time she had even approached the stables here, which lay just outside the palace compound, her guards had turned her aside. They were courteous enough, but they had their orders, and she could guess what they were. The queen must not be allowed outside the palisade—for her own safety, of course.

If she attempted to visit the stables with Æthelred's children and was turned away, they would quickly realize that she was a prisoner, and from that deduce that she was an enemy. The bonds between them—so fragile, so carefully forged during their time together in Canterbury—would melt like ice in the sun.

"Perhaps we can go tomorrow," she hedged, "if the weather remains fine." She would have to try, once again, to speak to the king. If she were in the company of the children, their attendants, and a score of guards, perhaps he would let her go.

She reached to her left to catch the ball that the boys' tutor had hurled from the other side of the circle, but it bounced against her hand and went off at an angle. Emma turned to retrieve it but drew up abruptly at the sight of the young man who captured the ball with easy grace.

"My lord," she said, unsettled by the steady gaze of Æthelred's eldest son.

"I advise you to take advantage of the sunshine, my lady," he said. "You cannot count on fine weather for the morrow. I, for one, wish to try one of the excellent mounts that accompanied you from Normandy." He tossed the ball to his brother. "What do you say, Edward? Shall we take the queen for a ride?"

"Yes!" Edward said, the ball game forgotten. "Edgar must come, too. We do not have to bring the girls." His tone became suddenly imperious. "They are too little. They would only slow us down."

He smirked at his sister Edyth, who wrinkled her nose at him and stuck out her tongue.

"We don't like horses, anyway," she said. "They smell. And boys smell even worse. We're going to play with the kittens."

She marched off to her nurse, nose decidedly out of joint, her sister Ælfgifu in tow. It appeared that the ball game was over.

Emma turned back to Athelstan, who, with a quick jerk of his head, sent his two younger brothers pelting for the stables. The sun lit his tawny hair with golden highlights, but that was the only thing warm about him. He did not smile, merely waited politely for her reply.

She did not know what to make of him, or of his invitation.

"The guards," she said, hesitating, "will not allow me to—"

"I will take responsibility for your safety," he said.

She understood then. She would still be a prisoner, escorted by the ætheling and his men rather than her Norman hearth troops. Nevertheless, she would be outside the city walls for a time, on her own mount, in the sun and the gentle summer air. It might not be freedom, but it was as close as she was likely to get.

"Do not leave without me," she said. "I will be with you directly." She beckoned to Wymarc and made for the passage that led to her apartment.

As she hastened to her chamber, her mind was busy. What had prompted the ætheling's generosity? On the few occasions that she had attempted to converse with Athelstan, he had been civil but hardly warm. She had given up trying to placate any of them—the king's grown sons, the ladies of the court, the king himself. She felt like a pariah at the table and in the hall, for the king ignored her, and everyone else followed suit. What, then, had prompted Athelstan to seek the company of his father's reviled queen?

She could not guess, yet she was certain that he had some hidden motive. Every word, every act, every gesture made at court was laced with cryptic intent. The very walls held secrets. And the king's eldest son had reason to mislike and mistrust her, for she might one day bear a son to supplant him. She wished that it were not so, that she could ride today with a carefree heart. But she knew better. She would have to be wary.

Soon the cluster of riders was making its way past the mill, stringing out in smaller groups when they turned south to follow the path of the River Itchen. Emma found herself at Athelstan's side, with Wymarc and Hugh—summoned by Emma because she wanted at least one of her Norman hearth guards with her—immediately behind them. Edward and Edgar, their rambunctious spirits kept in moderate check by two grooms, rode some way ahead, while the ætheling's well-armed outriders trailed at a discreet distance.

As she rode Emma studied the young man beside her, looking for traces of his father. Their coloring was the same—hair as golden as ripe wheat, although Athelstan, like most English youth, wore his cropped roughly about his ears, in contrast to his father's longer, perfectly groomed locks. They had the same high forehead as well, but there the similarity ended. Athelstan's dark brows, broad nose, and full, sensuous lips bore no resemblance to his father's thinner, more sharply sculpted features.

She studied his mouth and tried to recall if she had ever seen him smile. Not at her, certainly, which made her question again why he was riding beside her at this moment.

"I am grateful for your kindness, my lord," she said. "The palace garden is quite beautiful, but I have longed to explore the countryside."

"My mother, who designed the garden," he said, "did not ride. She had a contemplative nature, and the garden seemed to satisfy all her needs."

Emma considered what little she knew of his mother. The king's first wife, it seemed, had lived like a nun, except for the very secular task of conceiving and bearing eleven children. Her personality seemed to have had all the impact on the king's court of a finger drawn through water. Had she truly been content to live such a cloistered life, or had she been forced into it by the king? Emma could imagine that well enough. But perhaps the woman had never known any other kind of existence. Perhaps she had been raised in such a sheltered environment that she found the world beyond the garden walls terrifying and forbidding.

"Your mother came from the north, I believe," she said. "You lived there for some little time, did you not? Does it look very different? Are the people different?"

"The land," he said, "the people—even the language is different. They speak an odd mixture of English and Danish there, with occasional Norse thrown into the mix just for flavor. It is a harsher land, though, than this." He nodded toward the rolling green hills of the downs. "Not as rich. There are jagged peaks in the north, rising sheer sided, as if they'd been thrust up out of the bowels of the earth. To the west the land is gentler. That is the district of the lakes—God knows how many. They are cradled in green valleys, and when the sun shines they are as blue as sapphires. Toward the eastern coast, near Jorvik, the land is different yet again, for it is flat, but not without its own kind of wild beauty. In the spring it is a tapestry of flowers."

Emma, astonished at this sudden spate of near poetry from one who had barely spoken a word to her until now, said, "Your eloquence, my lord, makes me long to see for myself these northern vistas. Perhaps the king's progress will take me there some day."

Athelstan shook his head. "My father went that far north only once, and then he had an army at his back. It is a dangerous place. The folk there are often restive under the rule of Wessex. Our strongholds, our history, lie here in the south."

She recalled that Elgiva's father was ealdorman of the northern lands. *A dangerous place*, Athelstan had said. And dangerous men and women were bred there, it seemed.

"Is Elgiva a northerner?" she asked.

"Yes," he said hesitantly, "and no. Elgiva's family owns half of Mercia, most of their lands lying in the area below the Northumbrian border. It's what we call the Midlands, but the very northern edge of it. Mercia once had its own kings before it was conquered by Wessex, but that was in the distant past. Elgiva, though, often forgets that Mercia is no longer a kingdom, and that she is not a king's daughter."

Or a king's wife, Emma thought. But if Elgiva's family was so powerful, it would go some way to explaining why Æthelred singled her out for his favor.

"What are the Northumbrians like, then?" she asked. "The folk farther north?"

He frowned.

"Fifty years ago there was a northman named Eric Bloodaxe who ruled Northumbria and called it the Kingdom of Jorvik. He was driven out, but the folk there still maintain strong ties to the lands across the Northern Sea." He was not looking at her but kept his eyes firmly planted on the path ahead, so that his next words seemed casually offhand. "You have ties there as well, I think—of family and trade."

Sensing danger in spite of his apparent disinterest, Emma replied flatly, "My mother's people came from Denmark," she said, "but she grew up in Normandy."

They were treading perilously close to a conversational landscape where she had no wish to venture. She believed that the king's mistrust of her was rooted in her Danish forebears as well as in her brother's lucrative trade with Viking shipmen. Had the king confided his suspicions to Athelstan? If so, then she had just given them credence by showing such an avid interest in the north. She wished that she had kept silent.

"It is no secret," he said slowly, "that the Danish king, Forkbeard, has been entertained at the ducal palace in Normandy. I have never seen him, although I have heard a great deal about him. Were you there when your brother greeted him? Did you see the king?"

He looked at her now with steady blue eyes, but she saw no guile there, only curiosity. Still, she hesitated, uncertain what to say. She had no wish to emphasize her brother's connection to Swein Forkbeard, but if Athelstan already knew that Swein had been in Normandy at Christmas, it would be foolish of her to lie.

"I saw him last Yuletide," she said, "but only briefly. My mother kept all the women of her household well away from the king and his shipmen."

"Ah," he said. "Yet he and his men were there at your brother's invitation."

She looked at him, irritated by his smug assumption that he understood her brother's motives.

"Indeed, my lord," she said. "And what would you do if an armed host, vastly outnumbering all your hearth troops and with a reputation for taking by force anything they wanted, appeared at your door demanding shelter?"

It was his turn to stare now, brows raised in surprise. Then he smiled.

"I would invite them in," he said.

So she had made him smile at last. It lit his entire face and softened the hard edges of that square jaw. She had told him more than she would have wished, but, all in all, she thought that the result was worth the risk.

The conversation became less pointed after that. Emma questioned him about his brothers, eager to know more of Edmund and Ecbert in particular, whom she had had little opportunity to observe. He asked about her own brothers and sisters, and was curious about the training that her brother Richard had devised for his horses.

It seemed to Emma that the time passed all too quickly, and she was sorry when they halted before the king's great hall.

"Perhaps," Athelstan said, as he helped her to dismount, "we might ride together again. I would learn more of Normandy, if you would be willing to instruct me."

He stood facing her, his hands still at her waist exerting a gentle pressure to steady her. Only his touch did not steady her. It did the opposite, and when she looked into his eyes, far bluer than the sky, she felt dizzy, as if she were falling from some great height.

"I do not know if the king would give me leave," she answered, backing away from him, seeking solid ground.

"I will speak to him. He should have no objection, so long as he is assured that you will be safe."

Safe? Was there anywhere in this realm where she could be truly safe? It was a world peopled with men and women scheming for power and preferment, and her marriage had bred resentment toward her that could one day turn to enmity, and against which she had little defense.

As she watched him lead the horses toward the stable, she pondered the wisdom of riding out with him again. She still did not know why he had made this overture toward her, but, dear God, she longed to escape the suffocating world within the palace walls. Why should she not attend him, if the king allowed it? She needed to forge alliances within the court. Perhaps this was a beginning.

Or perhaps, she argued with herself, it was a trap of some kind, devised to destroy her already precarious relationship with the king. How was she to tell?

She turned to follow Wymarc, who was shepherding the younger boys into the private apartments. There was no one at court, she reminded herself, whom she could truly trust, except her own people. She must remember that.

But as she made her way up the stairs, slowly, for her legs ached from their unaccustomed exercise, she was troubled by a too vivid memory of piercing blue eyes and the sudden shifting of the earth beneath her feet.

Chapter Thirteen

October 1002

Winchester, Hampshire

When the evening meal had been cleared away, and the king's household, to ward off the autumn chill, had settled themselves around the central fire, Elgiva, with Groa beside her, contemplated the gathering from an unobtrusive alcove. Normally she would have claimed a place at the king's side to listen as his *scop* recited some thrilling tale. Tonight, though, because of her father's imperious demands, she had to forgo her treasured seat beside the king.

She was still seething from the tongue lashing her father's messenger had delivered earlier in the day. The thick, swaggering, self-important churl had rebuked her in her father's name for not attending to the task he had set her.

"You were meant to be his eyes and ears," the oaf had said, "but to judge from the news you've sent him, you've gone blind and deaf. My lord wishes to know if you've gone softheaded, as well."

She'd wanted to slap the fool. She had her own affairs to tend to and little time to play at being her father's informer. Aside from having to attend Emma whenever she snapped her fingers, she accompanied the king when he visited some shrine or hunted with a few select companions—a daily ritual while the weather held fair. How could she pay attention to the business of others when she was so caught up in her own?

But she would have to send her father something, if only to keep that oaf from haranguing her again. She glanced around the hall, taking mental note of how the members of the court had arranged themselves. The place she usually had at the king's side had been filled by Ealdorman Godwine of Lindsey and his wife, Lady Winfled, who was chattering away like a magpie. Æthelred looked bored, and Elgiva smiled. When she sat next to him he was never bored.

She would tell her father about Godwine, of course, but the man was no threat and no particular favorite of the king's, for that matter. As for whom the king favored the most . . . well, that was no business of her father's. She held out her arm and gazed with admiration at the broad gold band that graced her wrist—a gift that Æthelred had presented to her only yesterday. She had spun around before him in a new gown, and he had placed the heavy bangle on her hand. *To keep your feet on the ground*, he had said.

She wanted more than pretty presents, though. She wondered how long it would be until the king grew tired of his insipid bride and turned elsewhere for consolation. Not long, she thought. Already he visited Emma's bed less frequently than he had in the early weeks of summer.

She made a mental note to tell her father about that. She would also tell him that Emma's waist remained slender, cause for great speculation among the women of the court. It was whispered that if Emma remained barren, the king might be persuaded to put her aside and marry another.

She searched for the queen then and saw her seated at some distance from her husband. Æthelred's three-year-old daughter, Wulfhilde, her thumb in her mouth, was curled in Emma's lap, and her sisters sat nearby. Whatever Æthelred's feelings toward his queen, Elgiva thought, his daughters had taken to her like chicks to a hen. The girls were not important, though, and not likely to interest her father.

Of far greater interest were Emma's adult companions, and Elgiva regarded them with some surprise. She leaned a little toward Groa and whispered, "When did the Bishop of Winchester and the Abbess of Wherwell become so friendly with the queen?"

Groa, her fingers busy as always with wool and spindle, glanced at Emma.

"When she gave the bishop the relics of St. Valentinus for the New Minster," Groa replied, "and when she endowed Wherwell with a tract from her dower lands to found a cell near Exeter."

Elgiva did not like that news. Emma may be a prisoner, but apparently she was putting her brother's gold to good use.

"Why did you not tell me of this before?" she chided Groa.

"Because you did not ask, my lady, and so I thought you knew."

Elgiva wanted to shake her old nurse. It maddened her that Groa was so closemouthed. She kept her eyes and ears open, it was true, but she was so niggardly of speech that one had to prise information out of her.

"How would I know about it?" she demanded. "I have spent a great deal of time of late with the king, and I can assure you we do not discuss Emma and her endowments." She huffed with impatience. "Who else has the queen been courting that I should know about? Tell me, even if you think it is obvious."

"The king's children attend the queen almost daily when she goes riding out beyond—"

"The children mean nothing," Elgiva snapped. "What of her escort when she rides? Are they the same men every time?" Wealth and beauty were seductive, and Emma had both. At Æthelred's court, she had observed, loyalty was often for sale.

"Lord Athelstan and his men provide her escort, along with some of Emma's Normans," Groa replied. "The æthelings Ecbert and Edmund sometimes ride with them as well. Indeed, the æthelings' retainers have befriended many of the Normans."

Elgiva felt a prick of alarm at this news. She glanced quickly around the hall and found Athelstan seated at a game board across from Emma's man, Hugh. The Norman priest, Father Martin, was in deep, quiet conversation with the abbot of the New Minster, and as she gazed around she realized that the Normans—men and women—no longer sat in a group by themselves but were scattered among the English folk.

"How have I not noticed this?" she murmured.

"Do not fault yourself, my lady. As you say, you have been attending upon the king when he rides to the hunt. You have not seen the queen's party ride out after your departure, nor seen them return before the hunters have come back."

"But I do not understand how the Normans have insinuated themselves among us," Elgiva protested.

"They have taken great pains to learn our language, and that is what has done it. Even Emma's women speak only English now. Surely that has not escaped you."

Elgiva scowled, stung by this, for it had indeed escaped her.

"All my thoughts have been focused on the king," she said. "You have told me that one day I will be queen. How can that prophecy be fulfilled if I do not make myself the king's darling?"

"You will be queen," Groa assured her. "It has been foretold by one who has seen it."

Not for the first time Elgiva wondered who had spun such a royal future for her. But although she had pressed the old woman for the source of her knowledge, Groa had refused to divulge it. And that was not such a bad thing, Elgiva thought, for if Groa kept the secrets of others, her own secrets would be safe with her as well.

Her eyes strayed to Athelstan again, and she saw that his gaze was fixed upon Emma. The queen looked up, met his glance, and for the space of several heartbeats some mute understanding seemed to pass between them. Then Emma blushed and looked away.

Elgiva drew a long, slow, astonished breath, hardly able to believe what she had just seen. Was it possible that Athelstan, who should have been Emma's greatest enemy, lusted after his father's bride? How many hours had they spent riding together, then? And what had been shared between them? More than fresh air, to be sure.

Her suspicion was like bile in her throat. If it was true, then

Athelstan was yet another thing that Emma had taken that should have been hers. And it was yet one more reason why she hated the king's Norman bride.

The Feast of St. Æthelred dawned clear and sunny. On this day the palace, the Old Minster, and all the streets surrounding the royal compound buzzed with anticipation, as royals, prelates, and townsfolk came together to celebrate the feast day of the king.

Athelstan, waiting to take his place in the solemn procession forming in the palace courtyard, watched as the lead figures in the column set out through the gate. The bishop led the way, resplendent in a red cope embroidered with golden roods, his hands adorned with ruby rings. Behind him, ten priests walked two by two, each one garbed in a green chasuble for the celebration of the Mass. They were followed by a dozen white-robed acolytes, who bore a flower-strewn litter that carried the massive golden coffer housing St. Æthelred's relics. Following the saint, the king and queen stood ready to lead the royal family toward the minster, and behind the royal party the choir had already begun to chant a psalm.

Athelstan, in his place behind the queen, thought that she looked as lovely as he had ever seen her. Her hair was pulled modestly into a long, thick braid, barely visible through the opaque whiteness of her veil. The white of her chemise, gathered tightly at her throat and her wrists, contrasted starkly with the deep blue of the cyrtel that hugged her slim figure. She had accented her gown with nothing more than a rope of pearls that looped to her waist, and the only gold she wore was a delicate crown set with sapphires. Beside her, his father was resplendent in gold from crown to hem, to give honor to the saint whose name he bore—and to impress the crowd.

The procession made its way past throngs of silently reverent town and country folk, who had spilled into the streets to watch the parade of royals, prelates, and the stunning reliquary of the saint. Many in the crowd held crosses; others stood with wide-eyed children perched upon their shoulders.

As Athelstan entered the Old Minster it took a moment for his eyes to adjust from the brightness of the sunlight to the shadowy vastness of the church. He caught the scent of roses before he could see them. The sisters of Nunnaminster and the ladies of Emma's court had transformed the cold stone edifice into a bower, for every altar and column wore garlands of fragrant blossoms. High above, bright silk pennons billowed from brackets on the walls.

The massive organ poured out a solemn processional that echoed over the heads of the congregation as the king led his entourage upstairs to the royal chamber near the altar. Athelstan took his place behind his father and swept his gaze over the hundreds of worshipers standing below. Many of them would have spent the night in the church to claim a choice spot from which to gaze their fill on the glittering royals. Few of the faithful, he thought, observing their upturned faces, would have their minds on their prayers today.

In truth, his own thoughts were anything but prayerful, and they were far more carnal than was politic or wise. Emma knelt just before him and a little to one side, and to be so close to her when he could neither touch her nor even speak to her was a sweet torture.

For the thousandth time he reminded himself that she was his father's wife.

The words seemed to repeat in his head like a demented litany, but it did not matter. Yes, she was his father's wife, but his father did not love her, did not even want her.

And, God help him, he did.

Thou shalt not covet thy neighbor's wife.

Which commandment was that? And what about thy *father's* wife? If you fell into that sin, was there any redemption?

He did not care, because he did not want redemption; he wanted his father's wife, although he could never have her. She was as far beyond his reach as the moon.

Yet he loved her—a thing that still mystified him. In spite of the laws of God and of man, in spite even of his own will, he loved her. And he did not know what to do, because while his father lived he never could have her.

The service seemed to last an eternity. By the time it was over his dismal reflections on the hopelessness of his passion for Emma had driven him to near despair. The royal couple led the way out of the church, and he dutifully followed them outside, where they were met by a cheering crowd and a cacophony of bells. Forcing himself to school his eyes and his thoughts away from the queen, he noticed a movement ahead of him and to his right, like the ripple of a wind breathing across a field of wheat. Puzzled, he stared at the brightly colored crowd, and amid their hues of green and yellow and rust, he made out a lone black form moving, swift as a hawk's shadow, toward the king.

Chapter Fourteen

October 1002

Winchester, Hampshire

The wild pealing of the minster bells filled the square with waves of sound as Emma, walking at the king's side, smiled at the cheering folk who lined their route. The afternoon sun felt warm on her shoulders, and she wished that she could slow her pace and clasp some of the many hands that reached out eagerly to touch their queen. Æthelred, however, did not allow it. His firm hand at her elbow guided her briskly toward the palace gates.

She glanced at him and saw that his face wore its usual grim aspect. She did not understand it. This was his feast day. All of this rejoicing was in his honor. Could he not even smile at his subjects in return? And there had been good news this morning as well: The winds in the Narrow Sea had shifted in England's favor. There would be no threat from plundering dragon ships now, not until the water roads opened up again in the spring.

It was welcome news to her, if not to the king. All summer she had watched and waited for Danish raiders to attack, fearing that when it happened her brother would somehow be implicated, guilty or not, and that retribution would fall upon her—guilty or not. Now she felt safe, and she walked with a lighter step, as if a heavy mourning cloak had been lifted from her shoulders.

The first inkling she had of anything amiss was the sound of a single, discordant voice that rose shrill above the clamor of the bells.

There were alien curses in that cry, words that raised the fine hairs along her arms and turned her blood to ice. She searched for the source of that hideous sound, and as she did so she saw a knife flash above the heads of the nearest onlookers. Before she could even scream a warning, the king was flung headlong to the ground and Athelstan had lunged at a figure hurtling toward them from out of the crowd.

She cried out as the knife glinted again, its blade driving downward. At the same moment a handful of men-at-arms, their swords drawn, surged in front of her, jostling her backward as they formed a wall that separated her from the king and his son. Rough hands grasped her shoulders, and a cluster of king's guards surrounded her, propelling her through the gates and into the palace yard. There was no chance to protest, no opportunity to determine what damage had been done, for her guards did not slacken their pace until they had brought her to her own chamber.

"I must go to the king," she insisted, shaken by what she had seen and heard, terrified by what she feared. The knife had plunged toward Athelstan. Dear God, what had happened?

She made to leave the chamber, but one of the guards blocked her path.

"You will stay here, my lady," he said firmly. "Guards will be posted in the corridor to keep you safe." He reached for the door and shut it, cutting off her protest.

For a moment she simply stared at the place where he had been, trembling and afraid. Doubt inched like a worm under her skin and into her brain. Were the guards meant to keep her safe or to keep her from escaping?

Either way, she was a prisoner.

She began to pace, her eyes shut, trying to make sense of what she had seen, recalling with awful clarity the words that had risen above the incessant clanging of the bells. Time passed slowly, and she heard nothing except the sound of her own footsteps. It seemed like hours had slipped by before voices rang in the corridor.

She turned to the door as it opened and the king's steward, Hubert, entered.

"What has happened?" she demanded, before he had even finished his bow. Her heart drummed in her chest as she waited for him to speak.

"The creature that raised his hand against the king has been taken," he said.

"And Lord Athelstan?" she asked. "He is unharmed?"

He raised an eyebrow, and she realized her mistake. She should have asked after the king first. She said stiffly, "I thought I saw the ætheling take an injury."

His thin, almost colorless mouth curled slightly in a dismissive smile.

"An insignificant wound, my lady, that has been tended. The king, I can assure you, was unhurt. He commands you to speak of the incident to no one, and he orders you to attend him at the feast in the great hall as soon as you may."

She stared at him, not certain that she had heard him aright.

"The king would keep this secret? How?" It was not possible. There had been hundreds of people in the square.

He shrugged. "Few actually saw what happened, and measures have been taken to silence idle tongues. Those who need to know, of course, will be informed at the king's pleasure. He trusts in your discretion."

After a curt bow, he left her. Still shaken, she continued to pace, trying to puzzle out the king's purpose in suppressing the incident. Was it merely that he did not want his subjects to perceive him as a victim, and therefore weak? Or was there something else in his mind? She was no closer to fathoming what that might be when Wymarc glided swiftly into the chamber.

"Why are there guards at the door?" Wymarc asked.

She did not look frightened, merely confused. So perhaps Hubert was right and what had happened in the minster square was not common knowledge.

"It is of no moment," Emma replied, eager to deflect Wymarc's curiosity. "All is well."

The brown eyes studied her, then Wymarc shook her head.

"All may be well," she said, "but you are as pale as a wraith, my lady, and you are shaking like an aspen in a fierce wind. If you will not tell me what is wrong, at least let me get you a cup of wine."

Emma, recognizing suddenly that her legs felt as thin and weak as cattails, sank into her chair. She gratefully accepted the wine, although she had difficulty holding the cup steady, for she could not control the trembling of her hands. How she longed to escape from here, to ride Ange along the river until she reached the sea. But the king had commanded her to attend the feast, and she had to obey. Would Athelstan be there? She prayed so. Hubert had made light of the ætheling's injury, but Hubert would say whatever the king commanded, and so she feared for Athelstan in spite of the steward's assurances.

Her mother's voice, emerging from some hidden corner of her mind, echoed in her head. *You must never allow anyone to see your fear.*

She looked down at her shaking hands and took a deep breath, trying to reach a calm that eluded her. It was not only for Athelstan that she was afraid. The words of the attacker still rang in her ears. Few in the crowd would have heard them, and fewer still would have understood them, for the tongue that spoke them had been Danish.

"Death to the king! Death to the council!" He had shouted the words over and over. She could hear them even as she was being hustled through the palace gates.

Yet it was not the words themselves that frightened her. It was what Æthelred, who knew no Danish, was likely to do when he learned their meaning.

Æthelred presided over the feast with what he believed was creditable dignity. His sons and his house guards had dealt quickly with the villain who had tried to kill him, and those in the crowd near enough to see the attack had been bribed with silver and threats to hold their tongues. He did not want his enemies to know how close they had come to dispatching him.

Nonetheless, they had come far too close.

He ate little, for the specter of his own death gaped before him like a yawning pit. When he could bear the tension no longer, he rose to his feet and, bidding his guests to continue their revelry, pleaded weariness and left the hall. Calling for torches and candles—for he wanted no shadowy corners in his rooms tonight—he sought the solitude of his chamber.

Once there, pacing to and fro in the silence, no amount of light could wipe from his mind the image of a gleaming knife poised to strike. It was retribution, he had no doubt—recompense for the murder of a king.

Twenty-four years ago he had seen just such a blade glinting in a raised hand, a flash in the dark. No one had intervened that night; no champion had stepped forward to save a king's life. He had watched in horror from the shadows at the top of the stairs, a scream caught in his throat as Edward fended off that first blow. But there had been so many blows after that one. Too many. Edward had been butchered at the hands of men he had trusted.

He stopped his pacing to stand before the crucifix where Christ hung in agony.

Today's attack was a judgment upon him sent by God as punishment for that murder done at Corfe. His own hand had not wielded the weapons that killed his brother, but neither had he done all he could to prevent it. He had seen the riders coming, had seen the moonlight gleaming on their swords, and he had not had the wit to cry a warning to Edward. He had stood there, mouth agape with a cry that never left his throat.

When it was all over, he was given Edward's crown.

Yet today, his son—who so resembled that dead king—had seen the danger and had come to a king's aid. Athelstan might have been enthroned tonight if he had hesitated but a little. He had not. He had intervened in God's act of retribution. But God, Æthelred knew, would not relent.

He fell to his knees before the cross, closing his eyes and bowing his head, and pleaded a silent prayer for mercy. He had made reparation. He had encouraged the cult that revered his brother as martyr and saint. He had built a shrine for Edward's holy remains, had invested abbeys in the martyr's name. What more could he do that he had not already done?

Yet even as he prayed, a cold dread crept over him.

"Yea, though I walk through the valley of the shadow of—" But the psalm caught in his throat, and some force—like an invisible hand beneath his chin—compelled him to lift his head and gaze upon that familiar, tortured figure on the cross. To his horror he saw that the face gazing back at him was Edward's face. It was Edward's blood that poured from a dozen gaping wounds and Edward's eyes that glared at him with unspoken accusation.

Æthelred tried to look away, to escape the relentless power that held him, but he was trapped in that pitiless gaze. His vision blurred with tears, and a cold, searing pain scored his breast once, and again. The stink of burning flesh assailed him, and he wailed in terror, because he knew that it was the stench of his own punishment come upon him, and that death—and worse than death—awaited him.

For surely in that terrible night beyond the grave lay judgment, and his brother, Edward, would be waiting.

Elgiva, striding down the passage that led toward the king's chamber, heard Æthelred's bitter cry and quickened her pace.

She had not been duped by his assertion that he was weary and needed rest. Something unpleasant had occurred, she was certain of it. She had seen it in the uneasy glances that passed between the king and Athelstan and had read it in Emma's brittle, unsmiling face.

There had been whispers, too—vague rumors of some mishap on the minster green. Determined to get to the bottom of the mystery, she had slipped away from the feasting shortly after the king did. If there were some treachery afoot, her father would want to know of it.

She was nearing the king's chamber, relieved to see a door ward posted there who knew her well, and who might be persuaded to allow her in, when she heard Æthelred cry out. The guard stared at the door, horror struck, but made no move to open it.

"Did you not hear that, fool?" Elgiva demanded. "The king calls for aid; get you inside, man!"

The guard hesitated, then rapped heavily on the door. "My lord?"

When there was no response he rapped and called again, but Elgiva shoved past him and thrust the door open.

Æthelred knelt on the stone floor with his back to them, his arms flung wide, mirroring the image of the crucifix on the wall. He gave no sign that he heard them enter but continued to face the rood as if in a trance.

The door ward stopped in his tracks, looking as though he wanted the earth to swallow him whole. Elgiva put a finger to her lips and motioned him out of the room.

Alone with the king, she regarded the kneeling Æthelred with a frown. Whatever had happened today it must have frightened him to his very soul to bring him so to his knees. She would have preferred almost any other response but this. She was used to men drinking themselves into a stupor—her father did it often enough whenever he was troubled, so she had some experience at grappling with a man's reeling body. She was far less confident of her ability to grapple with a reeling soul.

Silently cursing men and their foibles, she knelt at the king's side and, not knowing what else to do, she spread her arms wide. She did not know what prayer Æthelred sent heavenward, but hers was a heartfelt plea that she would not have to kneel here for very long.

After a time she glanced at the king's face and saw, with mild disgust, that it was wet with tears. Embarrassed at the sight of such unmanly emotion, she began to gingerly pat his back, as she might a weeping child.

"My lord," she whispered, hardly knowing what it was that she said, "you must not despair." She groped for some reassuring words and snatched frantically at something the bishop had said in today's interminable sermon. "Our Savior hears and answers the prayers of even the humblest wretches who put their faith and trust in Him. How much greater will His compassion and love be for the king who holds all our care in his hands?"

At first he made no response, and she wondered if he was indeed in a trance and had not heard her. After some moments, though, he eased his rigid stance, sitting back upon his heels and dropping his face into his hands. Gratefully, she too relaxed.

"God has no compassion for me," he murmured. "He has allowed the devil's servant to smite me."

She could make little sense out of that except that whatever had happened, he seemed to believe it had been orchestrated by God Himself. That was a sin of pride if ever there was one. She suppressed a snort at Æthelred's vanity.

"Tell me what happened today," she whispered. "You may find that it eases your mind to speak of it," she said hopefully. "Come, my lord king. Will you not tell me?"

She would have liked nothing better than to rise from her knees and escort him to the plush comfort of his royal bed, but to attempt it might shatter the delicate spell that, for the moment, bound them. Instead she continued to stroke his back and shoulders, to ease her fingers along his neck and scalp. She saw the rise and fall of his chest as he heaved a great sigh, and he began to unburden his heart.

She listened to his account, struck by the audacity of the attack. The creature with the knife must have been insane, for surely he could not have expected to escape with his life. Only a madman would attempt such an enterprise.

"He was sent by heaven to punish me," Æthelred said, his gaze once more fixed on the figure of Christ on the cross. "He did not succeed, but others will follow."

She closed her eyes. What sin blackened Æthelred's soul that he anticipated such fierce, divine retribution? That would, indeed, be a secret worth knowing. She opened her eyes and considered the man beside her. His face was white and waxy with exhaustion, like a man who had been a long time ill. He was weak, this king, and she felt nothing for him but scorn. Yet, she reminded herself, all men were weak.

And he was still a king.

She scooted forward and turned so that she could gaze into his face.

"But my lord king," she whispered, "do not you see that this may be not a judgment sent upon you, but a warning to you? Even if God allowed this devil to pursue you, he did not succeed. Your son protected you, and surely that, too, was the work of God."

She had his attention. The creases on his brow deepened into a frown, and she could tell that he was digesting her words. She pressed her advantage.

"You are right to pray, my lord, and you must pray for guidance. As you have said, this man may be just the leading edge of some greater, more terrible wave about to break upon us. Do not you see that you must rouse yourself to fight this scourge?" She groped for something appropriately biblical. "You must be the David, my lord, who conquers Goliath. You must be the Sampson who destroys the Philistines. Be a king who is ruled by your courage and your passion, not by your remorse for acts that cannot be undone."

She held her breath. What if she had gone too far? Would he spurn her for presuming to tell him what he should do?

She looked into his eyes and saw a sudden flicker of heat there, but it was not the heat of anger or desperation. Encouraged, she leaned forward and gently grazed her tongue against his lower lip, and he responded by pulling her fiercely against him.

The coupling that followed was swift and rough. It gave her no pleasure, but she did not care. She had at last made her way into the arms of a king. She had roused him from his torpor, and surely he would reward her accordingly. Groa had predicted a royal destiny for her, and now she was certain that, before very long, all that she deserved would be within her grasp.

·   ·   ·

Emma slept little the night of St. Æthelred's feast, for the Danish curses howled by the king's assailant continued to echo inside her head. In the morning she asked to speak with Æthelred, and when she was denied, she grew uneasy. Why would he not admit her? Was he afraid of all things Danish now, including a queen whose mother had Danish blood?

Throughout the day she tried to discover what was taking place in the king's apartments, but she could glean nothing, and her apprehension grew. She felt as helpless as a mouse in a box, bereft of light and sound. She dared not speak to anyone about what had happened in the minster yard, for the king had forbidden it. She dared not even set her fears down in a letter to her brother, lest it should be intercepted.

In the afternoon, weary from an endless chain of questions that her mind continued to spin, she went alone into the palace garden in search of respite. All she could do was pace, a victim to doubt and misgiving.

She decided that she must find some way to speak with Athelstan. There was no one else to whom she could confide her fears, and surely he would know what was in the mind of the king. She longed to see him, to speak with him and draw comfort from his counsel.

She longed for a great many things, she thought, that she could not have.

Then she saw Athelstan enter the garden and approach her through the lengthening afternoon shadows, and it was as if some good angel had taken pity on her.

"I hoped to find you here," he said, his voice urgent. He drew her into the small, sheltered copse in the garden's farthest corner.

"Tell me what is happening," she begged. "I have been able to learn nothing, and I am afraid of what the king may be planning."

But he ignored her question to ask his own.

"You know what he said, don't you?" His eyes searched her face. "The man wielding the knife, you understood him."

She remembered her mother's advice, to keep secret her knowledge of the Danish tongue. *It will not endear you to your new lord, and may breed mistrust.*

When she made no reply Athelstan answered his own question.

"Of course you understood him," he said. "Your mother is Danish. Jesu!" He ran a frantic hand through his hair. "Does the king know?"

"Only Margot knows," she said, "and now you."

He drew in a breath and released it.

"Keep your knowledge of Danish secret, lady," he said. "Guard it carefully, do you hear me?"

"What is happening?" she asked again.

"The man who attacked the king is mad," he said, "his wits as shattered as broken glass. I have said as much to my father, but he will not listen. He is convinced that his throne is imperiled by Danish enemies within the realm, and he is taking steps to thwart them. There is to be no Christmas court. Tomorrow the younger children will go to the manor at Cookham, while I am ordered to Headington with Edmund and Ecbert. My father wants us scattered, so that we are less of a target." He grimaced. "There is more—and worse, I fear."

She said nothing, waiting for the next blow.

"He does not trust your Norman retainers," he said. "They are all to leave the court. Hugh will go to Exeter to act as reeve there for your dower lands. Your hearth guards are to accompany him, and your women as well, save one or two. You will be confined to the palace—to keep you safe."

He had confirmed her worst fears. They would leave Winchester, all of them, while she remained here, a prisoner at the mercy of the king. She would be powerless and friendless, suspected of some imagined infamy.

She felt him grasp her shoulders as if to steady her, and she looked up into the now familiar blue eyes.

"How soon?" she asked.

"Within the week."

She closed her eyes. How would she bear it? Without her own folk about her, the winter ahead loomed long, lonely, and frightening.

Without Athelstan, the days would be endless.

"Emma," his voice was urgent again, and she opened her eyes to meet his. "I cannot be certain that this is all of it." He frowned, his expression grave. "There is a darkness in my father's mind that I do not understand. You must promise me that you will be wary of him, that you will give him no excuse to cause you more grief. Promise me."

She was aware, suddenly, of the silence in the garden. Even the birds had fled, and for the first time, she realized, they were alone, without children or servants or attendants. There were no eyes to observe them, no tongues to interpret every gesture and expression.

She lifted her hand to caress his cheek, with its rough, close-cropped beard.

"I promise to be careful." She held her breath as he turned his head to press his lips against her palm. The tenderness of that touch made her heart dance with joy and her soul quail with terror. "You must go," she urged, "before someone comes. I pray God will keep you safe."

"Do you? I pray for something else—something that is a sin even to think about."

His hands tightened on her shoulders and he kissed her—a bruising kiss that was as fierce and angry and desperate as a curse. An instant later he was gone and she was left alone with her fear, with the prospect of the dark, lonely winter that lay ahead, and with a heart broken by hopeless yearning.

One week after his feast day, the king summoned a select group of trusted councilors to a late-night meeting. The small chamber, wreathed in broad banks of candles, glowed with light, while the rest of the palace, and most of the folk within it, slumbered in darkness. Half a dozen more candles burned amid a riot of drinking cups and pitchers of wine on the long table in the center of the room.

Æthelred, seated at the table's head, watched the men file in. He read the apprehension on their faces as they glanced nervously at the clerks behind him, who recorded the name of each man who entered.

He had given no hint as to the purpose of the council. They would find out soon enough.

He bid the men seat themselves, and as servants moved among them to fill their cups, the mood in the chamber lightened appreciably. He drank little himself but watched, satisfied, as cups were emptied and refilled. Sober reflection was not what he required of these men tonight.

Finally he motioned for the servants to leave the room, all but the clerks whose duty it was to record what was said here, and what would be decided.

"We are here," he said solemnly, fingering his beard, "to resolve the issue of the Danes who dwell within our borders. First I wish to discover the magnitude of the problem. What can you tell me?"

They needed little encouragement, for he had chosen these men with care. Each one had numerous tales of outrage to relate—incidents of stolen cattle, plundered churches, raped women, and all of it the work of renegade Danes. As the stories were told and the wine drunk, the anger around the table rose until it spilled out in curses and calls for revenge.

Æthelred let them vent their outrage unhindered. He had already made up his mind about what must be done. The creature that had accosted him in the minster square was merely a symptom of a much larger disease. England was littered with bands of restless Viking mercenaries, seasoned warriors with no allegiance to anyone but their own leaders and the gold that was paid them. They had been of use to him once. Now, having proved that they could not be trusted, they remained in the land like a contagion. Men like Pallig, with too little to occupy them and no ties of loyalty to control them, were cankers that sickened his realm. He had no choice but to cut them out before they formed an army and destroyed him.

At the far end of the table, Eadric of Shrewsbury described the theft of a herd of horses and the torching of a barn, and then slammed his fist against the board.

"My lord, these men live among us, but they remain outside the law," he said. "They answer to no one. We fear, and rightly, the men of the dragon ships who steal our food, our goods, and our women. But we should fear even more the like-minded devils that dwell among us who do not have to cross the Danish sea to murder us."

Æthelred nodded as cries of assent rumbled around the table. It was time for the final act. He signaled the door ward, and then he said, above the din, "My lords, I have myself been the victim of these godless men. They have gone so far as to raise their hands against your king." There were shouts of shock and outrage, and before they could die down he cried, "The foreign devil that would have slain me stands there!"

He pointed to the ragged, black-clothed figure that stood in the doorway between two guards. The creature's reddened, malevolent eyes searched the room, and when they found Æthelred the monster howled like an animal that scents his prey. Straining against his bonds, hands outstretched as he tried in vain to hurl himself at the king, he shouted the Danish curses that had been the only words to escape his lips from the moment he was taken.

The men seated around the table were struck dumb. The abbot made the sign of the cross.

Æthelred, assured that his prisoner had had the desired impact, gestured to the guards to remove him.

"You see the kind of vermin that we face," he said. "His words touch all of us, I warn you, for he threatens death to me and to my council and promises that the Danes will take England for themselves."

More shouts of protest and anger greeted this announcement, and Abbot Kenulf, seated next to Eadric, rose to his feet.

"These are not Christian men," he said, in a voice that resonated with spiritual authority. "Men such as this worship pagan gods and practice pagan ways. They have sprouted among us like cockles among the wheat, and we must rid ourselves of their foul contagion before it grows too strong."

The shouting began again, and Æthelred raised a hand to quell it.

"What you say is true, abbot, but the task must be carried out with care and with secrecy. If they suspect that we are preparing to move against them, they will meet us with force." And it was all too likely, he thought, that the Danes would win such a fight. "It is why I have called you together tonight in such secrecy. I propose to send messengers to my reeves in every town and village where such men dwell. My men will bear writs branding this man and all men like him as traitors to the crown. On a day that I shall name, all across this land they will be arrested and put to the sword. Are we agreed?"

Eadric slammed the table again and shouted, "Aye, my lord! You have my support!"

In a moment, the rest had followed suit, and Æthelred nodded, satisfied. His prisoner, mad though he clearly was, had played his part well.

Æthelred turned to the clerk nearest him.

"How soon can this thing be done?" he asked.

The clerk pursed his lips, considering.

"We will need at least fourteen days to prepare the writs, my lord," he said, "and several days after that to deliver them." He ran his finger down the page of one of the books that lay open before him on the table, then looked up at Æthelred. "Friday, November 13," he said. "St. Brice's Day."

Æthelred nodded his approval. On St. Brice's Day he would be rid of the enemies who troubled his days and tortured his nights.

He dismissed the councilors and went to his bed—and to the embraces of the Lady Elgiva—well pleased with the night's work.

A.D. 1002   The king gave an order to slay all the Danes that were in England. This was accordingly done on the mass-day of St. Brice, because it was told the king that they would beshrew him of his life, and afterwards all his council, and then have his kingdom without any resistance.

—*The Anglo-Saxon Chronicle*

Chapter Fifteen

ovember was the blood month, the slaughter time, when stock were culled, butchered, and dressed in preparation for the lean days of the winter to come. In Winchester the short days turned cold and wet, but Emma took little note of the weather. She left the palace only to attend services in one of the two great churches nearby, always escorted by members of the king's hearth guards, for her Norman folk had been sent away, scattered to her various properties across Wessex and Mercia. Hugh was gone to Exeter, and Emma missed him most of all, for he had given her good counsel about the management of her estates. Wymarc, she guessed, missed him even more, although she did her best to hide it.

"I could send you to Exeter as well, if you wish it," Emma had offered several days before Hugh and his men had departed. She had seen the affection that had grown between Wymarc and Hugh, and although her heart was heavy at the thought of losing her friend, she had no wish to deny her the happiness that her queen would never have.

"Of what use would I be to you in Exeter?" Wymarc had demanded. "My place is at your side, my lady, not in some fortress at the kingdom's edge. And if you are thinking I've a mind to follow Hugh, well, it will do him no harm to discover how dismal the world can be with only English women in it."

Yet when Hugh took his leave of Emma, Wymarc had followed him from the chamber, and when she returned her eyes were bright with tears, and she had the rumpled look of a woman who had just been well and thoroughly kissed.

On the morning of November 13, the Feast of St. Brice, Emma's English attendants clustered in her chamber in small groups like flocks of brightly colored birds. Emma sat to one side with Wymarc, Margot, and Father Martin—all that remained of her Norman retinue. They were eagerly sifting through a packet that had arrived from Rouen with news of the forthcoming marriage of Emma's sister Mathilde to a Frankish count. A letter from Emma's mother provided details, but Emma was disappointed to find no message from her sister.

Mathilde, she thought, still harbored resentment that she had not been the one sent to wed a king. She could have wept at the cruel irony of it, but weeping was for later, when she lay alone in her cold bed and recalled the nights she had shared with her sister in their chamber at Fécamp.

Father Martin began to read aloud what amounted to a sermon from her brother the archbishop, regarding a woman's duty to her husband, and Emma was relieved when he was interrupted by a servant bearing news, until she heard what he had to say. A nameless Dane had been put to death that morning for crimes against the king.

She knew what the prisoner's crime had been, and that his life had been forfeit for raising his hand against the king. There was wild speculation, though, among the ladies of her chamber about the execution.

Emma tried to ignore the threads of conjecture the women spun. None of them could know for certain what he had done or how close the poor mad wretch had come to murdering the king or his son.

She caught sight of Elgiva then, who was looking at her with an arch, insolent gaze. Elgiva, at least, did know what had happened that day in the minster square. Indeed, she must know a great many things, for Elgiva was sleeping with the king.

It was the greatest open secret within the court—that, and the fact that Æthelred had not visited the queen's bed for many weeks.

The tiny flicker of fear that always burned within her flared brighter as she considered the problem of the Lady of Northampton.

If the king's attentions to Elgiva continued to keep him from Emma's bed, she would never conceive a child. That would matter little to Æthelred. He had sons enough; duty did not compel him to seek his wife's embrace. Emma was the one who needed a son to guarantee her status within the court and to protect her should the king die.

And kings did die. Rulers sickened and died for no obvious reason. It had happened to her own father. It had happened to Æthelred's father, as well, when he was younger than Æthelred was now.

Over the past weeks, stripped of her Norman protectors, Emma had come to realize how precarious her position really was. She had not heeded her mother's advice. *Use your youth and your beauty to garner the king's favor,* Gunnora had told her. Yet she had not merely lost the battle for the king's favor, she had vacated the field before the battle began. The king had pushed her away, and she had gone willingly. Now it may already be too late. If she were branded as barren not even her status as queen would protect her. She would be locked away in some abbey, a bitter and disgraced bride trusting to her brother for her support.

The king no longer sought her bed. When she had first wed him she had at least been an unknown commodity, a mystery for him to unravel. Now he had become accustomed to her, and he had found her wanting where Elgiva was not.

She must find a way to entice Æthelred to her bed, no matter how distasteful the prospect. Yet she had not the least idea how to go about it.

The next day it was Father Martin who entered the queen's apartment with news. Emma and her women were seated around a frame that held a length of linen upon which a motif of flowers and vines had been drawn in lampblack. Gradually their busy fingers were transforming the black into vivid, silken colors.

It was well past midday, and the light was fading when Emma saw the priest hesitating in the doorway. She smiled up at him, but her greeting died in her throat when she saw the agitated look on his face.

"What is it?" she asked.

"News is coming in from all across the land of a great killing," he said, his voice taut with shock and his face stricken. "A massacre of Danes, at the king's command."

"A massacre?" Every tongue in the chamber had stilled, and Emma's words seemed to echo in the silence.

"Men, women, and children put to the sword," the priest said. "Merchants dragged from their businesses, farmers and wives taken from their homes, and all of them butchered. A monk from Oxford has brought a wretched tale of folk who sought sanctuary within a church only to have the doors chained shut and the church burned over their heads by a crowd mad with bloodlust. There were over fifty folk killed in Oxford alone, may God grant them rest."

Beside Emma, Elgiva spoke up even as she continued to pierce the linen with her needle.

"They were the devil's spawn," she said placidly, "and the enemies of the king. They would have murdered us in our beds if given the chance. The king was wise to strike those foes that live amongst us, before they can cause us harm."

Emma had dropped her needle and clasped her hands as the images of burning mothers and children filled her mind, and now she turned outraged eyes on Elgiva.

"What is it," she asked coldly, "that makes them our foes? Rumor? Envy? Strange customs? A different language? What is it that they have done to deserve such a horrible death?"

"They attacked the king on his feast day," Elgiva said. "The Dane who was executed yesterday tried to murder the king. It is his confederates who have been put to the sword, to prevent them from bringing an army against us."

Emma heard again the mad howl that had promised death and destruction. But it had come from the mouth of a single man with a broken, twisted mind, one more to be pitied than feared.

"There was never any proof of an army," she said.

"The king has no need of proof. You have not lived among us long enough, my lady, to understand the danger that the Danes are to us." And now her eyes met Emma's boldly. "We must be wary of them, for they are strangers among us."

Just as you are a stranger among us. The words remained unspoken, but Emma felt their force and their threat just the same.

She sat up late that night, disturbed by the day's news and by the lack of Christian compassion that she had witnessed within her own household. She had sent word to the king that she was ill and had taken her supper in her chamber, for she did not think that she could bear to listen to the kind of discourse that was likely to go on at Æthelred's table. By day's end the murder of the Danes, even of innocent women and children, was being hailed as a great victory. Any who thought otherwise kept their thoughts to themselves.

She was seated with only Wymarc to attend her when the king strode into the chamber. He had apparently come straight from the feast hall, for he was garbed in a short tunic of rich scarlet wool, belted in gold, and with gold rings on his arms and thick, gold chains about his neck.

"Leave us," he said to Wymarc, who, with a long backward glance at Emma, left the room.

When they were alone, Æthelred helped himself to a cup of wine. Emma, watching his unsteady hand as he poured, thought that he must have had a great deal to drink already.

"You are up late, my lady," he said.

"I am unwell and cannot sleep."

"Since you are wakeful," he said, "then it is well that I have come to keep you company, is it not?"

She gazed at him and remained stubbornly silent. She should welcome him to her bed, for that was the duty she owed to her husband, lord, and king. She owed it to herself, for she had a desperate need to bear a child. Yet she could not do it. She could not rid her mind of the images of burning children, and it was all she could do to keep her anger and loathing from showing in her face.

.   .   .

Æthelred studied his lady wife in the candle glow. Seated in her cushioned chair she looked every inch the queen. Even garbed in just her
nightdress she carried herself with a regal air in spite of her youth. The
soft, thick shawl of fine-spun black wool that she had flung about her
shoulders set off the whiteness of her skin. Her hair, loosened from its
modest daytime braid, hung about her in soft waves that fell like a
milky stream into her lap.

In the six months since their nuptials he had formed no particular
fondness for her, but he felt an enormous pride in owning something
so exquisitely beautiful.

Emma, though, did not fully appreciate her own good fortune at
having been chosen as his queen. There was something lacking in her
expression whenever she looked at him. Even now she regarded him
with distaste, as if the daughter of an upstart duke considered herself
better than an English king. He had thought to bend her allegiance to
him by sending her people away, but still she kept herself apart. When
she looked at him her glance was cold, with no glint of gratitude or
approval. Christ, it galled him.

He tossed back a mouthful of wine and sat down on her vast, curtained bed.

"It was unwise of you to absent yourself from the hall tonight, lady,"
he said, "for it was your duty as queen to be there. Surely you are aware
that the Danish tide that would have engulfed us has been checked.
God has made me the instrument of His Divine Will, and I have saved
all of us, even you, from a terrible danger. Your voice should have been
raised with all the others in prayers of thanksgiving. Yet you seem un-
moved."

"Indeed, my lord, you wrong me," she said.

He raised an eyebrow at her, awaiting her excuse.

"How could one not be moved," she went on, "by the slaughter of
innocents?"

Good Christ. The girl was either mad or a fool to speak so to him.

"Innocents? Is that how you name them? A barbarous people with no regard for life or property? Folk who burn, pillage, murder, and rape, and who would teach their children to do the same? You would fear them if you had seen the destruction that they have wrought upon our towns and villages."

Her eyes flashed at him now, and her mouth twisted in scorn.

"And with this act, have you not unleashed death and destruction upon your people? The church of St. Frideswide in Oxford should have been a place of sanctuary, yet it became a funeral pyre for women and children upon your order. If you fear the Danes so much, then you must fear me as well. My mother is a Dane, a barbarian as you say. Do you not tremble that I might slay all your children in their beds? I have heard it said that English princes have some cause to fear their stepmothers."

As soon as the words left her mouth Emma knew that she had gone too far. The king's anger toward her had been smoldering from the moment he entered the room, and now she had fanned the flames into fury. She knew, instinctively, that she should run, but she had nowhere to go. In an instant he had dashed his cup to the floor and covered the distance between them with a single step. He slapped her hard across the face, and before she could recover from the blow, he had grasped her roughly and pulled her to her feet.

"Do you threaten my children, you Norman bitch?" He shook her, and for the first time in her life she was afraid of what a man might do to her.

"My lord, I do not!" she gasped through rattling teeth. "I meant only to remind you that you have many folk in your realm, and not all of them are English." She tried to calm her voice, to speak with the gravity of a priest or a councilor. "If you hold all the Danes in your kingdom responsible for the actions of one man, my lord, then you do them a grave injustice. My blood, too, is Danish, yet I am loyal to my king. Surely I am not alone in this."

She looked into his eyes, and her stomach twisted with fear as she realized that he was too far gone in drink to listen to reason.

"I know your blood well enough, bitch," he snarled at her. "Best you be wary of mine. If you do not fear the Danes, then I suggest you cultivate some fear of me!" He shook her again, but although Emma writhed in his grasp, she could not get away from him. "I bought and paid for you with English gold, and I have yet to see any decent return for my money, not even the seed of a half Norman brat taking root in your belly. Perhaps I have been at fault, treating you too gently. Mayhap you prefer more barbarous treatment, in keeping with your ancestry."

"No, my . . ." she began, but he cuffed her again.

Dazed by the force of this second blow, she barely struggled as he wrestled her to the bed. When he threw her roughly to the mattress she tried to curl herself into a ball, but he used his knee to trap her legs. One of his hands sprawled against her face, stifling her scream and pushing her head down hard against the bedding. With his other hand he grasped the skirt of her gown, rucking it up to bare her legs and thighs, and she knew then what he would do. She felt his weight on top of her, driving the air from her lungs so that she had to struggle to breathe against the hand that covered her nose and mouth. She arched her back, trying to ease the agonizing pressure on her scalp from the tug of her long hair, trapped beneath the weight of their two bodies.

She pushed against his chest with her hands, clawing at him, desperate for air. But Æthelred had been wielding a sword since he was a child. His arms were strong, and her fists had no effect on him. Panicking, she feared that she must suffocate there underneath his weight, until finally he raised himself above her and she was able to snatch a breath. She used it to scream as he brutally thrust himself inside her over and over.

When he was done he collapsed on top of her once more, but he'd moved his hand from her face, and she opened her mouth on a sob to draw in a lungful of blessed air. He roused himself at that, grasping her head with both hands, holding her down as he covered her mouth with his and thrust his tongue inside her, robbing her of breath once more and making her panic swell again. He ground his mouth against hers, using his teeth to score her lips before lifting his head. When she looked at his face, only inches from hers, she saw her blood on his mouth.

"I should have done that from the first," he said, "marked you as my property. You are not a Dane, lady, nor even a Norman anymore. You have my English seed inside you, and that makes you an English woman and nothing else. Never forget it again."

He stood up then, and she turned onto her side, crawling up farther onto the bed and pulling her knees up to her chest. She did not see him leave.

News of the massacre on the Feast of St. Brice reached Athelstan as he was hunting in Hwicce Wood. He listened to the lurid reports in disbelief, then immediately set out for Oxford with a small company to discover what truth lay behind the grisly tales.

They approached the settlement of Pallig and Gunhild late in the afternoon of a mid-November day, accompanied by a dismal, steady rain. The outer palisade stood deserted, the gate yawned wide, and a rank stench filled the air. In the center of the compound, a gruesome pile of charred human remains, slick and wet from the rain, lay open to the sky. Beyond it, the great wooden hall and its outbuildings stood whole and intact, but devoid of any signs of life.

Athelstan dismounted, skirted the gory remains of the pyre, and went into the hall. The place had been stripped to the walls. All the furniture, the hangings—everything was gone. The hard-packed dirt floor had been dug up in several places in search, he guessed, of any hoard that may have been hidden there.

Setting his men the task of burying the remains in the dooryard, Athelstan made his way into Oxford town itself. He passed the burned-out hulk of St. Frideswide's church but did not stop to inspect it. He had seen enough to confirm the grim rumors. What he wanted to know was if anyone had escaped the king's wrath. He wanted to discover what had happened to Pallig's wife and infant son.

He found the shire reeve in the local tithe barn overseeing the sorting of clothing, furniture, cooking pots and utensils, tools, even armor and weapons. Athelstan could guess where it had all come from—confiscated from the poor wretches who had been slaughtered at the king's command. The administrative arm of his father's kingdom worked as efficiently as one could wish. These items would be cataloged and sold among the locals, with most of the proceeds going to the king. Nothing would be destroyed or wasted. Except lives.

His interview with the reeve was brief. The man assured him that he had fulfilled the king's command, and that no one had escaped the king's justice.

"We struck before dawn with over a hundred men," he said. "They had watchers at the gate, but we got to 'em before they could raise the alarm. Caught 'em sleepin', mostly, although that whoreson Pallig put up the devil of a fight before we gutted him. His woman was no easy mark, either. She could sling an ax like a woodsman, that one. Used it to try to keep us from that cub of hers. Murdered two of my men, for all the good it did her." He grinned and winked, then inclined his head in the direction of St. Frideswide's. "The ones in the church were townsfolk, living among us as if they belonged here. Filthy Danes." He turned and spat. "They thought the priest might save 'em, but he was with us. We had a goodly crowd by then, and Father Osbern himself set the thatch alight. The good Lord gave us a fair sky and, oh, it was a mighty burning!" He gave a nod of satisfaction. "I reckon it was a good day's work, St. Brice's was."

Athelstan cursed as he turned away. Good work, indeed. The men of Oxford had followed the king's orders to the letter. As for the rest of the country, even the king would likely never learn how many hundreds had been murdered and how many had managed to escape the sword, for surely not every Dane had been butchered. And just as surely, Athelstan knew, someone would carry word of the massacre to

Swein Forkbeard and tell him that his sister and her son were among the Danish dead.

There would be a price to pay for the slaughter of St. Brice's Day. Blood would beget blood, and Swein would not let this outrage go unanswered.

By the time Athelstan made it back to Winchester two days later he had heard many more reports of killings that had been carried out in London, Warwick, and Shrewsbury. With each new account his anger increased. Ignoring courtly protocol he strode directly into his father's inner chamber and slammed both hands on the table before the king.

"Why did you do it?" he demanded. "What possessed you to put so many innocents to the sword?"

His father looked up, pursed his lips, and with a flick of his hand dismissed his steward and the clerk who had been scribbling away at a table nearby. Sitting back in his great chair, the king folded his arms in front of him and gazed darkly upon his son.

Athelstan, watching his father, thought that he looked like the very picture of God that was in the psalter given to him by his grandmother. There he sat, the Lord of Judgment, granting redemption or damnation as he saw fit.

"The Dane who threatened me," Æthelred said slowly, "claimed that he was part of an army. You heard him. You spoke with him yourself."

"Yes, I spoke with him! He was mad! He raved! There was no army!"

"There is no army now." Æthelred's voice was calm. "My reeves have seen to that. They put only armed men to the sword."

"You are misinformed," Athelstan said stonily. "They put women and children to the sword. In Oxford they burned them alive in the church where they sought sanctuary."

Æthelred waved a hand. "That was done in error."

Athelstan gaped at him. An error, he called it. Yet there was no sign of regret on the king's countenance, only mild irritation.

"It was done in your name!" Athelstan cried. "The deed is upon your soul."

"Not mine alone. I took counsel from my advisers."

"Then you were ill counseled! Whose advice did you seek? Let me guess. Eadric of Shrewsbury, who makes no secret of his hatred of the Danes who settled near his lands? Æthelmær of Oxford, who will probably double the size of his holdings as a result of this? Abbot Kenulf—"

"I consulted the men who would be the first to die should our enemy attack us from within!" Æthelred cut him off. "The kingdom is safer now that our enemy has been destroyed. I am safer!"

Athelstan stared at his father. How could a king be so blind to the consequences of what he had done?

"You have not destroyed an enemy, my lord," he insisted. "You have created one. This act will come back to haunt you. Hundreds are dead at your behest. Pallig is dead, even though you gave him the gold to build his hall and granted him the land on which it stood. His wife, Gunhild, and their small child are dead. Think you that her brother, Swein Forkbeard, the fiercest of all the Danish warriors since Alfred's time, will not seek vengeance?"

"If so, then he will do it from outside the kingdom, not from within! I could not allow my enemies to dwell within my very borders, making themselves fat off our lands while they wait for a signal to turn upon us and attack. Wiser men than you have given their blessings to this action. They do not question the judgment of their king."

"The Danes living among us had no reason to attack, my lord. Now you have given them one. Mark my words, father, you will regret this unholy act. We will all of us regret it!"

"Your regrets interest me not!" the king spat. "We are finished here. Hubert!"

The king's steward stepped into the chamber, bowed to his lord, and stood next to Athelstan, staring at him pointedly.

Frustrated and angered by his father's resistance to logic, Athelstan slapped his hand on the table, turned, and stalked out of the room.

His father was a fool. He was wealthy, powerful, and blessed by God, yet still he was a fool. He was making decisions that would lead inexorably to disaster. It was like using Greek fire to douse a flame. And Athelstan greatly feared that now that the blaze had truly begun, they would none of them escape it.

Æthelred scowled as Athelstan withdrew from the chamber. His foolish son did not understand. How could he? He had not seen Edward's wraith, had not been burdened with the foreknowledge of his own doom—had not been forced to take measures to prevent it.

But with this act that his son found so repellant he had triumphed over his enemies and over the vengeance that his dead brother sought to exact from beyond the grave. He had preserved his kingdom and his crown.

And surely he had banished forever the hideous specter that so haunted and tormented him.

"My son chides me, Hubert," he said, "for defending the kingdom that he will one day inherit. He would pit his youthful wisdom against my experience and knowledge."

"He is seventeen, my lord. Consider that when you were seventeen you had been wearing a crown for over seven summers. Perhaps your son believes that he is just as capable as you were then."

Æthelred frowned. Athelstan was still a whelp. He did not have the experience needed to understand the minds of men.

"At seventeen I was much older than my years," he said. "My son, though, has not yet mastered the skills of a leader. He commands his few hearth guards, but he has not been tested."

"Yet, my lord, he did you a great service recently, did he not? Intervening when the Dane would have taken your life? Thus, he has shown skill and loyalty. Perhaps such a service should be rewarded with some form of recognition, some visible symbol of your regard for him."

"Grant him the Sword of Offa, you mean? Designate him my heir and give him estates to manage?"

"If my lord Athelstan is taken up with his own responsibilities, he may spend far less time brooding over yours, my king."

Æthelred rested his chin upon his folded hands and considered the suggestion. It had merit. Certainly his son deserved some recompense for his quick action that day in the minster square. To grant him the Sword of Offa would only confirm what was already commonly accepted—that the eldest ætheling would one day inherit the throne. As for the lands, it was perhaps time to give all three of his eldest sons more latitude in managing the estates they already held. It would keep them occupied and give them needed experience.

"At the next *witan*," he said to Hubert, "we will bestow the sword upon my son and grant him other offices as well. Let him test his decision-making skills on his own men, and we shall see how well he does."

Chapter Sixteen

Emma, wrapped in a warm, sable-lined woolen mantle and attended by Wymarc and Margot, walked slowly along one of the gravel paths of the abbey garden at Wherwell. This was her first venture out of doors for many weeks, and after covering only a short distance, Emma had to admit defeat. She was tired. She was always tired now. Her body, even her mind, was sluggish. Every movement, every thought, took enormous effort, as if her body and her brain fought against a buffeting gale. In the hushed darkness of the abbey chapel she had prayed for relief from this weariness of soul and of limb, but her prayers had gone unanswered.

She was grateful for the ministrations of the good sisters, and for the care that Wymarc and Margot had lavished upon her ever since the night they had found her as the king had left her—bloodied, bruised, and violated. They had tended to her physical hurts until she was well enough to leave Winchester, transported to Wherwell in a curtained litter, her ravaged face hidden behind a dark veil. The physical marks were gone now. Only this soul-numbing lethargy remained, so enervating that she could not remember how long it had been since she had come here. She had arrived well before Christmas, so it must be two months, she reckoned, at least. Time seemed to stand still, here within the abbey walls, but she knew that the little peace she had found here could not last. She could not continue to hide from the world like a frightened child, not least because the king had insisted that she make an appearance at the Easter court—for the sake of policy.

And so, for the sake of policy, she must return to Winchester. That disagreeable duty, however, still lay some weeks ahead of her. Ash Wednesday had come and gone, but Easter was yet weeks away. The garden around her, still winter bare, showed no promise of spring. The time of earth's renewal hovered in the future like a distant dream.

She came to a bench beneath a tree whose naked branches splayed like skeletal fingers against a blue sky. Shafts of sunlight sifted through the boughs, and Emma sat down and turned her face up to their gentle warmth. She nodded to her companions to join her, and for a few moments they sat in silence, until Emma, turning to Margot, reluctantly picked up the thread of conversation she had abandoned only a little while before.

"Tell me," Emma said, "how you can be so certain."

"The signs, my lady, are all there," Margot said gently. "One has but to read them."

Emma closed her eyes. She had thought that she might be slowly dying of some wasting disease, some insidious enemy that robbed her of strength and would not let her eat. For a time she had even hoped that it might be so. But in the same way that she knew of the existence of the sun even when it was hidden by heavy clouds, she had known the truth of what ailed her: She carried the king's child within her at last— the fruit of his cruelty and of her humiliation.

Opening her eyes, she looked steadily into Margot's seamed and worried face.

"I do not want this child," she said in a whisper, searching the old woman's eyes for understanding. "I fear that I will hate it, that every time I see it I will remember how it was begotten." There were ways to end it, she knew. Margot would know what to do.

The old woman returned her gaze, and her brown eyes did not waver for an instant.

"I know what you would ask of me, child," she said. "I also know that if you truly believed that I would grant your desire, you would not ask it."

Emma shut her eyes again. She was not certain that Margot was right. Nevertheless, she had her answer. She would have to carry this thing, bring it into the world and find some way to endure its existence. Others could tend it and rear it. She had but to bear it, yet that task would be onerous enough. Love it, she never could.

"Emma," Wymarc's voice, rough as broken glass, slashed across Emma's brooding thoughts. Emma felt her friend clutch at her hand, as if she would rescue her from drowning in a sullen, black sea. "The child is not the father. The child is a miracle and the answer to your prayers. You have grown to love the king's other children. Will you not love your own babe even more? Think of little Mathilda, if you doubt it."

The image of a sunny, blue-eyed imp flashed into Emma's mind. Mathilda, the royal daughter who had been dedicated to Wherwell at the age of two, had been Emma's nearly constant companion from the moment that she arrived at the abbey. Fascinated by the brilliant new-comers who had entered her convent world, the child had attached herself to Emma with the loyalty and trust of an adoring puppy. Emma had done nothing to encourage her, but the girl's devotion had been impossible to resist. Now they were all but inseparable, and Æthelred's tiny daughter had been the only ray of light in the darkness that was Emma's life.

And yet, she thought, folding her arms tightly beneath her cloak and rocking back and forth in her despair, she did not trust herself to love the child growing within her. The babe had been purchased at far too great a cost. She despised the brutal act that had planted the seed in her womb, despised the man who had perpetrated it, despised her-self for submitting to it. How could she not despise the child who would result from it?

She placed her fingers against her closed eyelids, remembering the days of her girlhood in Normandy, wishing that she could return to that simpler time. Her mother's image rose in her mind, but she banished it. It was Gunnora's fault that she was here now, saddled with grief, fear, and an unwanted child. She would forever hate her mother for sentencing her to this wretched fate.

Yet for her own sake, as well as for the sake of those who depended upon her, she had to wrest herself from the black thoughts that engulfed her. The time for weeping was over. She could not change the past, and she could not continue to brood over her pain like a green girl. She must think like a queen now, for if she did not decide what to do and how to act, others would decide for her.

Emma dropped her hands to her lap and took a breath.

"The king must be told of the child," she said slowly, planning her next move as if a battle lay before her, "but not yet. This will remain a secret until I can tell him myself."

Somehow she must find the strength to face him—not as a supplicant but as a queen whose fertility had been proven. She would demand the status to which she was entitled. She would insist upon complete control over her properties and her household. She would claim the freedom to come and go as she pleased.

She would be a queen, and no longer a captive.

Before the week was out Emma had sent a message to Ealdorman Ælfric, asking him to wait upon her. When he arrived he answered all her questions regarding events at court, and he told her of the present concerns of the nobles and the common folk who were the lifeblood of the kingdom.

She learned that the king had settled in Bath for the Lenten season and had marked Athelstan as his heir by presenting him with the Sword of Offa. She learned that Elgiva remained the king's favored companion in spite of the guarded disapproval of the prelates who traveled with the court.

"They fear the Lord's wrath at this sin," Ælfric said. "There are many, my lady, who would greet your return to court with rejoicing."

Emma considered his words carefully, weighing the will of the bishops and abbots against the desires of a willful king. When Ælfric left he carried with him a message to Æthelred, bidding him to attend her at Wherwell on his return journey to Winchester. In the weeks that followed Emma planned and prayed, gathered her strength, and sought to accept the promise of life that was growing within her but that seemed like a dark burden too heavy to bear.

Chapter Seventeen

Holy Week, March 1003

Wherwell Abbey, Hampshire

Elgiva rode on a plodding horse through a steady, drenching rain along a muddy track leading, she supposed, to Wherwell Abbey. She was miserable. It had started to rain at noontide, and now, three hours later, the waxed wool of her fur-lined cloak was sodden. Water dripped from the ends of her soaked hair, from her nose, from her elbows and fingertips. Her wet skirts clung to her legs, and she was bitterly cold. She longed to be tucked up, warm and dry, in a thick feather bed next to a blazing fire, but she had little hope that she would find such respite at the end of today's journey. She had been to Wherwell once before, and unless things had changed greatly, she would likely be offered nothing more comfortable than a straw pallet in the nun's guest dormitory.

At least they would not put her in a cell, she thought with a shudder. She had been afraid of small, dark spaces from the time she was a child—when her brother Wulf had lured her into her mother's clothes coffer, fastened the lid, and then forgotten about her. It had been hours before she was missed and rescued, and for days after she had been wretched and ill. The very thought of spending even a single hour in a nun's dark, tiny cell made her stomach heave.

She glanced at Wulf, riding at her side. Where, she wondered, would he sleep tonight? He would probably find himself a pretty girl with a welcoming bed somewhere in the village. The king, riding in front of her with the bishop of Winchester, would sleep in the chamber set aside for royal visitors. Sadly for her, she would not share it, for she was one of the pleasures that the king had forsworn during this last week of Lent.

Elgiva hated the Lenten season. The endless prayers of repentance bored her, and the Lenten rituals of bodily mortification drove her to near madness. She could understand why the priests would encourage it among the common folk. By the time Lent came around most of their winter food stores had been depleted. Urging them to fast for the sake of their souls was merely putting a good face on what they were forced to do in any case. But the king was wealthy enough to set a decent table even in the lean months, so why must his court live on a diet of boiled greens and fish?

Their rations on this journey from Bath to Wherwell seemed to Elgiva to be especially meager. She was hungry all the time, and the fasting did no more for her humor than did the wretched rain. Thank God that Lent was nearly done.

The past five weeks, however, unpleasant as they had been, were not an utter waste of time. She had spent many hours at the king's side, distracting him from the worrisome details of governance by telling him stories that she invented out of the thinnest air. She embellished tales that she had heard at her grandmother's knee, and she made up stories about kings and battles set in strange lands peopled with terrible monsters.

Her favorite story was that of the king whose queen was barren. In it the childless queen begged her husband to allow her to enter a convent so that she could offer prayers for the safety of his kingdom, which was under attack by invaders from the far north. And so, reluctantly, the king agreed. He sent the queen to a convent and took another wife, who fought at his side to save his people.

She had spun this story one evening in Bath as the king sat in the hall with a score of his thegns. When the tale was finished she turned to Æthelred and arched her brows at him.

"Could a king set aside a barren queen in such a way?" she asked, feigning ignorance, for she knew the answer.

Æthelred's face turned thoughtful.

"A king may follow his own desires where women are concerned," he mused. "The emperor Charles Magnus took five queens to wife, replacing them one after another when he wearied of them. He did not even need the excuse of barrenness to repudiate them, although several of them, I understand, were childless." He cocked his head at her. "Are you wheedling me for a crown, lady? Has your father set you on my lap to suborn me to his will?"

His face had darkened, and she hastened to reassure him.

"I wheedle you for nothing but your affection, my lord," she said archly. Then, glancing up at him, she sighed and said, "But I would not have to share your affection with anyone, if your queen should choose to enter a convent and relinquish her crown."

The king's expression became thoughtful again, and she smiled to herself. She had sown the seed. With patience, luck, and some encouragement, she would make sure that it flourished.

Clothed in dry garments but still chilled from the day's ride, Æthelred warmed his hands at the brazier in the abbey's finest guest chamber. He was in no great hurry to see his queen. Let her wait upon his pleasure. He had bowed to her demand that he break his journey here in order to meet with her—a summons gilded by Ælfric in eloquent words, but a summons nevertheless.

He shouted for hot wine. It would do no harm to fortify himself before he faced Emma. The last time he had seen his queen she had dared to upbraid him for his actions against the Danes, imagining that she could school him in the duties of a king. He had thought that he had disabused her of the notion that she could advise him about anything, but apparently he was mistaken. She clearly had some matter of great moment that she wished to discuss with him. Certainly she had not summoned him for the pleasure of his company—he had no illusions about that.

Quaffing the wine, he considered the girl who was his wife. Was it possible that she had come to the same realization that he had reached—that she would be far better off living in a convent than at his side? The nuns might have had some influence upon her during her stay here. Certainly they would welcome her with open arms—and greedy hands—should she retire here. She might even become abbess someday, who could tell?

He tried to imagine Emma as an abbess, and he thought that she might do very well at it. Indeed, he might be willing to settle enough gold on her that she could found her own abbey and adorn it however she pleased. And if Emma were to agree to retire to a convent, he could take a more fitting consort. The bishops could have no argument against it, for surely Emma was barren. He had done his duty by her and she had not conceived. He could put her aside with the church's blessing.

As he gazed at the coals in the brazier, they seemed to glow with a darkly malevolent light, and his thoughts, too, darkened. He must consider more than just Emma. Her brother Richard would have some say in his sister's fate. Richard might object to her retirement, might even want her returned to him to see if he could peddle her elsewhere. He would want her dowry back as well—an unpleasant consequence. And there was the additional problem of the Danes and their easy access to Normandy's harbors. Richard would have to be convinced, somehow, to keep those ports closed to the Vikings.

Æthelred frowned. There had been no coastal raids since Emma's arrival, so Richard appeared to be keeping his end of the bargain. Still, if Emma did not produce a child, Richard's goodwill would likely vanish.

He shook his head. This was a pointless exercise. First he must hear what Emma had to say. Then he could decide what to do about her.

The queen's chamber at the abbey had been designed by Æthelred's mother to meet her requirements, and her son was no stranger to its comforts. The embroidered hangings that lined the walls, the thick draperies around the massive bed, even the brass-bound garment chest at the bed's foot were all familiar. As soon as he entered, though, Æthelred felt an old anxiety begin to gnaw at him, for this was a world of female power—as foreign to him as if it were another country. His glance swept over the servant who sat in a corner with distaff and spindle, past the abbess seated to one side of the low brazier, and at last settled upon Emma.

She was sitting in a cushioned chair, garbed in a saffron gown, its bodice embroidered voluptuously in all the colors of the rainbow. Upon her head she wore a creamy veil fastened with a circlet that flashed golden in the candlelight. The veil framed a face even more lovely than he remembered.

She did not look like any nun that he had ever seen.

To his surprise she held in her lap a golden-haired girl dressed in the plain brown robe of the novice. The child gazed up at him with solemn blue eyes, and it dawned on him that this must be his own daughter, Mathilda. She was the right age, and she had the flaxen hair that marked all his brood but Edmund.

Upon seeing him the women rose, and he acknowledged the abbess first, accepting the ritual cup that she offered him. He was relieved when, after murmuring a brief welcome and muttering something about his daughter and his queen, she excused herself and slipped away. One less female to deal with, he told himself, as he eyed his wife and the child who clung to her.

"Sit," he said to Emma, going over to the chair that the abbess had vacated.

He glanced irritably at the child, who had curled up in Emma's lap like a contented kitten. He had forgotten about this girl, although he had brought her here himself after her mother died. He had had little to do with any of his children until they reached the age of ten, and nothing whatever to do with his daughters. This one was his, certainly, with her limpid blue eyes and bright hair, but he had no idea what he was meant to say to her or do about her. Faced with the two of them now, the child gazing at him with wide eyes, he felt as if he were up against some female mystery that he did not comprehend. His irritation grew.

"Send the girl away," he growled.

The servant scurried from her corner, plucked the now whimpering child from Emma's lap, and left the room.

"Pardon me," his wife said coldly. "I had forgotten that your children hold no interest for you. My own father took a great deal of pleasure in his children. Even his young daughters."

"Did you summon me here to counsel me in my duties as a father? It is somewhat late for that. I'm not likely to change my ways, particularly when it comes to a child, such as that one, who belongs to God now rather than to me."

"I have not summoned you to counsel you, my lord," she said. "Indeed, you have made it clear that you have no wish to listen to my views upon anything."

He had not expected penitence from Emma, and so was not surprised that he got none. Her eyes blazed at him, and she held her chin high and proud. She mystified him. She was but a powerless instrument, first in her brother's hands and now in his, yet she did not seem to understand how weak she truly was.

Unable to resist goading her, he said, "Advise me about your brother's dealings with Swein Forkbeard, and I promise you, lady, I will hang on your every word."

He was perfectly aware that her brother had confided nothing to her. What missives she had received from Normandy had passed through his own hands first.

Her face bloomed red, and he knew that his barb had struck home. Her chin, though, remained high, and her face determined.

"I must disappoint you," she said, "for I cannot speak to my brother's intentions. Yet I hope that the news I have to impart will be of some interest."

"Then I am eager to hear it," he said, pouring a cup of wine from the flagon on the table next to her chair and holding it out to her. She shook her head, and he looked down at her in some surprise. "Ah, you are abstaining from wine. Is that because of your Lenten fast or something more significant? I have been speculating that you may have taken a liking to convent life, and that you summoned me here to announce that you have chosen to immerse yourself in a world of prayer and contemplation. Dare I hope that this is so?"

Clearly it was not. Her face went white now, and she rose slowly to her feet to stand before him, her hands fisted at her sides.

"I must disappoint you again, my lord," she said, "for I have asked you here to tell you that I am with child."

It was as if a veil had suddenly fallen from his eyes. He could see it now: the gravid thickening of her waist and the fullness of her breasts. This was the source, then, of the confidence that radiated from her like light, for she understood only too well what new power it could give her.

He scowled his surprise and disappointment, and he saw her mouth twist into a bitter smile.

"This is customarily a happy occasion," she said, "but I see that you are not pleased. Did you think to set me aside so that you could wed your leman?"

He raised an eyebrow at that. He had been out of her company for some time and had forgotten just how clever the minx was—likely as clever as her damned brother. He would do well to bear it in mind.

Then a second revelation struck him, and he knew how much he had been deceiving himself. He could never be rid of Emma. Even if the child she carried died stillborn, even if the church should agree to his setting her aside, Richard would never stand for it. He would use such an act as an excuse to ally with the Danish king. They would carve England to pieces between them, something that his own weaker levies and fewer numbers would not be able to prevent. The great king-dom that he had inherited would disappear, devoured by a Norman-Danish tide, and his dead brother would have his revenge.

His own sense of helplessness infuriated him, and he eased it in the only way open to him.

"This seems a miraculous conception," he snarled. "Is it mine?"

When she flew at him he was forced to drop the wine cup in order to grab her wrists and prevent her from scratching his face. The glass vessel hit the stone floor and shattered.

"Of course it is yours," she hissed at him. "You planted this child inside me the night you used me like a heathen thrall. That deed has stolen from me any joy I might have had in this babe, and for that I will forever despise you!"

She pulled away, glaring at him with such a terrible fury that he almost pitied her. But unlike the wine cup, Emma did not shatter. There was a strength in her that even he had to admire, but Christ, she wearied him. They were wed—bound by a contract that neither one of them could break in this life. It made him feel older than his years to have to bear the burden of responsibility for the well-being of this girl queen, in addition to all his other burdens.

"You came to England as a peaceweaver, lady," he said wearily, "to bind the interests of our two lands. And when you took your wifely vows you agreed to be ruled by me in all things, for I am not only your lord, I am also your king. If you would but remember that, you would find the burden of this marriage easier to bear."

She made a noise like a strangled laugh.

"Think you so?" she asked. "I expect that it would make *your* marriage burden lighter, my lord, but it would hardly ease mine. Only death will do that." She placed a hand across her middle and lifted her chin. "But I am of good cheer. Childbirth often releases a woman from the travails of this life, does it not?"

Indeed it did. It was how his first marriage had ended, and a similar resolution to this one would not be unwelcome.

"If that is what you long for, lady, perhaps God will gather you to His bosom," he sneered. "In the meantime, we will leave for Winchester at daybreak. See that you and your attendants are ready."

When Æthelred was gone, Emma sank to the floor, resting her head on the seat of the chair beside her and allowing the tears of rage and disappointment to come, now that she was alone. She recalled her mother's warning—that she would face many trials in her role as queen. She had accepted that truth, yet she had not truly comprehended what would be demanded of her. She had not known then that she could ever feel this wretched. Yet she must endure it, for the sake of this child she bore if not for herself.

She lifted her head, wiping her face with the heels of her hands and gulping in air to force back her tears.

She would not just endure it, though. She would not pray for humble acceptance of her lot, nor curl herself into a ball and die, as the king must surely wish. Tomorrow she would return to Winchester, and there she would take her rightful place beside Æthelred. She would no longer relinquish that role to another.

It would not be easy. Æthelred's final words implied that he was determined to maintain firm control over her. She must proceed slowly, one tiny step at a time.

She would begin with her own household—and with the Lady Elgiva. She could understand why Æthelred, or any man for that matter, would be drawn to the woman. She had the kind of allure that tugged at a man's loins if not at his heart. She had a pouting, rosebud mouth, milky skin, and breasts that strained at the bodice of her gown—bodices purposely cut small to make her breasts more pronounced. It was a seamstress's trick, and that was what Elgiva was all about—trickery and illusion and deceit. There was nothing honest about her, and Emma wondered if that, too, added to her charm.

What, she wondered, did Elgiva get from the king, other than his attention? He was free with his gifts, surely, but was that all that Elgiva wanted? Emma did not envy her any golden treasures, for she herself had no desire for presents from the king. What she wanted from him was recognition of her true status as queen, something much more valuable to her than gold or silver.

She had no particular wish to keep Elgiva from the king's bed either, now that she was with child. She was determined, however, to keep the woman from the king's side, for that was the place that she intended always to fill, in public if not in private. She would have to make certain that Elgiva knew her place—and kept to it.

· · ·

Elgiva slept fitfully on her cold, uncomfortable convent pallet, waking in a foul mood to the steady patter of rain on the thatch above her head. Her rest had been interrupted ever and again by the snufflings and snortings of the other women housed around her, and by the bells that called the sisters to prayer in the dark watches of the night. Groggy and heavy-headed, she shivered as Groa dressed her hair by the light of a sputtering candle in the predawn dark.

"By the rood," Elgiva moaned, "we shall have another day of riding in the wet and the mud and the cold. Why did the king not stay in Bath for Easter?"

"You could linger here at the abbey, my lady," Groa suggested smoothly, "until the weather turns. The rain cannot last forever."

Elgiva shivered again and turned to scowl at the old woman.

"Because the queen goes to Winchester today," Elgiva snapped, "I cannot very well beg leave to remain here, even if I could abide convent life for another day—which I cannot, as you well know."

She despised the strict regimen that governed life within a convent, hated being told what to do and when to do it—all of which Groa knew perfectly well. Besides, she did not dare stray far from the king's side. There were any number of pretty women at court to catch his eye and take her place if she were not there to keep them at bay.

Within the hour, after a silent convent breakfast of bread and small ale, the royal company made final preparations for the day's journey to Winchester. Elgiva had wrapped herself as well as she could in the cloak that was still damp from yesterday's ride. As she stood amidst the other women in the abbey's narrow entryway, one of the sisters drew her aside.

"The queen," she said, "bids you to attend her in the royal wain."

She was given no time to reply, and a few moments later she was seated alone in Emma's cumbersome wagon, awaiting the arrival of the queen and the other women who would attend her. She saw with relief that despite the wet weather the curtains had been tied back to allow light and air—as well as spatterings of rain—into the compartment. She would not mind the damp so long as she did not feel boxed in.

She wondered if she had the king to thank for this mark of esteem. Grateful as she was for the luxury of cushions and shelter, she would have preferred riding at the king's side in the rain to spending long hours conversing with her lover's wife. Thankfully there would be others present, and she would be spared any private conversation with Emma that might prove awkward. Besides, unless Æthelred had succumbed to Lenten remorse and confessed all to his wife, Emma could not be certain either of Elgiva's relationship with him or her motives in pursuing it.

Nevertheless, she felt nervous when a figure cloaked in Emma's familiar, fur-lined blue mantle, its hood shrouding her face, took the seat opposite her. She felt even more apprehensive when the wain creaked into movement with a shudder, and she found herself all alone with Æthelred's queen. She let out a long, slow breath. This was not the king's doing, then. Emma clearly had some purpose in hand, and now she could only sit, stiff and trembling with cold, as she waited to discover what it was.

Emma, however, said nothing, not even a greeting. The silence between them lengthened unpleasantly, and Elgiva's mind filled with misgiving. What would she do if she were in Emma's place at this moment? How would she rid herself of a rival, if she had all the resources and powers of a queen?

There were many ways to make a person disappear. It would have to be done carefully, though, and secretly. No queen would dirty her own hands with the death of an enemy, although . . .

She remembered the stories about the dowager queen and the men whom she had paid to dispose of her stepson, Æthelred's own half brother, King Edward. Elgiva trained her eyes on the figure sitting opposite her in the shadows. Was that, indeed, the queen sitting so quiet and still, with her face and body all hooded? Or was it someone else? A henchman, perhaps, draped within the concealing cloak, with strong hands to stifle her screams and strong arms to pin her against the cushions—and do what?

Winchester, Hampshire

Athelstan entered the palace grounds at the head of his small troop with the sense of satisfaction that comes at the completion of a job well done. The beacons between Winchester and the sea had been inspected and readied for the coming summer. Should the Danes attack the southern coast of Hampshire at any time in the next six months, word would reach the king at Winchester within an hour of the sighting.

In the chamber that he shared with Ecbert, Athelstan found his brother seated on his bed and his younger brother Edward kneeling on the floor at Ecbert's feet. Edward was bent over a helmet, a scrap of wool in his hand and a bowl of melted beeswax on the floor next to him, polishing the helmet's nose plate with an energy that was likely to wear him out within minutes.

"What have we here?" Athelstan asked, throwing off his wet cloak and tousling Edward's hair. "Are you finally putting this troublesome brat to good use, Ecbert?"

"I am not a troublesome brat!" Edward protested, pausing in his task and turning an affronted face to Athelstan. "Since you have been gone I have been made cupbearer to the king. He says I am to have my own armor soon, and I must learn to care for it. Ecbert is letting me practice on his."

Athelstan raised his eyebrows at this and exchanged a grin with Ecbert. The king's hearth troops were expected to polish their own armor, a task that was tedious as well as tiring. It was something that Ecbert complained about regularly.

"Well, that's very generous of Ecbert," Athelstan said. "You can practice on my armor as well, if you like." He pulled off his helmet and byrnie, laying them across the chest that sat at the foot of his bed.

Apparently Edward did not yet find the task onerous, for he nodded happily and resumed his rubbing.

"What other news is there?" Athelstan asked.

"The biggest news, next to the ascendancy of Edward Ætheling here to the post of cupbearer to the king, arrived by messenger late last night. Queen Emma, it seems, is with child."

Athelstan paused, briefly, in the act of pulling off his muddy boots, but he did not look up.

"Is it so?" he grunted. The news should not surprise him. She was the king's wife. She shared his bed. It was what she had come here to do.

He threw his boot, far too vigorously, onto the floor.

"The royal party is making its way here even now," Ecbert went on, "for the king intends to dispense the Maundy Thursday alms to Winchester's poor tomorrow. Edward," he said, "go and fetch Athelstan something to eat and drink. It is some little while yet until the next meal, and he must be hungry."

"But it is a fast day," Edward protested. "The pantry will be locked."

"You are the king's cupbearer," Ecbert said. "Use your new influence to get your brother a loaf of bread and some ale, at least." He hoisted Edward to his feet and swatted him on the backside, and the boy scuttled out.

Ecbert waited until Edward was out of hearing range, then said, "You realize that this will change everything, do you not? If the queen has a son, she will want her child to inherit the throne, and she will play upon the king until he grants her that. We have no one to speak for us, no one to push our suit before the king."

Athelstan scowled. Ecbert's fears seemed a trifle premature.

"What makes you think that the king will listen to Emma?" he asked. "He has all but ignored her for months."

"If he were ignoring her, Athelstan, she would not be with child. And now that she is breeding, her influence must increase. If Emma insinuates herself and her babe next to the king, what place will there be for us?"

Athelstan pictured Emma lying curled on a bed next to his father,

her body white and naked, her belly rounded with his father's child. Shaking his head to dispel the unwanted image, he slammed the second boot to the floor.

"Let us assume, Ecbert, that you are correct. Let us assume, for the sake of argument, that the child is born and that it is a boy. Let us even imagine that the king agrees to name this child his heir. What then? Our father is not like to die any time soon, and by the time that unhappy event occurs, a great many things could have taken place to change the course of all our lives."

Ecbert leaned forward, rested his elbows on his knees, and peered earnestly at him. "And in the years between now and that uncertain future," he said, "you and I and all our brothers will fight and bleed to preserve this land whole from the Danes. Should we then turn around and hand it over to Emma's son?"

"Jesu! We don't even know that Emma will have a son!" Athelstan glared in helpless exasperation at his brother. "And what is your proposed solution to the problem of Queen Emma and her unborn children?" he demanded. "Do we drown them at birth? Or perhaps we should attempt to drown the queen before she can bear them!"

Ecbert raised empty hands, palms up.

"I have no solution!" he said irritably. "I just—God damn it! He is an old man! He has sons enough and whores enough! Why could he not keep his cock away from this queen?"

Athelstan barked a bitter laugh.

"Would you," he asked, "if you were in his place?" *He* certainly would not.

"Some men could! Edmund could, were he wed to Emma. He hates her."

There was some truth to that. Edmund's dislike of Emma had been immediate and visceral, and it was based, as far as Athelstan knew, on absolutely nothing except that she was Æthelred's queen.

"Edmund," he said, "is a pragmatist. If it were in his interest to wed and bed a woman, he would do it, like her or not. Even Emma. And so would you."

"Mayhap I would not bed her," Ecbert muttered, "if I had the Lady Elgiva to distract me."

"Truly? And you would be willing to settle for one woman when you could have two at the snap of your fingers?"

Ecbert collapsed backward on the bed and groaned. "No, I would not! I take your point, but Sweet Holy Mother, what are we to do?"

"Nothing," Athelstan said. "There is nothing to be done. Put the child out of your head, Ecbert. When it is born, weaned, and has learned how to use a sword, then let us speak of it again."

When Ecbert left, Athelstan prowled the chamber, his mind toying uneasily with his brother's news. He recalled, not for the first time, the doom foretold him by the seeress at the stone circle—that the realm would never be his. She had not been able to tell him, though, who would next wear England's crown. It lay in shadow, she had claimed.

What did that mean? That there would be many rivals for the throne? Or could it be that Æthelred's heir was not yet born? If he were to search her out again a year hence, after the birth of Emma's child, would the old woman's answer be different?

He scowled. He did not truly believe what she had told him, yet the prophecy gnawed at him, as galling as the image of Emma lying white and golden in his father's arms.

The Winchester Road, Hampshire

Elgiva held her breath as the cowled figure seated opposite her drew back the concealing hood, but she relaxed when she saw that it was Emma who gazed at her in the dim light and not some pitiless Norman henchman. As the wain lurched over the muddy, rutted road, Emma fixed stern eyes on Elgiva, and she grew uneasy again. The queen looked ill, her face drawn and cold. She clearly had something unpleasant that she wanted to say, and Elgiva wished herself anywhere but here.

"I have heard reports," Emma said at last, "that you have found great favor with the king."

Elgiva sat up a little straighter. This was no less than she expected, but clearly Emma was fishing. She could not know for certain of Elgiva's trysts with the king unless Æthelred had told her. She felt a tiny shiver of misgiving. Could the king have confessed his sin to his wife?

She cleared her throat and said, "I have been blessed with some skill as a weaver of tales, my lady—for which I thank God. My stories seem to amuse the king."

"Ah, Elgiva." It was almost a sigh. "You are, indeed, a storyteller." Emma folded her arms and her glance became appraising. "And you have beauty as well as talent. It is no wonder that the king values your . . . services. I hope that he rewards you to your satisfaction."

Elgiva looked demurely down at her hands. "The king's pleasure," she said, "is all my reward. I seek no other." She looked up at Emma with what she hoped was a chaste smile.

Emma smiled too, so sweetly that Elgiva almost believed it, but not quite.

"Nevertheless," Emma said, "we all have secret longings. I wonder what it is that you desire in your deepest heart."

Elgiva kept her face guileless and said, "I can think of nothing, my lady."

"Can you not?" Emma's head tilted to one side. "And yet, I am told that once you thought to be Æthelred's queen."

Emma's pale green eyes all but pinned Elgiva to her seat, and Elgiva could not turn her own away. Which one of them, she wondered, would blink first?

"It was my father who put me forward for that honor," she said. "I am innocent of any such ambition, my lady, I assure you."

Emma raised one eloquent eyebrow.

"You need not protest your innocence to me, Elgiva," she said. "My mind is entirely made up on that score."

Elgiva kept her expression perfectly bland. She understood Emma's twisted meaning well enough, but she would die before she would let Emma see it. She waited for whatever would come next.

"I wish to explain something to you today," Emma said, brusquely, "because I want there to be a perfect understanding between us." She leaned forward a little, so that her face was very close to Elgiva's. "I am Æthelred's anointed queen," she said, pronouncing her words so carefully that her Norman accent all but disappeared. "I will never step aside, willingly or unwillingly. The king will never put another in my place. Whatever hopes you may have, lady, you will never be Æthelred's queen."

Elgiva felt a momentary pang of compassion for Emma, because of course the queen was mistaken. If she remained barren nothing could prevent Æthelred from putting her aside.

"My only hope, my lady, is to remain in your service and to please you," she said. "I hope you do not doubt my loyalty to you. I pray daily for your health and for the blessings of children upon your union with the king."

Emma gave a short laugh, cut off as the jolting of the wain flung her back against the cushions.

"Then it will please you to learn that your prayers have been answered, Elgiva, for I have, indeed, been blessed. Even now I am with child."

It was the last thing that she had expected to hear, and for a moment she merely stared, stunned, at Æthelred's queen. How had the Norman bitch managed to conceive? She had been shut up in her convent for months, and even before that the king had had little to do with his wife. She herself had seen to that. Pulling herself together, she bestowed a smile on Emma.

"This is wonderful news, my lady," she said. "Indeed, I am very pleased to hear it. Who would not be?"

Emma's eyebrow flicked up again. "A great many people, I expect," she said, almost to herself. Then she said, "Because of the child, it will be necessary for me to make some changes in my household. I will want to have about me women who are experienced with babies and with childbirth. I am sorry to have to dismiss any of my ladies, but so it must be, in order to make room for others. As you, Elgiva, are yet a maid, I fear that you do not have the knowledge or experience that I will need in the months to come. I have already arranged it that tomorrow you will be returned to your estate in Mercia."

The wain gave another sudden lurch, and Elgiva felt her stomach clench, although it was not from the jarring. She licked her lips to respond to Emma, but her mouth had gone dry. So this was how Emma would rid herself of a rival. The plan had much to commend it, as it was innocent, painless, and bloodless. Emma would not be responsible for whatever might happen to Elgiva when she faced her father's wrath after such a dismissal.

Did the king know about Emma's plan? She suspected that he did not. With Emma pregnant and the Lenten fast behind him, Æthelred would be in need of a woman, and Elgiva had no intention of being sent away from Winchester when her services, as Emma had put it, would surely be required.

"You are all kindness, my lady," she said. "I think, however, that given your obvious lack of confidence in me, it would be best if I do not return with you to the palace. My brother Wulf, who rides today at the king's side, owns a town house in Winchester. He will care for me until my father can come to claim me."

For a moment, Emma looked nonplussed, and Elgiva drew some satisfaction from that. Nay, lady, she thought, you will not have it all your own way.

"As you wish," Emma said.

It was not as Elgiva wished at all, but for now it would have to do.

They rattled along the Winchester Road, the cart jouncing them up or sideways—a reminder that the day's journey would be long and far from smooth.

And pregnancy, Elgiva thought, contemplating Emma's worn expression, was much the same, fraught with dangers for both mother and child. Any number of things could cause a woman to go into labor too soon and lose her child. Any number of things. The queen may have won this little skirmish, but until she gave birth to a healthy, living child, the battle between them was not yet over.

Chapter Eighteen

Easter Sunday, 1003
Winchester, Hampshire

While the king was at Bath teams of workers had descended upon Winchester's great hall, and by Easter day the massive chamber was resplendent— newly thatched and freshly painted. The carved acanthus leaves that twined sinuously around the enormous oaken columns and roof beams had been regilded so that they gleamed golden in the torchlight. Silken streamers looped overhead from pillar to pillar in clouds of gold and white. The tables had been laid for the great Easter feast, covered with linens and garlanded with flowers, and upon the royal dais the high table wore a cloth of shimmering gold.

Emma, seated next to Æthelred on Easter day, toyed with the almond-stuffed honeyed dates on her plate and wished that she had more appetite, for the meal had been lavish. Assorted cheeses, sliced eels, a terrine decorated to resemble the tower of the New Minster, and four different kinds of fish had been followed by enormous bowls of lamb stewed with leeks and pulses. Finally, golden brown peacocks, spit-roasted to perfection, their tail feathers splayed behind them in wide fans, had been ceremoniously borne to the tables.

Now, as the tables were cleared, Emma gazed out at the dazzling array of sumptuously dressed men and women. They gathered in languid groups, milling about in a kind of food-induced torpor, drinking vessels in hand while the wine and the mead continued to flow unabated. Behind Emma the king's cupbearer, young Edward, was taking his new position quite seriously and had not spilled a single drop throughout the meal.

Her own cupbearer was Ealdorman Ælfric's granddaughter, Hilde, a slim young beauty of eleven summers who had joined Emma's household the day before. The girl's mother had died of plague when Hilde was but a babe, and of her father, Ælfric's son, the ealdorman would only say that the man was gone. Emma suspected a great sorrow there, and she did not press him. She found Hilde biddable, willing to please, and eager to learn palace ways. The girl, she thought, would do well in the royal household.

As she drank from the wine cup that Hilde replenished almost too frequently, Emma regretted that the child growing in her womb had robbed her of any pleasure she might take in food or drink. The wine, in particular—a newly arrived gift from her brother Richard—left a bitter aftertaste at the back of her throat. Nevertheless, she drank it—for she had need of the courage it bestowed.

The king's demeanor today was solemn and forbidding—hardly the mood for a celebration of spring renewal. They had had little to say to each other during the course of the meal, and it occurred to her that it was not unlike the Easter feast of the year before, when she had dined with him as a new bride and he had glowered through the entire meal.

There were differences, though, she reminded herself, apart from her pregnancy. Today the bishop of Winchester, Ælfheah, sat on her right, and his thoughtful and intelligent conversation contrasted sharply with the king's morose silence. And, in the crowd below her now, most of the faces were familiar. She could identify the factions that formed in little eddies around the room, and she could even guess at the topic of their conversations: They would be speculating about the child she carried.

She slipped her hand protectively across the small bulge at her belly.

She caught sight of Athelstan just then, standing with a knot of men that included his brothers Edmund and Ecbert. He seemed to feel her gaze, and he looked up and nodded to her. She smiled. As ever, her heart grew lighter at sight of him. She had missed him during her long, weary stay at Wherwell. She had missed their long rides and easy conversations, had missed the way he bent his head toward her when she spoke of Normandy, had missed the passionate intensity in his face when he spoke of his plans for the future of the realm.

She had missed him far too much during the short winter days, and in the long nights her rest had been plagued by the memory of a single kiss. Often she had knelt in the dark chapel and raged at God for binding her to the father and not to the son. Why, she had asked Him, must she bear a child that had been conceived in bitterness and fear instead of a child born from love and trust?

If God had answered her, she had not heard Him.

She bit her lip, drank again from her wine cup, and turned her gaze to the *scop* who had begun to play for the assembly. She did not dare rest her eyes or her thoughts any longer upon the king's eldest son.

Æthelred, sated with rich food and strong drink, regarded the throng in the hall with detachment. It turned to displeasure, though, when he saw his eldest sons in huddled conversation with Ælfhelm's brood and their northern companions. The bond that continued to exist between his sons and the Mercian nobles was likely to become troublesome if he did not find a way to break it. And what business was it that kept Ælfhelm himself in the north when he should be here at the Easter feast?

His glance fell on Elgiva then, and his displeasure grew. She was beguiling two of the Mercian lords who had lobbied in her favor during the debate over his choice of a wife—their support purchased, he suspected, by her father's gold. Æthelred wondered how much influence Ealdorman Ælfhelm, and by extension Elgiva, had now with the northern lords. He was no fool. He recognized Elgiva's thirst for power. It was a family trait, one that all her father's brood shared. He could easily imagine the uses that Ælfhelm might make of his daughter as messenger, as spy—as king's whore. She had pleased him well enough in that role, although of late his disapproving bishops had forced him to set her aside. But if she could whore for him, she could whore for someone else as well, and that might lead to alliances too dangerous to contemplate. What, he wondered, were his sons discussing with Elgiva's kinsmen?

He would have to put a rein on the girl. He could not allow her to stray too far out of his reach—a problem just now because Emma, empowered by the child in her womb, had dismissed her. That must not stand. He could not keep Elgiva's ambitions in check if she were not close at hand.

He would have to persuade Emma to bring the girl back. It was beneath him to meddle in the queen's household affairs, but he had no choice. He needed Emma's cooperation in this. Christ, he was going to have to woo his wife. How much was it going to cost him?

He took a wizened apple from the bowl before him, leaned slightly toward Emma, and said, "I would speak with you of the Lady Elgiva."

Emma stiffened. Well, he had known it would not be easy.

Carefully, he sliced the apple, offering Emma the first piece and waiting patiently until she took it.

"Have you considered," he asked, "why it behooves us to keep Elgiva here in Winchester?"

She bit into the fruit, and a small, thoughtful frown creased her smooth forehead.

"You fear a marriage alliance in the north," she said softly, "that might sunder the allegiance of your northern lords."

So she did recognize the danger. He had forgotten again how cunning she was, and that she, too, had her ways of discovering things.

"Even so," he said quietly. He gave her another slice of apple. "Your brother wed you, I fear, to a king under siege. The Danes press upon us from the east. The chieftains from Ireland strike at our western shores to grab whatever cattle and gold they can. Warlords who answer to Alba's king would snatch our northern borderlands all the way to Jorvik, if they could. My own nobles are restive. Their allegiances to each other are stronger than their oaths to me. Yet because my daughters are too young as yet to bind the more powerful ealdormen closer to me, I must use more," he paused, searching for an acceptable word, "unorthodox measures to control those most likely to conspire against me."

She looked straight at him, her expression solemn and grave.

"Whatever your political difficulties may be, my lord," she said, "it is not seemly for you to have two women at your side. A year ago you made me your wife, yet the Lady of Northampton would claim that which should be mine." She set down the slice of apple and wiped her fingers delicately with the edge of the tablecloth as if she were wiping her hands of Elgiva. "I have borne with that lady's ambitions for far too long and will do so no longer. I will not have a rival in my household."

He pondered this for a moment. Was it possible that Emma, who had never welcomed his attentions as her husband and lord, was jealous of Elgiva? He supposed that it could be so. It was possible to care little for something yet care very much that no one else should lay claim to it. Women were weak creatures, he had observed, and therefore susceptible to the most grievous of sins.

"I do not perceive Elgiva as your rival," he said, hoping to placate her.

"It is how others perceive her that concerns me," she replied. "Your attentions to her while you were at Bath did not go unremarked, I assure you. As your queen, soon to be the mother of your son, God willing, it is I who should be always at your side, not Elgiva."

Æthelred, irritated, tightened his grip on apple and knife, controlling each cut with precision. Would that he could control his troublesome queen so well. When he had agreed to marry Richard's sister he had hoped that he would find her pliable, willing to be ruled by him in all things. He had hoped for a young wife who would accept his favors gratefully and would meekly agree to all his desires.

Emma was none of these things. Yet he could not rid himself of this queen, and there were many at his court who would agree with everything that she had just said were he to give them the opportunity. The clergy, to his disgust, adored her, and the higher she rose in their esteem, the lower he fell. If anything should happen to Emma's child, or if the Danes should attack, or the crops fail, or a plague strike, the blame would be laid upon his shoulders. They would declare it God's punishment for his debauchery.

And so, if he wanted to maintain control over the actions of Elgiva and her kin, he was going to have to appease his queen and offer her a compromise. He did not like it, but he saw no alternative.

He placed his right hand, palm open, upon the table, and gave Emma a meaningful look. She raised a questioning eyebrow but placed her hand in his.

"I vow, my lady," he said, curling his fingers over hers, "that at every possible public function, in the church and in the palace and in the hall, I will keep you close to my side. In return for this you must find a way to keep Elgiva close to yours."

Emma considered the king's words, weighing her options. Even if she agreed to his proposition, she could not know for certain that he would keep his vow. And then there was the matter of Elgiva. She had no wish to keep that lady in her household, but if she refused the king's request there would be consequences. She knew him well enough now to recognize that, and she did not care to consider what form his reprisal might take.

So, knowing that she might be making a bargain with the devil, she nodded in agreement. She did not see that she had any other choice.

As the king raised her hand to plant a kiss upon her ring, Emma glanced out at the company below the dais. Elgiva was there, looking up at her with a cold smile that made the fine hairs on the back of her neck rise.

"Let us drink to our bargain," she heard the king say. He called for their cups to be filled, but after they drank, Emma set her cup down and pushed it away from her.

"I am learning that your child does not care overmuch for wine, my lord," she said.

"Then, lady," he replied, "you must give him good English mead instead."

Many hours later, in the dark watches of the night, Emma lay tangled in the clinging web of dream. She was riding Ange bareback along the beach at Fécamp in high summer. A hot wind blew against her face and the sun beat down hard, its heat radiating in visible waves from the white sand. Beneath her garments her body was drenched with sweat—her thighs clammy and slick with it as they pressed against the horse's hide.

Her legs ached from her efforts to control her mount, for Ange pelted headlong in a wild, unsteady gallop, and suddenly, beneath horse and rider, the sand turned to rock. Each hoofbeat sent pain shooting from Emma's tensed legs up through the core of her body, and the grinding agony of it grew so intense that she thought she must die. She tried to scream for help, but she could not force any sound past the fear that wrapped around her throat like a length of rope pulled tight.

Some tiny corner of her mind recognized the stuff of nightmare, and with an effort of will she opened her eyes. The darkness of her curtained bed replaced the burning brightness of her dream, but the searing waves of pain still clawed at her, and the scream of anguish that had stuck in her throat loosened at last and tore free.

Instinctively she drew herself into a tight ball around her womb. The child was coming too soon. She screamed for Margot, and then felt the covers ripped from her. Strong hands grasped her shoulders, and Margot was there, calling her name—her voice commanding and her face hard.

"You must push, Emma! You cannot save the child. Do you hear me? There is nothing you can do to save the child. It belongs to God already. Now you must save yourself. If you want to live, you must push!"

Afterward she would remember it as part of the nightmare—the pungent smell of blood and the crescendos of pain that crested and broke and crested inside her womb over and over. With Wymarc on the bed behind her for support and Margot reaching between her bloody, naked thighs, she braced herself against them, straining and pushing until she had freed her body of the tiny burden that it had borne for so little a time.

Released from the worst of the pain, but aching and empty, Emma lay desolate as her women tended her. It was only when she saw Wymarc take up the tiny bundle and carry it toward the door that she roused herself.

"Wait," she called. She would not have her babe disposed of like so much night soil. "Send for Father Martin. I want him to bless the child." It could not be baptized, but she could send it to God with a blessing. "In the morning we shall bury it in the minster garden."

It was such a little thing, this child, with no one to protect it but her. And she had failed at the one task that she had been given.

She turned to Margot, her vision blurring with tears that she wiped away with the back of a hand. "What did I do wrong?" she asked. "What did I do to hurt the babe?"

Margot sat at the edge of the bed and took her hand. "You did nothing," she said gently. "Do not blame yourself."

"But I am to blame! I told the king that I would hate this child because it was his." She closed her eyes at the memory. "It was not true. You were right. I would have loved the babe, yet God punished me for speaking such evil." She did not confess all of it. She did not speak of how she had raged at God for binding her to a man for whom she could feel neither respect nor love. In her heart she had wished her husband dead. God, hearing her, had taken the child instead.

Margot turned Emma's face so that she looked into the familiar eyes of the woman who had cared for her for as long as she could remember.

"I do not believe," Margot said, "in a God that punishes unborn children for a mother's hasty words. Nor should you. Think you that the Lord cannot read your heart? Surely He knows that you loved this child. We shall never know why such an innocent was lost to us, nor should we ask to know the workings of God. We can only thank Him for your safe deliverance and pray that your womb quickens with child again soon."

But God had, indeed, read her heart, and He had found wickedness there. She looked over at the tiny bundle still in Wymarc's arms, and her anguish at her loss engulfed her yet again. What would happen now? What if her womb never quickened again? Or what if it did, but she gave birth only to dead children? Her life would have been a complete and utter waste.

She turned her face into the pillow to stifle her tears, and a moment later felt a gentle hand upon her head and heard Margot's soothing voice.

"You must do your grieving now, my lady," Margot whispered, "and then I beg you to let this babe go. You cannot cling to it, not even in your heart. There will be other babes."

"But what if there are not?" She grieved for the babe, but it was not that loss that terrified her. It was her fear of what the future held that weighed upon her like a black cloud. She did not know how to dispel it.

"You will have more children," Margot said, and her voice held a matter-of-fact certainty that Emma clutched at with hope.

She turned to face Margot, searching for reassurance. The age lines in that familiar face seemed deeper than usual. It had been a long, weary night for Margot, too, yet her eyes were clear and bright, and when Emma looked into their brown depths they did not blink. "How can you be sure?" she whispered.

"Because," the old woman said, taking Emma's hand into her own and squeezing it, "there is no reason on this earth why you should not." She heaved a long sigh. "I speak to you as one who lost three babes, one after another, born before their time. Yet I saw six sons grow to manhood. Your mother, too, lost three babes in much the same way. Did you not know?"

Emma shook her head. She had been the youngest. All she knew of childbirth she had witnessed when Judith had presented Richard with a son after a labor so brief that even Margot had been astonished.

Margot was smiling now. "It will take no miracle for you to get with child again, my lady, so long as the king is willing. The miracle would be if you did not."

So long as the king is willing. And what of her willingness to give her body to the king? That duty was demanded of her by the laws of church and state, but she could not bear to think of it. Not now. With this child she had attained a small portion of the prestige that was due to her. Now all was lost.

She closed her eyes, numb with a weariness that she did not wish to master. She felt as though she had fallen into a deep well, and she could not convince herself that she had the strength or the will to climb out of it again.

On Easter Monday the Winchester market bustled with activity. Folk from nearby hamlets had been drawn to the spring faire to celebrate winter's end, and the Ceap was filled with buyers, sellers, and a fair number of gawkers. Merchant stalls lining both sides of the street displayed goods that came from as near as London and as far away as Constantinople.

By midday Elgiva, escorted by several of her brother's hearth guards, had been browsing the market for some time. Although the sun was bright, a chill wind blew from the south and was finding its way beneath her cloak. Elgiva felt cold to her very bones, but it had nothing to do with the breeze.

She had sent Groa to the palace close for news of the queen, and by her reckoning, Groa should have been back long before now. Any rumors about Emma would flash through the palace like wildfire. Groa had only to wander near the bread ovens or the brewing cauldrons to glean anything of interest, so where was she?

Nervously Elgiva fingered a length of gold-threaded silk, ignoring the mercer's eager prattle. What if something had gone amiss? She picked up a length of russet silk and saw that the merchant—a tall, thin man with a beaky nose and the eyes of a hawk—watched her with inordinate interest. Her hands were trembling so badly that the silk rippled, and she set it aside for fear that the merchant would notice her distress. A moment later she saw Groa hurrying toward her from the direction of the palace.

"Put this aside for me," she said to the mercer, pointing to the bolt of silk with as pleasant a smile as she could muster. She had been here too long; it might arouse suspicion if she left without a purchase. "I'll send someone for it later."

Gesturing at her brother's men to walk several steps behind her, she grasped Groa's arm and walked in the direction of Shieldmaker Street, where her brother's town house lay.

"What is the news?" she demanded.

"The child is no more, my lady," Groa murmured.

So it had actually worked. She breathed a long sigh of relief. The child was dead, and she would not be the only one in the kingdom to rejoice at the news.

"What of the queen?" she asked.

Groa shook her head. "I could learn nothing of the queen except that she had lost the babe. The king and his sons rode to the hunt today, so we can presume that she is well enough. It may be days before we learn if she has taken any hurt from the potion."

"And if she does?" Elgiva whispered. "Will there likely be any suspicion about the wine?"

"Nay," Groa murmured. "The queen's new cupbearer was too dazzled by the courtly glitter to take any notice of what I did near the flagon. And even if suspicions were aroused, how could anyone determine who was responsible? There are many at court who have no desire to see this queen bear a child, and that includes the king's own sons. Be assured that no one will question this loss, or even mourn it overmuch."

"Then it has turned out as well as we could have hoped," Elgiva said. "You have done very well."

"I have other news," Groa's voice was smug. "You are to be summoned back into the queen's service, perhaps as soon as today."

Elgiva slowed her step a little.

"This must be the king's doing." She had seen him watching her yesterday when she had been so attentive to Wulfgeat and Leofwine. She had set out to make him jealous, and apparently she had succeeded.

"He still desires you," Groa insisted.

Of course he desired her. She never doubted it. He would have her back at court, and Emma could do nothing about it.

How swiftly the queen's ascendant star had fallen with the loss of the child, and how quickly her own, now, would rise again.

The spring weather held fair and mild, and on the downs of Wessex the sheep and cattle grazed on thick new grass. In the forests along the river bluebells carpeted the ground with blossoms, and it seemed that there was a kind of blessing upon the land. When storm clouds did come they shed their bounty upon the earth during the night, while the days were awash with sunlight. So April slipped away, and when southerly winds brought no sign of dragon ships from the harsh northern lands, folk began to hope that this year Æthelred's realm might be free of fire and pillage.

For Emma, though, the beautiful spring days were almost intolerable. It seemed to her that she alone lived within a dark cloud. Her body had recovered quickly from the trial of miscarriage, but her spirit remained burdened with the pain of her loss. Each day she woke with a sense of despair and foreboding that she could not escape—a lassitude that bound her like a snare. She took little interest in the things that should have demanded her attention. Pleas for direction from Hugh in Exeter went unheeded; missives from her mother and her brothers went unanswered. She kept mostly to her chambers, imprisoned now by her own will rather than Æthelred's. Even the children could not draw her out of her lethargy. She could no longer join in their play or be their confidante and comforter. Instead it was Hilde who, hardly more than a child herself, supervised their care.

Occasionally she would catch a glimpse of Athelstan in the midst of his brothers and retainers, and sometimes his eyes met hers before he looked away. His face, in those brief encounters, was always solemn, and if there was any silent meaning in his grave expression, she could not read it. He never attempted to speak to her or send her any message, and it was as if the companionship that had once existed between them belonged to another life. The child that she had carried for so short a time, she believed, lay like an invisible wall between them, and that only added to her despair.

She rarely saw the king, except at the evening meal in the great hall when she took her place beside him at the high table. True to her promise to him, she placed Elgiva beside her there. If Emma noticed that Elgiva seemed not so content with her favored position as before— for the king's attentions to that lady had cooled considerably—Emma gave no sign. Her heart ached with such longing for the child she had lost that she paid little heed to the tempers and trials of the other members of the king's court. She responded listlessly to the king's inquiries about her health and dreaded his return to her bed, knowing that it must happen soon. As spring lengthened toward summer, Æthelred sent his own leech to examine her, and in spite of Margot's protests, the man bled her, then pronounced her well enough to attend to her lord's needs.

That evening Emma prepared herself for a visit from the king, but to her surprise and relief, he did not come. Instead, he sent word that the court would move to London within the week, and that she must prepare for the journey. It was a command, she knew, yet she did not see how she could obey it. She sent word to Æthelred that she did not yet feel strong enough to make such an arduous journey and begged to be allowed to remain in Winchester. Then she waited in an agony of suspense for his response. She had couched it as a request, but how Æthelred would interpret it would depend upon his mood at the time.

His response, when it came, was scrawled on a wax tablet. She had to study it for some time before she could decipher it.

I will grant this request, but push me no further. For too long have you neglected the duties owed to your king. My patience is nearly at an end.

So she had bought herself a little time—perhaps a month, but no more. She must content herself with that.

Almost as soon as the king and his court departed, the spring weather turned from sunshine to grim, unrelenting rain. Under its spell the mood in the queen's apartments became as somber and listless as Emma herself, and she could not rouse herself to change it. Elgiva, apparently irritated that the king had left her behind, was sullen and ill-tempered, using her tongue to lash anyone who crossed her. Servants whispered of a malignant spirit that had cursed the queen and so caused the death of her unborn child. Alarmed by the rumors, Wymarc insisted that Emma wear every piece of amber jewelry that she owned, for amber was a talisman against evil. Margot, too, sought to break the spell that held the queen, placing rosemary under Emma's pillow to give her pleasant dreams. Yet the shadow of hopelessness that seemed to enfold Emma like a shroud refused to lift.

In the end it was young Edward who drew Emma from her despair. An ague had kept him from accompanying his father to London, and a week or so after the king's departure, the boy's condition worsened. Emma ordered a servant to carry Edward into her own chamber, where she and Margot could tend him, and suddenly her days had a purpose and a meaning. Hour after hour she sat at Edward's bedside, placing cool cloths upon his fevered skin, coaxing spoonfuls of Margot's willow bark infusion past his chapped lips, lulling the restless boy to sleep with stories of Normandy. But Edward's condition did not improve, and Emma's heart ached at his suffering. She sent a messenger to London, advising the king that Edward's illness was grave; then she waited, daily anticipating Æthelred's return.

It was late one May evening that a royal party arrived within the palace grounds. The king, Emma surmised, had come at last. She glanced toward the shadowy corner where Margot, who would keep the long night watch, sat dozing. All of her other attendants were abed, and she saw no reason to summon them. The king's staff would see to his immediate needs, and it may be some time yet before he came to find his son.

Edward lay shirtless beneath the bed linens, and Emma repeatedly bathed his face and upper body with cool water in an effort to banish the fever that held him in restless dreams. His hair had been cut short so they could tend him more easily, and he looked far younger than his eleven summers. He moaned in his sleep, and as Emma took his hot hand in hers, a servant slipped into the room to whisper that Lord Athelstan was asking to see his brother.

She started at this, but in a moment her heart lifted, as if some great weight she had been carrying had suddenly slipped away. She bade the servant escort the ætheling into the chamber, then she tried to ignore the trembling of her limbs as she waited for him in the near darkness. There were a thousand things that she longed to say to Athelstan. Every day the pile of words that remained unspoken between them grew higher and broader. Yet the words she would speak were utterly forbidden, and so she must remain forever mute. Just to have him near, though, would be some consolation.

She rose as he entered the room, and in the dim candlelight she drank in the sight of him—the thatch of bright hair, the startlingly dark eyebrows, the wide mouth, the beard the color of raw honey, the solemn blue eyes.

He paused in front of her, and as their glances met she read there the same gravity—cold and distant—with which he had greeted her ever since her return to court. It chilled her like a winter wind.

He gestured for her to sit and, drawing a stool next to her chair, took his place beside her.

"My father received your message but matters keep him in London, and he sent me to learn how Edward is faring." Awkwardly, he touched Edward's cheek with the back of his hand. "Jesu, he is so hot."

"I am frightened for him," she whispered, studying Edward's face, as she had for days, looking for some sign of improvement. She did not find it. Flushed with fever, his nose thin and pinched with lack of nourishment, he barely resembled the brown-faced boy who had ridden with them along the Itchen the summer before. "My sister suffered from agues all her life, but I cannot remember that she was ever as sick as this. Edward complains of pains in his arms and legs, and of a scalding in his throat. Nothing we do eases him."

She glanced at Athelstan and saw a shadow cross his face. Her words had alerted him to his brother's danger, and it pained her to be the one to deliver such evil tidings. Yet it was better that he know now what may have to be faced all too soon.

"My father," he said, his eyes still on the boy, "has asked the bishop and all the clergy in London to offer prayers for his recovery. Do you hear that, Edward? All of London is praying for you now."

She, too, had prayed for Edward, but her prayers had sprung from a bitter heart, and God had not answered her.

"Perhaps God will listen to them," she said. "He has not listened to me." The rage that had lain coiled within her, suppressed in silence and in bitter tears, sprang suddenly to life. "Why is God so cruel?" she demanded, fisting her hands and beating them impotently against her knees. She longed to weep, but she would not give God the satisfaction. "Why does He punish innocent children for the sins of others?"

Athelstan heard the despair in her voice, and it smote his heart. She was his father's wife, and for that reason he had schooled himself to look upon her with a stern regard that showed neither pity nor compassion. He could not do so now. Her anguished eyes, bruised with weariness, were fixed upon Edward, but he guessed that she must be thinking as well of the babe that she had lost. If God was cruel, then Emma was as much a victim of His cruelty as poor Edward. She had lost her own child, and now she lived in fear of losing a son that she had embraced as her own.

He searched for words that would give her consolation, but what did he know of the mind of God? He was a warrior, not a priest. His duty was to fight, and it was up to the priests to sort things out with the Lord. Yet how was anyone to fight and win against the will of the Almighty? How was one even to recognize God's hand at work in the world when there was so much darkness and misery?

Emma, though, needed consolation, however clumsy it might be.

"We are God's instruments for vengeance or for mercy, are we not?" he asked gently. "So if you would look for the hand of God in Edward's illness," he took hold of her hand, and held it before her, "look to the hands that have given him relief from pain and have tended him with a mother's care."

It did not content her, though. She shook her head, drew her hand from his, and gently ministered again to Edward. His brother's thin face was no longer flushed but eerily pale now in the flickering light.

What if Edward should die? He had never thought much about death, in spite of the hundreds of sermons he had heard detailing man's ultimate fate in the most harrowing terms. Even now he could not reconcile himself to the prospect of a world without Edward, for he was but a boy. It seemed impossible that he should die. Yet children, even the children of kings, did die. His own father was the only one of three brothers to survive to manhood.

Unbidden, the words of the seeress at Warwick sprang into his mind. She had predicted that he would not inherit his father's kingdom. He could not fathom such an outcome—unless he were to die before his father did. Was that what she had been trying to tell him? Was that to be God's will—his destiny as well as Edward's?

He scrubbed his face briskly with his hands, trying to rid his mind of such morbid thoughts. At the same moment, Emma gave a small cry. When he looked he saw her leaning forward, her palms pressed against Edward's breast.

"What is it?" he demanded, tense with foreboding.

"I don't know," she cried. "Something has happened. Margot!"

In an instant the old Norman dame appeared from out of the shadows and shooed them away from the bed. She bent over Edward, setting her ear against his mouth, then touching his neck with her fingers. Athelstan held his breath.

Dear God. Had his mortal thoughts somehow beckoned Death to his brother's side?

When the old nurse called for a servant and turned to Emma, placing her hands on the queen's shoulders, he felt a chill run from his spine to his fingertips. He closed his eyes, and through a fog of despair and grief he heard the old woman rattle something in a burst of Norman

French. Although he could not comprehend her words, he knew that Edward must be dead.

He drew in a heavy breath and opened his eyes to find Emma before him, her face lit with joy and relief. She took his hand.

"The fever has broken, my lord," she said. "God has answered our prayers at last."

He looked past her to where Edward lay profoundly asleep, oblivious to the women who now went about the task of changing his damp, tumbled linens.

"Can it be true?" he asked, hardly daring to believe it. "Could the tide of his illness turn so swiftly?"

"He is far from well yet," Emma murmured, "but Margot says that now he should begin to mend." She smiled, but her eyes were filled with tears. "Perhaps he heard you when you spoke to him, and it was your voice that drew him back to us. He would do anything for you. You are his hero; did you know that?"

He shook his head, wondering what else Emma knew about Edward that he did not. She still gripped his hands, and for his part, he had no wish to let her go. He wanted to pull her close and enfold her in his arms as if he had the right to do so. But he did not have that right, and the awareness of it tortured him so that he loosed her hands and frowned at her.

"Edward's recovery is none of my doing," he said. "It was your care that saved him, and so I will tell my father." He glanced again at the bed. "I will leave for London in the morning. May I visit him again before I go?"

"Of course," she said, "but I cannot promise that he will be awake when you come. Can you not send a messenger to your father? It will do Edward good to have you here for a time, however brief it may be."

"I cannot stay. The king would have me return to London tomorrow." He saw that his curt reply had wounded her, but he could think of no way to dull the sharp edge of duty that must always lie like a sword between them.

"Of course, my lord," she said stiffly. "I will bid you good night then."

He nodded to her and walked quickly from the room. He was sorely tempted to stay, and that would be a grave error indeed.

In the moments after Athelstan left, Emma felt as cold and empty as a bell that has lost its tongue. She longed to follow him, to crawl into his arms and feel their warmth and strength, to feel the comfort of his touch once more. But there was no place for her in Athelstan's arms, for he was not her lord nor ever would be.

A moment later Margot was at her side, urging her to lie down and sleep, but there was something else that she must do first. She wrapped her shawl close around her, called for a light bearer, and made her way behind him through several passages to the tiny private chapel that had been set up by Æthelred's first wife. Emma did not like this place, for it was little more than a barren closet with nothing about it to offer comfort to a weary soul. Nevertheless, tonight she slipped inside and dropped to her knees before the altar. She whispered a prayer of thanksgiving for the gift of Edward's life, and she asked God's forgiveness for her doubts and her sins. She offered Him a promise as well. She would no longer shirk her duties as Æthelred's wife and queen, and she would shut her heart to temptation.

Chapter Nineteen

June 1003
Winchester, Hampshire

The king returned to Winchester at the head of a long train of retainers and under a fierce sun that had frayed his already short temper. A month spent in the bishop's London palace had forced him into celibacy, and to make matters worse his high eccleiastics had spent the time chastising him for ignoring his marital duties to his queen. He would rectify that soon enough, though. He would soon put her on her back, for she had kept him at bay for too long.

It was nearing twilight when he dismounted in the palace yard and tossed his reins to a groom. There would be food awaiting him in the hall, but he had business with the queen first. As he made his way to her apartments a small crowd of petitioners surrounded him, every one of them yammering pleas, none of which would have interested him even if he could have deciphered the gabble. He forced his way through them, although not before some enterprising lout had thrust a bit of parchment into his hand, which he palmed and then forgot.

He strode purposefully into the queen's quarters, ascended the stairs, and flung open the chamber door. Emma and her priest sat at a table covered with letters. A knot of women sat off to one side, fluttering and clucking until they saw him and fell into silent obeisance.

"Get out," he grunted.

Emma had already risen to her feet, and she nodded to the priest, who scrambled to gather up the scrolls.

"Leave those," Æthelred ordered.

The chamber emptied quickly, and he turned to Emma. She stood her ground, facing him with that stiff little chin of hers angled upward and one eyebrow cocked with curiosity.

He had a matter to raise with her that would wipe that smug look from her face, but it could wait. Grasping her wrist he made for the inner chamber, tugging her after him.

"Don't pretend that you do not know why I am here," he growled, slinging her toward the bed that lay hidden behind lush hangings.

He did not bother to ask after her health, for he wanted no excuses. The last time he had favored her with his intimacy she had resisted him. He would have none of that today.

He watched with satisfaction as she shed her gown and shift. Dropping the bit of rolled parchment he'd been handed, he discarded his belt, tunic, breecs, and hose. When he turned again to Emma, he was surprised at how quickly he was aroused by the sight of her lying naked on the sheets, her white thighs obligingly spread to receive him. He wasted no time, spilling his seed into her vigorously and swiftly. Afterward, spent, he lay sprawled on top of her enjoying the scent and the feel of her woman's flesh. Then he raised himself on his forearms to study her face.

The light in the chamber was dim, for only a single oil lamp hanging from a chain near the door threw its glow across the bed. It was enough, though, for now.

Emma shifted beneath him in an effort to push him away.

"May I get up, my lord?" she asked.

"Nay, lady. We are not finished yet, you and I." Her pale braid had come undone during their coupling, and now he toyed with a long lock of her hair, wrapping it about his finger absently as he watched her face. "Tell me what you know of your brother's new alliance with the Danish king."

She gave him a look as guileless as a child's. "I know nothing," she said. "My brother has not confided in me."

He cocked an eyebrow, considering her reply. It might be the truth. His spies had not reported any missives from Normandy that spoke of an alliance with Swein Forkbeard. Still, he did not quite trust her.

"Your brother has been remiss, then," he said, tugging at the blond tress so that she winced, "for he is, indeed, negotiating with Swein."

"Perhaps it is some matter of trade—"

"Even so," he said, and now he pulled harder to make sure that he had her attention. "What do you think they are likely to trade between them? I shall tell you. Poor English folk dragged from their homes to be sold as slaves, shiploads of silver, and booty from English towns."

And there was the little matter of Swein's revenge for the death of his sister on St. Brice's feast day. In London the bishops had railed at him interminably about the likelihood of the Danish king's vengeance, and though he had made light of it, his own fear of Swein's retaliation gnawed at his gut like an incurable, weeping wound.

Emma was squirming beneath him now in a vain effort to ease the pain he was inflicting.

"Stop it," she hissed.

But he had no intention of stopping. With his other hand he twisted another bright strand about his fingers and pulled that as well. She would have clawed him like a she-cat, he guessed, but he'd taken the precaution of pinning her arms at her sides.

"Earthly pain leads to greater glory in heaven, does it not?" he asked. "Be submissive to life's afflictions, lady, and you will find them easier to bear. I've told you that before."

"Tell me what you want," she said through clenched teeth.

He smiled, but he did not ease the pressure. It would take far more than this to break Emma, but he would master her eventually, hopefully before her belly swelled again.

"I would have you remember that you are the queen of the English and no longer a tool of the Norman duke," he replied. "You will write to your brother and remind him of his promises to me. It would be unfortunate if he should commit himself to an alliance that you, more than anyone else, might regret. Do you understand me?"

There were tears in her eyes now, though she did not weep. She was cold, this one. Even in her pain, Emma did not weep.

"I understand," she ground out.

"Good. I shall expect to see the letter tomorrow."

To remind her of her task, he snagged the tender flesh beneath her ear with his teeth. When she flinched, he grinned. His queen did not have Elgiva's taste for sexual adventure.

He rather missed Elgiva, but there were other women at court to satisfy him.

He rolled off of his lady wife and watched, amused, as she slipped from the bed, drew on a robe, and stalked across the chamber and well out of his reach.

"What were those letters I saw you poring over with the priest?" he asked.

"They are from my reeve in Exeter."

"Bring them to me. And light some candles. It is too dark in here." She lit a taper at the lamp, and one by one set all the candles in the room blazing.

"You have not asked about your ailing son," she said.

"What about him?" He reached for the flagon beside the bed and poured himself a cup of wine. "His fever is gone, is it not?" He tossed back the wine and poured more.

"He tires easily. I am concerned for him."

He grunted. The children were *her* concern, not his.

"He goes to Headington next week with the rest of them," he said. "He will be well tended there. Bring me those scrolls."

She fetched them, then began to dress herself while he sat on the edge of the bed, looking over each missive as he drank a second and third cup of wine. There were reports from her reeve, as she had said, as well as a petition from a host of Devonshire landholders urging Emma to visit her properties in the southwest.

Of course they would want her to make a royal progress to her dower lands. After all, it had been the southern nobles who had supported her as his bride in preference to Elgiva. They wished to curry her favor now, get her among them and fete her in the hope of solidifying her royal patronage. He'd had a letter from one of his Devonshire thegns some months ago suggesting just such a journey. He had dismissed it at the time. Now, though, he thought, fondling his cup as he considered the idea, things had changed.

If Duke Richard had allied himself with King Swein, then for the next four months all of England's southern coast would be at risk of attack from ships striking across the Narrow Sea, and England's fleet was too small to patrol that long sweep of coast. So what if he were to use Emma as a shield for the western shires? If he placed her in Devonshire and made certain that her brother knew of it, Richard would doubtless seek to protect Emma and her lands by urging his Danish allies to aim their strikes further east. That would leave him with only half of the coast to defend. It was perfect.

He tossed the scrolls onto the bed and began to dress.

"You will make that progress through your dower lands," he told her. "The southern lords would take it amiss if you refuse them. I will send Ealdorman Ælfric and his men to escort you. And now I think on it, you may wish to stop at some of the shrines along your route and pray that your womb will soon be fruitful again."

He watched her face as she weighed his words, and the consternation he read there amused him. Emma wanted a child. It was not obedience that had driven her to spread her legs for him today but the hope that his seed would take root within her. A son would garner her more lands, more money from his own purse, and even more support from the bishops than she had now. Once Emma had a son she would be a force to be reckoned with, something his damned bishops seemed unable to grasp. Well, they could hardly expect him to bed her if she wasn't here, which would leave him free to seek his pleasure elsewhere. And Emma would have to wait a little longer for that child.

She made no reply to his suggestion but turned away from him, fingers busily braiding her hair. He pulled on his breecs and his tunic, and then noticed the small scroll that lay on the floor. Languidly he reached for it, glancing quickly at its lines of script.

And now art thou cursed from the earth, which hath opened
her mouth to receive thy brother's blood from thy hand.

He stiffened, the menace in the words as palpable as a physical blow. Christ, what fiend had given him this?

He tried to visualize the faces that had surrounded him in the palace yard, but he had taken too little notice of the rabble. He read again the baleful words—the Almighty's curse upon Cain. As his mind quailed from the threat it carried, he felt, to his horror, a menacing cold come upon him.

He guessed what the chill portended, but surely he had to be wrong. He had freed himself of his brother's vengeful shade when he had rid himself of the Danes who had schemed to destroy him. The fetch was gone! It could not come again to hound him. Even God would not be so cruel!

He steeled mind and body against the panic rising within him, but the growing cold clasped him in its unrelenting embrace, its icy tendrils reaching beneath his flesh to clutch at his heart. The scroll slipped from his hands, and his eyes, frozen wide, could only stare into a void that swirled and spun. All light fled the chamber, and in the darkness his brother's glowering visage shivered before him like an unsteady flame, filling his soul with dread.

This time, though, he refused to succumb to the numbing terror. A rage sparked within him, bright as a glowing coal. He wanted to throttle the horror that faced him, to channel all his fear and fury into a lightning bolt of violence that would shatter this fiendish exhalation and send it back to hell. He struggled against the invisible bonds that held him, but he was spellbound, encased in a shroud of ice.

"Why?" he howled, wrenching the word out of the depths of his soul. "Speak, damn you! What do you want of me?"

There was no answer, and with a strangled curse and a supreme effort of will he raised his arm and dashed the wine cup at his brother's face. Edward's shade neither moved nor spoke but merely stared at him with empty eyes while time seemed to stand still.

In those endless moments Æthelred felt a desperate weariness come over him, and a chilling heaviness in his chest, as if a stone lay upon it. He tried again to shut his eyes, but he could only stare into Edward's bloodied face, until at last the shadow slowly receded and the chamber glowed with light and warmth again.

Freed at last from his brother's grasp, he sank to the bed and wept.

Emma stood transfixed, her eyes flicking between her weeping lord and the red stain on the wall where the cup had shattered. How many eternities, she wondered, had passed while she stood here, bewildered and aghast, watching as the king struggled against some invisible threat that drove him past distraction into madness?

She began to breathe again as she realized that whatever had held him in thrall seemed to have set him free now, for even the king's weeping had ceased. Yet she made no move to go to him. The memory of his petty cruelty was too fresh in her mind, and she could not be sure that he would not turn his rage upon her. So she stood, immobile, uncertain what to do.

"I am cold," he whispered.

The words held a plea that she could not ignore, pulling her from her trance. She snatched up her robe and went to him, wrapping the thick fur and wool about his shoulders.

"My lord, I fear you are ill," she said. His face was white and waxen, like a candle melted in the sun.

"Burn it," he whispered.

She frowned. Burn what? She glanced at the parchments tumbled around him on the bed.

"The scroll," he said, gesturing to something on the floor nearby. "Burn it!"

She spotted it then, a scrap the size of her finger. Was this the cause of his madness? Could so small a thing scatter the wits of a king? She picked it up, sorely tempted to unroll and read it first, but Æthelred was watching her with eyes sharp as blue steel. Obediently, she fed the scroll to the lamp's flame.

"What is it?" she asked.

"No business of yours. Just do what you're told, damn you," he said, his words slurred from the wine.

She watched it burn, aware that it might hold the key to the puzzle that was Æthelred of England, and it was with a bitter pang of frustration that she dropped the last bit into the lamp and watched it curl to ash.

She heard him heave a great sigh, and she turned to look at him. Some color had returned to his face, but the weariness had not left it. He looked sick and haggard, with dark crescents beneath his eyes. He was a man who slept but little, she knew, and not for the first time she wondered what dark dreams troubled his rest. Now she watched him slough off her robe and rise to his feet, but slowly, as if he were still burdened with a great weight.

"Tomorrow," he said, his voice leaden, "you will deliver to me the letter for your brother, and you will begin preparations for your journey to Exeter."

He left her then, his gait slow and heavy, while she stood in stunned silence, her ear attuned to the sound of his retreating footsteps.

When she was certain he was gone she went, trembling, to her great chair and sat down, steepling her hands in front of her as she considered what had just occurred. She knew little of men, for she had ever dwelt in a world of women. But she was beginning to know this hard and brutal man who was her husband and her king. And the more she knew him, the more she feared him.

Yet surely her fears were as nothing beside his. Æthelred, it seemed to her, feared everyone. That he mistrusted *her* did not surprise her. She was a foreigner, and in spite of her marriage vows, he could not be certain of her allegiance until she bore him a son, and perhaps not even then. She understood this. But Æthelred mistrusted and feared his counselors, and even his own sons. He perceived Athelstan, in particular, as a dangerous rival and a threat. Had there been some warning about Athelstan in the missive that she had burned? She could not believe it. Athelstan had a pure heart, and God knew, there were any number of enemies who might threaten a king.

Must every ruler keep himself so separate from those around him, even those whom he should be able to trust? Or was there something in Æthelred's very being that set him apart? It seemed to her that there was some fissure in this king's soul from which suspicion rose like a malevolent cloud, working on him like a poison—and it was well-known that when a king waxed ill the entire realm suffered.

Like a cold fog, the stories she had heard about the death of Æthelred's brother crept unbidden into her mind. A king had been murdered, and since that death England had been cursed with ill fortune. If Æthelred bore the blame, guilty or not, for the death of that king—and thus for the troubles that threatened the land—how many enemies he must have! And because she was bound to him body and soul, her fate wrapped within his, they were her enemies too, for all the years of her life.

She covered her face with her hands, and it seemed to her that the king's own fear still blanketed the room, and that its essence settled upon her like a suffocating mist.

The final details for the queen's removal to Exeter were all but completed. On the morning before her departure the ladies of Emma's household sorted feverishly through her wardrobe, debating among themselves which items would be necessary for the journey. Emma, seated nearby at her worktable, was absorbed by a map that Father Martin had found for her, its surface smooth beneath her fingers. Far older than she was, it had been commissioned by King Alfred over a hundred years before to show the royal holdings in Wessex. With her index finger she traced a line from Winchester to Exeter, wondering at the distance that she must cover in the next few weeks. Her finger paused, though, when she spotted the royal manor of Corfe marked near the southern coast. Corfe—where Æthelred's brother, King Edward, had met his death.

She stared at the crimson circle on the map. What had really happened there on the night that Edward was murdered? No one had been punished, no wergild paid for the death of that anointed king. And now, it was whispered, miracles had begun at Edward's new tomb at Shaftesbury: a lame child had walked; a blind woman had been given back her sight. There were stories that the martyred Edward had appeared in dreams to some who had known him, warning that those who were guilty of his murder must make restitution to avert the doom that was about to fall upon England.

Winchester's bishop had preached the day before of the need for all men to confess their sins and offer alms for the expiation of any crime, however small. She had watched the king as he had listened, stone-faced, to the voice that soared from the pulpit. He had never blinked an eye, never moved a muscle to indicate that his heart had been touched. Yet afterward he had bid her break her journey at Shaftesbury to offer prayers at Edward's tomb. He had given her a bag of gold to bestow upon the abbey in the name of the king, and of his dead mother, Queen Ælfthryth.

It made Emma wonder again if the king had had some responsibility for the death of his brother. If the stories could be believed, it was Queen Ælfthryth who had planned Edward's murder so that her own son could take the throne. But Æthelred would have been a child, only ten or eleven summers old. Surely he could not have taken part in that deadly pact.

Yet something, some unnameable terror, tormented the king. She could not forget his anguished cry as he stood in her chamber, transfixed by some foe that she could not see. She dared not ask him about it—not then nor any time since. Every night that he had come to her bed he had been more distracted, more silent and surly even than before. She did his bidding, and then he left her, but the memory of that strange and awful happening hung between them like a glittering dagger, its point aimed at her throat.

She longed to get away from Winchester, from the king and all his secrets, and from all the bitterness that lay between them. Tomorrow could not come soon enough.

When a servant entered to announce that Lord Athelstan wished an audience, joy soared through her. He had not accompanied the king from London, and she had despaired of seeing him before her departure. *Lead me not into temptation*, she prayed, schooling her face into a polite mask as she extended her hand toward him.

"Welcome, my lord," she said.

He bent to kiss the heavy gold ring that marked her as the king's possession, but his smile of greeting did not reach his eyes.

Immediately she was alert to something amiss. She gestured to a chair and glanced around the room. Elgiva, kneeling on the floor nearby as she packed gowns into a coffer, quickly turned away, as if to give the queen privacy. But Emma knew that Elgiva marked every conversation that took place in these rooms, and she suspected that Elgiva reported them to the king. Who else would take such a keen interest in everything that passed in the queen's apartments?

She did not dare breach the etiquette of palace politics by sending her attendants away so that she could speak to Athelstan alone. Much as she longed to do it, it would arouse suspicion that she could ill afford. She dismissed Elgiva from her mind and focused all her attention upon Athelstan.

He had not taken a seat but was fingering the map that lay open on her table. Now he nodded toward it. The smile was gone.

"You cannot go to Exeter," he said bluntly, as if he were giving her an order.

She looked at him, confused.

"Are you relaying a message from the king?" she asked.

"No. I am giving you the advice of a friend. You must give up this scheme, my lady. It is far too dangerous for you to even consider such a journey."

She heard the passion beneath his words, read it in his eyes, but she could not comprehend it.

"I thank you for your concern, my lord," she replied, "but surely there is little danger in such a journey as I intend. The king himself has assured me that—"

"I know what the king says," he snapped. "I have just come from his presence. He is blind to the danger, or indifferent, I know not which. That is why you must take heed! My lady, the Danes will attack this summer. Swein Forkbeard seeks vengeance for the massacre of St. Brice's Day, and every hour that passes makes it more likely that the next tide will carry dragon ships to our shores."

A chill settled on Emma's heart at the mention of St. Brice's Day. News of Æthelred's massacre of the Danes had spread to Europe, drawing protests even from the pope. Her brother Archbishop Robert had written a protest to the king, and in a letter to her had demanded to know why she had not used her influence with Æthelred to stop such a heinous act. Her mother had been more discreet. In a missive hidden in the slit leather cover of a psalter she had written: *What kind of Christian burns innocent women and children?* Emma had been unable to defend the king, had not even tried to defend herself. She should have known about his plans, should have been a voice of reason, should have counseled him. But he wanted none of her counsel, and that was her failure, her own burden of shame to bear.

Like everyone else in England, she had expected the Danish king to wreak some kind of vengeance. They had all waited, as the spring brought fair sailing, for the hammer blow of reckoning. So far, it had not come. And because folk cannot live always in constant expectation of doom, they had put fear of Swein away from them, packed it up the way they would a winter cloak during summer's dog days. The king insisted that with his stroke on St. Brice's Day he had rid England of Swein's supporters, and that the Danish king's next move would take years to plan. Clearly, though, Athelstan believed otherwise.

"How can you know that Swein will come?" she asked. "Is there some augur that you have been given?"

"No, I have no proof!" He slapped the flat of his hand against the table in frustration. "I can feel it, though. It is like a thrumming underneath my skin. I know not how to explain it. I can only tell you that I know it. Swein will come."

She looked up into his face and read the fear and urgency there. A prickling started at the back of her neck. She had been foolish to imagine that England could escape Swein's vengeance. There was good reason why her brother feared to cross the fierce Danish king. Of course Swein would come.

"But even if I grant that you are right," she protested, "it does not mean that Swein will attack Exeter. Surely the Exeter coast is the safest place to be. The town is well protected, and the countryside was attacked but two summers ago. There is little enough left to pillage from those wretched folk."

"It is not just booty that Swein is after, do you not see? He has a score to settle with my father. And no, there is no possible way to know exactly where he will strike, but strike he will. Has your brother Richard sent you any word, anything that might be seen as a warning?"

She gazed at him in surprise.

"No, my lord. He has sent me no word. Only my mother has written to me, to tell me that my sister's wedding to the Count of Blois will take place at midsummer." She frowned, trying to remember all that her mother had written. "Some time after St. John's Day both of my elder brothers will escort the couple back to the Duchy of Blois, which borders Normandy on the south."

His gaze sharpened at this news. "So Duke Richard and the archbishop will be away from the Norman coast in the weeks after midsummer," he mused. "If I were Swein, and if I wished to savage England's southern coast, that is when I would strike."

"But why strike the southern coast? Why not strike the eastern shires that face the Danish Sea?" She looked down at the map before her, and pointed to the empty space above Wessex that was marked East Anglia.

"The fens country, you mean?" Athelstan thought for a moment, then shook his head. "Swein is hungry for revenge. He will aim his blow at Wessex, my lady, for Wessex is Æthelred's heart. He will strike our southern coast," he said, bending over the map and running his finger over its lower edge. "Here, perhaps, near Pevensey." His finger stabbed at a spot near the king's manor at Beddingham. "Or here, at Exeter." His finger moved to the fortress that marked her own journey's end. "Swein will sail his ships down along the south coast of Denmark, along the coast of Frisia, and thence to Normandy. When the tides and winds are with him, he will launch his dragon ships across the Narrow Sea." He raised his eyes to hers. "If your brothers are in the far south of their land, how are they to prevent Swein's fleet from lurking in Normandy's northern harbors?"

Emma pondered this, trying to recall exactly what her mother had written in her last letter. Had her news about Mathilde's wedding, of Richard's decision to visit Blois, been a hidden warning? A cold thought struck her of a sudden. Had her brothers' plan to travel to Blois been deliberate, so that they could claim ignorance about what Swein might do? So that they could turn a blind eye to whatever use the raiders might make of Normandy's harbors? Surely Richard's purpose for accompanying the couple south was no more than to reinforce his support for an alliance he had long sought. Besides, Richard knew that she would be in Exeter. She had written to him that she would go to her dower lands there, knowing that he would approve of her determination to take responsibility for her properties.

No. Athelstan must be wrong about where Swein would strike. He was guessing, like the priests who had made dire predictions about the end of the world in the years before the millennium. They had warned that the sea would boil, that the land would fracture and mountains collapse. Yet nothing had happened. Life had gone on much as before.

"You cannot know any of this for certain, my lord," she said softly. "It is but conjecture. What must we do, hide behind our city walls for the next two months for fear of the Danes?"

"No, my lady," he said. "But if you see dark clouds and lightning in the distant skies, you do not climb the highest tree that you can find to watch the storm's approach! You must not go to Exeter or to any town that lies within striking distance of a Danish army!"

She sighed, exasperated by his vehemence.

"I have made my preparations, my lord, and I will go to Exeter. My responsibilities demand that I do so. Even the king demands it." She smiled at him, trying to ease the heavy atmosphere between them. "If it makes you feel any better, I promise not to climb any trees during a thunderstorm."

Athelstan gave her a cold glare. "What if I am right, my lady, and you are wrong?"

"At the first sign of a dragon ship I will get on a horse and flee. Will that satisfy you?"

"And if the ships come in the night? What then?"

"There will be a watch, surely. Ealdorman Ælfric will see to it."

Abruptly he pushed away from the table, agitated, frustrated. But what could she do? She could not acquiesce to his plea when the king had already bid her go. And, Sweet Virgin, she longed to be away from here, whatever the risk.

He placed his hands again upon the table between them and leaned toward her until his face was close to hers. "If you must go to Exeter, then I will ask the king to send me with you." He lowered his voice to a whisper. "I will trust no one else with your life. Do you understand me?"

She understood him only too well. And she understood her own heart well enough to know that if the two of them were to spend time together, away from the prying eyes and ears of the court, she would be in far more danger from Athelstan than she could ever be from Swein Forkbeard.

"I thank you, my lord," she said softly, "but I forbid you to do that. Promise me that you will not." Her voice broke, and she wanted to touch him, to place her hand upon his to ease the sting of her words. She could not. "Your father is a suspicious man, my lord. He sees enemies everywhere. He already mistrusts me. Who knows what evil intent he will read into your request?" She straightened her back and raised her voice. "Thank you, my lord Athelstan, for sharing your concerns with me. You may be assured that I will give them all due consideration." She looked at him with a reassuring smile, pleading with her eyes for him to leave.

He hesitated for an instant, then bowed and stalked from the chamber.

Emma gazed after him, waiting for the beating of her heart to slow. The chorus of voices in the room had risen again, and she welcomed its gentle susurration, like the sound of waves brushing the shore. She was trembling, as if she walked along a terrible precipice, exquisitely aware that the slightest false step would send her over the edge.

She saw Elgiva fix her with a curious stare. How much had she heard? How much did she guess? Emma drew in a breath and picked up the map again, but a moment later her servant returned clutching something in her hands.

"Lord Athelstan," the girl said, "bid me give you this. He says you must keep it sharp, and keep it about you always."

It was a sheathed *seax*, its hilt made of smooth, bleached bone. Taking it in her hands, Emma drew the knife from its sheath. Unlike the delicate blade that she used at meals, this was a weapon—unadorned yet beautiful in its brutal simplicity. The blade was broad and heavy, its single cutting edge tapering to a lethal point. The sheath had no loop to attach it to a belt, and she realized that it was meant to be hidden somewhere on the body—tucked into the leggings wound around the lower leg, or perhaps slotted into a stiff boot.

She would have no need of it, she was certain. But she would do as Athelstan asked, if only to have something always about her that had once belonged to him. At least, she thought wryly, no one could suggest that it was a love token.

Chapter Twenty

June 1003
Middleton, Dorset

The hamlet of Middleton lay nestled in a green fold of the southern downs, halfway between Winchester and Exeter. Precisely in the middle of nowhere, Elgiva thought, as she stood beside Groa to look down on the village from the path that climbed toward the birch-covered ridge above it. From this vantage point she could see the village, an abbey, the queen's pavilions—and nothing else except fields, forest, and sheep.

She shook her head in disgust.

"I will never forgive my father for forcing me to attend the queen on this wretched progress," she grumbled. "He could have spared me this. I have been an obedient daughter, and I do not deserve such punishment."

"Be patient, my love," Groa crooned. "You will be rewarded in the end. Every step you take brings you closer to a crown."

This had become Groa's standard response to anything that irritated Elgiva. Yet Elgiva could not see how she benefited from Emma's royal progress, and less so today than ever before. At least the queen's other stopping places—Romsey, Wilton, Shaftesbury—had been bustling market towns offering something more to see than a minster or an abbey. Middleton, though, was a green desert.

Beside her, Groa started up the gently sloping path again, and Elgiva followed, still brooding. When she had informed her father of the queen's intention to make this journey, she had begged him to find some way to release her from it. She had insisted that if she were forced to visit every wretched church and convent between Winchester and Exeter she would go mad.

But her father had sent back word that she must accompany Emma, and that she must take note of anyone of import who met with the queen, relaying their names to one of his several retainers who trailed their party like shadows. So when the queen and her retinue reached their stopping place for the day and finished their repast, Elgiva would slip away with only Groa for company. One of her father's men would find her—in the minster or the marketplace or by some holy well—and listen attentively to whatever she had to say.

For the past two days, though, there had been no messenger, and today, since there was no crowded marketplace, all she could think to do was to get out of sight of the pavilions and hope that her father's minion would find her.

She could not fathom why her father had such a keen interest in Emma's doings. It irritated her that she had to follow his irksome in-structions without even the benefit of knowing their purpose, particu-larly since, as far as she could tell, the queen's activities seemed unimportant.

Emma, she had observed, spoke to her traveling companions along the road, particularly Ealdorman Ælfric, who led the company. When they stopped at shrines along the way she apparently spoke to God, her head bowed in sanctimonious prayer. The only person of any moment whom she had consulted was the abbess at Shaftesbury when, last Sunday, the two women had been closeted together for some time. Elgiva could not know for certain what they had discussed, but she guessed that a generous amount of money had changed hands, for the abbess was smiling broadly when she bid the queen farewell.

Emma was no doubt bribing God with prayers and gold, hoping He would make her belly swell again. And if the queen expected that to happen while she was so far away from the loving attentions of her husband, then her faith was great indeed.

They reached the top of the hill, where a small chapel built of mortared gray stone stood in a clearing. A man cloaked in dark green glided toward them from behind the chapel, sunlight and shadow dappling his lithe figure as he moved. She did not recognize him, but he lifted his hand to show her father's ring on his first finger. She nodded to Groa, who would keep watch for any intruders, then turned to her father's man.

The face that peered down at her was attractive—sun darkened, with high cheekbones and liquid, brooding eyes. His curly brown hair was cropped short and his beard well trimmed. The shoulders beneath the green mantle were broad, but his body tapered to a slim waist, the tunic cinched tight with a wide black belt.

"Do you bring me word from my father?" she asked.

"He sends his greeting, my lady. I am to say that he hopes that you offered a Mass for him at St. Edward's tomb, and that you have not yet been driven mad by prayer."

Elgiva snorted at her father's idea of a jest.

"And is that all you are to say? Can you not at least tell me where he is?"

He shrugged. "When last I spoke with him he was with the king at Winchester, but that was some days ago."

Elgiva frowned, puzzling over what her father might be up to. Was he planning to make some move against the queen or did he merely wish to know who she met with and, presumably, influenced?

She sighed, still annoyed with her father, and considered the man in front of her. He was different from the other messengers her father had sent. They had been mere servants, barely raising their heads to look at her. This one was watching her with molten eyes, his mouth slanted upward in an arrogant half smile. She judged him to be not many years older than she was, and she thought him somewhat young to have such an obviously high opinion of himself.

"What is your name, fellow?" she demanded.

"Alric, my lady. My lands are in western Mercia, and your father and brothers know me well." So he was a man of some substance, then.

She eyed him as he inclined his head toward her in a slight bow, keeping his eyes on hers as if he thought himself her equal. The man was insolent indeed. Still, she rather liked the look of him. He was bold, and in a handsome man that was not such a bad thing.

"I have little in the way of news to give you," she said.

"Your father would know something of the queen's daily routine," he prompted.

She raised an eyebrow at him.

"Will you remember all that I tell you?" she asked.

"With pleasure, lady," he said, his voice a caress.

Honeyed words, indeed, she thought. He raked her with appreciative eyes, and she brushed past him, walking into the trees so that he would not perceive how his hungry gaze pleased her.

"Very well," she said, trying to dismiss him from her mind as she gathered her thoughts. "We begin each morning with ablutions just after dawn, followed by a prayer and our first meal. By the time the queen is ready to set out, the pavilions have been dismantled and are already on their way to the next stopping point. We ride at a leisurely pace for the most part, but messengers are sent ahead to every town through which the queen will pass to announce her imminent arrival."

As she recited the routine, it suddenly dawned on her what Emma was accomplishing with this progress. She was seducing the people of England! At every village and town she threw pennies to the throngs of folk who surrounded her, and she called out greetings that held only the merest trace of her foreign birth. And those simple, stupid folk, damn their eyes, would probably worship her for it! Whatever misgivings they might have about Æthelred, they would love their pretty young queen.

Elgiva stopped in her tracks and closed her eyes, remembering Emma's arrival at Middleton and the cheers of the crowd.

She felt Alric come up behind her, although he did not touch her. He was not that bold, at least.

"Tell my father," she said sharply, "that I believe that the queen gave generous gifts to the abbey at Shaftesbury. Tell him that not only do the good sisters love her, but that the townsfolk who have seen her are besotted with her. Tell him to beware if he is planning any move against the queen. Can you remember all of that?"

"Aye, lady." It was a mere whisper, for his mouth was next to her ear.

She caught her breath at the nearness of him, then turned to hold out her hand, signifying that their interview was over. But her hand trembled as he clasped it and brought it to his lips, his eyes once more raking hers.

He kissed her ring, then turned her hand palm upward and placed a lingering kiss there, too—a kiss that burned her like a brand. An instant later he was gone, his green cloak melting into the colors of the brush beyond the clearing. She stood there a moment, catching her breath, allowing her pulse to steady.

Alric. She smiled to herself as she whispered his name. Here was a man of no little worth.

As she made her way back toward the pavilions she forced her thoughts back to Emma, finally admitting the truth to herself. Æthelred would never set his queen aside. In that first year, while Emma had been perceived as a foreigner and had yet to prove that she could conceive a child, there may have been a chance. Now that chance was gone.

Elgiva kept her eyes on the ground, carefully avoiding piles of sheep dung. What had she to strive for now? Must she resign herself to a marriage with one of Æthelred's thegns, she who had been promised a crown? She clenched her hands into fists at the thought. She would not do it. Not while the king had marriageable sons, at any rate.

She would have to seduce one of the æthelings into wedding her. She would prefer Athelstan, of course, but he was bewitched by the queen. She wanted no man who was so moonstruck that he courted disaster for the sake of a woman—unless she was that woman. No, Athelstan had moved beyond her reach, but Æthelred had plenty of other sons. If it was indeed her *wyrd* to be queen, then she must find a way to bring it about.

"Groa," she said, pausing to wait for her, "what have you to say to Ecbert as a husband for me?"

"He would be," she paused, as if searching for the right word, "pliable, my lady. But will he ever be king?"

Elgiva pursed her lips. "You are right," she said slowly. "He would be pliable, yet he is not the heir—not yet, at any rate. As his wife, though, I think I could inspire ambitions in him that he does not yet entertain." She smiled to herself and drew Groa's arm in hers. "When we return to Winchester I believe that I shall pay particular attention to young Ecbert."

Yet the image of Alric remained in her mind, sharp and clear. She hoped that she would see him again, many times, before she returned to Winchester.

Winchester, Hampshire

King Æthelred, seated formally upon his ornately carved, brilliantly painted throne in Winchester's great hall, gazed upon the nobles come from all over his realm to witness the workings of the court. He knew most of them by name and had a general idea of their worth to him in taxable property. They were like children, he thought, who sometimes had to be appeased, sometimes coerced, sometimes placated, sometimes punished. He passed laws to protect them from each other and levied taxes to protect them from outsiders. Yet they perceived him as weak, because, for some years now, he had purchased peace with gold instead of with English blood. He did not doubt that if some brilliant warrior should rise to challenge him for the throne, offering to lead them in battle against their foes, many of his thegns would forsake him.

Brooding upon this dismal theme, Æthelred noticed his eldest son emerge from a knot of men at the back of the hall and make his way toward the dais. As Athelstan approached the throne and knelt at his father's feet, a shaft of sunlight slanted through the high windows to set the lad's golden hair aglow and burnish the ornate silver clasp at his right shoulder. Hardly a lad now, Æthelred reminded himself. Headstrong, opinionated, outspoken, yes, but a lad no longer.

He squinted at his son, trying to read the expression on his face. There was trouble brewing there. Of that much he was certain.

He nodded to his son to speak, and Athelstan rose and stepped to one side, turning so that all would hear his words.

"I would speak of our enemy, Swein Forkbeard, who now holds sway in both Denmark and Norway, and who seeks to add England to his northern realms." His voice rang through the hall, as sharp and clamorous as a warning bell. "It is likely that even now Swein is gathering his dragon ships in some Norman port, preparing to strike us. He will cross the Narrow Sea to plunder our lands and rape our women, for he has a sister's death to avenge."

He paused, and Æthelred could see that his son had snared the attention of every man in the hall, for they all feared the next Danish onslaught.

"Will we wait," Athelstan went on, "as we have so many times before, like huddled sheep for the blow that we fear will come and pray will not? I say . . ." He paused again, and he seemed to grow a little taller as he squared his shoulders, almost as if he were about to face an enemy. "I say that we do not wait for the dragon ships to strike. I propose that we send ships to Normandy, find the Viking fleet, and destroy it before it crosses the Narrow Sea. Let us torch their dragons like signal beacons, cripple them so that they cannot hit us."

The hall began to buzz with voices, and then a Kentish lord spoke up. "And who would undertake to lead such an enterprise?" he demanded.

"There are three of us," Athelstan replied, as Ecbert and Edmund stepped forward to stand with him.

And now a low roar swept through the hall like a rising wind. Æthelred cursed under his breath as he quickly weighed the likelihood of the success of such a plan and found it wanting. It was based on the assumption that Swein's ships could be found in their Norman haven, and then destroyed. The odds in favor of that were long, indeed.

On the other hand, if by some miracle the venture should succeed, he would have to look no further than his own son for the challenger to his crown. Was Athelstan not challenging him already, here and now, in making such an outrageous proposition before his court and council? Even as he considered how best to counter his son's defiance, though, he felt the weight of his dead brother's unseen presence. Edward's cold malevolence was snaking toward him from somewhere in the shadows while, standing before the dais in a shaft of light, Athelstan looked up at him with Edward's face.

This was all his brother's doing, he realized—Edward's vengeance working through the actions of his eldest son. He could feel his brother's menace all around him now, ominous as the silence before a thunderclap, and Æthelred braced himself against it. Almost as if a voice had whispered it in his ear, he understood at last what his brother wanted from him as expiation for his sin. But it was too great a sacrifice. Even Edward's black vengeance would not compel him to it.

Swiftly Æthelred rose to his feet, and pitching his voice so that it could be heard in every corner of the hall, he answered Athelstan's challenge.

"I will not send my sons, nor any man's sons, on such an ill-considered, perilous venture. The hazards far outweigh any gains, and it is not to be thought of, now or ever." He fixed Athelstan with a contemptuous look that brooked no argument. "There's an end to it."

He stalked from the dais, desperate to escape curious eyes and to shake off the clammy chill that enveloped him now like a fog. He knew, even without seeing it, that a shadow followed in his wake. Edward would show him no mercy, but God help him, the retribution that his brother demanded was far too high. He would not pay it, let his brother's bloodied shade do what he would.

Athelstan stared, thunderstruck, at his father's retreating back. The king had asked for no considered opinions but had treated his suggestion with contempt.

And when, he asked himself, had it ever been otherwise? His father had always dismissed his counsel. Even the king's gift of the Sword of

Offa had been an attempt to placate him, as if he were a mewling babe who could be silenced with a toy.

He turned from the empty throne and elbowed his way through the crowded hall, with Ecbert and Edmund at his heels.

"What are you going to do?" Ecbert demanded.

"Now that the king has humiliated me in front of the entire court?" he asked. "I am going to leave, of course. What other choice do I have?"

Ecbert moved quickly to plant himself directly in Athelstan's path. "You cannot leave the court without his permission!" he protested.

"Watch me," Athelstan said, shoving his brother aside.

"Surely you don't propose to fire the Danish fleet all by yourself." This from Edmund.

Athelstan barked a laugh. "Without a sealed writ from the king I am powerless to raise the ships. No, Swein's fleet is safe from me. I will wait for word of Armageddon at my estate at Norton." His lands lay within a half day's ride of Exeter, and if, God forbid, the Danish force should strike there, he could at the very least spirit Emma out of danger.

Suddenly he found Edmund once again blocking his way.

"Stay away from her," his brother said in a low voice, his face dark with warning. "She is not worth the risk that you are taking."

There was no need to ask whom he meant. Edmund despised Emma, and if anything should happen to her, he would likely rejoice, not mourn.

In that instant Athelstan felt his tenuous hold on his rage—against his father, against the Danes, against God Himself—give way. He lunged for Edmund's throat but almost immediately found his arms pinned from behind.

"Stop it!" Ecbert hissed in his ear. "We're on your side, you fool. You risk losing your properties and titles if you leave."

"If the Danes attack," Athelstan said, shrugging out of his brother's grasp, "the king will have far more to worry about than a son who disobeyed him by going off to confront the enemy."

He stalked away from his brothers. Already he had wasted precious time trying to persuade his father to make the first strike against Fork-beard. With midsummer less than a week away, and the Danish fleet perhaps already poised to sail across the Narrow Sea, there was little time to lose. He could make it to Exeter in five days with swift horses. His sense of foreboding, of some calamity about to befall all of them, was stronger than ever. Whatever was to come he would face it at Em-ma's side, or die trying to reach her.

Middleton, Dorset

It was the Lord's Day, and in St. Catherine's Church on the ridge above Middleton Abbey, Emma knelt before the small altar. The Mass was done, yet she lingered to pray alone for a time in the solemn quiet of the chapel. Early morning light streamed, honey colored, through the thick yellow pane of the window set into the wall behind the altar, and the sweet, heavy fragrance of incense hung in the air, masking, for the moment, the odor of damp that clung to the lime-washed walls and rush-strewn earthen floor.

When Emma had finished her prayers she stood up and turned to find that Ealdorman Ælfric, too, had lingered in the chapel. He rose when she did, bowing to her with grave dignity.

"My lady," he said softly, "may I speak with you a little?"

"What is it, my lord?" she asked, seating herself upon one of the benches that lined the chapel walls. She signaled to Wymarc, who had been waiting near the church door, and in a moment Emma and Ælfric were alone together in the quiet of the little chapel. "Pray, sit down," she said to the old man.

He lowered himself onto the bench next to her, his wrinkled brow even more furrowed than usual. Tall and gaunt, grizzled and gray, he reminded Emma somewhat of her father. There was the same gentle-ness in his face whenever his eyes lit upon her, and the same kind of genial smile of affection. Her childhood memories of her father had become so entwined with this man that she could not help but look upon him with the same regard that a daughter might.

He gazed at her gravely, large hands clasped together upon the folds of his brown cloak.

"Do you know aught of my son, my lady?" he asked.

"Your son?" she said, surprised by the question. "No, my lord. Only what you told me at Wherwell . . . that you lost him some time after Hilde's mother died."

"Lost him, aye," he said, nodding. "That is true enough. Yet it is not the entire truth."

This did not surprise her. She had often been forced to settle for half-truths at the king's court. She said nothing, though, merely watched the old man as he looked down at the strong, sinewy hands in his lap. When he trained his dark eyes upon her again he said, "My son is lost, although not dead."

He told her a piteous tale, then, of a headstrong son who after the death of his young wife had left his baby daughter in his parents' care and, in spite of his father's protests, disappeared from all their knowledge.

"We thought that he, too, had died, perhaps even among the many who lost their lives in the battle against the Danes at Maldon in ninety-one. Then, the year after Maldon, when Swein Forkbeard struck in Kent, the king called out the *fyrd* to meet the enemy, and I was to lead the ships that would cut off the Danes' retreat after the battle." He paused, grazing a hand across his brow as if he would wipe out the memories there. "The night before we would have set our trap, as our host camped on the Thames bank, my son appeared at my tent, hale and healthy. To me it was as if Lazarus had come back from the dead, for I had thought Ælfgar buried in the fens at Maldon. To this day I do not know if any of what he told me that night—of his capture by Danish shipmen and his repeated efforts to escape—was truth or lie. I did not bind him in chains, for I did not know then that he was Fork-beard's man, body and soul." He gazed at her, his eyes bleak with grief.

"It is said that the Danish king has a power in his gaze that captures and holds men's hearts. I think it must be true."

Emma recalled the power and calculation she had read in Swein Forkbeard's eyes. She could not speak to how it might affect the hearts of his followers. Swein had inspired her only with fear.

Ælfric again took up his tale. "My son slipped away again in the night, and although I followed with a party to capture him, by dawn he had alerted the enemy of our intentions, and their fleet had sailed. Only one dragon ship was set aflame. All its crew was slain but for one man—the traitor, Ælfgar. My son."

Emma swallowed, forced to ask the question although she dreaded to hear the answer. "What was his punishment?"

"The king, for the love he bore me, gave me my son's life. But they gouged out his eyes and left him all but dead. For ten years now he has been cared for by the brothers at Magdalene Abbey near Exeter, but in all that time I have not seen him, for fear of incurring the king's displeasure." He paused, and his eyes, when they captured hers, gleamed with unshed tears. "I would see my son again, my lady, reunite him with his daughter if he should will it. Hilde knows nothing of her father's treachery, but she must learn of it soon. I would rather that she heard it from me than from any other. And when she knows the truth"—he looked at her with pleading eyes—"she will need comfort, I think."

Emma though of Hilde, who had often sat with young Edward during his illness, telling him stories to distract him from his pain.

"I will stand by Hilde," she said, "and offer her whatever counsel she may need."

The old man did not speak, but kissed her hand. As Emma watched him leave, she pondered his willingness to risk his king's displeasure in seeking out a faithless son, whose actions had cast infamy on his father's name.

If the king's sons should commit some rash, misguided deed, she doubted that they would find their father so willing to forgive.

Chapter Twenty-one

When Queen Emma of England entered the royal *burh* of Exeter on Midsummer's Day, Athelstan watched the event from a lookout atop the city wall. The day was bright with sun, and as Emma approached the group of nobles waiting for her at the southern gate, all the church bells of Exeter began to peal, and a roar went up from the crowds that had come to watch.

Athelstan guessed that nothing like it had been seen in Exeter within living memory. Not since the days of King Athelstan, near eighty years before, would such an array of priests, soldiers, noblemen, and courtly ladies have made its way through the gates of the city's Roman wall, past the minster, to the fortress on the hill. The bishops of Crediton and Sherborne, rivaling each other in capes of scarlet silk, rode at the queen's side. Behind her, Ealdorman Ælfric's heavily polished mail tunic and helmet outshone not only the glitter of the prelates' garb, but even the gleam reflected from their shining tonsures.

Athelstan barely noticed them, for his eyes were fixed upon Emma, in her cyrtel of shimmering blue godwebbe. Her mantle was of a deeper blue, trimmed with white silk, and clasped at her right shoulder by a broach of gold inlaid with pearls. On her head she wore a delicate silk veil bound in place by a thin circlet of beaten gold. Perched atop her great white horse she looked stunning. It seemed to him that anyone who saw her must love her.

Yet even as he watched the queen make her slow way through the streets of Exeter, he did not for a moment forget the threat of Swein Forkbeard and his dragon ships. From where he stood Athelstan could see the River Exe as it flowed past the city walls toward the Narrow Sea. Ever and again his eyes strayed to the southeast, where a signal beacon was perched atop a hill crowned by the remains of a fort built by a people long vanished. Should Danish ships be sighted on the horizon the beacon would be lit in warning. But no trace of warning flare blazed on the hill. Athelstan relaxed ever so slightly.

His two companions, garbed as he was in fine, gray, knee-length woolen cloaks that covered their mail tunics, had been in his service from the time that they were boys together. He nodded to them to remain on watch, and he left them, making his way through the press of people and down from the wall. He skirted the crowds that flooded Ceap Street in the wake of the queen's procession, following the wall to the western gate, where his mount waited in the care of an old man who preferred the weight of silver pennies in his purse to the sight of a queen.

Athelstan mounted his horse and urged it out of the gate and away from Exeter, and from Emma. He had toyed with the idea of trying to see her at once, to be waiting for her at Hugh's side when her reeve welcomed her to the fortress at the top of the town. He had much to say to her, for they had parted badly and it had been his doing. She would grant him pardon, he was certain, were he to ask it. But this was neither the time nor the place to ask for pardon. He would have to be patient, for today she belonged to others—to the thegns and their ladies, to the bishops, to those who sought a boon from the white hand of the Lady. He would not seek a public audience with her. He had learned from his last, disastrous interview with the king that such a thing would be unwise. He must bide his time, and wait for an opportunity to speak with her alone.

And when they met, what would he say to her, beyond the words that he would use to beg for forgiveness? Would he tell her all that was in his heart? No, for it would be cruel to burden her with that. Did she not already have enough to bear? A husband who used her badly, a babe miscarried, and the fear of whatever horror the Danes might bring.

Would he burden her, too, with words of love? Already today the folk of Exeter had hailed her, cheering for their Lady Queen, smitten by the very sight of her. No, she did not need the burden of his love. He could offer his service, though. He would be the queen's man, if she would but let him. He would guard her and protect her, come what may, and ask for naught in return.

He spurred his horse northward toward his holdings at Norton. Soon, though, he would return and make his pledge to her, if she would have him.

Several days later, beneath a dismal sky, Emma stood upon the ramparts of the fortress that would be her home for the next two months. She would have preferred a chamber in St. Nicholas's Priory on the edge of town, but Athelstan's dire warning about the Danes had convinced her to be prudent. Here, atop this enormous bloodred rock, she would be protected by timber, stone, and sheer height from any danger. Except a high wind, she told herself wryly, as the thin silk of her headrail swirled around her face.

She pushed back the veil and studied the view before her. The city itself was surrounded by hills, and to the south the River Exe wound its way through them. From the city gate that faced the river the long Ceap Street, crowded with shops and lodgings, ran toward her in a straight line. On one side of the Ceap the walls of the minster rose above houses roofed with thatch, the red stone of the church sharply outlined against the green of the close and the fields that surrounded it.

From her vantage point she could just make out three of the great gates set into the city's high Roman walls. The fourth gate, Northgate, lay behind her, and, according to Hugh, once the gates were closed there was only one other way into the city—a secret door, its precise location known to only a few. *La posterle*, Hugh had called it, explaining that the door led to a tunnel that burrowed beneath the city walls. In case of an attack upon Exeter, defenders from the *burh* could slip out through *la posterle* to spring upon the enemy from behind. Its most recent use though, Hugh had said with a grin, had been by the former reeve who would slip through the hidden passage at night to visit his mistress in Northgate. Those forays had ceased when he returned to the *burh* one night to find his wife waiting for him beside *la posterle* with a switch in her hand, to the great amusement of the castle guards.

It occurred to Emma that it could hardly be a secret door if even the reeve's wife knew of it. Nevertheless, she had been given a tour of the entire fortress, and she had not been able to spot the tunnel's entrance.

She made her way past the guard who stood gazing stolidly toward the sea, and she paused to look down the wooden steps into the fortress yard. It was a stark contrast to the tranquil, royal enclave of Winchester. This was no palace, safely enfolded by the Hampshire downs and graced with the luxuries that the wealth of sixty years of peace and prosperity could provide. This was a fortress on the edge of Æthelred's kingdom, and there was little here of comfort or beauty, cleanliness or quiet. The enclosure below churned with soldiers, servants, horses, carts, and a never-ending line of tradesmen who came and went through a small door next to the main gate. Hugh had made his own quarters available for her use, and the high stone hall with its thatched roof sheltered not only Emma and her women, but its undercroft harbored a chicken coop, a small sheep pen, a dwindling store of grain, and assorted families of resident vermin that she preferred not to think about. Presumably, it hid the entrance to that secret tunnel as well.

She stepped carefully along the rocky path that led to the hall and climbed the stairs to its timbered door. Wymarc waited there for her, a pair of clean leather slippers in her hands and such a bright expression on her face that Emma had to smile. Hugh was responsible for

Wymarc's joy, she was certain. She had been witness to their reunion and to the looks of suppressed longing that neither had been able to disguise. She'd sent the two of them off on a trumped-up errand, just to give them some moments alone together, and Wymarc had been glowing like the moon ever since.

Emma was about to broach the topic of Wymarc's feelings for Hugh when a shout went up from the guard at the fortress gate. The massive bulk of the outer gate swung wide, and a group of horsemen rode in, but Emma saw only the man at the head of the troop.

There was nothing in his garb to mark him as the eldest ætheling and the heir to the throne, for he was dressed simply, cloaked in fine gray wool, his head crowned with only the golden sheen of his hair. Yet there was no mistaking the air of authority that proclaimed to anyone who saw him that this was a son of the royal blood.

So Athelstan had come, as she had known that he would. She wished with all her heart that he had not. She was not prepared to see him, for she could not feign indifference to him any more than Wymarc could pretend indifference to Hugh. She suspected that every word she spoke, every action, every glance was observed and noted. If she were to allow Athelstan into her presence, how long would it be before the king heard of it?

Æthelred and his sons were already at odds—had been since the day of her marriage. As peaceweaver was it not her duty to mend the rents in the fabric of the kingdom, reconcile father to son if she could? Yet if the king were to harbor suspicions about her feelings for Athelstan, her efforts would only sow more discord between them.

She would have to send Athelstan away, and she must do it in such a way that he would not attempt to see her again.

"Find Hugh," she said to Wymarc.

Athelstan placed both his hands upon the table in front of him and glowered at Emma's reeve. As the king's eldest son, he was not used to being thwarted, and he did not much like it. Beyond that, he had come to consider Hugh a friend and had not expected this man, of all men, to stand in the way of his desire.

"How can you know that the queen will not see me?" he demanded. "You have not even sent her word that I am here."

"She knows well that you are here. She has bid me tell you that, as she is certain that you have brought her greetings from the king, she thanks you for your courtesy. She hopes that you will comprehend the heavy matters that prevent her from granting you an audience with her, and she requires that any message you bear from your father be delivered through me. She asks me as well to urge you, upon your present return to Winchester, to bear the greetings of a loving and obedient wife to your father the king."

With an effort, Athelstan reined in his temper. He and Hugh had shared ale together in the king's hall and had told bawdy jokes to each other in the long hours of the night watch in the palace yard at Winchester. Hugh's face was wont to reflect his every thought, and the fact that right now it was as blank as a pool of still water told Athelstan a great deal. For the moment, Hugh was nothing but the queen's mouthpiece. He would say only what he had been ordered to say, and nothing that Athelstan could do, short of violence, would change that. In the great hall of her dower city, the orders of the queen overruled even those of the king's heir.

Hugh's formal greeting was meant for everyone within earshot to hear, yet Athelstan perceived a hidden message that washed over him like icy water. Emma greeted him not as a friend but as the wife of the king. That in itself was a wall placed between them as thick as the fortress walls of Exeter itself. She wanted to hear no pledges from him. At least, not in public, he told himself. And for reasons that he could only guess at, she was not willing to risk seeing him in private.

Was she afraid of what he might say to her? Or was she fearful of what others might say about her? When he entered the hall he had taken careful note of those present. The room was not overly large. Perhaps three of them could fit within the great hall at Winchester.

There were maybe thirty people milling about, and the conversations that had reached his ears as a loud buzz when he first stepped through the doorway had dropped, almost immediately upon his entrance, to a low hum.

The great hall was ever a breeding ground for rumor and gossip. Anything he said here was likely to be repeated, perhaps even into the ear of the king. He cared nothing for that, for himself, but he had to consider Emma. Clearly she wanted him to be gone, to return immediately to Winchester. Had his father threatened her in some way? Was the king, indeed, fearful of losing the wife he did not want to the son he did not heed? His father was ever one to misjudge where danger lay, a king who started at shadows. Nevertheless, he himself must be mindful of the queen. He would have to frame his response to her with the same care that she had used in couching her message to him.

He nodded brusquely to Hugh.

"Tell the queen that I apologize for my impetuous arrival today, as well as for all my other ill-considered acts. She will be able to think of many, I am certain. My father sends assurance," he could not refrain from a bitter smile as he stretched the truth somewhat, "of his confidence in the summer's continued peace. I will of course bear the queen's greetings to the king when I see him." This would not occur any time soon, but the audience around him need not know it. "Have you begun the repairs to the city walls as I directed?" he asked. At least he would make sure that the city's fortifications would withstand any assault.

"We started work today, my lord," Hugh replied.

"Good," he said. "There is one more thing. I understand that Lord Ælfric accompanied the queen to Exeter. Can you direct him to attend me at my Norton estate in four days' time?"

"My Lord Ælfric set out early this morning toward Torverton on some purpose of his own. He will return by nightfall, however, and I will give him your message then," Hugh said, rising from his stool to bow in acknowledgment.

Athelstan nodded and made his way out of the hall. The queen would know now where to find him. And if she had any message for him, of warning or of forgiveness, she would find a way to send him word. For the moment, he could do no more.

Elgiva, wearing a sober black cloak, and with her wanton curls bound in a demure braid and covered by a linen veil, stood in the shadows near the door of St. Mary Minster, pretending to pray. Her father's man was late today. She had been waiting here, cold and uncomfortable, throughout an entire Mass. Her feet hurt from standing on the hard stone floor, and every inch of her felt damp from the moisture that seeped through the wall next to her. Groa, silent and watchful, stood in front of her, shielding her from curious eyes and from the chill draft that came in through the open door. Groa's company, though, gave Elgiva little in the way of comfort. It was her father's handsome thegn, he of the searching eyes and arrogant mouth, who she wanted beside her. He had sent her word through Groa to meet him here, and her frustration and anger grew as the minutes dragged by and he did not appear.

A crowd had formed at the church door now, made up of priests and worshipers trying to make their way out as pilgrims tried to make their way in. The pilgrims, some moaning, some weeping, all of them wretched, advanced in a line toward the altar. Most of them crawled, brought to their knees by illness or devotion, others hobbled on crutches, and she could see one who was carried on a pallet. They all sought forgiveness or miracles—or both. They came to place their hands upon Mary's stone, reputedly taken from the tomb of the Virgin and placed in the floor before the altar of this church when it was first built. One of the old kings of Wessex—Alfred or Athelstan, she could not remember which—had purchased it and set it here. Countless folk, so the story went, had been healed of whatever miseries ailed them just by touching it, and so the believers continued to come in search of healing and peace.

At the moment there was little enough peace to be had. The shrill clamor from the pilgrims set Elgiva's teeth on edge, and she had just made up her mind that her father's messenger could go hang when a form clad in dark green separated itself from the cluster of folk at the door and moved to stand immediately behind her.

"What news, my lady?"

She recognized his voice, and a thrill of anticipation shot up her spine. But the church and the wait and the pilgrims had put her in a foul temper, and she was not to be easily appeased.

"You are late," she hissed. "Why have you kept me waiting so long?"

"Forgive me. I was on a mission, and I was delayed."

She caught his scent now, a pleasing man smell of leather and horse-flesh and sweat. The heat from his body displaced some of the chill from the stones beside her, but there was not enough remorse in his tone to pacify her.

"Do not keep me waiting again," she snapped. "My time is more important than any mission that you might have." She clasped her hands and bowed her head to give the impression that she was praying, should anyone chance to glance in her direction.

"Lady . . ." The word was spoken with a long, slow sigh. "There is nothing of greater import to me than the brief moments I spend in your presence."

Groa, standing beside Elgiva, snorted.

Elgiva glared at her. "Get you away from us a little," she spat at the old woman. "You know your business."

Groa moved away, and Alric urged Elgiva deeper into the shadows, until they stood against the church wall, hidden from all eyes by a massive stone column.

"I want you to tell me what my father is planning," she whispered. "I am weary of working toward an end that I cannot see."

"I would tell you if I could," he whispered back, "but I do not know myself. I am but a weary messenger. What news have you for me?"

He placed himself behind her, so close that the front of his body touched the back of hers. Gratefully, she eased her weight against his solid warmth, then she felt the edge of her veil lifted, and a finger gently caressed the back of her neck. She gave a little gasp of surprise and released it in a sigh of pleasure. He was taking liberties, to be sure, but why should she not receive some recompense for the tedious hours she had spent waiting for him?

"My news," she whispered, "is that Lord Athelstan waited upon the queen yesterday, but she refused to see him."

The messenger's cheek grazed hers, his beard pleasantly rough against her skin.

"Did you see him?" he asked.

Now his lips brushed against her neck, and she turned her head aside to give him easier access, shivering when she felt his tongue trace her ear.

"No, I did not," she said, allowing the slightest hint of a pout into her voice. "Dearly would I have loved to spend a few stolen moments with the ætheling, but alas, I was disappointed."

His hand found its way inside her cloak and began teasing her breast through the fabric of her gown. "I would make you forget your disappointment, my lady, if you would but let me," he whispered.

"I do not doubt it," she said, catching her breath at the exquisite torture of his touch. It had been long ere the king had taken her to his bed, and when he had, it had never been like this. She would like nothing better than to rut with this fellow who seemed to know his way so delightfully around a woman's body, but she dared not risk getting a babe from such a one as this. "I have other news," she said. "Would you hear it?"

"I am at your command," he said.

Ah, she would love to try that, but not today.

"Ealdorman Ælfric goes to see the ætheling at Norton tomorrow," she whispered.

The hand at her breast stilled.

"And what of the queen? Will she go to Norton?"

"No," she said, pressing herself against him, gratified when his hand began to minister to her again. "Nor am I to go. Ælfric takes his grand-daughter and the Lady Wymarc in his train, though, at the queen's behest. I am certain that one of them will carry a message to the ætheling from the queen."

"Think you that the queen will make tryst with him?"

Elgiva did not think it likely. If Emma had wanted to see Athelstan, she could have done so yesterday. It would be foolish for her to attempt a secret meeting, for there were too many people around her. Unless, of course, the queen and the ætheling actually planned to run off together. . . .

Elgiva opened her eyes to stare, unseeing, toward the front of the church. Was that what her father hoped—to catch the queen in a traitorous act with the king's son? She tried to puzzle it out, but the messenger's hand had moved from her breast, inching ever downward in a slow, desultory caress until she could not focus on anything but the sensations his fingers evoked. She reached inside her cloak and pulled his hand back up to her breast.

"I cannot tell," she said smoothly, "what message the queen will send the ætheling. Tomorrow she will journey to the estate of Lord Egwin for two nights."

"Who will attend her?" He nipped at the tender spot beneath her ear, then lifted the hem of her cloak and slipped a hand beneath it to press her feverishly against the hard root of him.

"All of her attendants will go, and a large armed force from the fortress is to serve as escort," she whispered, trying to keep her voice even. Beneath her cloak both of his hands stroked her now, one at her breast while the other moved insistently between her legs. She would have fallen to her knees like some pilgrim if he had not held her close against him. She shuddered in his arms, and her moans joined the plaintive cries of the faithful.

"So she travels with far more than a few trusted men."

She caught her breath and, languid with pleasure, forced herself to focus on what he had said.

"Her reeve insists upon it," she said, shaking her head a little to clear it. Why was he so concerned with the number of men guarding Emma?

"If you learn that she will venture outside the city walls with only a small guard . . ." Both his hands fondled her breasts, thumbs massaging ever so gently. ". . . you must send me word immediately. You cannot wait for even one hour."

A tiny shiver, this time of fear, coursed through her limbs. "Did you relay my words of warning to my father?" she asked. "Did you tell him to be wary of plotting against the queen?"

He kissed the back of her neck, but his touch no longer distracted her, and now she waited impatiently for his reply.

"I relayed your message, lady. Your father bids you to do all that he commands and to trust in his judgment. Whenever the queen leaves the city, send word to the inn on the Ceap, just below the fortress gate. Look for me there day or night, whether you have news to give me," he nipped her ear gently, "or something else."

He caressed her backside once, set her firmly on her own two feet, and slipped away. Elgiva bowed her head over her clasped hands. Her father's assurances gave her little comfort and his commands annoyed her. Still, her interview with his thegn, Alric, had certainly been worth the wait.

Ealdorman Ælfric's company spent a week at Athelstan's estate at Norton. When they returned to Exeter, Emma wasted little time in drawing Wymarc aside. Together they walked along the ramparts, where Emma could be certain that no one would overhear them.

"Lord Athelstan bid me say that he will not return to Winchester," Wymarc said. "He wishes to come here where he can be of service to you. I am to tell you that he cares not what his father may think, or believe, or command."

"But he *must* care!" Emma protested. "It is perilous to ignore the king's commands." Or his suspicions. Sweet Virgin, she was afraid for Athelstan, afraid of where the mounting tension between father and son might lead.

"He cares only about the Danish threat," Wymarc went on, "and he fears for your safety. He would have his own men, under his command, set in place here to strengthen the numbers of your guard." Wymarc frowned at Emma. "Perhaps he is right."

Emma shook her head. She feared the Danes as well, but Athelstan had already arranged for the repair of the city walls and set in place rigorous training sessions for the men who guarded the fortress. What more could he do here?

No, it was Athelstan who would be in danger if his father's suspicious mind should turn him against his son.

"How did you leave it with him?" she asked Wymarc.

"He bid me tell you that if you desire him to return to Winchester, then you must return there as well. He will return here within a sennight to consult with you."

That news made her want to weep. She longed to see Athelstan, a yearning that drove her to her knees daily to beg God for pardon. And for that very reason she could not allow him near her.

"He will be wasting his time," she said, "for I shall not see him."

She may not be able to prevent a conflict between Æthelred and his son, but she would not be the spark that lit that fire.

Chapter Twenty-two

July 1003

Exeter, Devonshire

In mid-July, Exeter held its summer fair, and one morning Elgiva made her way through the maze of booths set up along Ceap Street. Accompanied by Groa and one of the fortress guards, she quickly skirted the stockyard and the pens where the bear baiting and cockfights were held, and ambled among the stalls that offered locally made caps and ribbons as well as furs from Norway and leather goods from Spain. Many of the merchants, she noticed with disgust, displayed poppets made in the likeness of the queen.

Emma's popularity in Exeter seemed to increase daily. The ecclesiastics thought she walked on water because she had donated a magnificent silver cross to the minster. The townsfolk loved her because her guards tossed silver pennies to the crowds whenever Emma ventured beyond the fortress walls.

Elgiva hoped that her warnings to her father, which she repeated whenever she met with the delightfully nimble-handed Alric, had convinced him to give up whatever he might be planning. She feared what might result should her father make some move against the queen.

As she considered the purchase of an amber necklace, Elgiva glanced up to see Alric standing in the shadow of the South Gate, deep in conversation with two men. One of them, a thickset fellow with lank blond hair that hung about a face twisted in an unpleasant scowl, was someone she did not recognize. But the other man, hooded and caped in black, turned suddenly, and she realized with a shock that it was her brother Wulf.

Instinctively she moved toward the group, but they swiftly disappeared into the shadows of the gateway. What, she wondered, was her brother doing in Exeter? Why had he not sought her out? Surely he was here at her father's command, but to do what? And who was his disreputable-looking companion?

There were too many riddles, and she did not like riddles. Wulf must be part of her father's plan, whatever it was. When next she saw Alric she would demand to see her brother, and she would insist that Wulf tell her what her father was intending to do.

Emma stood in the doorway of the tiny wooden structure that served as the fortress chapel. In this quiet spot the clamor of life in the *burh* faded away, and she always found solace within its walls. As usual, her eyes were drawn to the sanctuary lamp that hung from a chain beside the altar, its flame aglow, like a star come to earth. As she grew accustomed to the dim light, though, she made out a slight form kneeling beneath the lamp, head bowed in prayer.

Hilde again. Emma had found the child here often since her grandfather Ælfric had left Exeter to return north. Emma felt sorry for the girl, certain that she was mourning the father whom she had so lately discovered—the father who, according to Ælfric, had no wish to see his child.

Emma placed a hand gently on the girl's shoulder. Hilde immediately sprang to her feet. Then, seeing who it was, she dropped back to one knee.

"My lady," she whispered.

Mindful of the promise that she had made to Ælfric at Middleton Abbey, Emma said, "Burdens become lighter if they are shared, Hilde. If you wish to talk to me, I will listen."

The girl did not reply, but a single tear coursed down the side of her nose, and she wiped at it with her fingertips.

"Come," Emma said, taking her hand. "Let us sit together for a while."

She drew her to a squat, wooden bench, and together they sat down, hand in hand, eyes drawn to the comforting light of the altar lamp. They sat in silence, for Hilde seemed unable to speak. At last Emma said, "If I were a girl whose father had forbidden me to see him, I think that I would be torn between grief and anger."

It was a gentle prodding, but it seemed to loosen the girl's tongue.

"He wants no part of me," Hilde said in a small, tight voice. "He is my father, my own blood, but he does not want to see me. He hates me, and I do not know why."

"Oh, Hilde," Emma said with a sigh, putting an arm around the thin shoulders. "He does not hate you. But you are part of a world that he left behind many years ago. Mayhap he believes that it is better for both of you that your worlds remain separate."

"It is not better for me," Hilde said, her voice breaking with her effort not to weep. "It is a punishment, but I have committed no crime."

"No, of course you have not," Emma soothed. But Hilde's father had committed a very great crime. The child was too naïve to recognize that Ælfgar, even in his blinded, lowly state, could be considered a threat to the king. The man had been condemned a traitor, and as such he cast a long shadow. Anyone who contacted him, even now, would be suspect.

In forbidding his daughter to visit him, Ælfgar was doing what little he could to protect her.

"Your father is but thinking of your future, Hilde," she said to the girl. "Because of his past actions, your kinship to him cannot help you, and may even harm you. I suspect he has forbidden you to see him because he sees it as his duty."

"But is it not my duty to visit a father who is ill and imprisoned? Is that not what God commands us? To honor thy father? To visit the sick?"

The face that looked up at Emma was filled with misery. Emma knew that she ought to respond with calm logic, to explain to Hilde that it was not God's will at issue here but the will of the king. She doubted that Hilde would respond to logic, though, and Emma could scarcely blame her for that. The girl was within a few hours' ride of a father she longed to meet, yet she had been ordered to keep her distance.

Even to Emma it seemed unfair. Hilde was but twelve summers old, still a child, really. What harm could it do to allow her to spend an hour with her father? And if it was managed with care, who would know?

A plan began to take shape in her mind, and she smiled down at Hilde.

"One day soon," she said, "I think that I shall go riding toward Torverton and Magdalene Abbey. You and several others shall come with me. Perhaps even Margot will want to come, for the abbey, I think, is known for its leechcraft. Once we are there, well, I cannot promise that we can convince your father to speak with you. But we can try."

Hilde looked up with a face that glowed as brightly as the flame burning beside the altar.

"Oh my lady, truly?"

"Yes, but listen to me now. This is to be our secret. I will mention it to Hugh tonight, but you must act as if you know nothing about it. Can you do that?"

"Aye, my lady."

"Good. Now get you to the hall. They will be setting up the tables soon, and you will be missed."

Alone in the chapel, Emma pondered what she knew about Hilde's father. He was a man who had betrayed his own father and turned against his king. When forced to choose between Æthelred of England and Swein of Denmark for his lord, he had chosen Swein. Why? What had driven a man of honor to make that choice?

She thought that it might be worth her while to discover the answer to that question. Hilde was not the only one who might benefit from this visit to Magdalene Abbey.

That evening Elgiva listened with half an ear to Hugh's tedious, nightly recitation of Emma's schedule of visitors for the following day. It was only when Emma raised an objection that Elgiva paid closer attention.

"I wish a day of respite, Hugh," Emma said. "I have listened to the complaints and entreaties of so many lords in the last month that my head is crammed with them." Hugh began to object, but she raised a hand to silence him. "No, I will not be denied this. I require one day outside the city with only my ladies and a few guards to attend me. It need not be tomorrow or even this week, but it must be soon, and you must arrange it. So look to your schedule and tell me when it is to be."

Hugh named a day a week hence, and Emma nodded, satisfied.

Elgiva bit her lip. This was what her father's man had been waiting for weeks to hear.

Do not wait even a single hour, Alric had cautioned her. Yet she could not simply stroll out of the fortress, particularly at night, without being stopped and questioned. She might be able to bribe one of the porters to let her out of the hall, but then she would have to cross the grounds, where a hundred or more men were quartered in tents with guards posted all around. She would never even make it to the gates.

No. It would be fruitless to attempt it now. She would have to wait until the morning.

Long before first light, while the queen and her other attendants yet slept, Elgiva rose from the bed that she shared with Groa. Shivering in the chill darkness, she pulled on an old gray kirtle and a shawl, fastened Groa's headrail clumsily over her braided curls, snatched up the knife she used at table, and silently slipped from the queen's bedchamber.

Averting her face from the Norman guard, she mumbled a Frankish greeting to him—one of the few phrases that she knew. In the hall the servants were already scurrying about, setting the tables and benches in place for the day's first meal. Elgiva snatched a ewer from the high table. If anyone asked, she was drawing ale for the queen. But as she scurried down the steps of the great hall, no one paid her any attention.

At the foot of the stairs she set the ewer behind some wooden casks, then made her way along the edge of the narrow inner yard. Her route took her behind the clay ovens, already giving off a pleasant warmth and glow in the darkness, as the kitchen slaves fed kindling into their mouths. She passed the cook fires heating kettles filled with water for the queen's morning ablutions, rounded the dovecote, and arrived at the gate that opened into the *burh*'s outer grounds.

She stopped there, acutely aware that she would be out of place should anyone spy her in this bastion of armed men. But she decided that the predawn darkness, lit by only campfires and torches, would hide her if she moved quickly. Keeping her eyes down, she walked purposefully along the path that ran beside the fortress's outer walls, avoiding the soldiers' tents, stepping aside for men bearing buckets of water or loads of wood, and holding her breath as she passed the pits where a line of men stood pissing and genially cursing the cold and each other. No one spoke to her or even gave her a second glance. At the gatehouse she stepped up to the burly guard posted there.

"I am on an errand for the queen," she said, "and will return shortly." She placed a silver penny in his palm. "You will know me again when I return, and let me in?"

He leered down at her. "I won't forget your face, sweetheart. Sure you wouldn't like some company, to keep you safe?"

She dodged his groping hands with a wave. And who, she wondered, would keep her safe from him?

The inn lay ahead of her, across the road, and she made straight for its broad, oaken door, still shut fast against the night. On the threshold, she paused. She felt suddenly as if she were naked, unescorted as she was for the first time in her life. A thin thread of anxiety crept along her spine at the thought of entering, all alone, a place that might harbor the roughest breed of men. But if she were to find Alric and deliver her message, she had no choice.

A voice from behind her made her jump and snatch for the slender knife at her belt. And suddenly, there was Alric, his face registering surprise.

"I thought it was the crone who accompanies you everywhere," he said. "Came you alone from the fortress, my lady?"

"Never mind that," she snapped, still ill at ease in the darkness. "The queen goes riding one week from today, with only her ladies and a small escort."

"At last," he murmured. "And the queen goes to. . . ?"

"I do not know. She wishes to leave unremarked, and so is likely to ride out the north gate, as it is nearest the fortress. After that, I cannot say which direction she will choose."

She saw him glance quickly to his right, and she realized that the big fair-haired stranger who had been with him at the market stood in the deeper shadows cast by the eaves of the inn, close enough to hear their conversation. At a nod from Alric, the stranger slipped into the darkness.

"I want to know what is going on," Elgiva hissed. "I want to know who that man is, and I want to know what my brother is doing here in Exeter."

Even as she spoke he reached past her to knock at the inn door. It was opened by a boy she recognized as a servant of her brother's. Alric, with a firm hand at her back, urged her through the doorway.

"Tell my lord that his sister wishes to speak with him," Alric said. The boy sprang across the antechamber and disappeared behind a drapery.

"My brother is staying here?" she asked. They were standing in the screens passage of the inn, and she could hear a murmur of men's voices from the other side of the partition.

"Your brother and his retinue are making use of this inn," he said, pulling her to one side as a line of servants passed them with platters of bread and cold meats.

She was aware of Alric's hand, warm on her arm, and then he moved away from her as her brother stepped through the draperies.

Wulf must have been roused from his bed. He was lacing his breecs, he wore neither tunic nor shoes, and his eyes were heavy with sleep.

"You have brought me news?" he asked. Then he frowned. "Why did you come yourself, you little fool? What if you are missed?"

"The queen will not look for me until after morning prayers, when she sits down to break her fast."

He drew her into a chamber that was little more than an alcove, unfurnished but for a wooden chest and a rumpled bed. A pretty, dark-haired woman stared at Elgiva from the nest of bedclothes. Wulf tossed some coins to the whore and jerked his head. When she was gone, he turned to Elgiva.

"Tell me," he said.

While he pulled on a *smoc* and tunic, she repeated her news, and when she had told him all she grabbed his sleeve.

"What are you doing here besides whoring?" she demanded. "What is it that you and my father are planning? I have done all that has been asked of me, and I am weary of working in the dark for I know not what end. Tell me what is going on."

Wulf, scowling, shook her off. "My father does not confide in me."

"You must know something," she persisted.

"I have my suspicions," he said, "and nothing more."

"Tell me your suspicions, then."

"I will not," he barked. "The less you know of his schemes the safer you will be should anything go amiss."

Dear God! These men and their secrets maddened her!

She did not let him see her irritation, though. Wulf had ever been easier to persuade with honeyed words than with curses. Besides, he had a wicked temper, easily set off, and for the first time ever Groa was not here to protect her.

"Wulf," she said sweetly, following him as he crossed the chamber to snatch up his belt. "How am I to avoid danger if I know not where it lies?"

But her brother's patience suddenly snapped, and he turned and cuffed her with the back of his hand before she could dodge the blow.

She cursed him as tears stung her eyes, but he paid her no heed.

"Now," he said, grasping her arm, "you will shut your mouth and listen to me. Do not go with the queen when she leaves the city. Plead illness, faint, do whatever you have to do, but do not attend the queen. Wait for me to collect you at the fortress, be prepared for a long journey, and say nothing to anyone."

"But what will happen when the queen returns and finds me gone?"

"That is not your concern."

She opened her mouth to object, but he raised his hand again and she snapped her mouth shut.

He pushed her toward the door. "I have told you all you need to know! Now get back before you are missed!"

Snatching open the chamber door, he called for Alric. Moments later, ignoring her spate of questions and protests, Alric escorted her up the lane to the castle gate and left her there.

Furious at the ignoble treatment she had received, she glared after him as he strode away, but he never looked back at her. In the end she had no choice but to edge past the gatehouse guard and make her way to the hall, cursing all the men who ever lived as she went.

Chapter Twenty-three

August 1003

Exeter, Devonshire

On the first Monday in August the morning mist gave way to a day of heartbreaking beauty. High clouds scudded across a blue sky, blown like thistledown by a southern breeze that rippled the waters of the River Exe and danced over the canvas awnings of the market stalls. The church bells had just rung terce, the third hour after sunrise, when the queen and a small party rode out of the fortress gates and turned up the high street toward the north gate of the city wall.

Emma rode with a light heart, relishing the beauty of the day and the unlooked-for absence of Elgiva, who had complained of illness and begged to be excused. With Elgiva safely tucked up in the queen's bedchamber, this visit to Magdalene Abbey was likely to remain a secret. Aside from herself, only Hilde and Hugh knew where their road would lead them today, which did little to appease Hugh. Emma was still smarting from the tongue-lashing he had given her when she'd revealed her decision to take Hilde to meet her father.

"You are mad to go anywhere near the refuge of a known traitor," he had railed at her. "If the king discovers it—"

"The king will not discover it," she had insisted. "And even should he do so, we will have stumbled upon the abbey by chance during our ride. No one in the party, aside from you, Hilde, and me, will ever know that it was our destination from the outset."

"My lady," Hugh had said, gentling his voice and obviously trying another tack, "if you wish Hilde to meet her father, then send the girl with me. There is no need for you to go anywhere near Magdalene."

She had not argued with him, for he would not understand her own need to speak with Ælfgar—to try to understand what had turned Ælfhelm's son into a traitor.

"I will take Hilde to Magdalene Abbey," she had said, her tone final.

Hugh had thrown his hands up in frustration.

"Let me at least send a warning to the abbot. I know him, and I trust him. Perhaps he can find a way to keep your arrival at his gates from turning into a pageant that will draw gawkers from miles around."

This morning Hugh rode at the head of their party, with Wymarc at his side. Emma, riding just behind them with Father Martin, eyed the couple speculatively. Something had flowered between Wymarc and Hugh during this sojourn in Exeter, and Emma wondered if it might bear fruit in the months to come. Had there been a handfasting between them? Probably. And if Wymarc asked to remain in Exeter when the queen's household returned to Winchester, Emma did not know how she would bear it.

As she watched Hugh lean toward Wymarc, saying something that made her burst into laughter, Emma recalled the times that she and Athelstan had explored the paths outside of Winchester, Wymarc and Hugh riding ahead with the younger æthelings, well out of earshot. She did not know what had been said between the two of them on those occasions, but she guessed that it was similar to what had passed between herself and Athelstan. They had come to know each other's minds and hearts. It was then that he had taught her much of what she knew about the people and the history and the policies of the kingdom. She in turn had told him of Normandy, of her brother's ambitious plans for his duchy, and of the alliances he had forged, through his sisters, to bring them about.

No such intimacies had ever been shared between herself and the king. Their only bond had been that forged in the bedchamber, and by any standard of measure, it was a failure. Was it her youth that told against her? Would the king have sought her guidance had she been ten years older? She doubted it. Æthelred had married her for policy only, had borne his marriage to a foreign bride as he would a noxious remedy against disease. He cared nothing for her counsel nor, in the event, for her person. She had come to England expecting to play the role of peaceweaver, to be a bridge between husband and brother. Yet the only communication that she had passed from one to the other had been her brother's outrage at the massacre of the Danes on St. Brice's Day and Æthelred's ominous warning to her brother regarding the alliance with Forkbeard.

How different her life would be now if Athelstan, and not his father, were king. How different this realm would be. There would have been no massacre of innocents, and folk would not now be living in terror of the Danish king's vengeance. They would have a king who was not afraid of shadows or rumors, or of his own sons.

Their road took them through several small villages, and eventually the track crested a long rise. From there Emma could see a wooden palisade that enclosed thatched buildings, an orchard, a garden laid out in neat rows, and, rising over all, the stone bulk of a small church. Beyond the settlement, fields of golden wheat undulated in the breeze. At the far edges of the fields two lines of dark figures moved slowly forward, and the tall stalks of wheat disappeared in their wake.

"Magdalene Abbey lies ahead of us, my lady," Hugh called out.

Emma glanced at Hilde, who rode with her eyes trained on the abbey walls, her face alight with hope. She wished now that she had found a way to speak with Hilde on this brief journey, to warn her that the upcoming interview with her father might not be all that the girl might wish.

Inside the abbey palisade they were met by two of the brothers, and Emma recognized one of them as the tall figure of the abbot who had been presented to her on the day that she had entered Exeter.

"Abbot Oswald," she said, "I hope you will not mind if we trespass on your hospitality for a little."

"You are most welcome, my queen," he said, with a low bow, "but I must ask your pardon for providing such a poor reception. We began the wheat harvest today, and every pair of hands is in the fields, so that only myself and Brother Redwald here are left to wait upon you."

And so, Emma thought, this clever abbot had emptied the abbey for her benefit so no word of her visit would escape its walls. She smiled at him, and at Brother Redwald, a short, thin fellow with a head as bald as a river stone, and who looked upon her with benevolent eyes set in a narrow face creased with age.

"I trust we shall not tax your resources too much," she replied. "My companions," she nodded toward Wymarc and Margot, "have a wish to explore your herbarium. As for myself, I have a mind to see the precincts where you care for the infirm."

"Brother Redwald knows every plant in our garden," the abbot said, "and can tell their names and uses in Latin, English, and French. The ladies will find him a willing guide."

The little monk led the two women down a path that ran between a fruit orchard and the long stone chapel of St. Magdalene.

Emma turned to Oswald. "How fares the Lord Ælfgar?"

"He is a man uneasy in mind and in body," he said. "This is his child?"

"This is Hilde," Emma said, "and she is eager to meet her father. But Hilde," Emma said, placing her hand upon the girl's shoulder and bending toward her, "I would speak with your father before you go to him. Can you be patient for just a little longer?"

Hilde nodded and remained with Hugh, while Emma followed Abbot Oswald through the abbey's deserted great hall, and then across a courtyard and into the guest chambers.

"I cannot promise that Ælfgar will speak coherently to you," he said as they walked, "or at all. I do not know what you wish from him, but you must understand that, although his body is weak, his will is strong, and, I regret to say it, malicious. Whatever you hope to gain from your converse with him, he is not likely to humor you."

"I understand," she said. "And his physical illness? What is it, exactly?"

"He was struck by the half-dead disease some months ago. There is a weakness on the left side of his body, so that he cannot lift his arm or his hand. It need not be a death stroke. I have seen others recover from it, especially if they are determined to fight off the bad humors and so return to their lives. But Ælfgar has no wish to live. Death offers him the only release that he will ever have, and he weakens more with each day that passes."

Emma knew this sickness. It had struck her father's steward so that he had been unable to speak or move. In spite of all that the best physicians could do, he had died within a week.

"Is his speech impaired?"

"He can speak, but at times we cannot comprehend him." He paused at a closed door, his hand upon the latch. "Are you ready?"

But Emma placed her hand over his. "While I speak with Ælfgar, would you do what you can to prepare Hilde for her interview with her father? You, more than anyone, can help her understand his illness and what she will be facing when she meets him."

"I will, my lady," he said.

"Go then," she told him, "and I shall beard the dragon in his den."

Ælfgar's chamber was somewhat larger than a monk's cell, and the hangings that draped the walls were plain and unadorned. A blind man, she reflected, had little need of visual distraction. A curtained bed faced her from the opposite wall, flanked by stools on either side, one of which held a small tray with a clay flagon and cup. A single, narrow window opening, its oak shutter flung wide, overlooked the orchard, and the summer-scented breeze filled the room with the fragrance of ripening apples.

As she stepped farther into the room, Emma could see clearly the ravaged face that lay pillowed within the shadows of the bed. The scarred eye sockets had sunk so deep that Ælfgar's head looked skull-like, and the gray hair and beard added to the impression of one already long dead. Bolstered by pillows and wrapped in furs in spite of the pleasant warmth of the day, he gave no sign that he had heard her enter. Emma thought that for the rest of her life, the scent of apples would bring to mind the wasted face before her.

"God's blessing upon you, Ælfgar," she said in greeting. "I am called Emma."

He did not answer her, and she gazed at the eyeless, lidless face in some consternation. How could one tell if such a man slept or woke?

She went over to the bed and pulled the stool close to it. It grated harshly upon the floor, and still Ælfgar did not move. Emma sat down and gazed at him. She was uncertain what to say next. It would be a fruitless conversation if she were the only one to engage in it.

"I have brought your daughter, Hilde, here to the abbey," she said, "because she wishes to see you. But I desire some speech with you before you meet with her." She studied the immobile face—the straight, thick, white brows above the scarred tissue that had once been his eyes, the seamed forehead and creased cheeks, the blue-white pallor of the skin, the mouth that drooped on one side in a permanent grimace. It was the face of nightmare, and her throat constricted with horror and pity. "I know that you do not wish to talk with me," she began, and then stopped as one side of his mouth twisted into a sneer.

"Are you so vain that you think you can read what is in my mind?"

His voice sounded like stone grating upon stone, and his breathing came labored, as if a hand grasped him at the throat. But there was no mistaking his words, slurred as they were, nor the language he had used. He had spoken to her in a queer mixture of English and Danish.

Was this what the abbot had meant when he said that Ælfgar might be incoherent? To one who did not know both languages it would sound like so much guttural nonsense.

"I cannot see into your mind," she replied in Danish. "If I could, I would have no need to speak with you at all, would I?"

Something close to a laugh emerged from the thin lips, but they did not smile.

"Does the king know that his queen speaks the language of his enemies?"

Emma did not answer him. Æthelred did not know that she could speak her mother's tongue. She had guarded that secret from all save Athelstan.

"So, lady," he said into the silence, "my father has told me much about you, but what I cannot grasp is what it is you want of *me?* Surely more than just to gaze upon your husband's handiwork."

Truly she wished that she did not have to look upon that ruined face; and the knowledge that Æthelred was responsible for such injuries was a grotesque reminder of just how brutal a king's justice could be.

"I wish to understand why you betrayed your king and pledged yourself to Swein Forkbeard," she said.

He grunted. "Why do you think, lady?" he asked. "I chose the better man."

She frowned. "And how did you make that choice?" she asked. "What did you know of either man?"

"Oh, I knew Æthelred well enough," he spat. "We were raised together, he and I, for we were nearly of an age. I am older by barely a year."

Emma started at this. She had never thought of her husband as young, but compared to Ælfgar, with his grizzled hair and wasted face, Æthelred was vigorous and strong.

"I was fostered at King Edgar's court," he went on, "and there I did Æthelred's bidding. I waited upon him, played whatever game he chose, even studied from the same books. When the ætheling was caught at some mischief, it was I who took the beating. King Edgar never knew about that; it was the queen's doing. She would not have her darling touched." He sneered again, an expression made even more sinister by his ruined face. "I complained to my father, but it was ever Æthelred who came first with him. When the old king died, it was my father to whom Æthelred turned for guidance. And when King Edward met his death, it was my trusting father who swore that Æthelred could have known nothing about it, even though I told him otherwise."

Emma's heart lurched. Here was something she had dreaded and feared.

"Aelthered was just a child," she whispered. "Surely he would not have been part of the plot to kill Edward."

"Ah, but he knew about it. Had he so wished he could have found a way to warn Edward. But he did nothing, because he feared his mother. He confessed as much to me, after it was all too late. And so Æthelred was crowned king, and thus he learned the price of a crown. He learned the price of everything, that one, for he is cunning when it comes to silver. Did he not purchase my own father's love and loyalty with gifts of land and power? Has he not bought peace from the Northmen, again and again? But he is accursed, as are all who follow him. Aye, Æthelred purchased himself a crown, but that does not make him a true king."

She closed her eyes. Æthelred may indeed be cursed, but unlike Ælfgar, she could not bring herself to lay the blame for the murder of a king at the feet of a child. Nor did she trust Ælfgar in his assessment of his own father. She knew Ælfric as a man of honor and generosity. Yes, he was loyal to Æthelred, but it was out of honor, not greed. And she had witnessed his love and grief for Ælfgar with her own eyes.

She looked again at the wretched face before her, and she could not blame him for his hatred. Æthelred had done this to him, and in pleading for his son's life, Ælfric had condemned him to a living death.

"If Æthelred was no true king, then why did you fight for him at Maldon?" she asked.

"I did not fight for Æthelred; it was Byrhtnoth's banner that we followed into battle. A great warrior that man was, and a leader of men. Yet the king should have been there. It should have been Æthelred whose body they hacked to pieces until the water below the causeway ran with his blood. The king was young and vigorous, with but twenty-four summers to his life's tally. Yet he sent an old man to face the Viking onslaught." The right half of his mouth twisted again. "Æthelred ever held his own life too dear to risk it in battle."

Emma said nothing, but she shook her head. Ælfgar's loathing for

Æthelred made him ignore the realities of kingship. If it had been the king who had been killed at Maldon, what would have happened to the realm? In that year Æthelred's eldest son could have been no more than a babe. If an infant had been placed upon the throne, the turmoil of a dozen years before that had led to King Edward's murder would have begun all over again. Whatever Æthelred's sins, and they were probably many, failure to wield a sword at Maldon was not one of them.

"Tell me what you know of Swein," she asked, for that was truly what she wished to hear.

"You would know your enemy, would you?" he asked, his voice weakening with the effort to speak. "Then you are wise, Emma, queen of England, for one so young."

He paused, breathing heavily, and she placed her hand upon the useless, crippled claw that lay upon the furs.

"I have wearied you," she said. "Forgive me. Rest a while, and we will speak again later."

"Nay, I would tell you what you wish to know, for my daughter's fate lies in your hands." He drew in a heavy breath. "I sailed with Swein and fought beside him, and I know him for a fearless, able leader who combines courage with honor. He understands men, and he knows how to rule them." He paused to gather breath again. "What's more, Swein turns to his nobles for counsel and weighs their words before he acts. Unlike King Æthelred, who listens to no one."

That criticism of Æthelred rang true. She would be the last person to deny it.

"Is King Swein," she asked slowly, "as ruthless as Æthelred?" She had already formed her own opinion about that. Swein had won his crown in a fierce battle against his own father. But she wanted to hear Ælfgar's reply.

"Every king is ruthless. It is the only way to rule. But Swein tempers it with justice. And for that reason, lady, he will not rest until his sister and those Danes who died by Æthelred's command on St. Brice's Day have been avenged. All in England will live to regret that foul deed." He lifted his good hand, index finger raised. "Mark me. Swein will sweep across this land like a storm of fire, destroying all who oppose him until he wears England's crown. And one thing more you should know: There will be many in the north of England who curse Æthelred and will welcome Swein." He dropped his hand and struggled to breathe.

Emma felt as if Death himself had spoken to her. She stared at the face upon the pillow, the mouth a rictus now as he gasped for breath. Was he right that Swein would be welcomed by folk in the north? If that were true, then if Swein loosed his armies upon England, the forces of two ruthless kings would face each other, and this land would be awash with blood.

She rose, went around the bed, and poured water from the flagon into the cup. She would have held it to his mouth, but when he sensed her beside him, he took the cup himself.

"Because I am Æthelred's queen," she said softly, gazing bleakly toward the light that streamed through the window, "those who curse the king will curse me as well." She was oath-bound to him; there was no escape, no matter what the future held.

"If you are wise, lady, you will get back to your brother's land while you still may. And when you go, take my daughter with you, for she will find no safety here."

"You would have me be an oath breaker?" she asked.

"Why not? You will be just one among many, I warrant."

Why not?

Because, she told herself, I am a queen. And to break my pledges to my king, whatever his weaknesses and sins, would destroy my honor and make my life, like this one, a living death.

The sun was well past its highest point in the sky when the queen's party set out for Exeter, accompanied by Brother Redwald, who promised to show Margot a patch of betony where she could replenish her dwindling supply. Father Martin and Hilde elected to remain at the abbey, for Hilde wished to stay with her father until the queen was ready to return to Winchester.

As they rode, Emma's mind ran upon all that Ælfgar had told her. He had spoken what he believed to be the truth, but how clear was Ælfgar's vision, warped as it was by his loathing of Æthelred? That enmity was so palpable that she felt it still, like a caustic upon her skin. He had nursed it for ten years, until it had all but consumed him. And Æthelred, she thought, must be consumed by fear of enemies such as Ælfgar.

How many enemies were there?

Surely Swein of Denmark was one of them, and he was just as ruthless as Æthelred of England. Ælfgar's insistence that Swein would not rest until he had taken England's crown for his own was something she could well believe, and in light of it, she weighed Ælfgar's advice. *Return to your brother now*, he had told her. Yet she could not abandon England. On the day of her wedding and coronation she had been given two rings: one bound her to the king and the other bound her to England, and to her duties as queen. She could not, in honor, forsake them.

For now she could only hope that Ælfgar was wrong in his estimation of Swein's might. That Swein would come she had no doubt. Athelstan, too, had said that it was merely a matter of time, and she had the uneasy feeling that time was running out. Still, it would take a great deal of wealth, of men and arms and ships, to wrest a throne from England's king. Had Swein so much wealth? Silver had, indeed, flowed from the towns and abbeys of England to Danish longships and so across the northern seas, but it would take a great deal of it to launch so ambitious an enterprise.

Or perhaps, she thought, it would take only the promise of silver. Swein had but to swear to his followers that great wealth awaited them at the end of the ships' road, and they would willingly follow him.

Lost in such dismal thoughts she paid little heed to the road and the passing miles. They were well beyond the abbey lands when Brother Redwald halted the company in a narrow valley between two hills. Ahead the road curved sharply to the left, and out of sight.

"The patch of betony lies on the far side of this hill," Brother

Redwald said, nodding to the hill on their right. A narrow track, only just visible through a break in the thick hedgerow that lined the road, led up the slope.

"Go with him then," Emma said to Margot and Wymarc, "and gather your precious crop." She looked behind her to where, some little way back, the branches of oaks formed a canopy over the lane and provided some shelter from the sun. "We shall await you in the shade there."

As the little monk and the two women urged their horses onto the track, Emma and the others turned back to the relief of the shade. The queen dismounted, and Hugh signed to the six guards to dismount as well. As Emma walked, stretching her legs, he handed her a flask of water.

"I fear," he said, "that your interview with Hilde's father was not a happy one."

She took a long pull from the flask and returned it to him. She did not wish to speak of Ælfgar's dire predictions. The weight of responsibility for the folk who had accompanied her from Normandy suddenly felt heavy upon her shoulders. How was she to protect them from Swein's fury when he struck against this land like a hammer upon an anvil? No one, she thought, would be spared. It seemed hard to her that she should have to face such a fate. And the question that raised itself now was whether her brother had suspected that such an event would occur. *You have the strength,* her mother had said. Was the coming conflict the reason why she and not her sister had been chosen to wed Æthelred?

"I thought," she said to Hugh, "when I was sent to this land to be its queen that I was coming as an offering of peace. I begin to fear that I was sent as sacrifice, and that my brother knew it."

She felt Hugh's eyes upon her, as if he were trying to read what was in her mind.

"Ælfgar spoke to you of Swein, did he not?"

She nodded, her eyes focused on the trees whose branches arched overhead, shutting out the sky.

"No man, my queen, can read the future, I think," he said. "Not Ælfgar, not your brother, not my lord Athelstan, not even the bishops who warned us of apocalypse some while back, and who were proved so wrong in their reckoning. The true prophet says *be not afraid*, and to his word we must cling. After," he said with a wry smile, "we have made certain that our city walls are strong and our swords are sharp."

His smile disappeared suddenly, and he raised a hand. Emma heard then the sound that he had already caught—men and horses coming toward them but hidden from their view by the sharp bend in the lane ahead and the thickets that edged the road.

"To horse, my lady," Hugh said, swiftly helping her to mount.

The guards, too, sprang to their saddles, and even as they surrounded Emma with drawn swords, a cart pulled by two horses and escorted by mounted riders, two in front and two behind, rounded the base of the hill and came briskly toward them, their speed assisted by the downward slope of the road. The foremost rider, a tall, dark-haired man in a green cloak, called out to his companions and reached for the bridle of one of the cart horses to halt them just at the entrance to the tunnel-like patch of shade where Hugh stood, his sword a bright shimmer in his right hand.

"My lord," the lead rider said to Hugh. "What's amiss? We are honest folk, not ruffians that you need draw your sword. Rarely do we meet anyone along here. It is lucky that you have no cart yourself or we should all be in a fine fix." He pursed his mouth, studying the width of the lane. "I fear we cannot go back, but if you string your mounts in single file along the side of the lane, I think you could get by us. Shall we try it?"

Hugh studied the problem for a moment, eyeing the road and the width of the cart. It seemed to Emma that there was little else they could do, for at this spot the hedgerows were too thick to allow the horses to break through in order to clear the road, and the last crossroads that she remembered was a good way behind them. The cart, which looked to be heavily laden, its mounded cargo covered by leather tarps, its wheels firmly embedded in the ruts of the lane, could go in only one direction—forward. Hugh, apparently coming to the same conclusion, nodded.

Emma's hearth troops sheathed their swords, and Hugh led them to the side of the narrow lane. Emma, nudging Ange into line behind Hugh's roan, noticed that none of the men in the other party had given her the merest glance but kept their eyes focused on her guards. This struck her as odd, for she was used to being stared at by the country folk as if she were some divine apparition from heaven. Still, she was dressed plainly today, she told herself, dismissing her apprehension as she edged her horse carefully past the wagon and then the horsemen. She had nearly cleared the last outrider when he reached out and snatched her reins. He tugged hard, almost pulling the reins from her hands, and she shouted in surprise and fright.

Ange reared, but the man hung on, and Emma could not get her mount free of him. She saw Hugh draw his sword and come back to aid her. Then, as her mount reared again, dancing and turning in terror, Emma saw three armed men erupt from beneath the tarps of the wagon. They set upon her Norman guards, who, caught between the wagon and the hedgerow, were unable to maneuver their horses.

Emma felt, rather than saw, the fierce grip on her reins momentarily slacken. She wrenched her horse away as Hugh shouted, "Fly, lady!" She kicked Ange sharply, and the mare flew up the lane and away from the maelstrom of horses and men.

Ahead of her on the right the steep track that Wymarc and the others had taken led off from the main road, but Emma ignored it. If she was pursued she did not wish to lead these men to the old monk and the two women. Instead she followed the road, taking its curve at a frantic pace. As the lane climbed upward she continued to spur her horse, confident that she could easily put some distance between herself and any pursuers. When she reached the top of the rise and saw three horsemen riding swiftly toward her, she felt a flash of relief. Surely they would help her. She slowed Ange, preparing to sue for assistance, when something familiar about the foremost rider made her breath catch in her throat.

She knew him, and she knew now that the riders coming toward her would offer no succor.

She wheeled her horse around, looking wildly for some way of escape. The hedges that lined the road, though, made a barrier that only a rabbit or squirrel could penetrate. Her only hope was to make it back to the hedge break and the narrow track that Wymarc and Margot had taken over the hill. Yet even as Ange obeyed Emma's unspoken command, dashing back the way they had just come, two horsemen rounded the curve of the lane. One of them was the man in the dark green cloak, and Emma knew that she was lost.

Once again she reined in her horse and reached forward to pat the sweating, shivering animal, and to whisper words of encouragement. Then slowly she swung her mount back around to face the three men who had blocked her escape. She found herself staring into the piercing black eyes of Swein Forkbeard.

Chapter Twenty-four

August 1003

Exeter, Devonshire

Elgiva paced the queen's bedchamber, back and forth, from window to bed, nervous and impatient. She was eager to be gone, to quit Exeter as Wulf had promised, but her brother, curse him, had not yet come to fetch her. It was long past the appointed time.

"Where is the fool?" she demanded of Groa, who did not look up but continued to hem a length of red silk that spilled across her lap like blood. "Likely he is dallying with that whore of his. What am I to do if the queen returns? How am I to explain all of this?"

She gestured toward Emma's bed, where a small casket and three satchels held the belongings that Groa had packed for their journey.

"He will come," Groa replied, so irritatingly calm that Elgiva wanted to throttle her.

Silently she cursed the old woman for being so maddeningly placid, and cursed Wulf for keeping her waiting like this. She wanted to howl with frustration, but at that moment a sudden, sickening thought struck her. What if something had gone wrong? What if her father's schemes had been discovered, and the king's men had taken her brother?

A wild shout from outside that was taken up by other voices and repeated over and over drew her quickly to the window, her heart in her throat for fear that she would see her brother in chains. Instead she saw men in the yard below dashing toward the fortress gates, pulling on helmets as they ran. Their mail glinting in the bright sun, they struggled to make their way out of the stronghold through waves of panicked citizens, who were trying just as desperately to get in. Some of the townsmen carried swords. Women were burdened with children and bundles.

In the great hall someone began to scream so piercingly that Elgiva's flesh puckered. Other screams joined the first, one after another, like geese sounding an alarm at the sight of a predator, and she placed her hands over her ears to block out the noise. Groa had risen and stood with her now at the open shutter, the scarlet silk forgotten as it fluttered to the floor.

On a distant hill a warning beacon sent smoke upward in a straight column through the still, blue air. From this vantage Elgiva could not see the city walls or the river, but there was no need. Only one thing could cause this kind of panic.

The Danes had come at last, and Exeter was under attack. Whatever her father's plans might have been, they were in ruins now.

She thought of Emma, safe outside the city with her Norman reeve. Hugh would see the beacons and guide the queen to some place of refuge, while she, who had thought to escape this wretched city today, was as likely as not to die here within its bloodred walls.

Æthelmær's Manor, near Exeter, Devonshire

Athelstan sat at table in the great hall of his father's thegn Æthelmær. He had come to this gathering of nobles of the western shires with some reluctance. Æthelmær, though, had been adamant that he meet with these men, insisting that as the heir to the throne and to numerous royal lands in the counties of Devon and Somerset, it would be to Athelstan's advantage to foster ties to the men who would one day serve him.

"The king concerns himself with affairs in Winchester and London,"

Æthelmær had said, "yet he is king of Exeter and Totnes, of Lydford and Dorchester as well. To have some commerce with the eldest ætheling can only solidify support for the throne."

And so two days ago he had journeyed here, to this pleasant manor an hour's ride north of his own extensive lands at Norton, and with every passing moment he became more ill at ease. It was not just that he disliked being at such a distance from Exeter while the danger from Danish raiders was still so high, although that was unsettling enough. But there was an undercurrent of dissatisfaction among these men and at the same time an effusive deference toward him that he found discomfiting.

The final, midday feast of the gathering had been consumed, and the men at the tables were drowsy with food and drink. The *scop* had taken his place in the center of the room and had begun to sing a tale that each of the listeners, Athelstan guessed, knew well. It was an old saga rarely recited in its entirety at one sitting. Today the *scop* began not at the beginning of the tale but at the description of an aging, joyless king who waged war against a mortal enemy. Then, clearly with some plan in mind, the singer slowed his rhythm and skipped ahead to the lines that introduced the brave hero of the tale. With a throbbing intensity he sang of the men who urged the young warrior to lend his aid to the ineffective king. And as the *scop* recited the verses that told of Beowulf's determination to assume control of the battle against the monstrous foe, Athelstan felt the force of a dozen pairs of eyes trained upon him.

Not a word had been spoken about his father's inability to protect the land from the ravages of the Northmen, or of the crippling taxes that the men at Æthelmær's table paid in geld to buy off the Viking raiders. Nevertheless, here in this hall he was surrounded by the most powerful of the nobles in the southwest, and this particular section from the old poem was a thinly disguised entreaty that he assert his authority against an aging father.

Point taken, Athelstan thought. And if he should act upon this appeal and challenge his father for the throne, would these same men support his claim against a father and king who would cling to his crown with all the sinewy strength of the fabled monster? Would they have the courage to follow the son, in spite of the oaths they had made to his father?

A stir at the bottom of the hall drew his attention, and he saw one of Æthelmær's retainers sprinting toward the dais.

"The beacons have been lit, my lords," he cried, even before he reached the high table, "coming from Exeter."

It was as if he had thrown a fireball into their midst. The hall came suddenly alive with chaotic movement and sound as men overturned benches and shouted for servants or bellowed for their mounts. Athelstan, who had eaten little and drunk even less, thrust his way through dozens of reeling men. With his own cohort at his heels he ran to the stable to find that their horses had already been saddled and bridled. Within a matter of minutes they were riding toward Norton where, he planned, he would gather the rest of his men and ride to join in the defense of Exeter. And as he rode he whispered a fervent prayer that Hugh had already sent Emma north and far out of harm's way.

Near Magdalene Abbey, Devonshire

Emma glared at the man who faced her from astride one of England's sturdy, native horses. Garbed in a tunic of finely woven scarlet linen, his deep brown cloak trimmed with martin fur and clasped at the shoulder by a silver brooch, her captor could pass easily for a well-to-do English thegn if one did not know that thin face. She knew it, and she knew, too, the thick white fall of hair and the pure white beard, forked and braided.

Did he recognize her? Had she stumbled somehow into a Danish force making its way inland and scouring the byways for mounts and treasure? She tried to steady her breathing, to still her trembling hands, even as she fingered the thin silver knife at her belt.

"Tell the queen," Swein Forkbeard ordered in Danish, "that she will not be harmed."

So he knew her, and this meeting was no accident. She schooled her face to blankness as the rider in the green cloak, who came from behind her to tear her reins from her hands and to snatch away the slender knife at her belt, spoke to her in the Frankish tongue, repeating Swein's assurance of her safety.

This was a planned attack then, and one carried out with ruthless efficiency. That they apparently had no awareness of her knowledge of Danish was to her advantage though, however small an advantage it might be. She kept her eyes focused on Swein, but she spoke in Frankish to his lackey.

"My brother once showed you great courtesy, Swein Forkbeard, in his bannered hall at Fécamp," she said. "I demand that you release me for love of my brother Richard. I am not your enemy."

Swein listened to the translation, and then replied, "Nay, my lady, you are no enemy. But you are, nevertheless, a very great prize. We shall see how much your king will pay to redeem you. Speaking for myself, I would give at least half my kingdom for the safe return of a bride such as you."

He smiled at her, waiting to see if she would respond to his courtesy. Emma listened to the translation but gave no reply. Would he be so bold as to demand half a kingdom as her ransom? And, indeed, if he were to do so, what would Æthelred's answer be?

She had little time to ponder the question. Swein himself snatched her reins and led her horse back toward the spot where her Norman guard had first been attacked. Another rider took his place close upon her left side, and she realized that he was no man but a tall, skinny boy, perhaps twelve or thirteen years old. His mane of red hair had been tied back with a thong, exposing a high, broad forehead above enormous eyes that were the same dark hue as Forkbeard's. They met her own, appraising her with a solemn gravity that made her question her own assessment of his youth. She recalled how Swein had bragged to her brother about his sons. This, then, must be one of them. Apprentice murderer and brigand. His father would teach him, firsthand, the thrill of savagery. Or perhaps he already knew it. Likely this one had been riding the deck of a longship since first he learned to walk. No wonder he had already acquired an aura of experience and command.

They rounded the curve of the lane and Emma's gorge rose as the metallic reek of blood struck her like a wave. Knowing that a greater horror was coming, she steeled herself against it. She could not afford to show a woman's weakness before these men. As they drew nearer to the place where the trees shaded the lane, she clenched her jaw tight to keep from crying out.

The men of her hearth troop—six Normans who had sailed with her across the Narrow Sea—had been butchered like cattle. Stripped of their armor and weapons, their bodies, bathed in gore, had been thrown into the bed of the cart.

Hugh, she saw with a mixture of relief and apprehension, still lived. What fate worse than death, she wondered, awaited him? He sat on the verge of the lane, the right side of his body drenched in blood, his hands trussed in front of him. One of the Danes knelt beside him, staunching a wound on Hugh's sword arm and wrapping it with a strip of linen.

"Don't want you to bleed to death before you get us into the fortress," she heard him grunt in Danish. The other men, busily garbing themselves in the byrnies and helms of her Norman guard, gave a shout of appreciative laughter.

She saw Hugh's gaze focus first on her and then on Swein, and she did not miss her reeve's sudden jolt of recognition. Yes, he would know Swein. Hugh had been at Fécamp when the Danish king had descended upon them that Christmas. Hugh's eyes slid to hers again, but she looked away. She could not bear to see the fury and the frustration in his face. This was her fault, for insisting on leaving the fortress with such a small guard. Her fault, but all of them would have to pay the price.

She wanted to search the hill for signs of Wymarc and Margot, but she did not dare. She prayed that they were safely hidden, and that they would stay that way. She did not like to think what Swein, who was out to avenge the brutality visited upon his sister and her family, would do to them if they fell into his grasp.

"How many losses?" Swein demanded.

"One, sire. Sigurd. He died well."

"He would have done better to live. We need every man. Leave the wain behind," Swein ordered, "and make haste to Exeter. The ships will already have been sighted, I'll warrant, and the beacons lit." He nodded toward Hugh. "Can he ride?"

"Aye, my lord," he said. "Halfdan! Help me get this piece of carrion on to his horse."

Once Hugh was mounted, Swein drew up beside him so that the two men faced each other.

"There is a hidden entrance into the fortress at Exeter," Swein said, while the man cloaked in green translated his words into Frankish. "You will lead these men into the city through that secret gate."

Emma kept her face passive, but her mind worked feverishly. So that was why they had spared Hugh. Exeter fortress—so well fortified, so painstakingly prepared by Hugh and Athelstan to withstand any assault by the Danes—might be taken with relative ease if even a small band of men made it inside and managed to open the gates to the larger force without the walls. Swein must have had spies in Exeter who had ferreted out the secret of *la posterle*.

Hugh said, "The passage you speak of is locked from within."

"Locks can be broken," Swein said, grinning. "Sometimes your God even works a miracle. Perhaps you will witness one." His smile disappeared. "Now, you will obey every order that these men give you. If I learn that you betrayed them by word, by deed, or by even the briefest glance, your queen, although she will live to be ransomed, will not remain untouched. Do you understand?"

Hugh's mouth, bruised and bloody, twisted into a sneer. "Not even Swein Forkbeard would be mad enough to harm Æthelred's queen and Duke Richard's sister," he said, his voice ringing with scorn. "There would be nowhere in Christendom for you to hide from their revenge."

"Harm her?" Swein smiled again, this time a taunting leer. "Nay, I would do her no harm. But we might have some sport together, she and I. Do you not think that it would be a great joke if Æthelred were to ransom his wife only to discover that her womb was quick with my child?"

Emma felt the bile rise again in her throat, while Hugh responded by spewing a torrent of Norman curses at Swein.

"I am already lost!" she shouted to Hugh in the Breton that she prayed only he would comprehend. "Do not aid . . ."

Swein turned with lightning speed and cuffed her so hard across the face that her ears rang. Hugh, even bound as he was, lunged his mount at Swein, but two men dragged him off his horse, raining blows upon him until he was subdued. Emma watched it in shock and rage, only dimly aware of the taste of blood in her mouth.

"Halfdan," Forkbeard barked, "you and the boy will ride with me to Otter Mouth to take ship. The rest of you know what to do. Gisli, if the Norman survives these next few hours, bring him with you to the ships. We may have further use for him."

Then he was leading Emma past the wain with its grisly cargo. The boy and one other followed in their wake.

Her mind a blinding thicket of terror, anger, and dread, Emma strove to grope past the burning pain of it, to calm herself into stillness and rational thought. She knew where she was being taken—to Otter Mouth, he had said, where a ship would pick them up. The River Otter lay to the east, between here and the River Sid. She remembered crossing it on her journey to Exeter. It would likely take them many hours to reach the river's mouth.

Somehow she had to escape before they reached the waiting ship. She could rely on no one but herself, for help was unlikely. Even if by some miracle Hugh could slip away from his captors, he had little chance of organizing a rescue. Unless, she told herself, the garrison at Exeter defeated the Danes and somehow managed to burn all the ships. But such a feat was unlikely, and if even one ship escaped, it would make for Otter Mouth and Swein.

No, there would be no rescue.

Swein set them an even, steady pace. As they rode, Emma cast an appraising eye on her captors' mounts. Sturdy and well able to carry heavy loads, they would be neither as fast nor as well trained as Ange. She would have an advantage there if it came to a horse race. At the moment, as she rode between Swein and his son, her fingers clutching her reins while Swein kept a firm grip on the lead rope he'd tied to her bridle, she had little opportunity to make a dash for freedom. Nevertheless, they had a long way to go before they reached the coast. All she needed was a moment of inattention, a loosening of his grip.

And if she could not escape, then she would find a use for the knife, Athelstan's gift, that was wedged firmly into her boot.

She whispered three prayers to the Virgin—one for herself, one for the folk of Exeter, and one for all of England. But she kept her eyes open and her head up, looking for an opportunity to bolt.

A.D. 1003   This year was Exeter demolished, through the French churl Hugh, whom the Lady had appointed her steward there. And the army destroyed the town withal, and took there much spoil.

—*The Anglo-Saxon Chronicle*

Chapter Twenty-five

August 1003

Exeter, Devonshire

Elgiva felt her panic rising as she watched the terrified citizens of Exeter crowd into the fortress. They had been through this before, so they knew only too well what lay ahead if Exeter's defenses failed: pillage, rape, murder.

She flung herself away from the window. "I have to get away!" she cried to Groa. "I will not stay here to be raped and slaughtered by some brute of a Dane."

"Nay, my lady," Groa said, "I would kill you myself before I would let that happen."

Elgiva stared at her in horror. Groa's eyes burned like coals in her withered face, and Elgiva believed that the old woman would actually murder her if it came to that. She took no comfort in the knowledge.

Behind her the chamber door banged open, and she screamed. But it was Wulf who strode quickly into the room.

"There is no time to lose," he said, grabbing Elgiva by the arm and urging her toward the door. "Come. There are men and horses waiting for us outside the city."

"How are we to get through that mob in the yard?" Elgiva demanded, as Groa wrapped a cloak about her.

"We cannot. There is another way out of the fortress. Be quick!"

"Wait!" Elgiva snatched up the small casket that held her jewelry before Wulf herded her out the door with Groa close on their heels.

Wulf led them into the great hall, clearing a way through the dense tide of women and children seeking shelter. The poor wretches, Elgiva thought, were looking for some corner where they could hide. This would be their last refuge from the Danes, this bastion perched atop the massive red mound that overlooked the city.

Even as she followed Wulf's lurching progress around knots of frightened townsfolk, and past mail-clad men who were trying to organize order out of the chaos, Elgiva shuddered. She could not have stayed here, her back against a wall while Vikings launched themselves against the city below. There would be no way to even gauge the course of the battle except by the sounds of fighting, and if the tide should turn against the defenders, there would be no escape. Death would come rolling into the hall with the sickening inevitability of a massive wave from the sea.

At the bottom of the stairs, Wulf turned sharply through one of the three broad archways of the undercroft, and then he stopped. Although it was dim within the cavernous space, there was enough light to see that the storeroom was filled to overflowing.

Over the past weeks the landholders all around Exeter had paid their farm rents to the queen. Elgiva could make out a pen where a dozen sheep had retreated, cowering, to a far corner. They shuddered and bleated in pitiful alarm—not unlike the terrified women upstairs, she thought. Directly in front of her, stacked end on end almost to the ceiling beams, stood casks of all sizes that likely held wine, salt, honey, or hard cheese. Nearby lay piles of sacks filled, she guessed, with wheat and barley. Next to them she could see ropes made of oiled leather, carefully coiled and neatly piled, and next to them bales of wool rising nearly to the rafters. In front of the wool a score of boxes held beeswax candles as long as her arm, and twice as thick.

"Where are we to go now?" she asked.

"There is a passage through the northern wall," Wulf said. "It is here, somewhere in this storeroom."

He darted forward, but Elgiva did not move. The reek of sheep dung and wool assailed her nose and her eyes. She watched as Wulf wedged himself between the casks and the stacks of grain, stamping his feet on the wooden planking of the floor as he went.

"It has to be underneath us," he said.

"But it could be anywhere," Elgiva protested. Groa was making her way among the boxes of candles, grunting as she heaved them aside to peer at the floor. "What if it is beneath the casks or buried under the bales of wool? There is no time to move all of that." Shouts and screams continued to shatter the air, and she set the jewel casket on a box so that she could put her hands over her ears to block out the sounds of panic.

"Emma's reeve is no fool," Wulf said, coming to stand next to her and turning with a frown to survey the vast chamber. "The door will be hidden but not inaccessible."

Elgiva followed his gaze to where the sheep cowered and bleated.

"The sheep?" she asked, incredulous.

"The sheep," he replied, with a curt nod. He glanced around and snatched up an empty sack that lay in a corner by the archway. Then he vaulted over the low wattle fence that hemmed in the flock, terrifying the already panicked sheep and scattering them. Their temporary paddock had been thickly strewn with straw, and as Wulf walked along the back wall of their enclosure, he swept the filthy stuff away with his boot. But there was no sign of an entrance to a passage.

Undeterred, he started along the west wall. After a few steps he crouched and used the sacking to clear a space in front of him, revealing a large iron ring. Half standing, he pulled at the ring, and a segment of the wooden floor rose.

It was made of thick oak, far too heavy for one man to lift alone. Elgiva, following Groa's lead, scrambled over the fencing and into the paddock as Wulf uncovered a second iron ring. Together, straining, they managed to lift the flooring away.

In front of them, a flight of stairs led downward into darkness.

Elgiva stared into the hole and froze. The old terror of small, dark spaces clawed at her like some feral beast. She could not go down there. If she went into that black maw, the earth would swallow her, and she would never come out again. She would be trapped inside the belly of the mountain, unable to breathe, unable to see. She would die there, clawing at rock walls, gasping for air. It would be better to die at the hands of a Dane.

Wulf had darted out of the storeroom, and now he returned holding a torch. Groa had retrieved the jewel casket, and she held it out toward Elgiva.

"No," Elgiva said, shaking her head and pushing the casket away. "I am not going down there. There is no need. The raiders will be stopped. They will not come inside the city gates. Wulf, you will protect me, and we will all be safe."

But her brother grabbed her arm, holding it like a vise until she squirmed with the pain of it.

"I will not be here to protect you, Elgiva," he hissed, his face close to hers. "I am leaving, as our father ordered. Like it or not, you are coming with me."

Elgiva tried to back away from the yawning darkness at her feet, but Wulf held her firmly.

"Groa!" he barked. "Help me. We have to move!"

Elgiva felt Groa pushing her from behind, while in front of her, still grasping her wrist, Wulf took the first two steps down into the darkness.

"I am afraid," she wailed, trying to free her hand from her brother's grip.

"Breathe, my lady," Groa whispered in her ear. "You must take slow, deep breaths. Sit down on the top stair and let your brother guide you down into the passage. I will be right behind you. Nothing will harm you, I promise."

Still she resisted, staring at the narrow black hole and the walls that appeared to lean inward, while her brother tugged at her wrist.

"Elgiva," her brother said, his voice fierce. "Move now or I will take Groa and leave you behind!"

Groa placed a hand on her shoulder and whispered, "You must watch the torch, my love. Look at the light and nothing else."

Trembling and nauseated, she crouched and managed to sit down on the top step. She had to cover her mouth with her hand and work hard to swallow back the bile. Then she turned and grasped Groa's skirt.

"You won't pull the boards over the entrance behind you?" she asked Groa. "We can come back?"

"I cannot shut it, my lady," Groa assured her, "it is far too heavy. But there will be no need to come back, my love. There is daylight below, I promise. Look at the light, and follow your brother. There's a good girl."

Wulf yanked her arm again, pulling her down into the darkness. She tried to take a deep breath, as if she were going underwater, but her lungs refused to fill. Then she was into the passage, and she nearly gagged on the stench of mold and rot. With her free hand she groped the rough, slimy wall, trying to slow her plunge into the dark. Shying and halting, she pulled against her brother's grip, barely holding her panic at bay as he drew her inexorably down slippery, uneven stairs.

Wulf cursed her, urging her to go faster, while Groa's voice floated down from behind her like a constant waterfall, encouraging and coaxing her. But as she descended, resisting every step, the sound of their voices faded while the roar of her terror grew and echoed in her ears.

She tried to do as Groa bid her, to watch the torchlight. But its brightness in the dark hurt her eyes, and so she closed them against the pitiless glare. Then she saw a different space, smaller even than this endless tunnel, and darker, and she was a child again, on her back, unable to move or even to breathe. She could not bear it, and she opened her eyes to escape, and she was back in the tunnel, where Wulf was a shadow against the torch's flame.

The walls twisted to the left, and she could sense them moving, sliding closer together. She could hear the rock breathing, alive and malignant. It would not let them escape now that it had them in its throat. Why could the others not see it?

She could not catch even the smallest breath, and panic bloomed in her breast. She had to go back, to crawl if she must, but she had to get out into the open. Gasping, she wrenched herself free from Wulf's grip and scraped both hands against the wall, trying to turn around. Her foot slipped, and she fell sideways against him. There was a clatter, the walls trembled, and then with a hiss the world went black. The scream that had been building in her throat tore loose, and she screamed and screamed until a hand slapped her into silence.

"You little fool!" Wulf's voice was as hard as the stone of the walls. "I swear I will leave you here if you do not shut up and keep moving."

He clasped her wrist again and once more dragged her relentlessly downward. She was blind now, and whimpering, helpless against both her brother and her fear. The darkness, like the rock, was a living thing, its wings beating at her like a host of devils.

She was going to die here, and she did not want to die. She began to wail, and Wulf jerked her arm.

"Shut up!" His voice was a snarl, and again she was struck in the face, and then pushed so that her knees crumpled beneath her, and she slid down the wall. She crouched on the step, sobbing, cowering with terror. She heard her brother cursing and a sound like mice scrabbling, and she began to scream again. The rock was bearing down on her from above, trying to crush her, to grind her beneath it. She lifted her face, and the darkness drew the breath from her body like a succubus, its black mouth shaping itself implacably against hers. She tried to fight it, but it was too strong. Like a silent wave it engulfed her, and beyond that there was nothing.

Norton Manor, Devonshire

When Athelstan led his men into the manor courtyard he called for fresh mounts and news.

"My lord," said the groom who took his horse, "one of the queen's ladies rode in only moments ago, asking for you. She was in a terrible state, and they've taken her up to the hall."

Athelstan ran, fearing he knew not what. He had not yet reached the hall when he saw Wymarc hurrying to meet him. Her muddied gown and tangled hair spoke of hard riding, while the terror in her face hinted at something much worse. In a moment he had reached her, and he clutched her shoulders to steady her. She was trembling violently, and tears streaked through the dirt on her face.

"What has happened?" he demanded. "Are you hurt?"

"Not hurt," she said hoarsely. "Please, my lord, I must speak to you alone."

Her agitation infected him. He drew her away from the furtive glances of his retainers in the forecourt, busy with preparations for departure.

"The queen?" he asked, steeling himself for the reply. Emma must be dead. Wymarc would never have left her side otherwise. It came to him not as a thought but as a shadow, black as the mouth of hell, that darkened the whole world.

"They took her. I don't know how many. It was a trap, and we could not help her. He wants half the kingdom." Her voice rose as each phrase tumbled incoherently on top of the last in her urgency, and she began to cry. "You must get her back, my lord, quickly. He threatened to rape her. You must go now. No one else can help her. There is no time."

Athelstan shook her. "Who has taken the queen?"

She looked at him, mouth agape in confusion and terror.

"Forkbeard."

He stared at her in stunned disbelief. Not dead then, but at the mercy of a vengeful Forkbeard. The shadow that had fallen over him deepened.

He questioned her closely, aware of the passing of every precious minute. He called to a servant to fetch the monk who had accompanied her, and between them they told him what they had heard as they lay hidden in a tangle of shrubbery that lined the narrow defile where the Danes had attacked Emma's guards.

"You are sure that you heard him say the River Otter?" he asked Brother Redwald.

"I cannot be sure that he meant the river," the little monk said in dismay, "for he was speaking in the Northman's tongue. But I heard the word *otter*, or what sounded to me like *otter*."

Athelstan considered it. There was no question that Forkbeard would make for the sea, for it was his only escape route. He would likely have a ship waiting for him somewhere along the shore. The Otter Mouth was a likely choice. The bank of red cliffs that faced the sea there would be a familiar landmark to any shipman with a passing knowledge of the southern coast. And the shallow caves that dimpled the landward face of the high, narrow spit that bordered the Otter's eastern bank offered shelter and protection to anyone who might wish to escape the notice of folk living nearby.

And if Brother Redwald had misheard?

Then he would search for them in the wrong place, and Emma would be lost. She would be lost in any case if he did not get to her in time. He may already be too late, but he had to make the attempt.

"How many men?" he asked.

"Forkbeard and two others," the priest said. "All the rest went to Exeter."

Yes, that felt right. It would take few men to guard the queen if one assumed that no rescue would be attempted. Swein might have a surprise in store for him if he underestimated Emma, though. Jesu, he hoped she would not do anything that would bring her to even greater harm.

He gave orders swiftly, and his men responded as they had been trained to do, with efficiency, silence, and speed.

He turned to Wymarc who stood braced against the wall, huddled in her cloak, her face in her hands, a picture of despair.

"You will stay here until you receive word from me. Tell no one what has happened."

Within minutes he had sent a force of twenty men riding hard toward the besieged city and ordered a culver sent to the king with word of the attack on Exeter. He kept six men behind to protect the manor and the folk who had sought refuge there when the beacons were spotted. Then he mounted his horse, and with three close companions he rode like the wind for the mouth of the River Otter.

Exeter, Devonshire

Elgiva opened her eyes to find Groa peering down at her. The light was dim, but she could just make out, above Groa's head, roof beams and smoke-stained thatch. She lay on a filthy wooden floor with her head pillowed in Groa's lap. The mountain had not collapsed upon them, then. They had managed to escape from the tunnel that she had been certain would be their grave.

"What is this place?" she asked. There was a vague roaring in her ears, and she felt giddy. She could see little, for the room they were in had no window openings and no source of light other than what leaked in through the eaves of the roof.

"It is a storeroom next to the sword maker's forge outside the city walls," Groa said. "A hidden door there," she pointed to one wall, "leads to the tunnel."

Elgiva sat up. The world seemed to spin for a few moments, and she had to close her eyes and pull in several deep breaths, but then her head cleared somewhat. She twisted around, looking for the hidden door, but the wall of fitted planks was so well made and the lighting so poor that she could not make it out. The room held numerous wooden boxes filled with ingots of iron, bales of wire, and assorted implements that she could not name.

"Where is my brother?" she asked.

"He has gone outside to see if the way is clear. Drink this."

Groa placed a dripping cup in her hands. She took a few sips of the water, not at all certain that, sick and dizzy as she was, it wouldn't rise back up again. But she felt better afterward. A moment later the outer door opened and Wulf slipped in. She realized suddenly that the roaring in her ears, like the steady rush of ocean waves, was the distant shout and clamor of men.

"They are ransacking and burning the houses that lie outside the city walls," her brother said. "It will not be long before they make their way here. We have no time to lose."

He pulled Elgiva to her feet and picked up the jewel casket and thrust it into her hands. Then he led her toward the door and out into the light of late afternoon. She blinked at the brightness of it, and then Wulf was pulling her after him, running along a track that wound through the little settlement outside Exeter's northern wall. Groa followed behind.

Elgiva thought it strange to see cottage after cottage deserted and silent, as if this were a place inhabited by ghosts. Everyone must have fled to the shelter of the city walls or deep into the woods at the first alarm. But abandoned curs growled and snarled at them, and more than one felt the flat of Wulf's sword and scuttled away howling. At one spot they had to step over the body of an old man. Elgiva saw no sign of blood on the body. She wondered if he had died of fright. It was, as she could attest, a formidable enemy.

Finally they came to the end of the cottages, and her brother paused to scan the outer perimeter of the suburb—a wide swathe of meadow that she guessed was the site of a local market. Beyond it lay the forest.

"My men and the horses will be waiting for us among the trees, somewhere near the river," Wulf whispered to them. "Take a moment to catch your breath, and then we'll make a run for it."

Elgiva pulled in a breath, but the reek of smoke was strong. God, she wanted to be away from this place! But first they would have to cross that wide, open space. How long would it take to get across it at a run? If the raiders spotted them, they would be at their heels like hounds on a fox. Wulf would be able to hold out against them for only so long.

Her pulse throbbed in her head. The smoke was all around them now, billowing from the cottages that had been torched behind them, and next to her Groa leaned against the cottage's wooden wall, gasping and coughing. A shout from somewhere close by warned that the attackers were getting nearer. She felt a surge of panic. There was nothing of value in this settlement, nothing to distract or delay the shipmen. What if they found her, and took her? How would she save herself?

She could barter the jewels. No, they would simply take the jewels and kill her, or worse. She would offer them information, then. She could show them the hidden entrance to the fortress. Surely that was worth her life. And she would promise them silver. Her father would pay for her safe return, more than they could get if they sold her into slavery.

Wulf grabbed her hand.

"Now!" he whispered, nodding over her head to Groa. He pulled Elgiva with him as he darted into the open space.

Elgiva ran as fast and hard as she could, but her thick skirts hampered her, for Wulf clasped one hand and with the other she clutched the casket of jewels. Desperate, she yanked her hand out of Wulf's grasp so that she could pull the clinging linen away from her legs, and then she was able to run faster. She had her eyes on the trees at the edge of the field, though, not on the ground in front of her, and she missed her footing, sprawling on the tussocky grass. The little casket bounced and flew open, spewing brightly colored jewels. She got to her knees and began to gather them up, and it was then that she realized that Groa had lagged far behind her. Glancing back she saw that the old woman had halted, hands clasped against her chest as she struggled for breath.

Someone would have to help Groa or she would never make it across the field before the Danes spotted her. Elgiva looked at the jewels in her hands, at Wulf who ran on, unaware that she had fallen, at Groa so far behind, and at the cottage on the edge of the field where flames had begun to lick at the thatch.

She could not go back, it was too risky. Groa would not expect it. Groa would tell her to run, to save herself.

She got to her feet, clutched the jewels and her long skirts to her breast, and sprinted after Wulf.

When she reached the shelter of the forest he was there, panting from the run and shaking his head as he stared past her.

"Poor old bitch," he muttered. "She's in for it now."

She turned round.

Groa had dropped to her knees, and as Elgiva watched, two men appeared from behind the nearest cottage. They pounded toward the old woman, but Groa did not see them because her eyes were fixed on the trees where Elgiva and Wulf stood hidden in the forest shadow. The men were huge, tall and broad-shouldered, shirted in mail, their heads protected by skull-shaped leather caps. Each one bore a long-handled broadax.

When they reached Groa one of them gave her a brutal shove, so that she fell forward onto her hands. He tossed up her skirts and threw himself on her like a dog, thrusting and heaving. When he was done he drew aside and watched while the other took his turn.

It lasted only a few moments. Elgiva told herself that they would leave Groa alone now. Why shouldn't they? She was harmless, not worth the effort it would take to kill her. But when the second man had rolled off of her, the first one raised his ax high. In that single instant before the downward stroke, Elgiva saw the ax head glisten, bright as a jewel in the sun.

Devonshire

Emma's captors led her steadily southeast. Swein rode on Emma's right, the leading rope of her mount wound tightly around the pommel of his saddle. His son—Cnut, his father had called him—kept pace with her on the left, and the third man, Halfdan, brought up the rear. They had been riding for some time when Emma saw, in the distant western sky, an ominous pall of smoke. Slowly the black stain grew and spread until it devoured the sun, and Emma knew that the walls of Exeter must have been breached.

Swein's men would have found *la posterle* and opened the city gates, and the carnage that she had witnessed this afternoon in the narrow lane between the hills was now being repeated in the streets of Exeter. The bitter certainty of it kindled in her heart a burning rage toward the Danish king, an anger that was fueled to a white heat by her helplessness to do anything about it.

She never ceased looking for an opportunity to escape, but as the miles passed her despair grew. She would need a miracle to get away. Her captors kept close watch on her, and the boy, Cnut, seemed to never take his eyes from her.

She could not tell how far they had traveled, but as the sky grew steadily darker, they drew ever nearer to the coast. At the crest of a low hill Swein checked his horse and brought the company to a halt while he studied the horizon. She followed his gaze and saw that the road ahead of them continued almost due south, where a cloud bank marked the shore, she guessed, of the Narrow Sea. A second, narrower track led downhill to the left, through a small village and then across a sheep-strewn meadow, until it disappeared into a dense forest of pines.

She looked eagerly for anyone who might come to her aid, but it was as if the land had been swept clean of everything human. She guessed that with the lighting of the warning beacons folk had grabbed whatever valuables they could carry and had gone to ground like rabbits in a thunderstorm. They would be hiding now, waiting for the storm to pass. Whatever belongings they had left behind would be free for the taking.

Swein gestured toward the hamlet below the hill.

"There is likely food to be had in the village there," he said to his companions. "We may have a long night ahead of us, so go see what you can find. Be quick. I will go on ahead with the lady."

As the boy and the guard wheeled their horses toward the village, Swein urged his own mount down the southerly track, drawing Ange behind him. This, Emma realized, might be her best opportunity to get away. She eyed Swein's strong, sturdy figure. He was a formidable man, to be sure, but she deemed that skill and the speed of her horse would be in her favor, if she could but break away.

Still, she hesitated. If her attempt should fail, she would never get another. Covertly she studied the man while the sheath of the hunting knife tucked into her boot seemed to burn like a brand against her skin. She dared not attack him directly, for Swein—bigger, stronger, and better armed—would overpower her in a moment.

No, she thought as she worked out each move, she would have to rely upon the sharpness of her blade, on her own strength and quickness, and on the element of surprise. Swein would not expect her to attempt to flee, for in truth, she had nowhere to go. She could only trust to her horse to outrun her foe so that she could lose him in the forest. Still, that was better than whatever awaited her at the end of this road.

Her mouth went dry as she slowly eased her trembling hand down the side of her leg until she had the hilt of the knife in her grasp. Then, deliberately slowing her mount, she pulled the knife free with a quick, fluid move and slashed it through the taut leading rope. Swein, shouting, lunged for her, but she wheeled her horse to the left and widened the gap between them. Kicking the mare into a gallop, she bent her head to its neck, urging Ange toward the eastern road. Her Norman horse, pursued by Swein's more stolid mount, ran as if the devil himself was giving chase.

Chapter Twenty-six

August 1003
Bishop's Waltham, Hampshire

"Although you have not asked for it, my lord king, I wish to give you counsel regarding your eldest son."

Æthelred did not much like the disapproving tone he could hear in Bishop Ælfheah's voice, and he shifted uneasily in his chair. He and Ælfheah were facing each other in the bishop's lodge, several hours' ride from Winchester. The hall was not large, but Winchester's canny bishop had made sure that the two of them could converse in private, away from the retainers and huntsmen who were gathered nearer the fire pit.

The day's sport had gone well, the feast that followed had been more than satisfactory, and although he could not expect to find a woman waiting for him in his bed tonight, he had been lulled into a pleasant languor by the bishop's hospitality. He should have guessed, though, that Ælfheah had more on his mind than merely reflecting upon today's wild chase and the hart that had been brought to bay at last.

"I thought you invited me here to hunt, not to give me unwanted advice," he muttered.

"When I see the need for counsel, I offer it," Ælfheah replied, "wanted or not."

Æthelred studied the man who had been giving him counsel, usually unasked, for more than half his life. The years had been kind to

Ælfheah—or, more like, God had favored him—for he looked far more youthful than a man of fifty years who had been a bishop for near twenty. His tonsured head was crowned with thick, brown hair and a smooth, seamless brow. He had an aquiline nose, a usually genial mouth framed by a short, dark beard, and his perceptive brown eyes bespoke a keen and agile mind. Those eyes were fixed on Æthelred now as if they would search his soul, and he glanced away.

This bishop lived in the light of God's grace. What right had he to judge a man who lived in the shadow of hell?

"So you wish to tell me how to deal with my son," he murmured. "Based on what, Bishop? How many sons do you have?"

"Many, my lord, for a bishop is father to all men in his care. Even kings."

Æthelred reached for the mead-filled cup set beside him and took a long swallow. That was the trouble with most bishops, and this one in particular. Ælfheah believed that his office gave him the right to put his nose into royal concerns where it certainly did not belong. Nevertheless, the bishop would have his say in his own hall, and even a king, for courtesy, had to listen.

"Go on," he said.

"I have heard rumors that Athelstan is to be punished for leaving court without your permission. I understand that you must discipline him, but I urge you, my lord, to be lenient. His departure, I believe, was not without provocation."

"Provocation?" Æthelred nearly laughed. "Because I refused to countenance his mad idea to cross the Narrow Sea and fire an imaginary Danish fleet?"

"Because you treated him with contempt before all your court. He is your heir, my lord, and if you do not treat him with respect, neither will the nobles of this kingdom. You are undermining his future."

Æthelred snorted. "You need have no worries about his future. Even now he is laying that foundation. Have your priest spies not told you what he has been doing in the west?"

"They report that he has been repairing Exeter's walls, readying the city's defenses against—"

"Against what? The Danes attacked Exeter two years ago but could not breach those walls. Think you they would try again and expect a different result? If they strike at all it will be farther east, and my forces there will be ready for them." He took another pull from his cup and waved it at the bishop. "Oh, I grant you, Athelstan may be repairing the damage from that last assault, but that is not his main purpose. He is building alliances, wooing the men of the western shires and assuring them that he will one day make them a better king than I." He scowled at Ælfheah. "His sins, Bishop, are pride and ambition. He thinks he can defy his father and his king with impunity. Mark me: If I do not continually slap him down, one day the cub is like to challenge me for my crown."

Ælfheah's face went blank with astonishment.

That, Æthelred reflected, was Ælfheah's weakness. His own goodness blinded him to the black intentions of other men.

"I think you misjudge him, my lord," Ælfheah protested. "I have often spoken with Athelstan—"

But Æthelred had ceased to listen, his attention claimed by a royal messenger who had entered the hall and came to kneel before him.

"What is it?"

"I am come from Winchester, my lord. We have had a bird from the royal manor at Norton with news that a Viking fleet has landed at Exeter."

He gaped at the man. It wasn't possible. He had been certain that of all the coastal towns in England, Exeter would be safe from Viking attack. Emma herself had written to her brother that she would journey to her dower lands. Surely the Norman duke would have cautioned his pillaging Danish allies to spare his sister's haven.

"At Exeter?" he asked, incredulous. "Has there been any word from the queen's reeve in the city?"

"No, my lord, not when I left Winchester."

Æthelred dismissed him, keenly aware of the bishop's eyes hard upon him.

"Is it King Swein, think you?" the bishop asked.

Swein—the Danish king who had a sister's death to avenge. The very name hovered in the air like a curse. But he would not believe it.

"Any Danish lord who can outfit a dragon ship might join with a handful of others to go a-viking. This is likely half a dozen vessels filled with desperate men out for whatever plunder they can grab. Let us hope that my ambitious son has completed the task he claims to have set for himself, and that the shipmen break themselves upon the city's defenses. In any case," he said, getting to his feet and gesturing to a light bearer, "I shall say good night, for I must return to Winchester at daybreak."

Ælfheah rose as well and now his smooth brow was furrowed with concern.

"But if it is Swein . . ." he began.

"If it is Swein, he will show us no mercy. He will make us bleed—first blood and then gold." And if he should break through Exeter's walls, Æthelred thought darkly, Swein will find an English queen within. "Batter heaven with prayers, Bishop," he growled, "that it is not."

Chapter Twenty-seven

Devonshire

Emma kept her eyes on the lane where it left the hamlet and bisected the meadow to disappear among the trees. She raced flat out, the wind tearing against her face. Sheep scattered away from her, bleating in alarm. She sensed that Swein was falling behind, and she felt a surge of elation. She whispered a prayer to the Virgin and shouted encouragement to her horse.

The hamlet lay on her left now, and she kept her mount in a diagonal line that would bring her to the lane at a point beyond the last house of the village. Just a little farther and she would have won her freedom. But as she neared her goal she saw another horse and rider fly out of the village, bolting along the lane to head her off. Swein's son. Unlike his father, he sat his horse well, and his lithe figure seemed to be one with his mount.

She did not slow down but veered to her right, away from the dirt track and heading instead straight across the meadow for the woods. If she could stay in front of him, she might still escape, for she had the faster horse. The trees loomed directly in front of her, and as she slowed her mount to enter the woods, she saw the boy urge his horse off of the track to follow her.

Then she was in the trees, keeping her head low to avoid whipping branches that might blind or kill her. She trusted to Ange to stay ahead of her pursuer, but the horse came to a shuddering halt at a cliff edge, and Emma cried aloud in frustration. A river swirled far below her in a deep channel. She took no time to gauge the distance, but slid from the saddle. Grabbing the bridle, she led Ange toward the steep ledge, but suddenly the boy was there beside her, and long, thin fingers clasped her wrist.

Using all her strength she wrenched her hand away and turned to face him, brandishing the knife.

"You will let me go!"

He halted, more in surprise at her use of Danish, she guessed, than in fear of the blade in her hand.

Perhaps he sensed that she had neither the will nor the instinct she needed to make a lethal strike. Perhaps he was simply reckless. She only knew that for an instant they stared at each other, frozen in time like figures carved into stone. Then, as she turned to fling herself down the ledge, he clutched her blade arm and dragged her backward, so that she lost her balance and fell against him. Regaining her footing, she twisted and kicked, trying vainly to escape his cruel grasp. Slowly, and with a careless strength that maddened her, he pried her fingers from the hilt of the knife and tossed it away.

Still she resisted him, more frantic than ever, but he dragged her from the cliff edge, and as she continued to struggle he finally grasped both her arms and shook her until her teeth rattled.

"No more!" he shouted at her.

He shook her again, and she had to stop struggling then, for she was dizzy and weak from frustration and rage. She looked into his face, into dark eyes that regarded her not with the contempt that she expected but with compassion.

"You have lost the battle, lady," he said. "You cannot escape. It was a brave attempt, but it is done."

Any thoughts she may have had about making another attempt vanished with the arrival of Swein and Halfdan. Swein dismounted quickly and strode toward her, his face hard. She knew instinctively that he would cuff her, and she had no wish to feel the brunt of his anger again.

As he raised his hand to deliver the blow she cursed him in Danish and followed it with a threat.

"If you strike me," she said, "when next I lay my hand on a knife I shall slit your throat."

Swein checked his swing, gazed at her in amazement, then lowered his hand and grinned at his son.

"By all the gods! Spoken like a wench from the stews of Hedeby." His grin faded when he turned back to Emma. "The more fool I for forgetting your lineage, my lady. I shall gladly stay my hand, and I shall make certain, as well, that nothing sharper than your tongue comes within your reach. May I," he asked with a mock bow, "assist you to your horse?"

She did not want him to touch her, but having avoided a slap, she decided not to press the point. She spoke softly to Ange as the mare stood trembling with the exertion of their pointless bid for freedom. Their journey continued just as before, except that Emma gave way to bleak despair.

They crossed the River Otter at a ford above another deserted village, then followed a track that led them along the river's eastern bank. The land rose slowly until they were riding atop a ridge. Emma looked southward, and she could see that the ridge curved around to the west like a crooked finger. Below her the tidal estuary of the River Otter glimmered like the shards of a mirror in the last of the dying light, but her senses registered nothing of its beauty. She was numb to everything now except the realization that her life as she had come to know it was over.

They had reached the sea. She could hear the lash of waves upon the beach and smell the salt in the air. Somewhere nearby, she knew, there would be salt pans and tiny huts where the seawater was boiled to extract the precious grains. There were numerous tuns of that salt, even now, sitting in the storehouse below Exeter fortress. Or perhaps, she reflected, they had already been carried to Forkbeard's waiting ships. In any case, the saltworkers would have fled to shelter at the first sign of the warning beacons. There would be no one on the beach now to come to the aid of a beleaguered queen.

The evening sky was clear, although a bank of clouds lay threatening just off the coast. A moon nearing the full shimmered overhead, and it was late, she knew. She had come to day's end, land's end, and, for the moment, journey's end. She was hardly grateful. Indeed, she wished that she could simply continue to ride until she and Ange both dropped, exhausted and senseless. Instead she would be forced now to dismount and wait for whatever her captors had planned for her.

As they drew within sight of the sea she searched the waters for sign of a ship, but she could make out nothing. Perhaps the Virgin had answered her prayers, and the ship was not there.

The guard had already dismounted and now he approached a tall, mounded shape that proved to be a tarp-covered pile of wood and kindling, ready for lighting. Using a flint and steel, he soon coaxed a spark, and then flames bloomed into the night.

"Take the lady down to the beach," Swein said to his son. "If she stays near the horses, she might take it into her head to run again."

The boy led her down a steep, narrow track that led to the shore. She took one quick glance back, to where the guard was stripping the horses of all their gear. That would go with them in their ship. Silver bridle rings and tooled leather would fetch a handsome price at the market in Rouen. No doubt Swein was sorry that he could not take her mare with him as well. Ange tossed her head and nickered to Emma, and then the boy tugged at her hand and forced her farther down the path, and she had to look to her footing.

On the beach she huddled in a fold of the cliff to escape the sharp wind that swept across the land toward the sea. Still, she was cold, weary, and heartsore. She gazed sullenly toward the dark waves, and after a time a single pinpoint of light appeared. The dim hope she had held onto—that the ship would not arrive to meet them—flickered and died.

Athelstan, leading his men along the western shore of the River Otter, saw a signal fire blaze into life on the promontory across the river. Soon after, he saw an answering light at sea that rose and fell with the surge of the waves. There was a dragon ship out there, drawing slowly toward the shore.

They had come to the right place, then. Somewhere on the other side of the muddy estuary Emma was Swein's captive. He would not give her up without a battle.

He halted his men. "Remember, Forkbeard is worth more to us alive than dead," he told them. "We want him and we want the queen, both alive and uninjured. There are at least two men with Swein, maybe more. If we hope to get out of here with our own skins intact, we had better be quick, because if we are still on the beach when that ship reaches shore, we are dead men. Is everyone clear? I want Swein alive," he repeated.

The three men grunted grudging assent. They had ridden for many miles with the stench of Exeter's burning in their nostrils, and Athelstan knew that his order to spare the Danish king galled them. But Swein was a great prize. He could be bartered to purchase peace for England for decades to come. That was assuming, of course, that they could win the skirmish ahead.

He grasped his shield, drew his sword, and urged his horse forward, slantwise across the mudflats. Ahead of him he could see the broad shore of the Narrow Sea, where moonlight glinted on smooth, round stones. They reached the shingle, and the noise of their horses' hoofbeats must have alerted the Danes, for as Athelstan drew closer he saw two men on the beach ahead, facing him with swords drawn. Two other figures lurched away along the shoreline, their progress slow and fitful because one of them, surely Emma, seemed very disinclined to go.

Good girl, he thought. Fight him every step of the way.

He spared a glance seaward and saw the ship's signal light rising and falling as the vessel's oars strained against the outgoing tide. Thirty Danes would be over the side and making for the beach as soon as the ship found shallow water, but with the tide and the wind against them they were making slow headway. There was time yet.

He focused on the two armed men who stood separated by several

feet now, their cloaks tossed aside and their feet set wide apart, ready
for battle. The man closest to the water was white-bearded, tall, and
fiercely sturdy. Forkbeard. The other warrior, younger and brawnier,
suddenly ran toward them with a roar, as if to intercept the riders before they could reach his companion. He raised his sword in both
hands, and as one of Athelstan's men surged forward to meet him, the
Dane struck a blow aimed not at the rider, but at the horse. The animal
screamed in agony as it crashed to the shingle, pinning its rider beneath it.

Athelstan skirted the downed man and horse and paid them no
further heed, for all his senses were focused on Swein Forkbeard. He
had dreamed of facing the man a hundred times, had thought of little
else for months. All his desire was to outwit, outthink, outmaneuver
this Danish pirate who called himself king. He might not have the skill
to beat him in single combat, but if he could hold him at bay for a time,
he and his men might be able to disarm him at last. He was probably a
fool about to lose his life, but he had two weapons that Swein did
not—his shield and his rage.

He saw the king's sword flash in the moonlight, and he wheeled his
horse to dodge the slashing, downward stroke. Before Swein could
raise his sword again Athelstan leaped from his mount to land on his
enemy, hammering his shield against the king's sword arm. Swein
grunted and staggered a step with the blow, but did not fall. Athelstan
pushed himself away from his enemy, knees bent, sword and shield
ready to meet the next thrust. He repelled it with his shield, following
it with a stroke aimed to disarm rather than kill. Swein sidestepped it
easily, and they traded more blows, so many that Athelstan's arms grew
weary as he parried and dodged, twisted and slashed, fending off a warrior skilled in arms whose mind was bent on slaughter.

Emma, desperate to escape Cnut's brutal grip on her wrist, threw herself to the shingle and was surprised that the tactic worked. Freed for
a moment, she scrambled to her feet and ran back toward where the

men were battling on the beach. One rider had gone down, but two others were trading blows with the big Dane. The third man had his back to her, moving with an agile grace, and it seemed to her that he did not fight Swein so much as use his weapons to fend off Swein's repeated sword strokes. She had barely managed to grasp all this when Cnut, with a curse, tackled her from behind, and she fell headlong. She clutched one of the smooth fist-sized stones beneath her, and when Cnut dragged her to her feet she smacked it against his ear and twisted out of his grasp again, stumbling toward the melee.

She had nearly made it to one of the horses when Cnut brought her down once more, so hard that she was knocked breathless. He landed on top of her, but he was up in a moment, pulling her arm sharply and causing her to cry out in pain.

A second cry rang out over the beach then, and both Emma and her captor looked in the direction from which it had come.

The king of the Danes was standing, disarmed, with his back to the cliff face. Two men in mail stood facing him, each with a sword point placed against his throat. A third man was running toward her on the shingle, and she saw that it was Athelstan. It was he who had shouted, and now he stood only a few steps away, sword pointed at Cnut. The boy made to reach for his own sword, but Athelstan's blade touched his breast, and Cnut froze.

"Tell the lad," he said to Emma, "that if he does not release you the king will die. Tell him to do it now, or Swein dies. Now!"

Emma translated the words, but Cnut was already looking past Athelstan, his eyes fixed on his father. She saw the desperation in the boy's face, as if he were trying to work out what Swein would want him to do.

"Now!" Athelstan repeated, and Cnut, understanding, pushed Emma away from him, toward her rescuer. She felt like a game piece, shuttled from one player to the next, only this game was deadly. Two men lay broken and bleeding on the shingle, and she realized with sudden horror that more were about to die, for now a chorus of shouts from the dragon ship drew all their eyes to the sea.

A score of men, determined to reach the shore to defend their leader, had thrown themselves into the black, raging water, struggling against the falling tide. Their armor and weapons dragged them down, though, and Emma saw several of them disappear beneath the waves. Still, others came on as the ship drew inexorably toward the shore.

Athelstan may have cornered Swein, but he had run out of time.

He ignored the oncoming Danes, though, and she realized now, as he must have known, that none of them would strike while Swein stood unarmed with swords at his throat. As Athelstan stripped Cnut of his weapons and motioned him toward Swein, she ran to gather the horses, her heart pounding. Athelstan held all of their lives in his hands now. What was he going to do?

A half-dozen Danes stood on the shingle at the waterline. They were well trained, for although wet and battered by the sea, they formed a shield wall as if by instinct. Swein had but to nod, and they would attack.

She moved so that she stood close to Athelstan's side.

"What now?" she asked.

"Now I barter for our lives," he said to Emma. "Speak for me so that all will hear."

She nodded.

"I will grant you your life, Swein of Denmark," Athelstan roared, and Emma repeated in Danish, "but in return I demand that you grant the queen her freedom. You will allow us to escort her unhindered to Winchester. And you will swear to this by all the gods that you honor."

Swein cocked his head to one side, his eyes hard on Emma's. She looked from Swein to Athelstan, who still held his sword against Cnut's breast. She knew that she should tell Athelstan that this was Swein's son, that the boy might make the perfect hostage.

Yet she said nothing, and she could not tell why, except that she could not bring herself to use the boy as she'd been used.

Long moments passed and Swein made no reply. Emma's heart beat hard against her ribs. Swein could order his men to take her and to kill her rescuers, but it would cost him his life and the life of his son. She did not think it was a price that he was eager to pay. But what if he lied? What if he promised to let them go, and then set his men upon them?

She remembered, then, Ælfgar's words: *Swein combines courage with honor.* If that were so, then Swein would be true to his word. Still, it was a risk.

Finally the Danish king called out, in a voice that all of his men could hear, "I swear by Odin, Lord of Valhalla, and by Christus, King of Heaven, that no one will harm the English or the lady! They may go where they will, and my shipmen will not follow or detain them. So I give them my pledge."

Emma nodded to Athelstan. He lowered his sword and saluted the king. And then, as if they were comrades in arms instead of mortal enemies, the Danes helped the English place their dead companion on a horse.

Before they rode north, Emma looked back once toward the beach. Cnut stood on the shingle, his back to the sea, his face upturned toward her. He stood motionless, merely watching her with dark, fathomless eyes.

"What is it?" Athelstan asked, worried no doubt that the Danes might have made some threatening move.

"Nothing," she said, her gaze still locked with that of Swein's son, wishing she could read his thoughts. "Will the Danes leave us in peace now, do you think?"

"If you mean will Swein keep his word and let us return to Winchester unmolested, yes. If you mean will he keep his dragon ships away from our shores, not a chance of it," Athelstan replied. "Not while my father is king."

Chapter Twenty-eight

August 1003

Ætheling's Lodge, near Otter Mouth, Devonshire

Athelstan placed another log on the fire to ward off the morning chill. Outside the walls of the hunting lodge—his own secret retreat from the world—the dawn was breaking over the fields and the nearby forest. He could not see it, but he could hear the birds' morning calls, could feel the subtle change in the air that came with the rising of the sun. Soon the kitchen servants, the herdsmen, and the grooms would be stirring, but no one would disturb him here until he called for them.

On the bed across the room, Emma lay asleep beneath a pile of furs. He had kept watch over her through the ragged hours of darkness, unable to sleep himself, for his mind was still busy sorting through the events of the long night and imagining the dire reckoning that the coming day was likely to bring. He had mourned his dead companion, Eadsige, who lay now at the Priory at Otterton. He had given the brothers there silver to offer prayers for his soul, to bury him in hallowed ground, and to forget that a nobleman and his companions had ever been there. Then he had sent Eadmer and Ælfmær to Norton with word for Wymarc that Emma was safe.

And beyond that, what? With Swein and his host prowling the western shires the dawn was not likely to bring good tidings. Swein had been robbed of his greatest prize, but he would find some other way to take his vengeance and fill his ships with silver. Exeter, he feared, was but the beginning. Swein's spies would likely have assured him that the king's forces were ill prepared to parry whatever blow he might strike, and they would be proved right.

Athelstan rested his head against the wall behind him and stared, unseeing, at the roof timbers outlined by the firelight. If he had taken more men with him yesterday, would he have been able to capture Swein? He did not think so. It was not lack of men but bad timing that had thwarted him. He had come to the shore too late. He could have taken Swein only if God had ordained it, and God had chosen otherwise. Perhaps the bishops were right, and the people of England were being punished for their sins.

Even so, he suspected that English hands had assisted Swein. How had he known that Emma rode out yesterday with only a small guard? How had he known where to find her? Someone in the queen's service must have fed information to Swein or his agents, and if they had done it once, they could do it again.

On the bed Emma stirred, and he glanced over to where she lay, half hoping that he had not disturbed her and half hoping that she would waken so that he could share his thoughts with her. They had spoken very little last night. He had brought her here, as far from Exeter and the coast as they could travel in a few hours. She had asked him about her people, and he had been able to assure her that Wymarc was safe at his stronghold, and that Margot had probably sought refuge with the brothers at Magdalene Abbey. He could tell her little more, for he had no certain knowledge of the fate of Exeter, although he feared the worst. After that she remained silent throughout the journey, offering not a word of complaint as he led her as swiftly as he could to this refuge.

Once here, though, whatever internal strength had supported her throughout her long ordeal finally gave out. She had wept, inconsolable, blaming herself for all of it—for the deaths of the guards who had tried to defend her, for the men, women, and children that she was certain must have died at Exeter, for her rash journey outside the fortress with a company too small to defend her properly.

He had wanted to comfort her, had tried to take her in his arms, but she had fought him like a wildcat. He could only stand aside and let the storm pass, mute witness to her self-recrimination and despair. Finally, her fury spent, she had succumbed to weariness and fallen into a deep sleep.

He sat forward and dropped his head into his hands. The blame for all belonged not to Æthelred's queen but to Swein of Denmark. And along with Swein, to Æthelred of England, for the slaughter last November that had drawn the Danish force to these shores. Emma's brother Richard had played a role as well, with his cunning neglect of his treaty responsibilities and a well-timed journey to his southern borders that had left his northern harbors at the disposal of the Danish fleet. Ranked against the deeds of men of such power, Emma's part in this disaster was of little account.

When Emma opened her eyes, she heard birdsong. She blinked. The nightmare of Swein and of Exeter, of blood and of terror had been all too real, yet here she was, safe in England, tucked into a warm bed inside a room that smelled familiarly of wood smoke.

She searched for Athelstan and saw him close by, his head in his hands as if he were praying. She recalled the night before, how he had tried to comfort her and she had raged at him. Such fury would have been acceptable in a man. A man could vent his anger through brute force, could throw things, fight, even murder his enemy in combat. A lady, though, and especially a queen, must ever be serene. A queen must channel her guilt into prayer and focus her rage into the lethal tip of her embroidery needle. Last night she had done nothing of the sort.

How would this man, whom she loved, look at her now that she had railed at him like a madwoman? But far worse than that—would he, or anyone, ever grant her forgiveness for the devastation wrought on Exeter because of her? She felt the tears welling in her eyes again as she thought of it, but she swiped at them quickly. Today she would be in control. Today she would be a queen again.

"My lord," she said, sitting up.

He raised his head and came to kneel at her bedside.

"How fares the queen?" he whispered, reaching out to take her hand.

His palm felt rough but warm as he drew her fingers to his lips and kissed them. It was the lightest of touches, that grazing of moist lips upon sensitive skin, but it told her that whatever she may have to face elsewhere, here there was forgiveness.

"I am myself again," she assured him. "But, dear God! I wish I knew of some way to go back in time so that I could relive yesterday. I would do all differently."

He sat upon the bed and squeezed her hand.

"Even could you do so," he said, fixing her with a steady gaze, "there is no guarantee that the outcome would be any better than what it is today. Mayhap it could be worse. Swein Forkbeard is a crafty enemy. What happened yesterday was likely only one of many plans he had devised for the assault upon Exeter and the taking of a queen. No one can know for certain what would have happened had you, or I, or Hugh or anyone around you acted differently than we did. Be thankful, as I am, that you are here, safe, and not in the bowels of one of Swein's dragon ships."

She regarded him with a kind of wonder. That he refused to fix any blame on her at all struck her as nothing short of miraculous. Yet even as she marveled at his generous words, her mind reeled at the memory of the peril that he himself had been in last night. Swein, had he but known it, had had not only Æthelred's queen within his grasp but the eldest ætheling as well.

"My lord," she said, "I am grateful to you for my life, and I am grateful to God that He guided you and held you in His hand. And yes, you are right when you say that the outcome could have been far worse. Had you been captured, or injured, or killed—"

He placed his fingertips upon her lips. "Let us be thankful for what is, my lady, and not waste breath or heart contemplating evils that have not come to pass."

She shook her head. "That is easier to do when one has nothing to regret."

"Regrets are useless, Emma. They force you to look always to the past. You would do better to look toward the future, to change what is amiss rather than weep over how things came to be that way."

She considered his words as she studied his face—the high cheekbones; the strong, square jaw with the closely cropped, fair beard; the blue eyes that gazed at her now, unblinking. It was a youthful face, yet the intellect behind that steady gaze was sharp as a blade.

"You have ever looked toward the future," she told him. "It seems that in the past few months you have been given some special gift of foresight. You knew what Swein would do, and you took precautions to thwart him. If your father had only listened to you, if I had only—" She stopped. "Ah, I am again guilty of looking backward. It is because I do not wish to look at my future, I think." She could foresee only discontent and sorrow in her future, bound as she was to a man whom she could not love, or even trust.

"What have you to fear from the future, my lady?" he asked, his voice no longer gentle but sharp. "Your role as Æthelred's queen is secure. You will return to his court and his bed, and you will bear his children, as a queen must."

She heard the bitterness in his words, and it savaged her heart. This man who owed her nothing had risked everything—his life, his honor—for her sake. How could she let that go unanswered? Could she not, for his sake, risk speaking the truth just this once?

He stood up and would have walked away, but she clutched at his hand and slipped from the bed to stand before him.

"Do you truly believe that the future you describe is the one that I wish to have?" she asked. "Do you think I would not thrust my crown aside if by doing so I could with honor grasp the prize that is dearer to me than anything?" She felt the tears welling, unbidden, but she was past caring now. She was speaking not as a queen, but as a woman. "Do you think that I have not wakened in the night, sick with longing for what will ever be denied me, and that every single day I wake and curse the *wyrd* that bound me to the father instead of to the son?"

She had said it aloud at last, had spoken the unspeakable. But she would not call the words back, no matter what the cost. For a moment he hesitated, as if he expected her to renounce every word. When she only gazed at him through her tears, he drew her fiercely to him. She went like a falcon trained to the lure, conscious of neither past nor future, oblivious to right and wrong. She gave herself up, as she never had before, to instinct and to appetite, and to the fierce demands of passion.

Chapter Twenty-nine

Exmoor, Somerset

Elgiva tilted her head back so that her dark hair floated behind her. She was naked, immersed to her chin in the chilly waters of a mere, and it felt wonderful after the sultry heat of the day and the filthy ride. It felt wonderful just to be alive.

She cast a glance toward her brother, who sat at the water's edge, his back against a boulder. He was staring off into the trees, ignoring her. He was in a foul mood. He had objected to her bathing, but she had insisted, and now he was punishing her with his morose silence. He was forced to attend her now that Groa was gone, and he resented it. Well, she did not like it any more than he did, and she was in a foul mood as well.

After all, she was in mourning. Groa had been her nurse, her confidante, and her willing slave, and she had lost her. It was not her fault, of course. She could not have saved Groa, even if she had tried to do so. She would only have put herself in danger, something Groa would not have wanted. Had she not promised to kill Elgiva with her own hand before she would let any Dane assault her? Groa would have urged her to run.

Already, though, she missed the wretched woman. It was cruel of Wulf to be so cold to her when she was all but distraught.

They had ridden almost all night long, until Wulf had finally decided, via some mental reckoning granted by God to men alone, that it was safe to make camp. His men were guarding the horses, and he was guarding her.

"Why do you not come into the water?" she called to him, hoping to coax him into a better mood. "There is a deep pool here. You must be as hot and filthy as I am, and surely we are far enough away from Exeter that we do not have to fear the Danes. We must be in some other shire by now. Even if the raiders should come north along this very same road, they could not travel at our speed."

"The Danish *hird* has scouts, Elgiva," he said with a scowl, "who can cover ground even faster than we can. And this is no pleasure trip."

"I never said that it was," she snapped, irritated by his implied criticism. "But I cannot count on another opportunity to bathe between here and Winchester. And as I have had little to eat and almost no sleep, and my companions are a group of filthy men and a surly brother, I shall take my comforts where I find them." His petulance bored her. "Hand me my cloak," she said, making her way to the water's edge.

He tossed the bundled cloak to her. Wrapping it around her shoulders, she sat down next to him.

"How many days," she asked, "until we reach Winchester?"

"We are not going to Winchester," he said.

She looked sharply at him. He had told her that their father was at Winchester, and she had naturally assumed that they would join him there. The king and his sons would be at the palace, and she had business with the ætheling Ecbert, although he did not yet know it.

"Of course we are going to Winchester," she said. "Where else would we go?"

"I have been ordered to escort you to Northampton, to Aldeborne, where you will be safe and well guarded."

"I do not want to go to Aldeborne," she protested. "Surely I would be just as safe in the royal city."

"If the Danes attack Winchester, you will only have to run again. Aldeborne is safer."

She stared at him, dumbfounded. "Surely they would not attempt to sack Winchester. It is too well defended."

"Exeter was well defended," he said.

She sniffed. "We do not yet know what happened at Exeter. The raiders may have been routed and forced back to their ships." She did not like being reminded of Exeter. She wished that she could forget yesterday completely—the screams, the horror of that desperate scramble in the dark, her last glimpse of Groa. She winced, as if she felt a physical pain. She hated to think of Groa.

"The Danes burned Exeter, Elgiva." Wulf sneered at her. "That glow in the sky last night was from the city's pyre."

She studied his face, its coloring and features so similar to her own. Yet there was something new there that she had never seen before. He had aged since the spring. There were shadows around his eyes, shadows so dark that it almost looked as if he'd raided her box of eye paints for his own use.

"You know something that you are not telling me," she said. "What is troubling you?"

He scowled. "There is a Danish army loose in the land," he said. "Is that not trouble enough?"

"Wulf," she said, placing her hand gently on his knee, "why will you not trust me with your secrets?"

He glanced at her hand on his knee, cocked his head at her, and raised an eyebrow. "I tell you everything, dear sister, when I deem that it is right for you to know it. For the moment I have nothing but conjecture, and of that I will speak to no one." Gingerly, he lifted her hand from his knee and dropped it into her lap.

She could see that he was determined to thwart her, but she would not give up just yet. Artlessly, she lowered the hand that gripped her cloak, revealing the pink bud of one plump breast. His eyes followed her movement, and she arched her back just a little in a wordless invitation to caress her. It was a game they had played often when they were children, earning her sweets and presents from her appreciative older brother, until the day Groa had caught them at it and had given Wulf a brisk thrashing. Since they were grown she had not had the nerve to tease him so blatantly. But today she was desperate to learn what he knew.

"You risk nothing by telling me," she said, "and you know that I would not deny you anything that you asked of me."

His eyes traveled from her breast to her face, and his mouth curved into a cold smile. Slowly he reached out, pulling her close to him, then pinching her nipple so hard that she cried out, her cloak tumbling from her shoulders as she struggled unsuccessfully to free herself.

"I am in no mood for your childish games, Elgiva," he snarled. "There is a great deal at risk here, and you, my little slut, are not to take it lightly. And when I want something from you, I will take it, whether you are willing to give it to me or not." He let go of her breast and grasped her head with both hands, kissing her roughly, his tongue plundering her mouth in spite of her efforts to push him away.

When he finally let her go she hissed, "You bastard."

"Endearments, sweetheart?" he said, getting to his feet. "Save them for the king. We are finished here. Put your clothes on and come back to the camp. Or have I aroused you? Shall I send one of my men to finish the job? Perhaps you would like more than one. I am sure they would all of them volunteer."

She spat at him, and he gave a harsh laugh before disappearing into the trees. She dressed herself, then sat down on the warm rock to think, rubbing her painful breast with her fingertips. She should have expected that kind of response from Wulf. There was a cruel streak in him. She had witnessed it often enough, but he only rarely turned it against her, and when he did Groa had always been there to protect her. She had taken that protection for granted, but Groa was dead now, and Wulf had changed into someone she hardly recognized. She would have to tread more warily with him.

Gazing morosely across the water, she tried to fathom what might be tormenting her brother. What could her father be involved in that he would not even share it with his sons? As she pondered this she saw a movement beneath the trees on the other side of the mere, and remembering Wulf's words about the Danish scouts, she tensed, ready to spring to her feet and run. But it was no shipman moving among the trees. A stag, its pelt as white as snow, stepped delicately into the sunlight and bent its antlered head to drink. Three more deer, all of normal coloring, followed the stag to the water's edge. Against their russets and browns, the pale stag looked ghostly—otherworldly. She could not even be sure that it was real.

Elgiva held her breath. Groa had told her that such creatures existed, but she had never expected to see one. *The white stag*, Groa had said, *is a creature of portent, a sign that the world is about to change—a vision granted to very few.*

Elgiva felt a shiver race down her spine. Surely this was a message meant for her to interpret. The world that she knew was about to undergo some upheaval that would change her life. For the better, she wondered, or for the worse? Was this a promise or a warning?

She closed her eyes, but the image burned against their lids was the flash of light from an ax head and the spray of blood as the thing met its target. She forced her eyes open.

The clearing across the water stood empty.

Chapter Thirty

August 1003

Ætheling's Lodge, near Otter Mouth, Devonshire

"We cannot stay here."

Emma heard the words whispered gently against her ear, recognized their truth, and then dismissed them. She turned to face Athelstan, and she nuzzled her face against his as their legs tangled wantonly beneath the linens.

"Can we not stay just for tonight?" she begged. They had stolen a few hours from the sun's arc across the sky, had made love as if time itself did not exist. She wanted more of it. No one knew where she was, nor even if she lived. For a little while longer, surely, she had no one to answer to except herself.

Yet even as the thoughts formed in her mind, she knew that time had run out, and that there were others to whom she must answer.

Athelstan tenderly swept a lock of hair from her face and kissed her. For too brief a time they clung together, and then he pulled gently away and sat up.

"We need men and arms, and a fortified haven," he said. "We will go to Somerset, I think, to Watchet."

He frowned, and she knew that his thoughts had moved far away from her.

"The fortifications there are in good repair," he went on. "We can gather a force as we go."

She sat up, too, and looked at him, puzzled. A vague apprehension began to gnaw at her insides. "A force?" she asked. "Do you think to lead an army against Swein? But will he not go east, think you, along the coast?"

He laughed—a harsh bark with no humor. "I care not what Swein does now. He can burn and pillage at will. Let my father order his ealdormen to throw whatever force they can gather against the Danes and stop them if they can." He reached out to run his thumb along her cheek, gazing steadily at her. "The army that I will lead will be for another purpose altogether."

She caught his hand and stilled it, her alarm growing. "What are you thinking?" she asked.

Once more he grazed her lips with his. "I am the eldest ætheling," he said, "and the heir to the throne of a king who is woefully incapable of protecting this land. The queen herself shares my bed, may even be carrying my child." He gently caressed the soft flesh of her belly. But his gaze was elsewhere, into some vision that she did not share. "If I challenge my father for the throne, the nobles of the west country will support me. I expect more will follow."

She stared at him, struck by the horror that such a plan conjured up in her mind.

She was to blame for this, too, then. He would not be harboring such monstrous ambitions were it not for what had happened here between them, beneath the sheets that bound them even now. She had given him her body, her love, thinking it a sin that would rebound on no one but herself. She should have known that it would not be enough to satisfy him. He aspired to a throne, and he thought that with her at his side he had but to reach out his hand and take it.

As she searched for words to express her terror he took her hand in his.

"Do not be afraid, Emma," he said. "I will find a haven for you where you will be guarded and protected, and where neither Swein nor my father can touch you. Then, when I reign as king in Winchester, you will be queen at my side."

She withdrew her hand and wrapped her arms about her body, chilled not just with cold but with the dread that seemed to freeze her from the inside out.

"You would really do this?" she said to him, modulating her voice to a calmness that she did not feel. "You would challenge your father, and between the two of you would pull this kingdom down around your ears?" He made as if to speak, but she stopped him, for the terrifying images of what might be were racing quick and fast through her mind now. "No, you must listen to me! Can you not see how it would end, my lord? Even if you should win your treacherous battles, what then? Will you sully your hands with your father's blood? Think you the *witan* will name you king if the bishops have condemned you as a murderer?"

He swept her objection aside.

"I said nothing of murder! It will not come to that."

"It can come to only that! Should you best him in a thousand battles, your father will not step down and bow to you. What king of your line has ever done so? You will be like stags in the forest, the young buck challenging the old for supremacy in a fight to the death. And who are these thegns whom you believe will support you in your bid for kingship? The ealdormen, who owe all their lands and their power to your father? Your brothers, who owe him their very lives? They are all bound by oaths, Athelstan, to the king. Not to you!" She took his face in both her hands and gazed levelly at him. "I am bound by oaths as well," she said evenly, "to him, and not to you."

He grasped her wrists and pinioned her hands in front of her.

"You have already broken one of those oaths today, my queen," he said coldly.

She saw anger, despair, and passion warring in his face, and she realized what folly it had been for her to come here alone with him. Their destinies were like two rivers that flowed ever in the same direction, within sight of each other but never meant to meet, to touch, to join as one. Yet it was beyond her power to undo what was done, as he himself had so recently reminded her. They had lain together, and she could not change that. It was the future that she must attempt to re-pair.

"You are right to chastise me," she said, pulling her hands away from his grasp to snatch up her chemise where it lay near her pillow. She extricated herself from the sheets and the low bed, turned her back on him, and began to dress. She could not, however, control the trembling that coursed all through her body. The firestorm that Athelstan wanted to set alight in this land was more terrifying than any threat that Swein Forkbeard could pose.

"I am not trying to chastise you." His voice grated with pain. "For God's sake. Emma!"

She rounded the foot of the bed to stand in front of him, half dressed, cold and controlled now, for there was too much at stake for her to make a misstep.

"I have committed a grave sin," she said, "and I am ready to make retribution for it. I will accept whatever punishment God sends me, but I will not compound my sin by encouraging you in this madness. All of England will suffer a terrible evil if you follow through with this de-sign." She dropped to her knees before him and clasped her hands. "I beg you, my lord. Do not break your oaths to the king. You are Æthelred's heir, and yes, one day you will be crowned England's king. But your time has not yet come. You must be patient. I beg you to wait."

He clasped his own hands around hers and looked upon her with such tenderness that she wanted to weep.

"And if I do as you ask," he said, his voice so coldly rational that he might have been presenting an argument to his father's council, "if I wait to take the throne, what guarantee is there that the throne will still be there to take? The Danes are bleeding us dry. It will be as it was in the days of Alfred, with ships and men and arms arriving with the summer winds like a plague upon the land, year after year after year. What had once been fruitful will be blasted and wasted, fields and flocks and villages plundered. Even the great Alfred was unable to stop their depredations until he bribed them with land where they could settle. My father is no Alfred! He has nothing whatever that he can use to placate Swein Forkbeard."

His face above her wavered as tears filled her eyes, for he was right about his father, about the Danes, about all except the solution.

"And would you add to the misery of your people by making them choose between father and son, by harrying the land with your own armies who will kill and maim and bloody each other, and who will take for sustenance whatever food and cattle the Danes have not already devoured? How many good men will fall to the sword, my lord? How many women and children are like to starve because you turned against your own?"

Her words, sharp as a volley of arrows, goaded Athelstan from the bed. He flung her pleading hands away and swept past her to pour a beaker of wine and gulp it down. He was furious with her for her blind loyalty to his father. He was furious with himself for telling her of the design that remained even now only half formed in his head. He should have simply taken her to some stronghold and held her there until it was all over. It was a royal courting practice not unheard of in Wessex, and whether the chosen bride was maid, wife, or nun made little difference. It had its advantages; even Emma would have been convinced of his righteousness once he had an army at his back and a crown on his head.

Why could she not see it now, though? He knew that she loved him. Had she not given herself to him with abandon, forsaken the stiff reserve that had for so long kept them apart? To him their coupling was not just a completion but a beginning, a new alliance that would sweep all past allegiances away.

Emma, it seemed, saw it differently. He set down his cup and began to don tunic and breecs.

"And what would you have me do," he asked her stiffly, "while I wait for my appointed time?"

She had risen to her feet, but she made no move to bridge the gap that yawned between them. "You have no need of me, my lord," she said softly, "to tell you that. You know it already."

"Yes, I do," he sneered, distilling all his pent-up anger and frustration into poisonous sarcasm. "Have I not been doing it for two years now? My role is to sit at my father's board like an obedient son and watch him lead the woman I love to his bed. And then I entertain myself by imagining his greedy hands pawing and groping at her white breasts, and his stiff cock tenderly suckled by—"

"Stop it!"

She was glaring at him, not with shame, which was what he had wanted, but with fury.

"Had enough, my queen?" He snatched up the wine and raised it toward her in a salute. "Well, so have I." He drained the cup and then hurled it to the floor, but it provided no satisfactory release for his rage.

"Your anger is misplaced, my lord," she said, her voice hard as stone. "Neither you nor I can control the destiny that keeps us separate. In taking me to wife your father has taken nothing that belonged to you. But Swein would take everything from you, if you let him. That is your true enemy, Athelstan. Be your father's right hand in his campaign against the Danes, and you will have earned the right to kingship."

It was the old argument again. She was ignoring the reality of Æthelred and his unwillingness to trust any counsel but his own.

"My father does not listen to me!" he shouted, enunciating the words with terrible clarity, as if by doing so he could get her to understand and accept them, and to make an end of it at last. "He treats me as a child!"

"Your father," she said softly, "is terrified of you."

He looked at her sharply, startled by her words. His surprise must have shown on his face, for she was nodding slowly.

"Your father gained his crown through the murder of a brother. Do you think he does not worry that God will strike him down? You have sensed some darkness within him, and I have seen it. He does not sleep, Athelstan! He fears for his life, and because of that, he fears even you." She gave a bitter laugh that was almost a sob. "It would seem, from what you have said to me today, that he is right to do so. But I will not believe, even now, that you would ever commit such treachery. You may chastise your father in your heart. You may even despise him. But you will not raise your hand against him. Oh my love, in spite of your anger you must convince him that you will not break your oaths to him. Can you not see that he may be testing you, looking for a reason to give you his trust?"

"You are raving, Emma," he said, running a hand through his hair. She was a woman and a Norman. What could she possibly know about how his father's twisted mind worked? "You are imagining that my father is wise, foresighted, and crafty rather than vain, lecherous, and brutal."

"Your father is all of those things, my love."

He almost laughed then, but she went on.

"Think, Athelstan! You already sit on his council. You demonstrated your courage and loyalty when last year you stepped between your father and a Danish blade, a mark in your favor. And then what did you do? You castigated him for his actions on St. Brice's Day. You were right to do so, yes, but you went about it at the wrong time and in the wrong way." She smiled bleakly. "I was no wiser, I fear. I knew him little then, and I spoke my mind without thought of diplomacy."

He saw a flash of pain cross her face. If she had spoken plainly to his father, Æthelred would have punished her for it. Another black mark set upon his father's soul, he thought, but Emma had not finished.

"Then, in front of his entire court and without consulting anyone, you advised him how to deal with Swein. Yes, I heard the story. You humiliated him before everyone. And when he reprimanded you, you fled the court without his leave. Is it any wonder, Athelstan, that he looks upon you with fear and distrust?"

"And supposing that you are right," he challenged her, "how am I to change the man's mind about me?"

"Not by taking arms against him," she said gently, walking toward him and placing a hand upon his shoulder.

"Nor by bedding his wife?" He pulled her against him, and she twined her arms around his neck. For a moment they held each other close. For a moment she belonged to him again. "If I do as you say, Emma," he whispered against her ear, "if I play the role of good son, bow to my father's will, what of us then?"

She took a step back and gazed at him, her eyes glistening with unshed tears.

"Whatever role you play, my lord," she said, "there can be no *us*."

She would have pulled away from him, but he would not let her go.

"And if you are even now with child? What then?"

She was silent, but he read the answer in her eyes. He released her then, and she turned from him with a brisk step.

"I must get to Winchester as soon as may be now, especially if I am with child."

She had to get the king's prick between her thighs, so that if there was a child, all would believe it to be Æthelred's.

His hands so itched to grasp and shake her that he dared not allow himself within reach of her, for he was not his father—it would give him no pleasure to cause her pain. He wanted Emma to come to him of her own will, to place her hands within his and pledge herself to him, body and soul. Yet he knew that she could not, for that pledge had already been given.

In that moment he faced the stark truth about himself: He did not want his father's crown so much as he wanted his father's woman. But she had made it clear that while his father lived she would never be his.

Chapter Thirty-one

August 1003

St. Giles Priory, Sidbury, Devonshire

Eager as Emma was to return to Winchester, she had first to gather the remnants of her company, for she could not leave them to fend for themselves with a Danish army abroad in the land. She rode with Athelstan to the nearby priory of St. Giles, and from there sent messengers to Wymarc and Father Martin.

At the priory she found survivors from the sack of Exeter, refugees who had sought haven within the priory grounds. They told of the city's destruction, and many swore that Exeter would never have fallen but for the treachery of the queen's reeve. It was Hugh the Norman, they said, who had betrayed the city to the Danes.

Once within the walls the shipmen had plundered homes, ransacked churches, emptied shops and warehouses, and despoiled the king's minters of their silver. They murdered all who opposed them, set the city ablaze, and turned their fury even upon the surrounding walls, reducing them to little more than piles of rubble. When the Danes returned to their ships, Hugh the reeve was seen in their midst. He had betrayed Exeter, it was said, and left behind a ravaged city.

Emma listened to the stories, sick at heart. She searched among the ragged survivors for faces that she knew, for folk who had journeyed with her from Winchester in June, but she saw only strangers. She was able to learn nothing of Elgiva and Groa, and as she listened to the tales of horror, she began to lose what little hope she had for their survival.

Four days after the fall of Exeter, Emma and her retinue set out swiftly for Winchester, driven by the rumor of war at their backs. The Danish ships had gone, but no one knew where they might strike next.

At Emma's insistence she and her women were garbed in the plain robes and hooded cloaks of the sisters of St. Giles. Escorted by Athelstan and twenty of his armed men, they followed the king's paved highways, camping wherever they found themselves when darkness fell—always off the road and hidden, with stern-eyed men in mail set to watch during the long hours of the night.

It was in those dark, lonely hours that Emma met with each of her companions and heard what they could tell of the events that she herself had not witnessed. She learned how Margot and Wymarc had hidden and had listened to what unfolded in that ill-fated lane near Magdalene Abbey, and how, when all was quiet and they were certain it was safe to come out, they had found the cart and its grisly cargo. Margot had urged Wymarc and Brother Redwald to go with all speed to search out the ætheling at Norton while she waited with the dead on that lonely road until help arrived. She had accompanied their bodies back to Magdalene Abbey, where Father Martin saw them buried in hallowed ground.

Wymarc told of her agonized wait for news of Emma, and for word of the fate of Exeter. Her voice faltered when she spoke of Athelstan's returning hearth troops, for they brought word that Exeter had fallen swiftly to the Danes but could tell her nothing of Hugh. She wept in Emma's arms, and the queen wept with her for the man whom they had both come to admire and to trust, and whom Wymarc had learned to love. It seemed to Emma then that they had reached a moment in time where love had no place. It was something to be snuffed out, burned, and discarded, and there was only room in the heart for hatred and fear and, at best, the occasional cold alliance. Her own love—for the child she'd lost, for Athelstan, even for her Norman kin—had brought her nothing but pain. Love belonged to some other world. Perhaps it could be found after death, but it was unwise, she thought, to look for it here.

Father Martin's tale was of Hilde's father, Ælfgar, who had shown neither surprise nor satisfaction upon learning that Swein's forces were abroad in the land. Swein's coming, Ælfgar had said, was as inevitable as the tides. He had predicted, like some soothsayer from ancient days, that Æthelred and his sons would be swept away like so much flotsam. Emma shuddered when she heard this and whispered a prayer to ward against such an evil augury. *No man can read the future,* Hugh had assured her. Yet there had ever been prophets who had some foreknowledge of what was to come. She recalled the feral words howled by the knife-wielding Dane who had tried to murder Æthelred. *Death to the king! Death to the council!* She wondered now if his words had been ravings, as Athelstan thought, or something more dire. Could they have been a foretelling? There was a Danish army in England now, promising dark days ahead for the king and all his people. Once more she whispered a prayer for protection and mercy.

At last Father Martin told her of Hilde, who had been heartbroken when her father had refused to allow her to stay with him, telling her that she meant less than nothing to him. Hearing this, Emma wondered again if love could exist in a world such as this one.

She herself never spoke of the hours she spent as a captive of the Danish king, except to tell those who knew of her capture and escape that they must never speak of it to any human soul. She trusted them to keep that secret, for they knew that if word of her abduction were whispered abroad, all would assume that she had been sullied by her captors, and she would no longer be considered a fit wife for a Christian king.

As for the hours that she had spent in the embrace of her husband's son, that secret she kept locked in her heart.

On the sixth day after leaving St. Giles, the queen's company arrived at Wherwell Abbey, ten miles from Winchester's city walls. There they rested and refreshed themselves, and Emma, with the aid of the nuns, was gowned and groomed so that she could present herself before the king. On an August evening, lit by a sinking sun, she returned to the city of Winchester, where Æthelred and his court awaited her.

Chapter Thirty-two

Æthelred, seated upon his throne in the great hall, watched Emma approach with an impatience he found difficult to conceal. This welcome was mere formality, for he had received messages the day before informing him of the queen's safety and of her impending arrival. *Te Deums* had replaced the prayers of entreaty that had been offered for the queen's safe deliverance from Exeter, and from the moment she had set foot within the city, the bells in every church had rung with clamorous rejoicing.

Only moments before, though, word had come from the south that Dorchester had been sacked and burned. His kingdom was under siege, and the gravity of the peril weighed heavily upon his mind.

The members of the council who had been summoned to advise him were clustered now in small, buzzing groups while Æthelred stood to welcome his queen with the solemnity due her. She had clothed herself in a gown of finely woven linen that was as black as the night sky. Its only adornment was a wide silver border at the hem and delicate silver embroidery upon the silky black veil that covered her pale hair. A thin, silver cross hung on a chain between her breasts. She looked travel weary, but she was still as beautiful as he remembered. Her face seemed to glow from the dark folds of her raiment, but her eyes were red-rimmed, as though she had been crying.

She had reason enough to weep and to garb herself in mourning. Her sojourn in Exeter—which he had hoped would deter the Danes from attacking her lands—had ended in calamity, brought about by the perfidy of her Norman reeve.

He frowned, for the attack on Exeter still puzzled him. He had expected Richard to warn Swein away from Emma's lands, and so he wondered if there was more at work here than he was able to discern. This was not the time, though, to consider the problem.

He kissed Emma's brow in greeting, but he did not wish to prolong this rite of welcome any longer than necessary.

"You are tired, my lady," he said. "You will rest now, and we will speak on the morrow. When you say your prayers, beseech God to bless all that we do here tonight."

He expected her to take her leave, but her eyes locked upon his, and something glinted there that he could not interpret. Was it anger? Fear? Resentment? Then it was gone, and she had bent her knee in submission.

"As you will, my lord," she said.

He watched her leave the hall, his brow furrowed. Something about her had changed. She had ever been a mystery to him, but now, with one glance, it was as if a veil had been drawn aside and then quickly dropped again. He sat down, irritated by the unease that she could raise in him with just a look. She distracted him, damn her, when he had need of all his wits to deal with more pressing matters. The Danes had struck in the west while he had prepared for a landing in the east, and now he had to decide what to do.

He slid his gaze toward Athelstan, who stepped toward the dais now, flanked by half a dozen of his hearth companions. Æthelred signaled to the gathered nobles that they should be seated. He would waste no more time with pointless ceremony, but he wanted the entire court to see this contentious son of his get the welcome he deserved.

Emma approached her chamber with a brisk, angry step. Once again she would be imprisoned within palace walls, and she did not know if she could bear it. For the past three months she had tasted freedom and responsibility. In Exeter she had been the one holding court, seeking advice, and making decisions. How was she to content herself again with nothing but the minor details that came within her small sphere of power? In the great hall below, the king and his council were deciding the fate of the kingdom, while she was expected to kneel in her chamber in silent prayer.

By the time she reached her apartments, she had come to a decision. She would not be treated like a prize jewel—placed in a dark casket and tucked safely away. She would not allow herself to be distanced from the affairs of the court and the king. And if her lord forbid her to be present at his council, then she would find some other means of making herself privy to the decisions that were made there.

She beckoned to Hilde and drew her aside from her other attendants.

"You will go back to the hall," she ordered, "and you will mingle with the servants who bring in food and drink for the king's counselors. You will attend to all that is said among the great men there, and afterward bring me word of all that you see and hear. Do you understand?"

The girl looked at her with eyes that held no trace of guile. She was, indeed, the perfect little spy.

"Yes, my lady." She turned to leave, but Emma placed a hand on her arm to stop her, for there was yet another duty to be performed tonight.

"When the meeting is ended you must search out the ealdorman Ælfhelm. Do you know him?"

The girl nodded.

"You are to bring him to me. Say nothing of Exeter, Hilde, even if he asks. I would have him hear from my own lips what little can be told of the Lady Elgiva. Do you understand?"

Hilde nodded, and Emma watched her go with a heavy heart. She did not relish telling Lord Ælfhelm that his daughter had been left behind in the ruins of Exeter—to a fate that none could know but all could guess. Nevertheless, it was a duty that she could not escape.

Duty, she thought, was the price of queenship. And not for the first time she recalled with bitterness the anguish in Athelstan's eyes when she had refused to support his bid for the crown. That, too, had been her duty. For the rest of her life she would be bound by duty, and forced to pay that price again and again.

Æthelred studied the square, handsome face of his eldest son—the thick, dark brows that stood out, bold and startling, below his golden hair, the beard that had thickened and darkened. The young man's likeness to his dead uncle struck Æthelred anew. He read the same proud determination in Athelstan's eyes, and a defiant boldness that he hated and admired all at once. This was a son to inspire pride in a father's heart—aye, and wariness as well.

The cub had too high an opinion of himself. He would ask pardon, no doubt, for deserting Winchester without leave, but there was no remorse in his eyes. He did as he pleased and expected that all would be forgiven. But there would be no pardon granted today. He must be punished in a way best suited to teach him proper humility, if not remorse.

"I am told," he said slowly, "that you directed the queen's reeve in preparing for the defense of Exeter. Is this so?"

Athelstan frowned, as if trying to grasp the point of such a question. Nevertheless, he did not hesitate to answer.

"That is true," he said. "I consulted with—"

"And yet," Æthelred cut him off, "in spite of your best efforts, Exeter has fallen. Word has reached us that it has been destroyed utterly and that many have died. How do you, who were so deeply involved in planning its defense, explain such a catastrophe?"

Something flickered across his son's face—a flash of indecision or confusion. Then it was gone.

"I cannot explain it, my lord," he said.

"You cannot explain it." Æthelred inflected his voice with disapproval, although the answer suited his purpose well enough. "You cannot recognize, even with the evidence stark before you, that it was your own inadequacy that led to the destruction of a thriving town. Are you so blind to the measure of your own failings?" He paused to allow the question to ring in the still air, registering the displeasure of the king in the mind of every person present. No one moved or spoke, and Athelstan's mouth set in a grim line.

Yes, his son was smart enough to know when to keep his mouth shut, for nothing he could say would allow him to save face now.

"Perhaps, then," Æthelred went on, wielding his voice like a weapon to flay the pup that knelt before him, "having left my court without my leave, you have come back now to give me tidings of some moment. Mayhap you can tell me the number of enemy ships?" He did not wait for answers but flung his questions like daggers, each one louder than the last. "How large is the army? Who leads it? How well is it armed? Pray, Athelstan, what can you tell me that I can use to my advantage?"

Athelstan felt his face burn with humiliation. It was all he could do to keep his mouth shut, to resist his father's baiting. He knew how it was that Exeter had fallen, for Hugh had been forced to lead the enemy into the fortress. And he knew that it was Forkbeard who had brought the enemy fleet to England's shores. But he could not speak of these things without compromising the queen. Any hint of her abduction by Forkbeard would give his father cause to set her aside. Much as Athelstan might welcome such an outcome, Emma would not. Emma would be queen and peaceweaver, and she would relinquish neither role, not even for love of him. She had demanded an oath of silence from him, and he had pledged it. Now he must keep it, whatever the cost.

He looked into his father's face and read the triumph there. Jesu, the man was a fool! His mind should be bent toward the defense of his realm, yet there he sat, preening himself like a bird of prey and baiting his son for his own twisted amusement.

"I can give you no information about the enemy host, my lord," he said through clenched teeth. It was capitulation, and he knew it. His father had beaten him once again at this, his favorite game. It was ever a skirmish for mastery between them, which Æthelred always won. If Emma was right, and his father feared him, he had yet to see any sign of it. "I await the king's pleasure," he said, but he did not lower his gaze. Let his father read the anger there. What did he care?

"Tonight I consult with my council regarding the Northmen's threat," Æthelred said. "Since you have nothing of value to report, take your seat. Do not," his voice dripped vitriol, "presume to offer advice unless you are addressed. Is that clear?"

Athelstan made his way to a bench, his gut tight with rage. He glanced around the hall, taking note of who was present. His brothers Ecbert and Edmund eyed him from across the room. Edmund's face was unreadable, but Ecbert flashed him a compassionate glance that he answered with a grimace. His brothers knew what it felt like to be on the receiving end of their father's wrath.

Arrayed near the king were all four of his ealdormen, with their supporters and retinues close by. Old Ælfric of Hampshire looked pale and drawn, and did not meet his eye. Next to him, Leofwine of Hwicce sat with his usual solemn expression. They were the old guard, older even than his father. They would do their best to give good advice, and his father would ignore them.

The third ealdorman, Godwine of Lindsey, thin and scrawny, toying nervously with the thick ring that was his badge of office and far too big for his womanish hands, would have little to offer. Next to him sat Ælfhelm of Northumbria, as big and hale as ever.

Jesu. Ælfhelm would want news of his daughter.

He muttered a curse under his breath and hoped that he would not have to be the one to tell him that Elgiva had been left behind in shattered Exeter.

He signaled to a servant to bring him mead. There was no reason why he should not get drunk. The king did not want his advice, although his counselors were abysmally few in number tonight. There should have been five more ealdormen, but his father had chosen to leave those positions of power unfilled, because, in his wisdom, he mistrusted any who might challenge him. The king wanted to keep his nobles weak and maintain power and wealth in his own hands, and he had succeeded most admirably.

Now, in Forkbeard, the ealdormen and the king faced a formidable foe, although they did not yet know the extent of their peril. Athelstan doubted that they could win a confrontation against the Danish king, and it was all too likely that one or more of these men was supporting Forkbeard in secret. Did his father suspect that?

Of course he did. His father suspected everyone.

After a series of interminable prayers, the messenger from Dorchester stood before them and relayed his news. It was precious little. The city had been attacked and set afire. The raiders had struck at night, and the messenger himself had no knowledge of who led them nor how many of them there might be. That announcement was followed by a debate over whether the shipmen would march inland from Dorchester or return to their vessels and strike farther along the coast.

Athelstan signaled for his cup to be refilled.

The next debate was over the size of the force that should be raised. After that they addressed the issue of leadership, and after that they wrangled over which shires would contribute men and arms to the land force.

Three hours later, Athelstan had emptied five cups of mead and the council had come to a momentous decision: They would decide nothing tonight. The king proclaimed that there would be time enough for them to consider what actions to take once the raiders had made their next move.

Athelstan, too, came to a decision. He decided that he was drunk, and that he liked it. It provided an excuse to wave off the questions of his brothers and avoid Ælfhelm. Ignoring everyone, he stumbled vaguely toward his chamber. When at last he found it he threw himself, fully dressed, upon his bed.

He slept fitfully, troubled by dreams of Emma standing amidst shattered, flame-scorched city walls.

While the king's council met in the hall, Emma and her household shared a quiet repast in the women's quarters. The gloom that the travelers had carried with them from the south seemed to descend upon the chamber like a black fog, and there was none of the usual bustle that came with unpacking after a long journey. Indeed, Emma thought, glancing about her, there was little to unpack. Jewelry, gowns, furnishings—all had been left behind. And that was the least of it. Her heart lurched as she thought of the men who had died at the hands of Swein's shipmen, and of so many others who were missing.

They could not all be dead, she told herself. Some of them must have escaped, must have hidden or found some way to barter for their lives.

She beckoned to one of the kitchen servants who she hoped might have news.

"Has there been any word from Exeter, Ebba?" she asked.

Ebba, her broad, red face aglow with self-importance at being so addressed, said eagerly, "Oh, aye, my lady! The whole of Exeter is burned, and all the folk in it are dead. Dorchester is burned as well, and it is only by God's grace that we'll escape being murdered in our beds. The friar who preaches outside the Old Minster has said that the Northmen will kill us all, that it is God's—"

Emma raised a hand to stop her, cursing herself, because the woman's ranting would do more harm than good. "Who told you that Dorchester was burned?" she asked.

"A messenger came from the south tonight with news for the king. He stopped in the kitchens for a bite and some ale, and he said that Dorchester was afire."

Emma frowned. So, Swein Forkbeard had struck two towns now, both of them with stout, heavily defended walls. He must have a large host, then. Would he be bold enough to attempt to capture Winchester? She feared that he might, and looking about the chamber, she realized that she was not alone in her fear. She could see the wine goblet trembling in Wymarc's hand, and even Margot looked deathly pale.

"We must not despair," she said. She was frightened, too, but she did not believe that Winchester could be destroyed. It was unimaginable. "Doubtless the king will lead a force against his enemies soon, and drive them back to their ships."

And what of her, then? What if the king should send her away for safekeeping—to join his children at Headington, perhaps?

She folded her hands beneath her breasts, where even now a child might be quickening. Her dilemma was minor compared to the enormity of the threat from the Danish army, but she must determine how to deal with it. It had been a week since she lay with Athelstan, and she had only a little window of time now to make sure that, if she did bear a child nine months hence, it would be recognized as Æthelred's. She must find her way to the king's bed, and soon.

Which of his favorites, she wondered, was sleeping with him now? And how was she to displace her? Æthelred would think it strange if she showed a sudden ardor for his embraces, so she would have to be patient. There was time yet. He had said that he would speak with her on the morrow. When she saw him she must be obedient and compliant. She must offer him comfort and respite from the troubles that beset him. She must welcome him to her bed.

And could she imagine that he was someone else?

Her courage faltered at that. The father was not the son, and never would be. Yet what else could she do? She must be a wife to the man that she had wed—and never forget that he was the king and held her fate in his hands.

For the next few hours the talk swirled among the women like the water in a stream, touching lightly on topics as if they were stones, then flowing onward to something else. Emma noticed that Wymarc alone did not join in the conversation but remained wrapped in a grief that she bore in silence. There was nothing that anyone could do or say to help her, and Emma feared that Hugh's loss—for she was certain that he was either dead or a prisoner of the Danes—would weigh heavily upon Wymarc for many long months to come. She grieved for her friend, and wondered again if there was a place in this world for love.

It was very late when Hilde returned, followed by Lord Ælfhelm. Emma had sent all her women to their beds, and now, alone with Elgiva's father, she contemplated the man before her.

He was not an easy man to deal with, or even to look at, this Ælfhelm. His face was seamed and scarred, with large, irregular features—the kind of face that frightened small children. His wild black mane of hair hung to near his shoulders, and his thick beard was shot through with streaks of white. It had always astonished her that such a man could have sired three such beautiful creatures as Elgiva and her brothers.

He was built like a bear, and he had a belligerent manner, cowering to no one, not even the king. Indeed, she had seen him look upon Æthelred more than once with an expression of subtle contempt—something she suspected her husband suffered because he had no other choice. Rich in land and silver, Ælfhelm was the most powerful of the king's ealdormen, and the kind of man who could instill fear with just a glance.

He was looking at her now with hooded eyes. She clutched her hands together, anguished by the pain she was about to inflict.

"My lord Ælfhelm," she said, "I must be the bearer of ill tidings tonight. It grieves me to tell you that your daughter was within Exeter's fortress when the city was attacked. Groa was with her, and I continue to hope and pray that they were able to escape, but I do not know their fate."

She looked on him with pity, steeling herself to cope with his grief, yet, to her bewilderment, it did not come. His face, as hard as granite, showed no horror, no sorrow, not even surprise. It was like a blank wall, and she could not read it at all. Could a man, even one as unfeeling as this, be so stoic? Did he care nothing for his daughter?

"You should turn your prayers to better purpose, lady," he said, his voice dull and flat, "for my daughter is well enough."

Emma gazed upon him now with wonder and with sudden hope. If Elgiva had escaped the sack of Exeter, perhaps she had brought others with her.

"She is safe then? She is unharmed?"

"Oh, aye. The shipmen did not rape her, and for that I suppose I must be grateful. Never mind that for near a year she was the king's whore," he snarled, "when she should have been under your protection." He must have seen her start of surprise, because he raised an eyebrow. "Did you think I did not know? And after the king wiped his hands of her, did you think I would entrust her to your care again without taking measures to ensure her safety? I am not such a fool, lady. My men shadowed you all the way to Exeter, and my son kept watch there to protect his sister against any threats. When the beacons were lit, Wulf spirited her away, while you, I am told, were safe outside the city." His eyes glittered, cold and hostile, but his face remained expressionless. "Would you hear Groa's fate? She died under the blade of a Danish battle-ax." He bared his teeth, but it was not a smile. "Is there anything else you wish to know? Lady?"

Emma merely stared at him, assaulted by his words and too stricken to attempt a response. When she remained silent, he bowed and turned away. She watched him stalk from the chamber, her mind reeling from the force of his loathing.

How he must hate her. She had ever known that Elgiva was her enemy. Now she realized—and she should have known it long before this—that Ælfhelm, too, was her foe. And he was far more dangerous than any of his children.

Chapter Thirty-three

August 1003

Winchester, Hampshire

There was no dawn the next morning. Heavy black clouds blanketed the sky, and a drenching rain turned the palace grounds and all the streets of Winchester to thick, flowing mud. Æthelred, his black-robed queen at his side, led a procession of ealdormen and clergy, of noblemen, their wives, and as many townsfolk as could walk or hobble, in a solemn procession from the palace steps and down the dripping, tree-lined path that led to the Old Minster. Inside this, the largest church in England, beneath the massive golden shrine of St. Swithin, Bishop Alfheah led them in prayers of supplication.

Æthelred gazed in despair at the magnificent, gem-studded, gold-and-silver reliquary that his father had commissioned to honor St. Swithin. King Edgar the Peaceful, his father had been named. He had honored God and the Church, and his reign had been marked by peace and prosperity instead of the constant threat of fire and sword.

Æthelred had tried to follow his father's example, had granted land and income to the bishops of Christ's church and appointed able men to positions of ecclesiastical power. He had even erected the high stone tower that housed the sixteen bells now tolling in mourning for his wretched people. But God had rejected all his efforts and would not listen to his pleas. His sin was too great, his brother's voice beyond the grave too strident.

All about him the cloying scent of incense mingled with the sobs and wails of the congregation as they prayed for God's mercy. Æthelred, his face cradled in his hands, strove to empty his mind and heart of all despair. Surely such an outpouring of prayer and grief as this around him, such a thundering upon the gates of heaven from so many voices, would reach the ears of the Almighty.

He begged for forgiveness while the Latin chanting of the clergy rose and fell like the tides of the sea. *Pater noster qui es in coelis, sanctificetur Nomen Tuum.* Our Father, who art in heaven, hallowed be Thy Name.

He imagined his own father, seated at the side of the Lord in a blissful heaven, raising his hands to quell the storm that threatened his son's kingdom. Was this not a vision? Was it not a sign of God's forgiveness? In the comforting words of the Pater Noster he heard a promise that all would yet be well, and as Æthelred joined in the swelling music of the prayer, he was lifted at last out of his fear and bitterness. His heart grew lighter, for if God forgave him, what had he to fear from Danish raiders or blood-soaked phantoms in the night?

When the service ended, a messenger, soaking wet and filthy with mud, was waiting for him in the minster's west porch. Æthelred regarded him with misgiving. The wretch could not have brought him ill tidings, for he had prayed. They had all prayed.

"Well?" he asked.

"The Viking army is coming this way, my lord, three thousand men strong and led by the Danish king."

The solemn mood of the morning was shattered as if by a lightning stroke. A physical shudder of movement and sound rippled through the crowd behind the king and, impatient for more information, Æthelred raised his hand for silence.

"Have they crossed the Stour?" he demanded.

"Yes, my lord. Early this morning."

That meant that in four days' time Swein's army would be at the city's gates. He dismissed the messenger and, as the congregation behind him dissolved into panic, he made for the palace. He must rely on himself now, for God had abandoned him utterly.

Immediately he summoned his counselors to his private chamber. He called for maps, and with his nobles grouped around him at the trestle table, he studied the parchments set before him. With his index finger he searched for Dorchester, but the news of Forkbeard's advance had seared his mind like white-hot steel, and he could not focus his thoughts upon his task. The calm that had descended upon him in the church had deserted him, replaced by a growing sense of doom.

"Forkbeard's army," he said, "will reach the gates of our city in a matter of days unless we find a way to stop it." Even now he found it hard to believe that such a monstrous calamity could be about to engulf them.

"Offer them enough gold," Ealdorman Leofwine muttered, "and they will skulk back to their ships soon enough." He folded his arms across his chest, as if he considered the matter settled.

Æthelred scowled.

"Think you that they have not already taken gold and silver from the ruins of Exeter and Dorchester? Nay, they want more than our treasure. They want to fall upon us like ravening wolves and swallow us alive. They would destroy everything of beauty and of value in this land. In Exeter they left not one stone standing upon another. If we do not stop them, Winchester will suffer the same fate."

They stared at him, denial in their eyes. They still did not perceive their peril.

"My father is right." It was Athelstan who spoke, and Æthelred regarded him with surprise, for that phrase was not one his son was wont to use. "Forkbeard seeks vengeance for the murder of his sister and her family. Already he has speared his army deep into Dorset, farther than ever before. We must bring together a force that will match the Danes' and engage them before they can make it to our gates."

At this there was a clamor of voices, but Æthelred ceased to listen. The golden circlet upon his head had grown heavy and leaden, and now his temples throbbed with a piercing pain. Beneath the pain lay the chill finger of dread that bespoke the silent, looming wraith of his brother.

He could not see Edward, but he could feel him watching from the shadows with fierce, triumphant eyes. Was it the fetid scent of fear that brought him here? Surely the terror of death had been the last emotion that Edward had known upon this earth. Did his shade long to smell it now upon his brother's still-living body?

He tensed his shoulders against the pain that forked from his head to his neck, borne, he was certain, on Edward's baleful gaze. The words that he had read months before on a scrap of parchment surfaced in his mind to plague him again with their message of doom.

And now thou art cursed from the earth, which hath opened her mouth to receive thy brother's blood.

Who had written those words? Was he here, a member of his council, perhaps even one of his sons? How many of these men, he wondered, resting his gaze hopelessly on one face after another, would throw their bodies in front of a sword to protect him? Which of them would even feel sorrow if he should die? Ælfric, perhaps, he thought, glancing at his father's old friend. As for the rest of them, if they should see him cut down he had little doubt that they would quickly rally to Swein's side.

Today his nobles would demand that he lead them against Swein. But he would not place his life in their hands.

He could trust none of them.

When the rain had been swept away and replaced by a golden afternoon, Emma sought the haven of her garden. She had spent much of that morning directing the servants in sorting through the myriad items that had to be packed up and readied for removal in the event that the Danes attacked the city. Silver candlesticks, golden plates and chalices, jewelry, glittering hair ornaments, gem-studded gowns and robes, fur cloaks, beautifully illustrated manuscripts—all the trappings of royalty had to be itemized and packed away.

She had been glad to have something to distract her from thoughts of what must be occurring in the king's chamber—the council session to which she had not been invited. Indeed, she had had no discourse at all with the king, in spite of his promise that he would meet with her this morning. The news from the south had disrupted everything, and she wondered if normal life would ever return. Her need to speak with Æthelred, to lay the foundations for drawing him into her bed, nagged at her, setting her already frayed nerves even more on edge.

This morning at the minster she had read the terror in her husband's eyes when he learned that his greatest enemy was loose in the land. She guessed that Æthelred's fear of Forkbeard could not be any greater even if the Danish king sprouted horns and a tail, and she mistrusted her husband's thinking when he was frightened. It was fear that had led him to the ill-considered and ignominious massacre of St. Brice's Day. Now that events were spiraling out of Æthelred's control, she dreaded what his response would be. He was not likely to think things through, and he could not be expected to listen to advice from anyone, least of all from her.

She was brooding upon these thoughts when she saw Athelstan enter through the gate and make his way toward her. He took her hand in his to kiss her ring, and she made a conscious effort not to cling to his fingers for even the briefest moment. She was the one who had set the boundaries between them—she could not cross them, no matter how much she longed to do so.

"What has been decided?" she asked.

He told her, briefly, of Æthelred's battle plan.

"You were right about my father's fear," he said. "He is mad with it, I think. He trusts no one, not even his ealdormen, except for Ælfric. I think he is afraid that if he allows anyone else to lead an army they are likely to join forces with Forkbeard instead of fight against him. The king's entire defense hinges on whatever troops Ælfric can muster from Hampshire and Wiltshire in a matter of days."

"Has he cause for such fear of his nobles?"

He looked at her squarely, his strong, dark brows set in a scowl.

"Of course he does. My father's ealdormen do not trust him any more than he trusts them. But, dear God, if Ælfric should meet the Danes and lose—"

"But Ælfric is a good leader," she protested, "and loyal to your father."

He swept her words aside with an impatient gesture. "It is not his loyalty that worries me. Ælfric will have to face a Danish shield wall of three thousand seasoned warriors, while our army will be made up mostly of farmers and householders with little training in battle and God knows what in the way of armor and weapons. How will they be able to withstand the Danes? There is likely to be a slaughter, and all because we have not prepared to face so large an enemy host. My father insists on holding his hearth troops, men who can truly fight, in reserve here in Winchester, as a last measure of defense. He is wrong. It would be better to throw as many experienced, well-armed men as we can against the Danes in the first attack rather than divide our forces this way. It would be best of all if the king should lead the army, or at the very least ride at Ælfric's side. The presence of the king would stiffen the resolve of our warriors."

"Have you told him any of this?" she asked.

"He will not listen to me! I have offered to add my hearth troops to Ælfric's force, but the king will not allow even that. My brother Ecbert goes with Ælfric. I am bid to stay behind and arrange for the city's defense, to make up for the debacle at Exeter."

She knew how he must chafe at that. It was bad enough that the sack of Exeter had been laid at his feet, but now he must watch his brother ride off to battle while he stayed behind. Yet she was glad that he would remain. If the worst should befall them, she wanted him near.

"If your father has put you in charge of our defense," she said stoutly, "then he has done at least one thing right."

"You are wrong," he said, looking utterly defeated already. "There is nothing that feels right about this. Emma, listen to me." He took her hand in his. "You must leave the city now, for only God knows what may happen in a few days' time. Go to London and prepare a ship, so that if the Danes should have the victory, you can seek refuge at your brother's court in Normandy. There is no reason why you should stay here."

She read the urgent plea in his eyes, but before she could even frame a response, she saw that the king's steward, Hubert, had entered the garden and was hurrying toward them. She stiffened and pulled her hand from Athelstan's grasp, but she could not tell what the steward had seen. Hubert, whose long, pointed nose always made her think of a rat or a weasel, addressed Athelstan.

"My lord," he said, "the king requires your presence in his chamber."

The smooth face beneath the fringe of brown hair gave no indication that he had noticed anything amiss between the queen and the king's son.

"I will come directly," Athelstan said, and then turned to Emma. "Think on what I have said, my lady. Act upon it, I beg you."

When he was gone his plea echoed in her ears.

Leave. Seek refuge in Normandy.

He was not the first who had urged her to run. Ælfric's son, the blinded, bitter Ælfgar, had said much the same thing.

She could imagine what lay ahead. The savagery that had taken place in the lane near Magdalene Abbey would be as nothing compared to the carnage to come.

She covered her mouth with hands that trembled as she thought of Groa, and of all the others who lay dead in the rubble of Exeter and Dorchester—walled cities that had not been able to withstand the Danish onslaught. Why should Winchester be any different?

She was afraid of what was to come. Dear God, she wanted to flee, to take ship across the Narrow Sea, driven by her fear and by the fury of the Danish king. But she knew what kind of welcome she would receive in Normandy. Her mother, who had chosen her for this role of queen, would despise her for her weakness.

And her mother would be right. The queen's place was here, no matter what the danger. She might, even now, be carrying a child—a son of the royal blood who might one day rule this kingdom. This realm would be that child's birthright. She would not take him away from it.

She placed her hand beneath her breasts, resting it upon the fine green linen of her gown. She prayed for courage, and that her womb might be quick with Athelstan's child.

It was very late when, summoned at last by the king, Emma entered his bedchamber. Æthelred sat at the long table on one side of the room, stands of glowing candles all around him, a cup and flagon near to his hand. His steward, Hubert, sat at the table as well, laboring over an official-looking document. He cast her a furtive, ratlike glance that made Emma shiver with sudden trepidation.

The king ignored her altogether, and so she stood where she was, a heavy cloak wrapped around her linen nightgown, her feet cold inside her thin slippers as she awaited her lord's pleasure. She was uncomfortable in this chamber, this fortress of sovereign privilege. It was Æthelred's retreat, and she never ventured here unless summoned. Tonight she had been roused from her bed to attend him, and that had not happened before.

Again she felt a slight shudder of unease, and a finger of cold crept along her arms despite the cloak she wore over her nightshift. Nervously she glanced toward the far end of the chamber where the candlelight could not reach. The flickering darkness there preyed on her imagination, for she seemed to sense movement in the shadows whenever she was not looking directly at them.

It was just a trick of the light, she told herself, or the play of a draft fingering the thick curtain that was strung there from wall to wall. Behind that dark drapery were the chests and caskets that held much of the king's personal treasure. Æthelred's wealth was legendary, and his kingdom a prize coveted by men who would wrest it from him if they could.

She looked at him, smitten of a sudden with compassion for this man who saw himself as so beset by enemies that he could not trust even his own sons. He seemed to sense her gaze upon him, for he lifted his head just then and met her eyes. His were hollowed, and it seemed to her that the lines of his face too were deeper tonight than they had been this morning. But perhaps that was merely a trick of the wavering light, for the shadows in the room seemed to stretch and shudder like living things as the steward picked up a candle from the table and used the dripping wax to seal the document that he had just completed.

The king motioned to the monk to leave, and the little man rose, bowed, then gathered up his writing materials and slipped out of the room. He cast a sly glance at her before the heavy oak door groaned shut, leaving her alone with the king, and with the shadows that threatened from outside the circle of light. Emma felt another stirring of apprehension.

Æthelred tossed back whatever it was he had been drinking and rose slowly to his feet. He was clad in a nightshirt of fine embroidered white linen, with a thick, dark, woolen cloak thrown over it for warmth. He offered her no words of greeting, nor any invitation to be seated, and the expression on his face was forbidding.

"I have written to your brother," he said, "to inform him of the attack upon Exeter by Swein Forkbeard, although I do not doubt that Richard knows of it already. Indeed, he may have had word of it even before it happened."

He shot her an appraising glance, as if he were daring her to contradict him. She wanted to tell him that he was wrong, wanted to assure him that her brother could have known nothing of what Forkbeard intended. Yet she was not certain of that herself. Her brother might, indeed, have turned a blind eye to the Danish ships massing on his northern coast. Athelstan had suggested as much, and the possibility that this could be so had gnawed at her all summer long. Yet even if it was true that Richard had known Forkbeard's plan, she could not imagine how he could have stopped it.

She had no answer for the king, and seeing it, he smiled a cruel, hard smile.

"Do you not think it interesting," he went on, "that the Danes attacked your dower city, my lady? I have been pondering this, and I begin to think that Forkbeard was aiming at England's queen rather than its king." His face was speculative as he awaited her reaction to his suggestion.

Emma feigned puzzlement, but she felt her blood run cold under that gaze, for his words pricked her like the point of a blade. Did Æthelred know of the hours she had spent in Forkbeard's hands? Was the letter to her brother written to inform Richard that the king was setting her aside?

"I cannot think what you mean, my lord." She forced herself to speak through lips that had gone suddenly dry.

"Can you think of nothing?" he asked, raising quizzical brows and twisting his mouth into a sneer of disbelief. He moved slowly toward her, took her left hand in his large paw, and began to toy with the ring on her third finger that was the symbol of their marriage bond. "For myself," he said, "I cannot help but wonder if your brother might have promised your hand in marriage to someone else prior to bestowing it upon me."

He fixed his watery blue eyes upon her face, looking for her reaction, but she was so astonished by his words that she merely gazed at him with blank incredulity.

"Swein Forkbeard has two sons," he continued. "Did you pledge yourself to a son of the Danish king, Emma, and then break that vow when my emissary made a better offer?"

"I did not, my lord," she protested. "Nor did my brother make any such pledge, I assure you."

He smiled, but there was no warmth in it. "Then perhaps it was the Danish king himself who won your . . . admiration, shall we call it? I asked you on our wedding night if you were a maid, and although

I believed you when you assured me of your innocence, I have to wonder about it now. Did you perhaps bestow your favors upon Swein Forkbeard before your brother granted your hand to me? Did I purchase used goods for my bride? It is your lands that Swein has ravaged, Emma, not mine. A spurned lover's revenge perhaps?"

Her first instinct was to slap him, but with an effort she governed her rage. This was Æthelred's fear speaking. He was like a dumb animal cruelly baited, and so lashing out at anything within reach. If she gave him an excuse to hurt her, he would do so with savage glee. She must not lose her head now, for she was completely in his power.

She wrenched her hand from his grasp and said, icily, "I was a virgin when I wed you, my lord king, and I was pledged to no one before I gave you my hand. As for Swein Forkbeard's choice of target, I would not presume to guess what is in his mind. Surely he would see all of Wessex as the property of the king." She folded her arms against her body. The room was cold, and the king's sour smile made it seem colder still.

"Nevertheless," he replied, "the destruction of Exeter will, I fear, adversely impact your income, and I have so informed your brother. You would do well to consult with him regarding some means of additional financial support, since you will receive little from your Exeter holdings until the devastation there has been repaired. I promise you that you will receive nothing more from me until you complete the task that, virgin or no, you were sent here to do. Shall we?" He gestured toward the bed.

She stared at him. This was a man who had paraded first one mistress and then others before her, almost from their wedding day. Yet now, based on acts that he had spun out of his own foul imagination, he would brand her a whore. She despised him. She did not want him to touch her, did not even want him to speak to her. Whatever compassion she had felt for him had evaporated, and she wanted nothing more than to get away from him.

"Are you not afraid, my lord," she said, with as much cold disdain as she could muster, "that I will contaminate your hallowed sheets?" Perhaps he would merely cuff her and throw her out of the room.

There was no flare of anger in his eyes, though. All she saw in his face was cold calculation and, to her astonishment, a kind of grim amusement.

"You are right," he said. "Why should I sully my bedding with a Norman whore? You need no bed to fulfill your role as royal vessel."

He grasped her arm and shoved her toward the long table. For a moment she was bewildered. Then, with deliberate, steady pressure upon the back of her neck, he forced her head inexorably downward. She reached out instinctively to brace herself against the hard wooden surface, but she could not resist him—could do no more than turn her head to the side just before her face hit the table.

"I can call my servant in to hold you down, if you like," he whispered in her ear. "Or you can do your duty like a good wife. Which will it be? You must tell me."

He demanded an answer, she guessed, because he craved her complete submission to his will. Absolute power over someone else was, for Æthelred, the ultimate arousal.

"I shall do my duty," she grated through clenched teeth.

She felt him lift her gown so that her warm flesh was exposed to the cold air. His hands grasped her hips to pull her hard against him as he entered her. She clung to the edge of the table with her fingers, and with each deliberate thrust she watched the candle shiver.

When he was finished, as she lay there, stunned and humiliated, he wiped himself with the hem of her robe.

"You will attend me here tomorrow night in this same fashion," he said, "and you will continue to do so until you can inform me that you are with child. Get out."

She pushed herself from the table and adjusted her skirts, but she did not hurry. She would not give him the satisfaction of running from him, and she would not show him any fear. She glared at him, her chin held high, then stalked toward the door.

"Emma." His voice stopped her before she could lift the latch and escape from his loathsome presence.

She did not turn to look at him. She had not the stomach for that.

"You will stay away from my son," he said. She could hear him filling his cup again. "Do you understand me?"

So. This was more than punishment for some imagined, long ago tryst with the Danish king. This was some phantom, feral competition between the king and his son. What did he guess of her feelings for Athelstan, or of his for her? Surely if he knew the truth her punishment would have been far worse.

"Do you understand?" he repeated, more sharply.

"Yes, my lord," she said.

For the next three nights Emma attended her husband in his chamber, returning afterward to her own bed, where she lay curled protectively around the womb that she prayed held the seed of a child. On the fourth morning she woke to find her linen stained with blood. There would be no child, and she grieved her loss with an aching heart and secret, bitter tears.

A.D. 1003   Then was collected a very great force which was soon ready on their march against the enemy; and Ealdorman Ælfric should have led them on; but as soon as they were so near, that either army looked on the other, then he pretended sickness, and he began to retch, saying he was sick. . . . When Swein saw that they were not ready, and that they all retreated, then led he his army into Wilton, and they plundered and burned the town.

—*The Anglo-Saxon Chronicle*

Chapter Thirty-four

August 1003

Winchester, Hampshire

The city of Winchester lived in a fog of apprehension and fear for seven agonizing days. On the horizon to the southwest a thin smudge of smoke showed a sickly yellow-brown against the relentlessly gray skies, for the invaders burned every village, hamlet, and croft that lay in their path. A steady stream of refugees brought word of the Danes' northward progress.

Winchester itself had been bled of most of its able men, for they had taken up arms and marched west with Ealdorman Ælfric to make a stand against the foe. Those left behind took their turns upon the city walls, watching for signs that the invading army was drawing near. All commerce stopped. Shopkeepers and craftsmen shut their doors. No one was left to work the mills, and bread became scarce. Only the huge stones of the palace mills turned, and they worked from first light to full dark. At midday the gates of the palace were flung wide and servants distributed flour to the citizens who formed a line that wound past the Old Minster, through St. Thomas Gate, and up into Ceap Street. Inside the walls of the two great churches and the confines of St. Mary's Abbey, the monks and the nuns stormed heaven with prayers for mercy.

On the eighth day after the Danes had attacked Dorchester, the fate of Winchester was decided on a plain to the west, near the town of Wilton. Two days after the armies met, Athelstan and Edmund heard an account of what occurred from Ecbert, who had witnessed it firsthand.

"We came within sight of the enemy in the early afternoon." Ecbert spoke from his sickbed, and Athelstan moved his stool closer to hear him better. "Christ, we were close to each other. We were close enough to see their faces, the ugly bastards." He stopped and swallowed several times before going on. "The men on both sides were in a frenzy, ready to fight. We were taunting each other, shouting insults and curses. Not that we could understand each other's words, but the meaning was more than clear." He tried to fake a grin, but it twisted into a grimace.

"I hope you picked up a few Danish obscenities," Edmund said. "They might come in useful sometime."

Ecbert laughed, then groaned.

Athelstan, impatient to hear the tale, growled at Edmund. "Don't interrupt him. What happened next?"

"We had stopped midmorning so the men could have something to eat. Ælfric had called his battle leaders, a dozen or so of us, to break fast with him. I forced myself to swallow some bread and meat, and while we ate, he laid out his plans for the coming battle and gave each of us our orders. We knew what to do, how to place our men. . . . We knew it all. But we never got the chance to do it."

Ecbert stared at the opposite wall, as if he could see the events recurring, right there in front of him. A fine sweat dewed his forehead.

"We were not yet into position," Ecbert went on, "and I was still mounted when I first realized that something was wrong. The Danes had already formed a shield wall, and they had begun to bang their swords against their shields, ready for battle. It was like thunder, that sound, only it was as if the thunder was inside my head. I closed my eyes against the pain of it, but it would not go away. When I opened my eyes again I saw Ælfric only a few steps from me. His thegns had surrounded him, and he was on the ground, on his hands and knees, spewing his guts out."

He closed his eyes and placed a big hand over his face.

"I just sat there, staring at him, with this awful pounding in my head and a gnawing gripe in my belly. I remember feeling dizzy, and then I saw Osric, who had been sent to parley with the Danes, ride up and just slump off his horse, as if he had been struck by an invisible arrow. My own pain had gotten so bad that all I could think of was that I had to dismount before I fell, too. I made it to the ground, and then I was retching, and my hands shook so that I could not even hold onto my reins. Christ, the pain in my head and my gut was so awful that I would have welcomed the thrust of a Danish sword to put an end to it."

Athelstan studied his brother as he lay there, limp and spent. Ecbert was not yet recovered although the events he related had happened two days before.

"The men are saying," Athelstan said slowly, hating to burden his brother with the news but knowing that he would hear it sooner or later, "that Ælfric was terrified at the sight of the Danes."

Ecbert cursed. "Even sick as I was I could hear the men around me muttering, calling me a worthless, puling coward." He sighed. "In truth, that's what it must have looked like."

He sat up and grabbed Athelstan's arm, but his grip was weak.

"I was afraid, Athelstan," Ecbert whispered. "That much of the calumny is true. But it was not fear that struck me down, I swear to you! It was some kind of curse, some heathen magic that drove us to our knees. I do not know how they did it." His voice broke, and he sank back into his pillows. "I do not even know what happened after that. The rest of it you must tell me."

"There were ten or so men stricken like you," Athelstan said. "You and Ælfric, Osric, Edric, Brihtwold, Lyfing. All the leaders, do you see? When the leader is sick, the whole army is hindered. There was no one left to command, and so the entire host fell back. The Danes won the battle without lifting a sword."

"It must have been treachery," Edmund insisted. "Some Danish spy made it through the lines and poisoned the food or the drink."

"But it had been hours since we had eaten," Ecbert protested. "Surely poison would have worked sooner than that."

Athelstan said nothing, for he had no answers to give. Some force, he was certain, was assisting the Danish king. He had no idea, though, if it was the hand of God, of man, or of the devil. He sighed, frustrated and disheartened. They had suffered a defeat, it was true, but in the end it was not as bad as it could have been.

He told his brother the rest of the tale, all the events that Ecbert had not seen, because he had been lying in a covered wain, lost in fevered dreams as he was carried back to Winchester.

Ælfric's great army, leaderless, had been forced to retreat. Many of the men had drifted away to return to their homes and farms. Most of them, though, had stayed together, making their way to the royal city.

"The Danes swarmed first into Wilton, and then Salisbury. They looted homes and businesses, and they took a massive haul of silver from the minters' workshops and storerooms. That booty seemed to content them," Athelstan said dryly. "They did not attempt to lay siege to Winchester. We owe thanks for that to the remnants of Ælfric's host, who joined us on the walls as we prepared to defend the city. The Danes, seeing that, bypassed Winchester completely and went south along the Avon. We sent men in their wake, and I expect we will soon hear that they have taken ship for home."

"So our father will not have to bribe them with yet more silver to go away and leave us in peace," Edmund said.

"If we gave them any more silver," Athelstan growled, "their vessels would likely sink with the weight of it." He looked at Edmund and saw in his brother's eyes his own fear reflected there. "The Danes will not leave us in peace for long. You and I both know what Forkbeard will do with all his newly gained wealth."

Edmund nodded. "He will build more ships, and he will buy more men."

"And then," Athelstan said grimly, "he will come back."

Chapter Thirty-five

September 1003

Aldeborne Manor, Northamptonshire

It was Ealdorman Ælfhelm who carried word of the sacking of Dorchester, Wilton, and Salisbury to his sons and his daughter in Northamptonshire. Elgiva watched her father's arrival from the doorway of the great hall, flanked by Wulf on her right and by her eldest brother, Ufegeat, on her left. The autumn air was chilly, and she held the welcoming ale cup ready in her hands as their father dismounted and made his way up the steps toward them.

She had not set eyes on him since the spring, and she was struck by how much older he seemed to her now. Had her father really aged so much, she wondered, or were her senses merely more acute? Ever since she had been granted the vision of the white hart it seemed to her that everything looked different—older, darker, even threatening. Was this the gift granted by that vision? If so, she would just as soon give it back.

She had ordered a meal prepared, and as her father sat down to his meat and ale, all three of his children listened attentively to his tale.

"It is certain then," Elgiva said, after he had described Ælfric's untimely illness and the English retreat, "that the Danes have left our shores for good?"

Ever since her return from Exeter her brothers had kept her mewed up within the palisade that surrounded the estate, for fear of Danish raiders. Whenever she did get leave to set foot beyond the walls, whether to ride into nearby Northampton or to hunt within their own woodlands, she was accompanied by an armed force and, invariably, one of her brothers. She was heartily sick of her brothers.

"It is certain that they have left our shores, for now," her father replied. "Anyone who believes that they are gone for good is a dreamer or a damned fool."

"And in which category would you place our beloved king?" asked Ufegeat.

He held his cup out toward Elgiva and motioned for more ale, as if she were no more than a serving wench. Her eldest brother's arrogant attitude maddened her, although, truth be told, he treated her as he treated all women—as if the whole purpose of female existence was to cater to him. She poured the ale into his cup but muttered a curse under her breath.

Ufegeat sat back in his chair with his brimming cup and waited for his father to respond to his quip.

"Æthelred is a dreamer *and* a fool, as you well know," her father grunted. "You saw it firsthand in Cumberland two years ago, did you not? When the fleet ran into a storm and was unable to meet with the land force at the appointed time, the whole action turned into a debacle. It was a waste of time and money, all because Æthelred had neither the imagination to foresee what might go wrong nor the intellect to plan for it. And because he is so damned unlucky, invariably something does go wrong, and the result is disaster. It has happened over and over again. This episode at Wilton is just the latest example. It is hardly a wonder that our king has no stomach for fighting. Instead he prays and weeps and dreams that all will be well. But he cannot dream the Danes away. They will hit us again next summer, to be sure. The only question is where."

"They will not strike us here, will they?" Elgiva asked, afraid, eager for reassurance. And if they did come, sailing up the Nene from the Wash or marching northward from Wessex, there would be warning beacons lit, surely. There would be time to run.

"Have no fear," her father said. "They will not strike anywhere near here."

She saw a glance pass between her father and Ufegeat, just the briefest knowing look, so swift that she wasn't even sure that it had really been there.

"You sound very certain of that, my lord," Wulf said.

Her father shrugged. "Swein would not strike so far inland unless he was mad, or unless he was prepared to challenge Æthelred for the entire kingdom. He is not mad, and I do not believe that he has the numbers of ships and men that he would need to overrun all of England." He lifted his cup to his lips and muttered, "Not yet, at any rate."

Elgiva stared at him. "You think that is what he wants?" she asked. "You think he would make himself king of England as well as king of Denmark and Norway?"

It was a terrifying thought. If it were true, there would be no place to hide from the fighting. No corner of the kingdom would be safe. Dear God, her father would likely shut her up in a convent for safekeeping, and then she would go mad.

Her father waved a dismissive hand.

"Do not trouble your head about it, daughter," he said. "Your brothers and I will protect you, whatever comes."

Elgiva snorted. "My brothers have been protecting me for weeks, now, and I find it unspeakably tedious. I wish the Danes would stay at home in their own halls. I shall pray that if this Forkbeard sets out a-viking to our shores again, a storm will come along and swallow up his entire fleet."

"Forgive us, Elgiva," Wulf said, "if we do not count on *your* prayers to be answered. I've observed that you tend to be rather lax about saying them."

She ignored him. She did not really believe in the power of prayer to effect change in the lives of men. Why should God care what mortals did to one another? It was not as if what happened in this world could affect Him, for good or for ill. Besides, were not all Christians praying to the same God? Was the Almighty supposed to choose one side or the other in a battle, designating reward or punishment by the number of prayers sent heavenward? Such a concept of God could only have been invented by some arrogant male, someone like her brother Ufegeat, who had already founded an abbey for the specific purpose of praying for his immortal soul. He seemed convinced that this would allow him to disobey all ten commandments while on earth yet still find a place reserved for him in God's heavenly kingdom.

She herself had no interest in the halls of paradise. She was much more interested in what was happening in Æthelred's hall now that the Danish threat had passed.

"What news of the queen?" she asked her father. "Has she asked for me?"

"She was pleased enough to learn of your escape from Exeter," he said. "She thought you were dead." He turned hard, assessing eyes on Wulf. "I would learn more about what happened that day," he said, "and I expect you to give me a full accounting."

There was a chill in his voice, and Elgiva did not envy her brother. He would have to confess that he had been delayed in rescuing her from the *burh* at Exeter because he had been dallying with his whore. That, however, was his problem.

"Has the queen sent me a summons?" she begged her father. "Am I to return to the court?" She longed to be in Winchester and away from the stifling boredom of her father's manor. She would swear that the hall itself was shrinking daily, little by little.

"The queen did not summon you," he said. "Indeed, you would find little there to amuse you. The Lady Emma is in mourning for those who were lost at Exeter. She has very few women in attendance upon her, for she cannot afford it. Her income has been greatly reduced because so many of her properties in Exeter were plundered and burned by Swein's army. Rumor has it that she has applied to her brother Richard for funds. What's more, she has lost favor with the king. He treats her with cold civility and continues to bar her from his councils."

Elgiva toyed thoughtfully with the salt spoon. If Æthelred had tired of Emma again, it was even more imperative that she return to court.

She could influence the king in ways that her father never could. Besides, the æthelings would be there, and she still hoped to beguile her way into Ecbert's bed.

She folded her hands on the table before her, leaning urgently toward her father.

"I am weary of living so far away from the court," she said. "If the queen can find no place for me among her retinue, my brother's house in Winchester will suit me very well. Surely you will join the king for the Yule celebration, and then I could—"

"I shall not join the king's court for the Yule," her father interrupted her. "He would have me there, to be sure. He wants all his ealdormen close by his side, but I have danced attendance upon him through the summer and I see no reason to court him through the winter season as well. He pays no heed to my words, and I'll not waste my time."

"All the more reason then," she urged, "that I return to Winchester. The king has favored me in the past and I may be—"

"You, my girl," her father snarled, reaching across the board to grab her wrist so tightly that the pain and shock made her cry out, "will be less generous with your favors henceforth. I know well enough how the king has favored you, and that you welcomed him like a bitch in heat. I looked the other way while I thought it might be profitable, but it has brought us nothing, and now it will stop. I will see to that! Your old nurse is not here to pander for you, and you will not find it so easy to cozen me."

He thrust her away from him, and Elgiva scowled, rubbing the sting from her wrist. She sat in stony silence as he took a long pull from his ale cup and wiped his mouth with the back of his hand.

"The king will not dally with you, in any case," he said with a belch. "The bishops have got their claws into him and have persuaded him that a chaste ruler is most likely to win God's favor. The queen is the only woman to visit the king's chamber now."

"I thought you said he treated her coldly," Elgiva grumbled.

"He does," her father growled, "but that need not stop him from swiving her. He hated his first wife, yet he got a dozen children on her. God forbid this one should be so fruitful," he muttered.

"The king cannot live forever," Wulf said. "We should be currying the favor of his sons."

Elgiva thought this an excellent idea, but she knew better than to voice her opinion now. Her father was drunk, past the point where she could persuade him with honeyed words and smiles. She could do nothing but sit here and listen—and hope that she learned something to her benefit.

"The king has looped his purse strings about the necks of his eldest sons," her father said, slurring his words and staring dully into his ale cup. "He has taken control of their estates and their income and, what is more, he has set spies upon them. They cannot so much as take a piss without the king knowing about it."

"He suspects them of some treachery, then?" Ufegeat asked in surprise.

Her father gave a shout of laughter. "Whom does he not suspect?" he asked. "For the time being," he said, spearing another haunch of meat with his knife, "we will be patient. We will watch and wait and listen. You," he pointed his knife at Ufegeat, "will go to Jorvik for the Yule. There are some matters there that need attending. You," he pointed his knife at Wulf, "will stay here with me, and together we shall guard our family's greatest asset. And you," Elgiva saw the knife aimed at her, "will resign yourself to a life of quiet solitude. Be thankful that you do not have to count your pennies like Æthelred's queen. And if I catch you cocking your eye at any man, no matter who he is I will shave your head and dress you in sackcloth with my own hands."

She gaped at him in horror.

"What have I done to deserve such a fate?" she cried.

"It is what you are destined to do that concerns me," her father said, "and I will not have you making any move that might foul my plans. Now get you to your chamber. I have matters to discuss with my sons."

He waved his knife drunkenly toward the door, but Elgiva did not move. She could feel the storm of blood surging to her head like an angry red tide, and it swept her past all caution.

"Nay, father. I have some matters to discuss with *you*," she said, leaning across the board to hiss at him. "I would know what use you made of the news I fed you about the queen's doings on that wretched journey across Wessex. I would know what my brother was about when I saw him speaking to a Danish thug in Exeter's backstreets. And most of all, I would know what plans you have made for me without my leave."

Her father froze, mouth agape, while the juice from his meat dripped down his chin and into his beard. But it was her brother Ufegeat who responded by striking her a hard blow across the face. While she was still too dazed to move, he grabbed her arm and dragged her from the bench.

"You have ever made too free with your tongue, girl," he snarled, "and your cunt." He shook her so that she grew dizzy. "This time you have gone too far. You will shut your mouth, keep your legs together, and do as you are bid. Get out!"

He thrust her away from him so that she fell off the dais and onto the hard slate floor. She lay there for a moment, waiting for the room to stop spinning, assessing the damage. Her hip and her elbow hurt where she had landed, and she tasted blood in her mouth. She saw Wulf glance at her, but he made no move to aid her. He was too much of a coward to defy his elder brother.

Her father did not even look at her, and Ufegeat had already dismissed her. Slowly she drew herself to her feet and limped toward the door, cradling her arm.

Ufegeat would never have touched her if Groa were still alive. They, all of them, had feared the old woman, wary of her knowledge of herbs, knowing that Groa would take her revenge should anyone injure her darling.

Well, she may not have Groa's knowledge or her skill, but she would find a way to make them pay. She did not know how to do it, nor how long it would take her, but one day she would make them repent their treatment of her. Let them have their plans and secrets. Let them try to mew her up like a kenneled hound. Their prize bitch had a vicious streak, and someday they would discover, to their sorrow, that she could bite.

October 1003
Winchester, Hampshire

It seemed to Emma that the king's icy attitude toward her had seeped into the very walls of the palace. She had few friends among the nobility, and even the servants treated her with a brittle courtesy that she found difficult to bear.

Like the king, they held her as somehow responsible for the Danish raid, as if, like the pull of the tides, she had inexorably drawn the invaders to England's shores. It was whispered about that her Norman reeve, Hugh, had with his own hand opened Exeter's gates to the Danish shipmen, and so the destruction of the city was laid squarely upon Emma's shoulders. The massacre of St. Brice's Day the year before, set in motion by the king's command, had been forgotten. Instead it was the foreign queen who was to blame for all.

As a result she lived like a stranger among them. The king never sought her out, rarely even addressed her—not even when she made her nightly visits to his chamber to gratify his sexual demands. She knew, as she carried out that particularly odious function, that she was doing her duty as wife and queen, yet she felt sullied by the act, for there was no affection or warmth conveyed by it in either direction. It seemed to her that they were little better than animals trapped in the same pen for the sole purpose of copulation.

In spite of Æthelred's coldness, however, she saw much of him, for she refused to form a second court, as she had in the first year of her marriage. Sensing that the king would be only too happy if she hid herself away in her quarters, she took advantage of every opportunity to accompany Æthelred wherever he might go. She attended him at Mass and she hunted with him daily. She sat beside him at his board and rarely left before the king himself sought his chamber. She met his icy disdain with stoic patience, steeling herself against him like a fine-edged sword. She bore ever in her mind the recognition that she was a Norman duke's daughter and an English queen, and she used that knowledge as a whetstone to sharpen her will against the king.

She saw much of Athelstan as well, but she took care that they were never alone. A single glance from him still had the power to stop her heart, but she had grown adept at disguising her thoughts and her emotions. The king's warning about his son still rang in her ears, and she would give him no reason to suspect that she held any special regard for Athelstan, for the ætheling's sake as much as her own. She cultivated, instead, the few friends that she had at court—the ealdorman Ælfric and Bishop Alfheah among them. They were her allies, and they imparted to her the news of events occurring within the realm that her husband, in his cold silence, withheld from her. With their assistance she was able to keep her finger upon the pulse of the kingdom, from Canterbury to Jorvik, from London to Exeter.

Nevertheless, it was a dreary existence, and in late September Emma looked forward with eagerness to the return of the king's children from their sojourn in Oxfordshire. She was not foolish enough to hope that their presence would somehow thaw the mood of the king and the court toward her, but at least the children would distract her. And so it proved.

The little party arrived late one afternoon. Emma, in her chamber with Wymarc, Margot, and Father Martin, had been dictating letters that would go to her brother in Rouen. The churches and abbeys in and around Exeter were desperate for money in order to begin repairs and, more important, to provide food and shelter for so many who had suffered at the hands of the Danes. They looked to her for help, and she had little to give.

As she pondered how best to frame her request to Richard, she heard a commotion outside the chamber door. A moment later it was flung open, and Æthelred's children swooped on her like a flock of starlings. Four-year-old Wulfa immediately demanded to be lifted into Emma's lap, while her two elder sisters insisted that she settle a dispute over which of them had grown the most over the summer. She had just pronounced that Ælfa did indeed appear to be a little bit taller than her elder sister when Edgar, now ten and accordingly bloodthirsty, held his new knife under her nose for inspection. He offered to demonstrate its edge by slicing off one of Ælfa's golden curls. This resulted in tears and a howl of protest from his victim, who sought safety behind Emma's chair.

"Put your knife back in its sheath, Edgar," Emma exclaimed, while Wymarc distracted Ælfa and Edyth with a coffer filled with silken ribbons. "Now," Emma said to Edgar, as she shifted Wulfa on her knee, "show me the hilt of your dagger. What is the design on it?"

"It is a dragon," he said eagerly, unbuckling the belt and holding the sheathed knife so that Emma could admire it. "Look how its body wraps all the way around the grip. And see, there is flame coming out of its mouth. I call it Firedrake."

"It is beautiful," she said, tracing with her fingertip the delicate silver inlay that formed the dragon. "Where did you get this princely gift?"

"Edward gave it to me before we left Headington palace," he said. "The smith there has boxes and boxes of weapons stored away in a special room, things that once belonged to my uncle and my grandsire. He gave this knife to Edward as soon as we arrived, but Edward said that he had no use for a dagger, and so he gave it to me. I have a shield, too. I can show it to you. Shall I get it?"

"I will look at it tomorrow," Emma said, vaguely apprehensive at hearing Edgar's description of his brother's generosity. When did a boy ever not have use for a dagger, especially one as beautiful and prized as this? "But where is Edward? Has he gone to find your older brothers?"

"No," Edgar said with a scowl. "Nurse took him straight to his bed. He is always tired now. He never plays with me anymore." Then his face brightened. "But he said that I am to be the king's cupbearer now, because it is too hard for him to stand up for so long."

Alarmed, Emma thought back to when she had last seen Edward. It had been June, and he had not yet fully recovered from the illness that had felled him in the spring. Had he not improved over the summer months? She glanced at Margot who, understanding, nodded and slipped away. Margot would check on the boy, and Emma was confident that the old nurse would find some remedy for whatever it was that ailed him.

But it quickly became apparent that Margot had no potion that could restore the health of the young ætheling. As Emma sat with him later that day, his hand in hers, she was filled with foreboding. It was as if some vital spark within him had dimmed, and she sensed that before long it would be extinguished altogether.

Chapter Thirty-six

April 1004

Winchester, Hampshire

All through the winter and into the spring Margot searched for a cure for Edward's illness. She rubbed his chest with an ointment of rue and aloe seethed in oil that seemed to give him brief respite from the pain in his chest. A cream of wormwood and bishopwort boiled in butter eased the aches in his knees and fingers. An ale laced with parsnip was meant to strengthen him and dispatch his blinding headache, but it did little more than help him sleep.

The leech sent for by the king insisted on bleeding the boy, and this remedy seemed to do more harm than good. Edward, who had been able to walk around his chamber for a little while each day, could not even sit up for two weeks after the cupping, and he never regained the strength to leave his bed. All through the autumn and the yuletide he kept to his chamber, tended by the queen and her attendants.

Emma spent an hour with him every day, regaling him with stories that she remembered from her childhood. Sometimes she brought her harp and sang to him, telling him afterward what the words meant, although often the music lulled him to sleep. Slowly, what little strength the boy had faded away, and she watched his slow decline with a heavy heart.

The king rarely ventured into Edward's sickroom, and this indifference toward the boy angered Emma. She complained bitterly of it to

Margot and to Wymarc one afternoon in late spring, as a dull rain thrummed upon the roof thatch. That morning, in a voice that was little more than a whisper, Edward had confided to her that he knew his father disliked him, because his visits were so infrequent.

"I told him that he must never doubt that his father loves him. A king, I said, must care for every single person in the land, and for that reason he is prevented from spending his time the way he might wish." She stood up and went over to the window. Its thick, greenish pane gave a lurid light to the unrelenting April rain. It had been many days since they had seen the sun, and she had begun to think that, like her own spirits, the clouds would never lift. "I do not understand," she said softly, "how the king can be so cold to the boy. Does he not realize that the child is dying? Athelstan visits his brother nearly every day, yet the boy's own father cannot sit with him for even a few brief moments in a week. It is heartbreaking to see how much Edward longs for his father."

She turned away from the greenish light and saw Wymarc, heavy with child, look up suddenly from her embroidery, her brows shrouded with grief. Emma bit her lip and wished that she could take back her words. Wymarc's child would have no father. They had all come to accept now that Hugh must be dead, slain by some Danish hand. And even if he had somehow managed to escape that fate, he would not likely make his way back to England ever again.

"I think," Margot said, "that in this instance you do the king an injustice." She was sorting through a pile of gowns that had belonged to Edyth, looking for those that could be cut down for the king's younger daughters.

"What do you mean?" Emma asked.

Margot paused in her task and gazed thoughtfully at Emma.

"I do not say that I agree with the king's manner of dealing with Edward's illness," she said at last. "It would not be my way of addressing the death of a child. But I think, my lady, that it is not unusual. The king is protecting himself from the pain of parting from Edward by drawing away from him. I think that he cannot bear to watch this lingering death that weakens the boy day by day. Tending the sick does not come naturally to a man, and if they have never been taught, they do not know how to act in the face of it."

"No one asks him to tend the boy," Emma said bitterly, "merely to treat him with a father's affection."

"And what," Margot replied, "does he know of that? His own father died when Æthelred was but a child."

This gave Emma pause, for there was some truth to Margot's words. King Edgar had died when Æthelred was very young, only six or seven years old. What could the man remember now of his father's love? And yet she could not help but compare again the actions of the king with those of his eldest son, and she found the king lacking. Showing affection for a child was not a trait that one learned. Like compassion and tenderness, it dwelt in the heart and soul of a man. Whatever seeds of such emotions may have been planted once in her husband's breast, she guessed that instead of being nurtured, they had withered and died.

She placed a hand upon her belly where a babe had once more taken root. She hoped to present the king with a child early next year, but she had no expectation that it was a gift he would contemplate with much favor. He was not likely to show her child any more affection than he showed his other children; perhaps he would show this one even less, because of his disdain for the mother.

The thought sent a chill through her, and she stepped away from the window, and, pacing, pulled her shawl closer about her shoulders.

And what of her? Would she love this child less because its sire was Æthelred and not Athelstan? She remembered, with a sudden pang, her anguish at the loss of the half-formed babe that had been wrung from her little more than a year ago. The pain of that was still sharp, and she knew with a certainty that the father of the child made no difference. The babe would be hers, and she would lavish it with all the love her heart could give.

In the end it was Emma who watched alone at Edward's bedside one morning in late June as the boy took his last, shallow breath. She had come to Edward's chamber the night before, sleepless after being wakened by the mewling of Wymarc's week-old infant son, and she had found Edward in a heavy sleep. When at daybreak she could not awaken him, she had summoned Father Martin to anoint the child with the blessed chrism, and had sent word to the king that Edward was close to death. Then she held his small hand in hers until it turned cold in her grasp.

She wished, for Edward's sake, that the king had been there to bid his son good-bye. But he had gone with the three eldest æthelings to the port at South Hampton to greet the newly appointed archbishop, Wulfstan, upon his return from his consecration at Rome. She hoped that Wulfstan would not come back with them—not yet. The archbishop, whose shock of white hair and fierce expression perfectly matched his fiery sermons, would likely have little in the way of consolation to offer the grieving family. And although it would not matter to Edward, whose lifeless body lay in the Old Minster now, hands folded over his breast, with candles burning at his head and feet, Wulfstan's overbearing presence was more than she thought she could bear.

She kept watch near the bier with Margot and Hilde while a flock of sisters from Nunnaminster chanted the prayers for the dead in one of the side chapels. Earlier, as she had washed the wasted legs and arms that had once been so agile, she had wept for the boy who had been her first friend at court. Edward had embraced her as an older sister, if not a mother, and her tears were for herself as much as for him. Now, listening to the sibilant voices of the nuns, Emma's eyes were dry. Watching Edward suffer had been the difficult part. At least, for him, the worst was over.

As she prayed, the minster's massive wooden door opened, and she turned to see the king, who walked down the length of the nave, his cloaked figure silhouetted in the light from the doorway. He came unescorted, and she guessed that he had ordered the others to wait so that he might have some moments alone with his son. Believing that he would wish her away as well, she motioned to her attendants to leave. Before she could slip away, though, Æthelred called her name. Surprised, she went over to him and saw that his eyes were glazed with tears as he looked upon the body of his son. She touched his arm in mute sympathy. Whatever differences lay between them, they were united in their grief at the death of this child.

For some time they stood together in silence while the Latin chanting of the nuns echoed softly in the great church. Finally the king spoke.

"I owe you a debt, my lady," he said, looking not at her but at the face of Edward, as white and still as if it had been carved of marble, "for your tender care of my son."

Listening to these words she could not help but reflect on his own coldness toward the boy, and his unwillingness to reach out to Edward when the child had such a need for some sign of affection from his father. What good now was this display of sorrow, when the boy could not know it? But she held her tongue. Even to Æthelred she could not be so cruel.

"He had need of a mother's care," she said, more stiffly than she intended, "and his sisters were not old enough to provide that office. I did it willingly, for Edward seemed to me like the younger brother that I never had."

Still he did not look at her but turned his gaze meditatively on a dark corner at the side of the altar. She followed his glance but could see nothing there except shadows that grew and shrank in the flickering light of the candles.

"Yet it is not every woman," he said, his eyes still on the shadowy darkness, "who has a heart that is large enough to embrace a child who is not her own."

Emma studied his face, and she saw that his eyes were dark with emotions that she could not name. She wished that she could see into his mind, could read the memories that clustered there. Was he speaking of his mother, who had ordered the murder of that other Edward, Æthelred's half brother, to claim a crown for her own son?

Emma shivered, as if cold steel had brushed the back of her neck. As yet she had no child of her own to place in her heart above the children of her husband. Would she, one day, be capable of plotting the death of one of the king's sons for the advancement of her own? That she might even imagine such a thing terrified her. She could not contemplate bloodying her soul for the gift of a crown.

Then another, more frightening thought slipped into her mind on the heels of the last. Might not the children of Æthelred see her own child as a threat to their power? If she were forced to raise her hand against the king's children in order to protect her own, would she do so?

Dear God, she prayed silently, *never let me be put to such a terrible test.*

The king's voice called her back to the present.

"It speaks well of you, lady," he said, following his own train of thought, "that you showed such compassion for this child. God grant that you will have a child of your own one day."

Emma hesitated. Was this the time, when he was grieving for Edward, to tell him that she was, indeed, with child? And yet, what better time? For the moment, at least, they were in accord.

"My lord," she said, feeling as if she were standing at the edge of some dark abyss, "I am with child even now. Indeed, I hope to bear you a son before winter's end."

She waited for his response, still unsure if she had picked the right moment to tell him. His face registered neither surprise, nor joy, nor satisfaction. He did not even look at her.

"If it is a boy," he said, "we will call him Edward." He turned his gaze once more toward the flickering shadows. "Leave me now. I would be alone."

She watched him for a moment, astonished at the ease with which this man could replace one son with another. She turned to leave but stopped when she saw that Athelstan stood just within the doorway, watching her, stony faced. She read in his eyes that he had heard his father's promise to bestow Edward's name upon the child in her womb, and that the knowledge had created a gulf between them that neither one could ever cross. His eyes glittered coldly at her before he looked away.

She swept quickly past him, pressing her hand against her heart, keenly aware that she might be carrying Athelstan's rival for the crown of England.

. . .

Æthelred contemplated the pallid face of his dead child and wondered if this was God's retribution—the sins of the father visited upon the son. Or was it merely Edward's *wyrd* to leave this life so soon?

As father and king he had done all that he could to protect his children from perils that they might suffer at the hands of his enemies. But there were other dangers in the world that men could neither explain nor comprehend. Edward had wasted away before his eyes and he had been powerless to prevent it, king though he was.

He glanced toward the shadows beyond the bier, sensing his brother—that other Edward—lurking in the gloom there like a great brooding bird of prey. Christ, how he hated the thing! It stank of the grave, sickly sweet beneath the candles' honeyed fragrance. It carried the stench of his own eternal damnation.

Fear of that specter's malice clawed at him. His skin was clammy with it, yet even as his spirit quailed, he was consumed by a bitter rage. What business did his brother's fetch have here beside the lifeless form of a child who was innocent of any crime? Had the dead king, who had never sired a son, come to revel in a father's grief? Was he drawn to the scent of corruption?

Or had the murdered Edward come to lay claim to the soul of this boy who bore his name?

He grimaced into the murky darkness, and as the familiar painful heaviness blossomed in his chest, he sank to his knees, felled by the combined weight of dread and pain. He closed his eyes, his brain dulled and clouded. Yet he struggled against the torpor that enveloped him, searching for some way to quiet forever his brother's restless spirit. Was it possible to strike a bargain with the dead? Could he offer his brother some boon in return for respite from this endless, creeping horror?

He flicked a dry tongue across parched lips, and he reached out a hand to clasp the simple wooden rood that stood beside the bier. "I will grant you a son," he whispered, "another Edward, consecrated to you.

He will be your heir, your ætheling. I swear it by the Cross of our Savior. Will you not be content with that, and leave me to rule in peace?"

He held his breath, searching the darkness for some sign that this
vow would free him from his brother's implacable vengeance, but the
shadow was gone, the fetid smell of decay had disappeared, and he
could hear nothing but the mournful chanting of the nuns.

He drew a breath and looked one last time upon the face of his dead
son, and he envied Edward, for he had gone to God an innocent. He
had never known suspicion or fear, and he had never been riddled with
the burrowing worms of jealousy and hate.

Out of respect for the king's family, Archbishop Wulfstan delayed his
arrival in Winchester by some weeks, and when he did appear the cel-
ebrations were subdued. He spent a full month at the king's court, for
his departure was hindered by the rain that continued throughout the
spring and now seemed to threaten the summer months as well. There
was concern far and wide that the harvest would be meager, and ever
on people's minds was the fear that the Vikings would return to divest
them of what little they had.

At last, in early June, and in spite of the filthy weather, the archbishop prepared to set out for Jorvik. Accompanied by a dozen clerics,
by fifty of his own armed retainers, and by the three eldest sons of the
king and their retinues of armed companions, his escort was fit for a
prince of the church who was arguably the most influential ecclesiastic
in all England.

Athelstan, who would ride at the head of the archbishop's train,
waited with his brothers in a drenching rain for the order to set out.
He was eager to be away from the cloying intimacy of the Winchester
court, eager to meet with the men of the northern shires. He wished to
measure the temper and allegiance of the folk in Northumbria in particular, toward his father as well as toward Wulfstan, their new spiritual leader.

The entire company waited upon the archbishop now, who stood with the king and queen beneath a canopy on the steps of the great hall as he prepared to take his leave. Athelstan, his eyes drawn inexorably to the queen, watched as Archbishop Wulfstan raised his hands in blessing above the heads of the royal couple. Emma was gowned in black, for since Exeter she wore no color else. The darkness of her raiment today, though, only served to accentuate the bright gold of the thick bracelets at her wrists—gifts, he had no doubt, from his father, in anticipation of the birth of her child.

No official announcement had been made as yet, and certainly no casual observer would be able to ascertain from looking at her that Emma was quick with child. She was still tall and remarkably slim, and so fair that she seemed lit from within. No, it was the attitude of the king toward her that spoke to the queen's condition. Even now Æthelred stood with his hand supporting her arm, laying claim to her as if she were a long-held possession that he had suddenly found to be of some worth. Indeed, Athelstan had noticed the change in his father's behavior toward the queen from that very moment in the minster when she had sought to comfort him for Edward's death by announcing that she would soon replace the child that he had lost.

Sometime in the winter, with God's blessing, Emma would at last attain her heart's desire. How many times, he wondered, had she sought her husband's foul embrace to achieve that? She had made no secret of her nightly visits to the king's great bed. Athelstan himself had seen her, more than once, as she padded down the narrow corridor outside the king's door, pale as a ghost in the dark watches of the night.

It maddened him to think of it, yet he could not put it out of his mind. Distance and time must work that miracle for him. As for his own plans, for the moment he would follow the advice that Emma herself had given him not so long ago. He would be patient, he would plan, and he would do whatever he must to win his father's trust, even as he prepared himself to someday rule the kingdom. His father could not live forever.

A.D. 1004 This year came Swein with his fleet to Norwich, plundering and burning the whole town. . . . The enemy came to Thetford within three weeks after they had plundered Norwich; and, remaining there one night, they spoiled and burned the town.

—*The Anglo-Saxon Chronicle*

Chapter Thirty-seven

September 1004

Aldeborne Manor, Northamptonshire

A cold draft fingered the hem of Elgiva's woolen gown as she stood before her father, nervous and expectant. For weeks now there had been nothing but bad news on the wind—foul weather, poor harvests, and tales of Danish savagery on the eastern coast. She had been witless with fear, for her father's wooden palisade seemed to her a pitiful defense against Danish broadaxes. The gruesome stories coming out of East Anglia, of towns burned and English folk driven in chains to Viking ships, had recalled that black day in Exeter so clearly that she could smell the smoke from the burning and hear again the shrill, panicked screams.

Surely her father would send her away now, far from the reach of another Danish army that, if rumors were true, was coming straight toward them.

He looked at her with reddened eyes, and she noticed then the flagon and the half-empty goblet on the table at his side. Whatever he had to say to her, he had needed to fortify himself with strong drink in order to do it. She held her breath and waited.

"I have news of your queen," he drawled, "of your Lady Emma."

This was not what she had expected. What news could there be of Emma? She was with the king and the court, safely tucked up in one of the royal *burhs*, no doubt, far from any Danish threat.

"Well?" she said.

"She will soon give our king another brat for his collection. This time, though, it will be a Norman brat." He reached for his cup and waved it at her. "If its brothers have any sense, they will kill it before it can walk."

She glared at him. Such news might have tormented her once, but it was meaningless now.

"Why should I care about the queen or her brat?" she snapped. "Before the year is out I will likely be dead at the hands of some filthy Dane."

He threw her a bemused look.

"Are you so afraid of them?" he asked. "You need not be."

"Why not?" she demanded. "Do you not fear them?"

He waved his cup at her again, brushing away her question. "The fens will swallow them long before they can reach us."

His slurred assurances, though, did not quiet her fear.

Over the next few weeks, as the enemy drew nearer, Elgiva's fear grew. It became her constant companion, especially in the dark, malignant nights when she woke from nightmares that were filled with blood and fire, and were haunted by the face of Groa, her mouth open in a silent scream.

Finally, word reached them in October of a great battle between the Danes and a force of East Anglians. The defenders had suffered great losses, but they had driven the Danish army from the land at last. For now.

Elgiva could learn little more than that, for her father was niggardly with his news. For a more detailed account she had to wait until November when, to her surprise and elation, Athelstan and his eldest brothers arrived at their gates seeking a night's lodging as they journeyed south from Jorvik toward Oxfordshire.

As they dined on roast boar and a pottage of pulses and vegetables, Elgiva studied the æthelings. They had been sorely tested since last they came within this hall, yet the misfortunes of war, and even the death of their young brother, seemed to have left them unscathed.

Athelstan still wore an air of command, far more striking now than before. Even her father and brothers seemed somehow diminished in his presence, as if they instinctively recognized a quality of leadership in him beyond what his position as heir to the crown conferred upon him.

Edmund, she decided, was much the same. He had always been a changeling child, far darker than his brothers and with no look of Æthelred about him at all. His skin was still swarthy and his beard dark.

It was Ecbert who had changed the most, but she was not certain that it augured improvement. Sporting a fair, somewhat scrawny beard, he had lost his quick smile and puppylike enthusiasm. There was a sober thoughtfulness in his mien now that she found worrisome. She still harbored thoughts of wedding him, and he would suit her purposes far better if he did not think too much.

Athelstan's voice, responding to some question of her father's, drew her attention.

"It was Swein Forkbeard who led the attack on Norwich and Thetford," he said. "He could not resist the lure of the mints and their silver."

"Think you he knew of the mints?" her father asked casually, his attention focused on his meat.

"Consider the towns that Forkbeard has targeted," Athelstan said. "Norwich and Thetford this year, Exeter, Dorchester, Wilton, and Salisbury last summer. All of them sites of my father's mints. Forkbeard knew exactly which towns would yield the most treasure. The question is, how did he know?"

He sat back in his chair and looked at the ealdorman. Elgiva, watching the two men, felt a subtle change take place in the mood at the table. She saw that a pulse had begun to beat at her father's temple, and she knew from long experience what it signified—tension, distress, anger. Danger. Next to her Wulf stiffened, his gaze flashing back and forth from his father to Athelstan. The knuckles of the hand that held his small knife were white.

"Forkbeard," her father said slowly, his eyes focused on Athelstan now, "is a hero to many in the Danelaw. They are more Danish than English there, and Forkbeard's exploits are woven into most of the tales sung in every hall north of the Humber. Many men living in Northumbria, or even Mercia, would gladly supply him with any information that he might desire about English silver. Your father's new archbishop at Jorvik will have his hands full coaxing that brood, most of them Viking spawn, into submission to the king's laws."

"The archbishop will need assistance with that, to be sure." It was Ecbert who spoke now, measuring out his words slowly, as if he chose them with great care. "You, as Northumbria's ealdorman, will be in an excellent position to offer him aid. Has not your son, Ufegeat, been hard at work there, making himself well-known among the landholders, and even the freemen? Can we assume that he is laying the foundation for their allegiance to Wessex in the event that Forkbeard should ever challenge my father for his crown?"

Elgiva's heart began to race. She had not been able to learn what her brother was about in Jorvik. Yet again she wondered what schemes her father and brothers were weaving.

"My son is there by my orders, yes," her father said lightly, "testing the wind, you might say. When the moment comes"—his eyes flashed at Athelstan—"assuming that it does come, we will need to know whom we can trust. Some men, I fear, may need persuading."

Athelstan had kept his gaze fixed on the ealdorman, watching for some sign of discomposure, but he could see nothing. The man was as impossible to read as the blank face of a boulder. Ecbert had played his part well, his words suggesting links between the family of Ælfhelm and the Northumbrian men sympathetic to Forkbeard, and still the old man had given nothing away.

It was possible that there were no links, but Athelstan had heard and seen enough during his stay in Jorvik to make him doubt that. All three of them had sensed it—that sudden silence fraught with menace whenever they walked into a gathering of men. The silence would last only moments, but the menace lingered like a foul smell.

Jorvik was a city rife with secrets, filled with men of uncertain allegiance. It was the likeliest place to find men who might aid Forkbeard, as someone had certainly aided him when he abducted the queen last summer. Men in the north were restive, and this man, Ælfhelm, bore a grudge against the king, however expertly he might conceal it. Ælfhelm had gambled that the king would wed his daughter, an alliance that would increase his own prestige and influence. When the king wed Emma instead, and then took Elgiva to his bed, Ælfhelm made no protest. He must have imagined that he would be rewarded for his generosity, but the king had done the unthinkable. He had taken the girl and given nothing in return. She was granted no status as either wife or concubine, and Ælfhelm's gamble had brought him nothing.

How Archbishop Wulfstan must have raged at the king for his dallying with Elgiva! Athelstan wished he could have been there to hear it. He had thought little about it at the time. In Jorvik, though, the archbishop had warned him that Ælfhelm might seek revenge, and had explained why. Athelstan had realized only then the depth of the enmity between his father and this man, and slowly events had begun to fall into place.

Someone in the queen's company at Exeter had kept Forkbeard informed about the queen's movements. That could have been Elgiva, or her handmaid Groa. Someone supplied the Danish king and his retainers with horses, had hidden them and fed them and housed them. Ælfhelm had two sons who could have arranged such matters while their father remained at court. Many things pointed to Ælfhelm and his family as supporters of Forkbeard, yet Athelstan could not accuse any of them of disloyalty to the king, nor could he point to any specific act of treachery. He could prove nothing. He would have to wait.

He nodded to Ælfhelm.

"You are correct that some men will need to be reminded of their oaths to their rightful king. It would be wise, I think, to assist you in that by forging stronger ties between the House of Wessex and the Ealdorman of Northumbria. I will speak to my father."

He purposely gave no hint as to how such ties might be forged. Let Ælfhelm think there may be a marriage offer forthcoming. If nothing else, it might prevent him from taking any precipitous step in Fork-beard's direction. Dangling the prospect of a marriage alliance might buy them a little time. He might even convince his father to make some conciliatory gesture toward Ælfhelm.

He turned to Elgiva and smiled.

"I hope that you will accompany your father to the Christmas *witan* in Oxfordshire next month," he said, loud enough that Ælfhelm could hear him.

She turned to him with an uncertain smile.

"I hope for it as well," she said, "for I have been kept under lock and key here all summer because of the Danish threat. Still, I do not know if my father will give me leave to go."

There was only a hint of dissatisfaction in the gentle lilt of her voice, and she wore the demure expression of a submissive daughter. Athelstan had to stifle a laugh, for Elgiva was as submissive as a wildcat, and every man at the table knew it.

"Then my brothers and I must hope," he said, "that your father will brighten our Yule feast by bringing his most beautiful treasure with him."

The girl cast a glance at her father, and Athelstan, too, looked at the ealdorman to see if he would respond. But Ælfhelm's visage remained as dark and unreadable as the sea.

Chapter Thirty-eight

December 1004

Headington, Oxfordshire

Elgiva urged her horse onto the bridge that spanned the River Cherwell, following in her brother's wake as he led their little company toward the king's palace. The riders had to cross the narrow bridge one at a time, and as Elgiva reached the middle of the span, her nervous mount tossed its head and sidled, frightened by the rain-swollen torrent raging below. As she struggled to keep the horse from crashing against the wooden railing, Elgiva could see the water surging hungrily toward the wooden planks beneath her, and she cursed the horse under her breath. Finally, she made it to the other side, and then she cursed her brother, who merely grinned and told her to get used to it.

He was right, she thought. She would have to cross this wretched bridge every time she wished to attend a royal function at the palace. It was her father's fault for settling her in a convent instead of in the apartments of the queen, where she rightly belonged. Emma would surely have welcomed her if her father had asked, but he made no secret of the fact that he wanted Elgiva where he could keep close watch on her. Apparently he would prefer to see her drown as she tried to cross the river rather than trust her alone within the walls of Æthelred's palace.

This morning she had heard her father order her escort, composed of Wulf and five of her father's men, to take her directly to the queen's chamber door and to stay with her at all times. It would have been humiliating if she had thought for one moment that they could actually do it. The men, however, would not be welcome in the apartments of the pregnant queen. And later, when the feasting and the drinking in the great hall began, it would be easy to lose herself amid the crowd. As for the serving girl who plodded along behind her on a donkey, Elgiva had plied her with enough silver to keep the girl mindful of where her allegiance lay.

For a time they rode along the river, and it was not long before her cloak was spattered with mud. Jesu, she was sick of the mud. It was inescapable, more persistent even than the rain that, for the moment, had dwindled into mist. When she left Northampton six days ago she had imagined that as she traveled south she would find the sun, or at least a break in the rainfall. But they had seen nothing but foul weather, and the journey had taken two days longer than it should have. It had been a wet summer and fall, and it seemed that all of England had turned to bog.

She peered sideways through the drizzle at her father's man, Alric, who now rode beside her. A year had passed since she had last seen him, on that morning in Exeter when he had deposited her so abruptly at the fortress gate. He had trimmed his hair and shaved off his beard so that he looked completely different—and not nearly as handsome as before. His attitude toward her today was different as well. He had greeted her with a cool solicitude that was nothing like the smoldering attentions he had lavished upon her in Devonshire. Even now he would not meet her gaze, and she wondered what horrible punishment her father had promised to any man who cast a lecherous eye upon his daughter.

She looked past Alric to the masses of colorful tents and pavilions that had sprouted like mushrooms upon the meadows of the royal estate. They would house the retinues of the men who served on the king's council, and she saw her father's banner set amidst a flock of tents on the higher ground, a choice spot set aside for the retainers of the most powerful of the king's ealdormen.

The muddy road curved and began to slope upward, and as their company neared the palace a pack of yelping dogs shot through the gate, followed by a troop of horsemen who gave little heed to the folk scurrying out of the way. She recognized the king, his saffron-colored cloak flying behind him, and she picked out Athelstan's bright head, as well as her father's grizzled mane. She glanced at Wulf and saw him scowl at the riders. No doubt he would prefer the excitement of the hunt to the boredom of waiting for her beside the queen's chamber door.

Good. He deserved to be as unhappy with his lot as she was. When he helped her from her horse a few moments later, she gave him a sour look, and he returned it in kind. Then she climbed the steps to the queen's apartments.

To her surprise, the men-at-arms at the queen's door wore the king's badge on their tunics. Then she remembered that Emma's Norman retinue had been numbered among the dead in the rubble of Exeter. The queen would have to depend completely on English folk now for servants and retainers. How loyal, Elgiva wondered, would they be to their Norman mistress?

Shedding her male escorts along with her muddy cloak, she stepped through the screens passage into the queen's apartment and breathed a sigh of relief. For the past year she had been under constant surveillance by her father or her brothers or their spies. There were probably spies here as well, but at least they would not be tattling to her father.

She peered around the room, which was brightly lit by banks of candles as well as by the blazing central fire that sent smoke wafting upward, where it lay like a mantle among the roof timbers. The place was even more mobbed than she had expected. The king's summons to the *witan* had drawn all the powerful nobles of the kingdom to Headington, and all their wives and daughters must be housed in these apartments. All but the Lady Elgiva of Northampton, she thought bitterly.

The women stood in knots of five or six, some with toddlers clinging to their skirts, some whose servants were burdened with babies.

Their chatter was subdued, except for the squeals that emanated from a group of young girls seated on the floor near the door where the king's three daughters held their own little court.

Gesturing to her maid to walk ahead and clear her passage, Elgiva threaded her way through the chamber. She passed a long embroidery frame that had been set up along one wall, where a number of women plied their needles, some industriously, others with the kind of weary boredom that Elgiva herself suffered whenever she undertook such a task.

She knew some of them, but many faces were unfamiliar—an indication of how far out of touch she was with the lines of power near the throne. She would have to remedy that.

She found the queen at last, in a far corner of the apartment, where a tall screen protected her from the heat of the fire and provided a modicum of privacy. She almost did not recognize Emma at first. Her face, which Elgiva had always considered too thin and pale, had grown round, and was flushed, she presumed, from the closeness of the room. There were blue crescents of fatigue beneath her eyes, and the smile that she turned on Elgiva looked strained.

Elgiva had little experience with pregnant women, but if it meant looking like this—bloated and haggard—she did not think that she would like it at all. The queen half-reclined on a bed, her body bolstered by cushions and pillows. Margot sat on the floor in front of her mistress, with Emma's feet in her lap, rubbing briskly at the queen's swollen ankles and calves. Nearby Wymarc sat in a low chair suckling a babe.

She regarded the babe with mute astonishment. She had not heard that Wymarc had borne a child, or that she was even wed. Who was the father then? Could it possibly be one of the æthelings? She was still contemplating this as she bent her knee before the queen.

"Welcome, Elgiva," Emma said. "I have longed for some time to see you, if only to prove to myself that you survived the terrible events at Exeter last year with no hurt." She paused as Hilde, who had appeared from behind another screen, offered Elgiva a cup of wine.

"I thank you, my lady," Elgiva said, accepting the cup and taking the stool next to Emma.

"We all suffered some hurt, though," Emma continued, her eyes exploring Elgiva's face, "because of those we lost at the hands of the Danes. Groa's death must have caused you great pain, I think. We have mourned her, and we still remember her daily in our prayers."

Elgiva could think of no reply to this. Groa, who did not believe in Emma's God, would hardly have thanked Emma for her prayers. Indeed, she had had little love for the queen, and had not balked at murdering Emma's unborn child. Would the queen still offer prayers for the old woman's soul if she knew that?

She schooled her face to an expression of grief, but she did not grieve for Groa. She was still too furious with her for allowing herself to be run down by those two bastard Danes.

"It is true that we have all suffered loss," she murmured. "Even the king lost a child who was dear to him." She twitched her face into earnestness. "But you, my lady, will give him another son very soon, I pray. I see that many have come to be witness to your joy and assist you at the birth." She gazed expectantly at Emma. This was the moment when the queen should invite her to attend that birth.

Emma smiled. "I fear that I am surrounded by more ladies than will likely be of any use," she said, "and far more than I desire. The king has given me leave to seek a private retreat for my confinement, and I will do so soon."

"Indeed." Elgiva felt her bid for a place at the queen's side slipping through her fingers. "But will it not be unwise for you to travel, my lady?" she asked. "I have been on the road myself for some days, and every mile of the journey was fraught with peril. The roads are mired in mud, and all the rivers are swollen. Just crossing the Cherwell today seemed a great risk. Surely, in your condition, to travel any distance would be far too great a danger, both for you and the child."

And how strange was this, that she should be urging her greatest enemy to have a care for her safety!

Emma tilted her head ever so slightly, as if contemplating the suggestion. "You may be right," she said. "I will consider your advice." She rearranged herself on her bed, the topic of her confinement obviously closed. "I fear, Elgiva, that you have missed the opening sessions of the *witan*, but the great welcome feast is set for tomorrow, and you are in good time for that. And since you are here with us now, you must dine with us today."

"It would be my pleasure, I thank you." She had not been dismissed, exactly, but it was not the invitation that she had looked for. She hid her disappointment behind her wine cup, eyeing Emma as the queen leaned back against her cushions and closed her eyes.

Emma may have been living in penury a year ago, but her status had obviously improved now that she was ripe with the king's child. Her wrists were covered with golden bangles, and the golden necklace at her throat was studded with garnets. The embroidery of her gown, too, was gold, and the hems of her sleeves were liberally sprinkled with jewels. The shoes that Elgiva could see peeking out from beneath the bed were lined with fur. Add to that the number of women she was so generously accommodating within her apartments, and Emma's wealth appeared to be great indeed.

Elgiva swirled the wine in her cup and stared into its depths. Emma might be victorious for the moment, but even the birth of a son would do her little good in the end. Her child would never inherit his father's crown; there were too many older brothers in the way. When the king died, one of his elder sons would claim the throne. An infant king and a widowed queen would be of no use to anyone, and Emma would be lucky to end her days in a convent presiding over a clutch of nuns.

She looked up at Emma again, and found the pale green eyes fixed disconcertingly upon her.

"Perhaps," Emma said, "you would tell me what happened to you that day in Exeter. I never did learn how it was that you managed to escape when others, even Groa, did not."

It was a veiled accusation, and Elgiva felt a tiny knife thrust of alarm. She dropped her eyes to avoid Emma's intent gaze.

"Groa, too, would have escaped, except that she was too old to run, and the Danes were hard on our heels. She bid me to get away, even though she could not keep up." She clasped her hands tight in her lap. That was what had happened, wasn't it? Groa had called out, had ordered her to run so that she, too, would not be cut down. "What is it you wish to know, my lady?" she asked, modulating her voice to a mere whisper. "It pains me to speak of it."

"Pray, do not dwell on Groa's loss," Emma said, "but tell me how you were saved."

Wulf had already schooled her about what to say should she be asked, and so the lies came easily. She made no mention of the secret passage beneath the fortress or of the hidden door left unlocked behind them when they fled—a door that, she had realized later, must have given the Danes entry into the very heart of Exeter. Emma's reeve, Hugh, would forever bear the blame for that, but as he was surely dead, he would not care. Instead, Elgiva spun a tale of slipping through Exeter's northern gate before the guards closed it, embroidering the story with her very real memories of screams and the stench of burning.

Emma listened to Elgiva's words, studying her face as she described her flight from Exeter. The young woman's eyes were glazed with tears, and her expression was one of grief and pain, but Emma suspected that there were other thoughts hidden behind that sorrowful expression, although she could only guess what they might be.

Of one thing she was certain, however: Elgiva's allegiance did not lie with king or queen, with family or retainers. She did not hunger for love or wealth or even happiness. Elgiva hungered for power, and her allegiance belonged to herself alone. Clearly she wished to attend the coming birth, but only because she yearned to insinuate herself among the powerful, a place that she believed was hers by right.

Emma had no intention of granting Elgiva's desire; it would be like wrapping a viper around her wrist. Certainly she would have to make a place for Elgiva eventually, for the king wanted her bridled to prevent her father using her to forge some dangerous alliance. But a few more months would make no difference.

When Elgiva had finished her story, and had moved to a seat beside Wymarc, Margot sat down upon the stool next to Emma.

"I doubt that we will ever learn the real truth of what happened in Exeter that day," Margot murmured.

"We all have truths to hide about that day, have we not?" Emma asked.

And she had more to hide than anyone. She rarely saw Athelstan now, but every time she did her heart seemed to shatter anew. There was no warmth in his glance when he looked at her, and surely he had repented of ever having loved her. She loved him still, though, and she could not banish him from her heart. The sin she had shared with him remained unconfessed, a stain upon her soul because she could not bring herself to repent.

"Elgiva has given you good advice, though," Margot said, "in urging you to stay here for your confinement."

Emma sighed. She and Margot had argued about this before.

"I do not wish to bring my child into the world amidst a crowd of strangers," she said. "Is a queen not entitled to privacy when she labors to give birth?"

"The child that you deliver," Margot said, "will belong as much to them as to you. They have a right to be present. Aside from that, the journey to your manor at Islip, however short, puts both you and the child at unnecessary risk, especially now, when travel is so treacherous."

Emma did not argue anymore. Margot was right. It was a queen's duty to grant the women of the court the privilege of witnessing the birth. Yet the manor at Islip, although she had never seen it, remained in her mind a quiet haven and a refuge, and it was only with reluctance that she let it go.

Chapter Thirty-nine

December 1004

Headington, Oxfordshire

Two hundred men and women gathered in the king's great hall on the day of the welcome feast. Christmas was still a week away, so the courses served this night would be meager compared to what was to come. Nevertheless, the rafters and the shuttered windows of the hall were festooned with boughs of holly, ivy, and pine, and a fire roared in the central hearth. Huge banks of thick candles scented the air and filled the dark spaces with light.

Æthelred cast an approving eye upon his queen as he led her toward the dais. She had gowned herself in a festive kirtle of dark green. Her headrail was woven of some gauzy stuff that was shot through with golden threads, and her solemn expression was appropriate to the occasion, although she herself was unaware of the important role she was about to play.

He guided her up the steps, then he turned to look upon the nobles gathered before him. These were men whom he had raised to prominence and to power, though as he gazed on their faces, he all but despaired. They all demanded a piece of him, would suck the very blood from his veins if they could. He was like a mighty oak infested with mistletoe, supporting upon its limbs an enemy that would, in the end, drain it of every vestige of life.

And in return they conspired against him. Oh, he knew of their treachery. His spies kept him apprised of their plots and their schemes.

He could trust no one, his sons least of all. They had conspired with Ælfhelm of Northumbria, had met with him in his hall to forge an alliance that would allow Athelstan to seize the throne.

They denied it, of course. They had protested, Athelstan loudest and hardest of all, that they wanted only to support the king, their father.

I beg you to bend toward Ælfhelm, Athelstan had said. *Listen to his counsel. Find some way to show him favor. If you do not, you will sow the seeds of your own destruction.*

Thus he had been forced to listen to threats from the mouth of his own son, the child of his loins. He had been patient with the ætheling, had suffered his willful words and actions far longer than any man had a right to expect. He would put an end to it now. He would free himself from the parasites that sought to fell him, and he would keep the vow he had made to the vengeful soul of his dead brother.

He raised his hands, and the din of noise in the great hall slowly dwindled from a low roar to a rush, then to silence. He felt a sudden surge of power, filled with the knowledge that only he, of all the folk gathered in this room, knew what the next moment would bring. Even Emma, who had grown weary with the weight of the child inside her and sat now at his side, even she had no idea of what was coming.

The faces below him looked upward expectantly, for he stood on the dais as if to conduct a prayer. Canterbury's archbishop, who would usually have led them in an invocation, was watching for a summons to the king's side and looking puzzled that it had not yet come. The æthelings stood together in a group directly beneath him, the places of honor. Closest to the king's person of all save the queen, they, too, watched him, silently waiting.

Æthelred took a scroll of parchment from the clerk who stood at his elbow. He had written the words on that scroll himself, for he had wanted no one else to know what it said. Grasping the document, still bound, in his left hand, he turned to his queen, and gently taking her arm, he raised her to her feet.

"Queen Emma," he announced, making certain that his voice could be heard in even the farthest corner of the hall, "sister to Richard, duke of Normandy, will soon bear my child. I desire from each man in this hall today a solemn oath of allegiance to this child, if it should be a boy, as my royal heir to the throne of this land."

The king's words fell on Emma's ears like a clap of thunder, and for once she was grateful for his hand at her elbow. If he had not grasped her fiercely to keep her on her feet, she would certainly have collapsed. She managed, with the assistance of his arm and through sheer determination, to maintain her composure in the face of his announcement. She allowed not one muscle to twitch, and she kept the expression on her face calm and sober.

The crowd of men in the hall below, though, made no effort to curb their shock and outrage. Shouts of surprise and protest rang through the hall. Someone near the screen at the back of the room bellowed a curse that was directed not at the king but at Emma. Even the ecclesiastics looked dismayed, and Canterbury's archbishop glared at her with thunder on his brow.

The tumult of it washed over her like an enormous wave, and she clenched her teeth against it, and took long, deep breaths to contain her fear. She looked at the king's sons, standing so close that she could have touched them. She looked to Athelstan for compassion and found his eyes fixed on her with surprise and speculation. Beside him, Edmund regarded her with loathing.

Dear God, she thought. What demon had planted this scheme in Æthelred's mind? Every man here would believe that she was behind it, that she had somehow convinced him that her son, child of a consecrated queen, should be favored over the sons of his uncrowned first wife. They would not look past the obvious. They would not see that with one stroke Æthelred had separated her from everyone else in this room—had isolated her as thoroughly as if he had placed her in a convent on an island in the middle of the sea. The grievances, plots, and intrigues that had swirled around the palace with the king at their center point would now send their malignant impulses toward the queen and her child.

"I must sit down," she whispered to Æthelred.

He nodded, steadying her as she lowered herself to her chair. He seemed unperturbed by the turmoil he had aroused. Implacable, he beckoned the archbishop to his side and handed the parchment to him. The king removed the golden cross that he wore upon a chain around his neck, and looked to his eldest son.

Athelstan hesitated, and Emma held her breath as father and son glared at each other across a gulf that seemed to widen even as she watched. At last Athelstan stepped forward and took the cross in his right hand. Before he could begin the oath, though, Æthelred reached for his son's left hand and placed it against Emma's swollen belly. She felt the babe inside her kick, and she saw Athelstan's face color in response. He did not look at her, though, but kept his gaze fixed on his father as he repeated aloud the oath that the archbishop read to him.

She could have wept with frustration and misery. Athelstan knew her better than anyone here, and even he must now believe that she was behind this move, that she was his enemy. No one in this hall could imagine that Æthelred would do this except to please his queen.

One by one every man came forward to take the oath, one hand on the cross, the other upon her. She looked into the faces of the æthelings as they gave away their birthright to this unborn brother: Ecbert, eyes hard with resentment; Edmund, glaring at her with fierce, unmistakable hatred; Edrid and Edwig looking bewildered; eleven-year-old Edgar, the youngest, who cringed when his father ordered him to speak louder so that all could hear him.

She ceased to pay attention after that. At first she looked about the chamber, noting the men and women who were present as a way of distracting herself from the line of men, most of them scowling, that had formed before her. Elgiva stood not far from the dais with her brother Wulf at her side. Just behind her stood a man with features that Emma found familiar, though she could not put a name to his face. Clean-shaven and handsome, he looked harmless enough, yet something about him struck a deep chord of alarm in her. The source of her disquiet eluded her, though, and, frustrated, she gave up trying to puzzle it out.

She sent her mind elsewhere, across the Narrow Sea to Fécamp, to the massive church hard by her father's great hall. She was five years old, and her mother was leading her to the side chapel, bidding her place her hand upon the marble plinth where an angel had once stood. He had appeared there in the year of Emma's birth and had left behind the imprint of his foot in the stone. It had been worn even deeper since then, by the hands of the faithful that had touched it in reverence.

If marble could be worn away by the laying on of hands, what would happen to a woman? Would she bear a bruise from all the palms that touched her today with obedience and resentment? And what of the babe? Would the hostility that she could feel like a hot wind cause her child to be born misshapen and twisted?

The face of Ealdorman Ælfhelm suddenly loomed before her. His eyes, black and cold as a serpent's, raked her with undisguised hatred.

She knew in that moment that she must leave this place. She would not deliver her child surrounded by enemies. Tomorrow, she vowed, she would go to Islip.

The following morning Athelstan stood flanked by Edmund and Ecbert and watched from beside the swollen River Cherwell as their father escorted Emma to the vessel that awaited her. It was a sullen day, clouds hanging heavy in the sky and rain an ever-present threat. The queen walked, even this late in her pregnancy, with a firm step and erect figure. Ealdorman Ælfric, whom she had asked to escort her on the short voyage to Islip, straddled the wooden dock and the gunwale of the *Trinitas*, his hand extended to assist the queen aboard. She grasped his hand, stepped onto the deck, and walked gingerly to the small shelter midship without even casting her husband a farewell glance.

That was just as well, Athelstan thought, for the king had turned away as soon as he handed his wife, like so much cargo, to someone else. Æthelred was already making his way back toward the crowd of thegns and their ladies who had accompanied him to the water's edge. His face was set in a grimace, and he walked with the brisk stride of a man who has just relieved himself of a heavy burden.

Athelstan, though, watched as the cluster of women and servants who would accompany the queen boarded other, smaller vessels for the short voyage upriver. At last the crew of the *Trinitas* maneuvered the craft away from the nearly submerged dock and into the river's deeper central channel.

Beside him, Edmund turned and spat.

"We're well rid of her," he grunted. "She must have poisoned the king against us. If she should die birthing her Norman whelp, you won't catch me weeping for her."

Athelstan gritted his teeth, but he had given up trying to defend Emma to Edmund. Besides, in this instance Edmund may very well be right. It could have been Emma who had convinced their father to disinherit his elder sons, for it was Emma, through her child, who would gain power and standing from such a move.

"Pray God she bears nothing but daughters," Ecbert muttered.

"Even if she should bear a son," he reminded his brothers yet again, "it can do us little real harm as yet. Our father is still hale. He is likely to wear his crown for a good many winters yet, and change his mind about his heir a hundred times over."

"Unless some mishap befalls him," Edmund said darkly. "The saintly King Edward met with an early, violent death that he did not anticipate."

Athelstan snorted.

"Think you that a group of England's nobles would strike our father down to place a babe on the throne?" he scoffed. "Emma has few supporters, and none that I could imagine raising his hand against the king."

"Do not underestimate ambitious mothers," Edmund growled.

Athelstan flicked him a sharp glance. The hand behind their father's rise to the throne had ever been shrouded in mystery, but everyone had heard the rumors that pinned the blame on the dowager queen. Did Edmund believe it?

"Remember, too," Ecbert added thoughtfully, "that Emma has supporters across the Narrow Sea. If the king should die, it will be Emma's
brother who will control her fate. You have said yourself that he may be a
pawn of the Danes. Who can tell what plans Duke Richard may already
have in hand in the event that our father meets an unanticipated death?"

Edmund grunted assent. "It would not surprise me to learn that
some of Richard's gold has already found its way into the hands of
some of our northern nobles. There are rumors that he is eager to see
England under the sway of Normandy and Denmark."

"That is ludicrous!" Athelstan protested. "Your arguments cancel
each other out. You cannot insist that the queen is positioning her unborn child to take the throne at the same time that you have her brother
pledging her widow's hand to some foreign power whose first act would
be to murder her child. And you imagine that she is planning all of this
while her husband yet lives and she is queen in England."

Ecbert shrugged. "We are merely suggesting possibilities," he said.
"Yes, they may seem ludicrous, but far more unlikely events have determined the disposition of a crown. Who would have guessed when our
father was born that he would one day sit upon the throne? He was the
third son of a young, healthy king. Yet our father went from third son
to second son to king in but a few brief years."

"Emma's son, should she even bear a son," he said, "will have seven
grown brothers ahead of him."

"Six," Ecbert said. "You forget. Edward is already dead."

Athelstan flinched. Edward's death was still a raw wound.

"If the declaration that our father made last night stands," Edmund
insisted, "Emma's child will have first claim to the crown, before any
of us."

"With no real supporters at hand beyond a widowed queen," Athelstan repeated, "other than your imagined Norman puppets somewhere in the north."

"What of the ealdorman Ælfric?" Edmund asked. "He would
surely feel compelled to honor the oath he made last night, and there
must be others who would follow his lead."

Athelstan gazed out at the river and at the ship that would, in a moment, round a bend and disappear from view. How deep did Ælfric's loyalty run? Was he bound more to the king now, or to Emma?

"Men keep oaths," he said, "only so long as they benefit from doing so. What benefit would there be to Æthelred's thegns to place a babe upon the throne? England needs a strong king, one who would protect its shores from the ravages of the Danes."

"Then why would our father demand our oaths in favor of Emma's child," Ecbert demanded, "unless it was at the urging of the queen?" He shook his head. "I have seen him look at her. He does not love her, so it cannot be for love. I think she has bewitched him."

"Whatever the motivation behind it," Edmund said, keeping his voice low as they turned to make their way back toward the palace, "this oath makes it difficult for you, Athelstan, to gather support in any bid you might make for the throne. You would not find it easy to rally men to your banner."

"That is my thought as well," Athelstan said, "and I warrant that we need look no further than that for last night's oath taking. The king mistrusts me, and I know not how to win back his esteem. Still, as long as I possess Offa's Sword, I can lay claim to the throne. If need be I shall wield that sword against anyone who threatens England, even if it is the king himself."

As they reached the gate to the palisade, a steady rain began to beat against the already waterlogged earth. Athelstan barely noticed it. His mind had raced back to the words of the seeress at the ancient stone circle.

Sword you may wield, but the scepter will remain forever out of your reach.

He had indeed been granted the Sword of Offa, as she had said, but many things had changed since that winter day when she had read his future. Could not his fate have changed as well?

It seemed suddenly imperative that he find out. There were men in the south willing to fight for him now, if he should reach for the throne. His brothers, too, would back him, in spite of the oaths that they had sworn to Emma's child. But if Emma should bear a daughter, if the Danes should strike in the spring so that all England rallied behind the king, if he could regain his father's trust, then there would be no need for rebellion. In the fullness of time the scepter would fall into his hands without his having to wield a sword to attain it.

When he took leave of his brothers he strode toward his lodging, but he was already determined that within the hour, he must set out along the king's road toward Saltford.

As the oarsmen maneuvered the *Trinitas* away from the quay, Emma did not glance back toward the receding shore. No one there would be sorry to see her go, and she felt only relief at this departure, for she was eager to leave Headington and all its ill will behind her.

The churning river, though—its brown water swirling and frothing around the ship's hull—gave her little reason to think that her brief voyage would be either easy or pleasant. The swell was running fast against them, and in the distance she could see a dark veil streaming from the clouds to the horizon. Likely they would be in for a soaking before long.

She was seated in a tent midship that might have kept her dry if she had been willing to close the flap in front of her. But her cloak was already slick with mist and river spray, and she could not bear to travel blind, especially aboard a ship. Better to be cold and wet than suffocated and sick. Margot seemed unperturbed by the motion of the vessel, for she had braced herself in the protective lee of their makeshift shelter and already seemed to have fallen into a doze.

Emma drew her cloak closer about her as the swift current grabbed the stern and the vessel gave a sudden lurch. The babe within her kicked, as if protesting this new mode of travel, and Emma saw her belly ripple as the child squirmed. Her back ached, had been aching all morning, and in spite of the brisk wind she felt heavy and torpid. She adjusted her seat on the bench, trying to ease into the rhythm of the ship, but it was impossible, for the vessel merely rocked and shuddered.

The oarsmen struggled against the river, cursing it and the wind, using sheer brute strength to maneuver the craft against the swell.

A sharper twinge of pain in her back forced her to adjust her position on the cushions once more. In the corner, Margot began to snore softly in spite of the surging of the craft.

She lost all track of time as she peered out at the landscape gliding past. A line of ash trees rose out of the water on either side, for the river had spread far past its natural banks. The fenlands, she thought, must look like this. It was a watery world, and the ground that should have been winter-brown glittered wet in the sullen light for as far as she could see. She might have found it beautiful if it did not presage famine and hunger by spring.

"Sweet Virgin," she whispered, the beginning of a prayer for mercy. But before she could continue, the ship, which had begun to move smoothly forward with each stroke of the oars, rose, and then sharply fell, as if some unseen hand had lifted the prow out of the water and then dropped it. Her stomach pitched at the unexpected motion, and nausea gripped her by the throat. Margot woke with a start, crossed herself, and settled back to sleep again.

Emma swallowed hard, willing her stomach to behave. She tried again to adjust her body to the rhythm of the oar strokes, but she had little success. The ship bucked and heaved, struggling as if it fought a living, writhing creature. Something scraped the hull with a loud, grating noise that brought her heart into her throat, and then the ship hit the curtain of rain—a slantwise, needling spray that made her flinch.

The pain in her back grew savage, turning into a fierce cramping that shot down through her belly and caused her to gasp and double over. She felt a wetness between her thighs, and she remembered that other time, when she woke to find herself slick with blood. It was happening again. Dear God, it was happening again.

She cried aloud with pain and fear, and instantly Margot's hand was at her elbow.

"What is it?" she demanded.

"I am bleeding," Emma whispered on a sob. "I am losing the baby, just like before."

But Margot was already rooting frantically among the cushions beneath Emma's cloak.

"Nay, my lady, it is not blood. It is your waters that have broken. The child is coming."

Emma clasped Margot's sleeve and clenched her teeth against the pain that gripped her.

"But it is too soon," she protested.

"Aye, well," Margot murmured, "God has determined otherwise."

Emma's ear, attuned from childhood to every nuance of the old woman's voice, caught the note of anxiety that she wasn't meant to hear. It planted a hard kernel of fear in her heart. As the pain eased a bit she drew breath to ask a question, but Margot's hands had begun to move along the mound of her belly, as if she were communicating with the child through some tactile alchemy.

"The babe is still too high." She pursed her lips and looked hard at Emma, her brown eyes sharp. "I'll not lie to you, my lady. You have hard work ahead of you to push this child out. We must trust that the Virgin will aid you, and thank God that you are young and strong."

Strong! She did not feel strong. She felt weak and afraid. She wanted Wymarc and Hilde about her, wanted to be safe within the shelter of thick walls. How was she to do this thing on a ship, in freezing cold and rain, surrounded by rough men? All of it was wrong.

Margot had turned to pull the curtains to shut out the rain, and Emma would have objected, but another contraction clawed at her and she closed her eyes, concentrating on enduring the grinding pain inside of her.

"Why does it hurt so much, so soon?" she demanded through gritted teeth while that kernel of fear grew and blossomed inside of her. "Wymarc's pangs did not start like this."

"Every birth is different," Margot said. "Wymarc was ripe and the birth passage wide when her waters came. You have not been so lucky."

She began to massage Emma's back. "Rest between the pains, child. You will need all your strength before we are done."

Emma felt panic rising within her as the contraction peaked. She wanted to stop the pain, to turn away from this ordeal. It was too hard. God had turned against her, and she knew, with a dread certainty, that she was going to fail. The baby would die, and she would die with it.

"I am afraid," she cried, clutching at Margot's hand.

"Of course you are afraid," Margot soothed. "Every woman is afraid when her time is upon her. But you must remember who you are." She took Emma's face between her hands and gave her a hard, fierce look. "You are the daughter of Richard of Normandy. You are the queen of all England. You have Viking blood in your veins, child. Will you allow your fear to defeat you?"

Emma looked into the brown eyes that she had trusted all her life, and she found no anxiety there now, only determination. Margot spoke the truth. She had to remember who she was and why she had been chosen for this task. If she allowed her fear to overcome her, she would fail in her duty as queen, in her duty as daughter, and, worst of all, she would fail her child. She could not do that again. She could not allow another child of hers to die, not without a fight. If *she* should die, so be it. But she would not let this child wither inside her.

"Tell me what I must do."

"You must walk to move the babe into position, but you cannot do it here. As soon as we get to Islip—"

"I will not wait until I get to Islip," Emma said. "Now! I want to walk now." The sooner she started walking, the sooner this child would be born. She was still fearful of what lay ahead of her, but she wanted it over as soon as could be.

"You cannot walk in the rain on a deck all awash with water!" Margot protested. "You need not even fall overboard to drown in this."

"This is not the open sea," Emma said, heaving herself to her feet and clinging to a post for support, "and I cannot sit still. The pain will be easier to bear if I am moving, will it not? Bid Lord Ælfric come to help me."

"But my lady—"

"I have to move, Margot!" she cried, as another wave began to engulf her. "Get Ælfric, I beg you!"

For the next hour, with one hand clinging to Ælfric's strong, steady arm and the other grasping the yard with its furled sail, Emma walked six unsteady steps forward along the heaving deck, then six steps back. The rain stung her face, and her sodden cloak and wet skirts hampered her movements. Whenever the wave of a contraction rose so high that her knees buckled with the pain, she stopped to lean against the solid bulk of the ealdorman. She bore each wave in silent agony, for she had been reminded that she was England's queen, and she knew her duty. No man would hear her cry out, not even the seamen who glanced uneasily at her as they plied their oars. She focused her mind inward, and like an animal that bites off a paw to escape from a snare, she endured the pain and the cold, the rain and the movement of the ship. Everything outside of her own body disappeared as she labored to bring forth her child.

At last the craft docked at Islip, and with Margot and Ælfric assisting her, she trudged through thick mud up to the manor, although she took little notice of its sheltering walls. She was stripped of her wet garments and wrapped in thick, warm linens, and would have been put into a bed but that she refused to lie down. She walked, driven by the relentless pain that bullied her. Sometimes, in the brief intervals of relief, she rested in the arms of Margot or one of the other attendants, snatching a few moments of sleep. Sometimes she dropped to the pelts that had been hastily scattered on the wooden floor, crouching on her hands and knees like a beast until the urge to pace dragged her to her feet again.

In this way the hours passed, yet the babe did not come.

Chapter Forty

December 1004

Near Saltford, Oxfordshire

t took Athelstan the better part of two days to reach Saltford on roads fouled by relentless, heavy rain. The light was draining from the cloud-dark sky as he approached the ridge and its standing stone, but for the moment, at least, the rain had let up. He had left his companions at Saltford, and now he dismounted and gazed once again upon the circle set in the clearing below.

A figure stood in the center of the ring, her face lifted toward his. She was swathed in a cocoon of shawls and bathed in the lurid glow of a small blaze that crackled amid the hearthstones at her feet. She did not move, merely waited, and as before, he felt that she was waiting for him.

He led his horse down the gentle slope and into the grove, tying the reins to a branch of one of the oaks that edged the clearing. He could see the brown wattle and daub walls of her croft rising out of a sea of mud on the far side, sheltered among the trees. Moss covered half of the thatching on its roof, and the dwelling looked in sore need of repair.

He stepped between two of the giant stones and into the circle, half expecting to hear a crash of thunder as he did so. But there was no sound at all, and that struck him as even more ominous.

He nodded to the woman, who gazed at him with eyes that bore no hint of welcome.

"Why have you come, king's son?" she asked, her rough voice muffled by her wrappings. "Are you so lost that you must come to me to find your way?"

It dawned on him that this was, indeed, why he had come. He was lost. It seemed to him that numerous paths lay before him, and without some guidance he could not discover which one was the best to take.

"I think, mother," he said, "that anyone who seeks you out must be lost, in one way or another." He glanced at the house and shook his head. "Does no one else visit you these days? You look ill prepared for the winter cold."

"Folk share what they can," she said, "and this year there is little enough to go around."

He drew a purse from his belt and held it out to her, but she made no move to take it.

"You told me once," he said, recalling all too clearly her words on that other occasion, "that I would hold Offa's Sword but that I had not the strength to wield a scepter. I have come now to ask you to read my future once more, to tell me if my arm has grown any in strength."

Still she made no move to take the purse but kept her eyes focused on his. Then she pulled the shawl away from her face, and now he could see her clearly. He realized with a shock that she was not aged, as he had thought. Her cheek and brow were smooth, although her skin was dark and not Saxon fair. One of the race of Old Ones she must be then, he guessed, who dwelt in this land before the first Saxons came from across the sea. She was far nearer in age to him than he would have guessed—so much so that he thought it was perhaps a different woman. But the voice was the same. He had heard it only once, but he could not mistake it.

"If you think to bribe me to speak sweet words to you," she said, "you will have wasted your coin. I speak only truth, for good or ill. Silver will not change it."

"Take the silver then, lady," Athelstan said, "and give me your truth in return. For I am at a crossroads, and I do not know which way to go. Perhaps you can help me to choose my path."

She stretched out her hand and he dropped the purse into it. Then he took off his glove and held out his empty palm for her to read. But she merely grasped his hand with her own and looked into his eyes, as if she could look through them into his soul and read whatever was written there.

After several long moments she closed her eyes, and for a time she stood statuelike, her thin, cold fingers grasping his. When she spoke at last her voice was deep and strong, and it resonated through his blood and bones, just as before.

"You will bear both sword and shield," she said, "but the crown and scepter will remain beyond your grasp. For whoso would hold the scepter of England must first hold the hand of England's queen."

Athelstan started at these words, doubt and hope warring within him all at once. He had tried to wrest the queen's hand from his father's grasp, and he had failed. What if he should try again? Would he succeed?

But the woman before him opened her eyes and gazed steadily into his own. He read sorrow there, and a terrible compassion.

"A bitter road lies before the sons of Æthelred," she whispered. "All but one."

Chapter Forty-one

December 1004

Islip, Oxfordshire

Within the queen's manor at Islip, the passing of two nights went unremarked by the queen and her attendants, for they dwelt in an endless, torch-lit twilight as Emma labored to give birth to the child that refused to be born.

For Emma it was a twilight filled with agony and increasing weariness. Supported by the women she trusted most, she walked endless miles back and forth across the room, stopping again and again to breathe through the pain that was turning her existence into one long nightmare. After what seemed an eternity to her she yearned for a release, even if it meant her own death. At last, too exhausted to walk anymore, she allowed them to lead her to the bed.

"I would see Father Martin," she whispered to Margot, as the wave of pain began to rise again, "to shrive me of my sins."

But Margot gripped her hand hard, as if she could, by her very clasp, bolster Emma's strength. "Your work is not done, my lady," she said. "Your child is coming. I will not let you despair."

As the pain gripped her, Emma clutched the worn hand with both of her own and cried aloud. When the contraction had subsided, she dredged up a weary smile for her old nurse.

"Aye, Margot," she said, "but I am not afraid of asking a higher power for help."

Momentarily freed from the labor pangs, she closed her eyes. When she opened them again the priest was at her side, marking her forehead with the sign of the cross.

She grabbed his hand and gripped it as another contraction tore at her. His clasp was warm and strong, and they rode the wave together until she had reached the other side.

"I must confess a great sin," she whispered, her throat so dry that the sound emerging from it was pitifully weak. He had to bring his ear close to her mouth to hear her.

"Peace, my lady," he said, tracing the sign of the cross on her lips. "I have already forgiven you all your sins. There is no need to speak."

She smiled her gratitude. She had only to beg forgiveness now from the child that she was unable to deliver, for in spite of Margot's care and her own will, her strength was almost gone. Once more she closed her eyes, but she was pulled out of sleep again when the next wave struck.

Margot and Wymarc were at her side now, and she clutched at their hands, screaming as she felt the urge to push the pain away from her.

"Aye, you must push, my lady," Margot croaked, in a voice as hoarse as Emma's own. "Come! Up now!"

They drew her from the bed and placed her on the birthing stool, and from some place inside her that Emma had not known existed, she found an unlooked for well of strength. Clinging to Wymarc's hand, she pushed at Margot's urging. It seemed to her that time, which had stood still for so long, now flew by as, at last, with a final great effort, she pushed her child into the world. She heard a baby's cry, and then Margot's voice seemed to come from a great distance, pulling Emma out of the haze of exhaustion that enveloped her.

"You have a son."

In another moment a tiny, squalling bundle was placed in her arms, and she peered through a prism of tears at this tiny miracle of a child. She had seen few newborns, but this one seemed desperately small to her. Yet he appeared lusty enough, red-faced and howling with rage at being forced into an alien world.

"Will he live?" she asked anxiously.

"He is small, to be sure," Margot said, "but his lungs are good, and he looks well enough. His wet nurse will have him fattened up in no time, my lady."

"No wet nurse," Emma whispered. "I will nurse him myself." She would not trust this son of hers to the care of any other, for all her future was wrapped up in his. He had been named the king's heir, and his enemies were legion. It would be her task to protect him, and to prepare him for the role that would one day be his.

She grazed the baby's head with a kiss, then she watched, enraptured, as he nuzzled her breast and began to suck.

"You are the most beautiful thing that I have ever seen," she breathed. And she realized that she already loved him with a fierceness that threatened to overwhelm her. In the light of this love, the grim oath taking at Headington took on a different cast.

When she had been pregnant and helpless, Æthelred's attempt to weaken all of his perceived enemies by naming this son as his heir had seemed a sword of peril pressed against her throat. Now, though, she was the mother of the only son born to Æthelred of a consecrated queen. She would have more power than she had ever looked for, and certainly more than Æthelred had intended. She had not asked for it, but the seeds of destiny had been placed in her hands. It would be her task to sow and nurture them, for her son's sake.

"I would send a message to my brother," she said to Wymarc. She must get word to him that she had borne a son who was heir to England's throne. Richard would, if she asked, send her more hearth troops, men who would be loyal to her alone. "And send a message to my lord the king," she said, "that God and the queen have given him another son."

Chapter Forty-two

On the Feast of the Epiphany, in a ceremony held at the palace of Headington, Edward Ætheling, the son of King Æthelred II and Queen Emma, made his first appearance before the royal court. The king's hall was crowded with bishops and abbots, with the king's most trusted thegns and their wives and children, and with several score of servants. All of them were eager to see the young queen and the child that Æthelred had named as his heir.

The Lady Elgiva, befitting her rank as the daughter of the powerful ealdorman of Northumbria, stood at a table just below the royal dais, flanked by her brothers on one side and by her father on the other. As she gazed up at the royals, she was impressed by the mummery of family unity on display. No one in the room, she was sure, could be stupid enough to believe it, but it was impressive.

The queen stood at the king's right hand with Æthelred's three daughters in a solemn line next to her. Edyth, the eldest at age eleven, looked boldly out at the assembled nobles, one eyebrow arched, as if she were taking the measure of each person in the hall. Ten-year-old Ælfgifu looked bored as she stifled a yawn. Seven-year-old Wulfhilde fidgeted, craning forward every so often to gaze with wonder at the baby in Emma's arms.

On the king's left, his six sons stood as solemnly as the king and queen, in the order of their ages and rank—Athelstan, Ecbert, Edmund, Edrid, Edwig, and Edgar. They were all of them handsome lads, each in his way. But all of the royal children, in their sober-colored, sable-trimmed finery seemed to fade into shadows cast by the queen, for Emma glittered in the torchlight like the sun.

She wore a fitted kirtle of golden godwebbe that was embroidered with silver thread and studded with gems that banded the neckline and the long, draping sleeves. The gown hugged her waist, now slim again, and molded her breasts so tightly that Elgiva realized, with a shock, that Emma must be nursing her own baby. On her head the queen wore a long, woven silk veil of a pale, shimmering yellow, and above it a delicate crown of twisted gold hung with pearls. That had been a gift from the king, Elgiva knew for a fact. He had given Emma lands as well, in addition to what he had bestowed upon his newest son. And all of it would be controlled by Emma.

Elgiva tore her eyes away from the queen's crown and considered the child—a brat wrapped in a blanket embroidered with golden thread, and so scrawny that he looked like a poppet, asleep in his mother's arms.

"I think," she whispered to her father, as the rest of the assembly recited the Latin of the Lord's Prayer, "that the elder æthelings have little to fear from this one. He looks as if the slightest breeze will send him to heaven."

"He may be a weakling," her father replied grimly, "but we all have a great deal to fear, for the queen has proved now that she can bear a living child—and a son, at that. If she gives Æthelred another six sons, one day we are likely to wake up and find ourselves in the midst of a royal battle for the throne. We will all of us have to choose sides then, and the last ætheling standing will win."

"Well, surely it will not be that one," Elgiva hissed, glancing up again at the tiny creature clasped in Emma's arms.

"Perhaps not. But there may be other children, and even a sickly son can be used as a pawn in this royal game. Much depends on what support the queen can rally about her now. Look at her. She's dripping gold, and not all of it came from Æthelred."

Elgiva turned her gaze upon Emma once again. Everyone at court knew that the golden gown was Norman work, and that it had been part of a shipment that had arrived from Normandy months ago, when the queen first announced that she was with child.

"I'll wager," her father continued, "that Richard of Normandy is determined to see Emma's son on England's throne. He will likely be sending the queen more gifts, now that her child has been named Æthelred's heir. With her brother's gold the queen will be able to purchase the allegiance of a great many men for her son."

"But people still blame her reeve for the attack on Exeter," Elgiva protested. She had heard as much from the nuns at the wretched abbey where she spent her nights, and for the nuns to know of it, the matter must be discussed everywhere. "Her reputation has suffered from that. She is not so popular as before."

"She will always be popular," her brother Wulf leaned over to whisper, "while she is young and beautiful and the mother of the ætheling."

Elgiva snorted. "I would rather be wed to an ætheling than be the mother of a puling babe such as that one." She flicked her glance from Emma and the babe to where Athelstan stood on the king's left hand. "The king's eldest son still retains Offa's Sword, does he not?" As long as that symbol of the king's favor was in Athelstan's possession, he could use it to rally his own supporters, even among those who had so recently pledged their allegiance to his baby half brother.

Now it was her father who snorted.

"Offa's Sword may influence some, but when the time comes, it will be the strong arm of the man who wields the sword that will determine England's next king. And you, girl, had best put all thought of marriage to an ætheling out of your mind, for Æthelred will allow none of his sons to wed while he lives. The king may be foolish, but he is not that foolish. And when you do marry, it will be to a man of my choosing, not yours."

Elgiva bit her lip, suddenly apprehensive. If what her father said was true, then all her dreams of a throne must perish. She could not wait upon the death of Æthelred to marry. That might take years and years, and who would want her when she was too old to bear children? She feared that her father had no husband at all picked out for her. He was the ealdorman of Northumbria. The only alliance of real advantage to him would be with a king's son, and if that option was closed to her, then nothing was left. She gave him a swift, covert glance. He would not put her in a convent, surely? She would kill herself if he should place her behind abbey walls.

She gazed again at Emma, bedecked in gold and cradling her new son in her arms, and she felt her old envy toward the queen swell and ripen. On the long list of people who would someday taste Elgiva's revenge—a list that included her father, her brothers, and even the king and his sons—Queen Emma's name stood at the very top.

Æthelred, standing at the center of his family upon the high dais, stifled his impatience as Wulfstan's interminable benediction droned on. The elaborate ritual had been the archbishop's idea—a consequence of his recent journey to Rome, where the importance of ceremony had been impressed upon him in the gilded halls of the pope. Wulfstan was correct, of course. It was important for Æthelred's family to present a united front to the world, but surely the prayers did not have to go on for so long.

He shot a glance at the child sleeping in Emma's arms—the only member of this family, he suspected, who was truly content. The rest were merely putting on a brave face for the benefit of the court. It was what he had demanded of them, and they had no choice but to bend to his will. He had even given instructions as to how they should dress. Let the queen and her son shine tonight. What harm could it do?

To be sure, the child that Emma had given him was a mixed blessing—a son to keep the Norman duke Richard mindful of his duty to his sister, and an heir to keep his own sons uneasy about their futures. That was well enough. But he had not anticipated Emma's reaction to the child. His first wife had birthed her babes and handed them off to others, and then had had little more to do with them. That

Emma should choose to nurse her child worried him. It bound her to her son, forged a link between them that might prove dangerous.

He would have to send the child away, to one of the great abbey schools perhaps, far from the queen's influence and out of the reach of jealous elder brothers. Mayhap the boy would learn to pray in a manner that would elicit some response from God other than tribulation piled upon disaster.

He shot an irritated glance at the droning Wulfstan, who seemed to read it correctly, because he brought his prayers to a ringing conclusion. As the company sat down to the feast the king looked out over his gathered court with something akin to satisfaction. His people appeared content for the moment, about to fill their bellies at his board. Even Ælfhelm of Northumbria, usually so intractable and belligerent, had acquiesced to all his proposals at the *witan* sessions. The havoc wrought by the Danes in the summer and autumn would be forgotten by next spring, and this new Edward, consecrated to his martyred uncle, might yet become the symbol of England's rebirth.

He set to his meat, but as he raised his cup to join in a toast to his queen and newborn son, he could feel his arm begin to tingle with cold while his heart gave a sudden, painful lurch. He set the cup on the table, and, looking warily into the middle distance before him, he could see the air rippling like water as his brother approached, every wound on his body gaping like a bloody mouth.

Still he torments me, he thought, clutching at his chest to still the pounding of his heart. It had been madness to believe that he could strike a bargain with the dead.

Forced to stare into his brother's burning eyes, he silently cursed the horror that held him in thrall. The martyred Edward, he knew now, would never settle for a golden shrine, nor even for a king's son consecrated to his service. *An eye for an eye*, the Bible said. A crown for a crown. His brother and his God demanded restitution, and nothing less. There would be no forgiveness, no peace, until he relinquished the power that should never have been his.

And that he would never do.

He would never surrender his crown—not to his sons nor to the Danish king who sought to destroy him. He would resist until his dying breath, and whatever terror his dead brother's foul wraith might visit upon him, he would resist that as well.

He grimaced into the fetch's glittering eyes and exulted when the thing looked away, as if beaten by his defiance.

Then he realized, with a start, that the martyred Edward had turned his countenance upon the æthelings, one by one. There was doom writ in that livid gaze, an omen of ill intent directed toward the sons of the king. Æthelred saw it, knew it for what it was, and felt his soul pierced with black despair and a bitter, burning rage.

Athelstan, having endured first the ceremony orchestrated by Wulfstan and then the ordeal of a meal in his father's close company, left the high table as soon as was politic. He made his way to the foot of the great hall, counting on the song that his father's *scop* had begun to keep the attention of the gathering focused away from him. He wanted to think.

The elaborate show of family solidarity that his father had demanded had chafed like a burr against his skin. He wished that he could see into his father's mind to decipher what plans he had for his children and for his kingdom. He mistrusted his father's foresight. And of late, he had begun to mistrust the queen.

He looked up at her, from where he stood in the shadows. Her babe had awakened, but instead of passing the child to its nurse, Emma continued to hold him. She looked, to him, like the Madonna with the newborn Christ, and the loving gaze that she turned upon her son struck Athelstan to the quick. Just so had she looked at *him* once.

But that was in the past. Whatever Emma may have felt for him had been drowned in the tidal wave of maternal love that she felt for Edward. Anyone with half an eye could see that her babe was all the world to her. What man could hope to gain ascendancy in her heart now that she had this son to love—this son who could have been his?

God help him, he loved her still. He had promised himself that he would strike her from his heart, but it seemed to him that the mother was even more desirable than the bride had been. The tenderness that few had been allowed to see was now apparent to anyone with eyes in his head.

As he watched, she grazed her child's temple with her lips and ran her fingertips along his cheek. He saw her laugh as Edward flung his hand free of his loose swaddling to clasp her finger.

And, in that moment, the words of the wisewoman came back to him.

Whoso would hold the scepter of England must first hold the hand of England's queen.

Athelstan stared at the mother, and at the child who clutched her finger.

A bitter road lies before the sons of Æthelred. All but one.

Was Edward, then, the son whose *wyrd* lay in sunshine and not in shadow?

No! He would not believe it. It was not possible that all six of Æthelred's sons should step aside or die so that this child of Emma's would become king.

Yet he could not rid his mind of the forboding words. He turned his back on his family, and on the feasting, and he left his father's hall.

Emma saw Athelstan leave the dais, saw him stand alone for a time and watch her from the darkness, saw him turn and make his way to the door. She could not tell what it was that upset him, but when he strode from the hall she felt a tugging at her heart, as if she were a jetty and he a ship straining at its moorings to be free.

Yet they had never been truly bound to one another. They had committed a great sin, but what she had felt for him, still felt for him, could never be spoken of nor acted upon. Never again. Not because she was Æthelred's queen, but because she was Edward's mother. The vows that bound her to Æthelred were as nothing to the invisible bonds that tied her to this babe. He was her treasure—her present and her future, her beginning and her end.

All her happiness was wrapped up in this child in her arms. And now she had become like Æthelred, trusting no one, not for fear of her own life, but out of fear for the safety of this child who needed her love and protection for his very survival. She must keep him safe, must guard his future.

Emma thought of her own mother then, and of how she had believed her heartless and cruel for sending her youngest daughter to a tragic land and to the cold bed of a sinister king. *You must go because you have the strength to do it,* Gunnora had told her. And Emma had thought she could never forgive her mother for that.

Yet she realized now that Gunnora had done what any truly loving mother must do—she had given her child the opportunity to fulfill her best, her highest destiny.

That is what she would do now for her son. Whatever sacrifices must be made, whatever alliances must be struck, she would pursue them to one end. For she was Emma, queen of England, and she had given England a son who would be king.

Author's Note

Some time around A.D. 1040, Emma of Normandy commissioned a Flemish monk, probably a member of her household, to write a book about her life. An eleventh-century version of that remarkable manuscript, *Encomium Emmae Reginae*, still exists. The document, however, begins in medias res, in the year A.D. 1017, when Emma must have been about thirty years old. Although the writer refers to Emma as a great queen, he makes no mention at all of her husband, King Æthelred II, or of the fifteen years of Emma's marriage to him.

Granted, the encomiast had good reasons for this huge omission, which I will not go into here, but those missing years, shrouded as they are in the mists of time and veiled by Emma's silence, became the focal point of my interest in this enigmatic English queen. This novel, the first in a trilogy about Emma of Normandy, is the result.

Because Emma's birth date was never recorded, she could have been as young as twelve or as old as twenty in the spring of A.D. 1002 when, as *The Anglo-Saxon Chronicle* relates, "Richard's daughter came to this land." What we can be certain of is that Emma's marriage was arranged very quickly, unusually so, within months of the death of King Æthelred's first wife. Although little else is known about Emma during the early years of her marriage to a king who has been described as mistrustful, violent, and haunted, much can be imagined, and I have done so.

The history of England between the years A.D. 1002 and A.D. 1005—the period covered in this novel—has been distilled from chronicles, wills, sermons, laws, charters, and other documents of the time. All of the ealdormen, the nobles, and the prelates who populate my book have been plucked from those records, but most especially from *The Anglo-Saxon Chronicle*. It is important to note, though, that all of the *Chronicle* entries that deal with Æthelred's reign were written some years after those events took place, by chroniclers who had distinct points of view, and who seemed to look upon Æthelred with either disapproval or despair.

King Æthelred did in fact attain his throne because of the murder of his elder half brother, Edward, in A.D. 978, and the common belief at the time seems to have been that Æthelred's mother was behind the deed. There is a twelfth-century account of Æthelred weeping at his brother's death, but there is no record of what he may or may not have known about the plot that led to it. This is one of those wonderful blank spaces in history that are so tantalizing to novelists. Certainly the cult of that martyred King Edward, fostered by Æthelred and involving the building of a shrine and the reburial of the saint's body around A.D. 1001, hints at, if not a guilty conscience, at least an attempt to solicit Edward the Martyr's goodwill in a time of extreme turmoil and danger in England. It was in that light that the character of Æthelred, haunted and guilt-ridden, began to take shape for me.

Regarding Æthelred's sons, royal charters provide their names and a rough idea of their birth dates. The likelihood that the eldest ætheling, Athelstan, was about the same age as Emma triggered irresistible romantic possibilities in my mind as I plotted my novel. Indeed, one rumor that echoes through the centuries is that there was little love between King Æthelred and his Norman bride, and the idea of a romance between a despised queen and her husband's rebellious son was just too fraught with delicious conflict for me to ignore. Aside from their names on the charters, though, nothing else is known about Athelstan or his siblings in the years covered by this novel, so I have had my way with them.

The fourth character viewpoint in the novel belongs to Elgiva of Northampton. In historical documents she is Ælfgifu, but I have chosen to use the variation Elgiva (it rhymes with Godiva) to differentiate her from Æthelred's first wife and one of his daughters, both named Ælfgifu. We know that Elgiva was Ælfhelm's daughter, and that by A.D. 1016 she had at least one child, but there is no indication of her age or her relationship to the major historical figures in England before that date. Nevertheless, because the names of the women who would have been part of Æthelred's court do not appear in the annals, it is quite possible that Elgiva could have been one of them, especially since her father was the leading ealdorman for many years. I have also placed Elgiva in the king's bed, for which, I confess, there is no evidence at all, except that King Æthelred had a somewhat notorious reputation where women were concerned, at least in later histories, as did his father before him.

Of Emma's Norman retinue, sources indicate that a woman named Wymarc and a man named Hugh were among those who sailed with her from Normandy. Hugh was appointed Emma's reeve in Exeter, and the Chronicle says that it was through Hugh's perfidy that Exeter was demolished by the Danes in A.D. 1003. The chronicler is mute as to how this came about, and so that part of my story is pure fiction. To my knowledge there is no tunnel under what was once the burh of Exeter, but there are underground passages beneath the High Street that date from the fourteenth century, and their existence gave me the idea for the dark escape route taken by Elgiva, Wulf, and Groa.

Which brings me to Swein Forkbeard and the Vikings. Could Forkbeard have seen Emma in Normandy before she departed for England in the spring of A.D. 1002? It's possible. Forkbeard's exact whereabouts in those years are unknown. At the end of A.D. 1001 he may have been on the Isle of Wight, where a marauding Danish army had settled to await a payoff from the English king. If the winds were favorable, it would be an easy voyage from Wight Isle to Fécamp, even in winter.

The St. Brice's Day Massacre, which some historians believe led Swein Forkbeard to wreak vengeance on the English king, occurred on

Friday, November 13, 1003. How many Danes were killed is unknown, but the massacre became legend, with gruesome details added (possibly invented) as the story was told and retold. Nevertheless, the horrific slaughter of the Danes who were trapped and burned in Oxford's St. Frideswide's Church did indeed occur, and this event was described in one of Æthelred's charters as a "most just extermination," which seems a pretty clear indication of how the king viewed the matter.

Emma's kidnapping by Swein is fictional, but it was inspired by an actual event that took place in A.D. 943. In that year the Danes attacked Tamworth and abducted the very wealthy Wulfrun—Elgiva's grandmother—presumably for ransom. Indeed, because of this event Wulfrun is the only woman other than royals and abbesses who is mentioned by name in *The Anglo-Saxon Chronicle*.

Regarding place names: I have chosen to use the modern versions except in a very few instances, when the eleventh-century name was wonderfully descriptive or just too different from what the place is called today. Saltford, which is modern-day Salford, was in the eleventh century exactly what its name indicated—a ford on the road that led from the salt deposits at Droitwich to the southern shires. Middleton (middle town) is the Anglo-Saxon name for today's Milton Abbas; Otter Mouth, where the River Otter flows into the English Channel, is modern-day Budleigh Salterton, and lucky for me, the word *otter* is pronounced the same way in Danish as it is in English, all the way back to the eleventh century. I chose to use the Scandinavian name Jorvik for the northern city of York because I wanted to set it apart a little from the southern Anglo-Saxon world that Emma would have known. The great stone dance where Athelstan and Groa meet with the seeress is based on the Rollright Stones near the border of Warwickshire and Oxfordshire.

The Queen Emma who commissioned the *Encomium Emmae Reginae* in the fourth decade of the eleventh century was at the height of her power—a power that the young woman who arrived in Canterbury in

A.D. 1002 to wed a troubled king could hardly have imagined. The tides of history, though, seldom ran smoothly for Emma of Normandy. The years of her marriage to Æthelred were beset by conflict—within the royal family, the court, and the realm. It must have taken a woman of strength, courage, and determination to thrive in that often brutal world, but thrive she did, and there is much more of her story yet to be told.

Acknowledgments

No manuscript makes the journey from idea to publication without assistance, and mine is no exception. My first thanks go to my husband, Lloyd, whose love and encouragement have helped me to realize so many of my dreams, including this one, and to our sons, Andrew and Alan, who kept me grounded in the modern world while I was so often lost in the past.

Thank you to my steadfast and brilliant agent, Stephanie Cabot, for believing in this book and for helping me angle the story in the direction it needed to go; to Stephanie's assistant Anna Worrall and to everyone at the Gernert Company who helped guide the manuscript to publication; to my U.S. editor, Emily Murdock Baker, who has been such a pleasure to work with, and to her team at Viking and Penguin; to editor Louisa Joyner and her staff at HarperCollins UK; and to Keira Godfrey, all of whom have been so enthusiastic.

I am indebted to fellow writers Christine Mann and Deborah Griffin, who read the first draft, and whose questions and observations helped shape the characters and story; to Matt Brown, for his wonderful map of Æthelred's England; to Linda Watanabe McFerrin, for her guidance about all aspects of writing and publishing; to the members of Left Coast Writers®, for their passion for the written word; and to Janice Baeuerlen, MD, for her unflagging interest and expert advice. Every novelist should have a psychiatrist for a next-door neighbor!

I am grateful to Professor Andy Orchard, renowned medieval scholar and engaging teacher, whose 2007 summer course at Downing College, Cambridge, illuminated some of the darker corners of the Anglo-Saxon world. Thanks, too, to the many academics who answered questions and offered encouragement over lunches at the International Congress on Medieval Studies at Kalamazoo and whose extensive research and writings helped inform this book, especially Professor Gale Owen-Crocker and Professor Maren Clegg Hyer. Special thanks to Professor James Earl, whose translation of *The Anglo-Saxon Chronicle* entry for A.D. 978 opens the book.

I am indebted to Lloyd Bracey for whisking me in October 2009 from modern-day London to the reenactment of the Battle of Hastings; to Maria Faul for answering all my questions about parchment; to Gillian Bagwell for sharing her knowledge of swordplay; to Sara Latta, Jean Langmuir, Margret Elson, Karen Carlson, Dorothy Mondello, and Ron Leavens for their willing ears and for cheering me on; to Joanne Lopez, Joan Harper, and Mary Wieland for decades of friendship, encouragement, and prayers; and to Jane Pitcock, whose memory will live always in my heart.

Of the many books that I consulted while researching the history behind this novel, several deserve special recognition. Pauline Stafford's *Queen Emma and Queen Edith: Queenship and Women's Power in Eleventh-Century England* was invaluable and was my primary resource; *Encomium Emmae Reginae*, edited by Alistair Campbell, introduction by Simon Keynes; *Anglo-Saxon England* by Frank Stenton; *Æthelred II* by Ryan Lavelle; *Æthelred the Unready* by Ann Williams; M. K. Lawson's *Cnut*; David Hill's *An Atlas of Anglo-Saxon England*; and *The Death of Anglo-Saxon England* by N. J. Higham. Two recent biographies of Emma, *Queen Emma and the Vikings* by Harriet O'Brien and *Emma: The Twice-Crowned Queen* by Isabella Strachan, were sources of inspiration, and would make excellent reading for anyone wishing to learn more about the life of Emma of Normandy.